Degrees of Love:

a novel

L I S A   S L A B A C H

PUBLISHED BY BOOKBABY
2017

Olivarez Media, Inc.
10 N. East St., Ste 106
Woodland, CA 95776

Print ISBN: 978-1-54390-721-6
eBook ISBN: 978-1-54390-722-3

Degrees of Love is a work of fiction and is a creation of the author's imagination. Names, characters, places, and entities are fictitious or are used fictitiously. Any similarities to real people, living or dead, or actual incidences are wholly coincidental.

For the three great loves of my life.

Degrees of Love

The sea hath bounds, but deep desire hath none.

–William Shakespeare

Chapter 1

I fired up the engine of my BMW, and listened to it purr while I inhaled the leathery new car scent. Last week, I'd come home in love with my handsome ride, but ever since I'd felt guilty about the indulgence. Not so much anymore. I wanted one minute, a mere sixty seconds, simply to sit and savor my success, but I had to go. I'd promised my boys I'd cook dinner. I also had to break the news of my promotion to my husband, and hoped he wouldn't object.

Putting the car in gear, I drove out of the San Francisco International Airport parking lot and wedged my way into the stream of commuters nudging south. It took about an hour to drive the paltry thirteen miles to my home in San Carlos. After a long day of travel and meetings, I was too tired for any kind of TGIF joie de vivre.

I stepped out of the car just as Micah ran out the front door. "Mom's home!"

Jason followed close on his heels. "Mommy!"

I hugged them close. The boys were getting so big, and I wondered how much longer they would race to meet me or call me *Mommy*.

"Hey, give Mom a chance to get inside before you tackle her," Matt half-heartedly ordered from the doorway. He stretched over the boys and pecked my cheek as I passed him.

As soon as we walked into the house Micah asked, "So what's the dinner plan?"

I was fried and really wanted to order a pizza, but I'd already used my free pass the night before with Chinese takeout. Rallying energy, I threw on an apron and dug red bell peppers, zucchini, and chicken out of the refrigerator while my guys settled around the kitchen table.

"Glass of wine?" Matt already had a bottle of Sangiovese sitting on the counter.

"Love one." My stomach clenched, but I went for it. "I got the call."

Matt paused with the wine in one hand and the corkscrew in the other. "What call?"

"The job." I took a breath. "I was offered the promotion."

"Oh." He glanced at me as if surprised and returned his attention to inserting the screw.

"I don't have to accept." I tried to sound as if it wasn't a big deal, but it was. I'd worked hard for that promotion and in the marrow of my bones needed a change for reasons I couldn't even begin to explain.

Matt meticulously poured an equal portion into each glass and handed one to me. His lips bent up, but his eyes weren't smiling. "Take it. Sounds like a great opportunity."

"You sure?"

He took a drink, and his smile became more genuine. "Absolutely. Congratulations."

"Thank you." I took a gulp from my glass and the lump in my throat receded.

"So, what will your new title be?"

"Senior Vice President."

"Impressive. When do you start?"

"Monday, since I'll already be in New York, and I'll meet my new boss." I knew almost nothing about Reese Kirkpatrick. Monday was his first day with Global Security. I didn't want Matt to know I had any qualms and asked, "How was your day?"

"Dad said we're going camping 4th of July." Micah looked at Matt. "Right, dad?"

Jason's face lit up. "Yeah, he said we'd catch fish and eat s'mores at night."

"Oh, really?" I raised my eyebrows at Matt.

Matt shrugged and this time he changed the subject.

After dinner, Micah and Jason wandered off to watch a movie while Matt twisted in his chair. He knew he was in the doghouse for promising the boys we'd go camping.

"How's work? Did you get your test results?"

The left side of his mouth lifted. "Yes, the preliminary reports are very promising, but I won't bore you with details you don't understand."

His superior attitude grated on me. Still, I probably wouldn't understand. Matt's work was difficult for most people to grasp. As a computational biologist, he studied genetic sequences in proteins. His work chemically linked the relation between depression and chronic illness, and was equal parts biology, mathematics, statistics, and computer modeling.

Funny, I understood when his colleagues explained what they did.

"I'm happy for you." I emptied the remaining wine into his glass. "So, camping? What happened to La Jolla and the Cove? Snorkeling and a condo with indoor plumbing?"

"I found a campsite along the Truckee River with great trails and fishing. It has flushing toilets and showers." I didn't bite and he threw me a bone. "You don't have to go."

He knew I wasn't big on camping, our vacation time was limited, and now I would be the bad guy if I didn't go. "Some choice you've given me."

"I thought it'd be nice to go someplace where you couldn't use your laptop."

He looked at me with his wide blue eyes and I melted. My vacations were never truly vacations. I always kept up with e-mail and joined important conference calls. Knowing the level of dedication expected by my company didn't alleviate the mom guilt. "You're right." A surge of affection for him filled me. I sat on his lap, and kissed him.

He leaned his forehead against mine. "So you'll come?"

"Will you clean the fish?"

"Always do."

"Then I'll go." I kissed him again; then moved to get up. He tugged me back on his lap and hardened underneath me. "The boys are awake."

"They're watching a movie," he murmured close to my ear.

This was not Matt's typical behavior, but I liked it and my body responded. I led him by the hand to our bedroom. Before the door shut, Matt had his shoes kicked off and was unzipping his jeans. I locked the door and undressed too. I pictured a pre-show of tasting and touching before the main event. Matt had a different agenda. He thrust his tongue in my mouth and thrashed it around as if we were having a tongue war. The strange thing was it didn't feel like it stemmed from passion. It was habit. I pulled away.

No matter how many times he did the crazy tongue thing, or how many times I jerked back, Matt never clued in that I hated it. I wanted to tell him just how much it turned me off but was afraid of wounding his ego. In a blink, he mounted me and a few blinks later, collapsed on my chest. He pecked my cheek and murmured, "That was great." Then, he went to the bathroom. No kissing, no cuddling, no post-coital chat.

A weight on my chest kept me down. I should've been happy. I'd just finished having sex with my husband. It hadn't been great, but not horrible either. At least we had sex.

Matt walked back in the room. "You tired?"

"A little bit."

He pulled on his boxers with his back to me and looked over his shoulder. "Think I'll watch the movie with the boys. You mind?"

"Go ahead." They were watching *Cars* for at least the hundredth time. I got up, finished the dishes, and went to bed.

The next morning, Matt slept snoring beside me while I lazed in bed daydreaming about the guy who worked at the Safeway fish counter. He had deep dark eyes and, while not great looking, exuded manly sexuality. I imagined how our first contact would be made.

"May I have four trout fillets, please?" I asked.

"You got it! Do you have a good recipe for trout?"

"No, I thought I'd just throw them on the grill."

"If you'd like, I'll write one down for you."

"That's very kind."

"My pleasure." He handed me the recipe with a rakish wink.

Instead of a recipe, it's a confession that he watches for me. If I'm interested, call him.

Silliness. Even though it was Saturday, and my bed was comfy, I got up. Maybe I could get through at least one cup of coffee in peace before Saturday morning cartoons started blaring from the television. I made a pot of coffee, poured a cup, and headed for the back porch. The cool air bit my skin, but curling up on a lounge chair, I was comforted by the early sun on my face. As I sat enjoying the morning, sipping coffee, my thoughts wandered back to my increasing awareness of other men.

Last week, I had even caught myself checking out a Safeway bagger's butt. He couldn't have been more than twenty, but his chinos looked good on him. I imagined myself as Blanche DuBois. *"Young man! Young, young, young man ... I just want to kiss you once, softly and sweetly on your mouth!"* How pathetic. I shook my head clear.

Everyone who knew Matt and I would attest we were happily married. We didn't fight. Neither of us indulged in excessive bad habits. Matt wasn't abusive. He didn't cheat. As my mother repeatedly said, I was lucky to have a man like Matt. So polite, so steady ... so reliable.

He'd changed very little since we'd met while attending Northwestern University. I was getting my master's in Acting, and he was getting his in Biological Engineering. One day I decided to eat in the cafeteria. When I couldn't find an empty table, I hunted for any open seat. Then I caught Matt staring at me. He was sitting alone, and he was pretty darn cute.

I walked up to his table and smiled down at him. "I saw you looking at me. Would you like to invite me to sit down?" He chuckled and turned a deeper shade of red. I noticed the serious pile of books on the table. "It's too noisy in here to study anyway."

As long as I could remember, I'd had a weakness for smart men. The fact that Matt was blue-eyed and blond was a bonus. His eyes were pools of clear blue water, and they crinkled adorably when he smiled. After half a dozen coincidental meetings, he asked me out. I'd thought it was fate, but Matt later confessed he sought out places where he guessed I might be. He thought I was exotic with my dark features and second-hand-store-chic clothes. I never considered myself particularly unusual; however, being an actress, I had been *dramatically* different from the women he had dated. He had been different for me too.

There was never any great passion between us, but we were compatible in our way. His apartment became my haven from the craziness of my theater friends. He calmed me. My roommate, Serena, thought he was a looker, but *flat*. That's what she called him. "Flat." As in absence of fizzle. If being even-tempered and reliable was *flat*, then it was good with me.

I was twenty-three when we married. At the time, Matt loved me, adored me even. I remember the moment I sensed a shift in him. It was at our wedding reception. I had envisioned us inseparable as we celebrated our big night, but Matt wanted to catch up with college buddies.

"I have the rest of my life with you. I just want to talk to my friends."

Not wanting to appear needy or selfish, I kissed him and let him go. Subtle though the change was, a moment of absolute clarity hit me. I had transformed to a fixture in his life that no longer required special attention. We were married, and I would be there when he finished with other things. I supposed that's what marriage was. I just never thought it would happen so soon after we exchanged vows. It didn't mean Matt stopped loving me. Things simply had changed.

Now here we were, thirteen years later. Lucky thirteen. Last week our wedding anniversary came and went without much fanfare. After the boys had gone to bed, I presented Matt with a watch. He gave me nothing, not even a card. The next day I bought the BMW on impulse. I told him it was an early birthday present for me.

"Mom, where are you?" I turned and Micah stood all of three feet from me.

"Right here." I knew what he wanted.

"Oh. What's for breakfast?"

"French toast and bacon sound good?" It was a rhetorical question.

"Mmmmm. Thanks, Mom. Can I watch cartoons?"

"Sure, but keep the volume down. Daddy and Jason are still sleeping."

Less than a minute later, the television blasted. I jumped up and followed the noise.

"Micah, turn it down." He didn't respond. "Micah, that means now."

I think I was louder than the television. His face scrunched, but he did as told. I went to the kitchen to start breakfast and heard Jason stumble out of bed and make his way to the family room. A minute later, Matt loped in looking sleepy eyed. He headed straight for the coffee.

He took a sip and smacked his lips. "Good coffee." I dropped a slice of battered bread in the pan, and it made a pleasing sizzle. Matt leaned over and inhaled the scent of vanilla and cinnamon wafting from the skillet. "Mmmm, smells delicious. You make the world's best French toast."

His unexpected compliment brightened my mood. "Thank you," I said and pecked his cheek. "It's such a beautiful day. Let's take the boys to Bean Hollow Beach this afternoon. We haven't been there in ages."

Matt looked at me a bit confused. "We're going to the A's game."

"You didn't tell me, but it sounds fun. What time do we leave?"

Matt looked at the coffee mug in his hand and then back at me. "I only got tickets for the boys and me. I thought we'd have a boys' day. You don't mind, do you?"

How could I object? Matt went to the bedroom to get dressed. I fought an urge to fling the spatula in my hand at him, but I flipped the French toast instead, wiping a tear before it dripped into the pan. I shouldn't have been so angry and hurt. I wanted him to be a good father, but I *was* hurt. The game was something I could do with them, too.

I told myself it didn't matter. A week's worth of laundry waited for me. Besides, since the guys would be gone all day, I could treat myself to a shopping trip in San Francisco. Recently, I'd recommitted to an exercise plan and lost fifteen pounds. None of my suits fit properly, and I wanted to make a good first impression when I met my new boss.

After breakfast, I helped the boys find their A's caps and baseball gloves, and then lathered them up with sunscreen. Just before they climbed into

Matt's Honda minivan, I gave everyone a hug, including Matt. I was still upset with him as they drove away. I hated that minivan. I had encouraged him to buy an SUV or Jeep.

Once inside, I missed the noise that had worked my nerves only moments ago. The quiet wasn't peaceful. It seemed inexplicably loud. I turned on the radio to drown it out, and a familiar tired restlessness crept over me while a weight settled in my chest. As I moved from room to room, gathering laundry, I kept expecting the impatient, heavy feeling to go away. It didn't until I walked into Neiman Marcus, my place to go when I really wanted to splurge.

Beyond pleased that the size 6 suit hung unattractively on my body, I asked the sales girl to bring me a size 4. It was perfect. "I'll take it," I declared and started to get undressed.

She gathered my selections and asked, "Anything else I can help you find?"

"I could use something for going out. Not for Business." I don't know where that came from. I didn't have plans to go anywhere.

She was back in a flash with an armload of clothes. After I dismissed her first few suggestions, she held up a printed wrap dress. It reminded me of something my mother might have worn in the seventies when she was a young divorcee on the hunt for a new husband.

"Who's the designer?"

"Diane Von Furstenberg. You've got a rocking figure and can pull it off."

Flattery always helped. I put it on and she was right. The dress was low cut and emphasized my newly flattened stomach and slenderized waist. I turned for a side view.

She studied my reflection. "Have you ever tried a push up bra?"

Okay, that was not flattering. My breasts weren't as perky as they used to be. Breast feeding two boys and gravity had taken its toll. I tried the suggested miracle bra with the dress.

She echoed my thoughts. "It's very sexy, but still sophisticated."

I had to hand it to her. She was good. I floated out of *Needless Mark-up* on heady shopping high with two suits, a dress, a bra with the matching underwear, and two pairs of shoes.

I hustled home to put my things away before Matt saw them. It wasn't because of how much I'd spent. Matt handed me the bills years ago when I started making more money than him. Other than the car, I'd always managed our money responsibly. It wasn't the money. It was the dress. I was embarrassed by how provocative I looked in it and wasn't sure what possessed me to buy it. If I wasn't comfortable modeling it for Matt, why did I bother?

I knew. I thought about it while I packed the dress in my bag Monday morning. When I looked in the fitting room mirror at Neiman Marcus, I saw who I used to be, and maybe still was under my standard little sweater sets, which I accessorized with my little pearl necklace. After Matt and I had married, I adjusted my style to please him. I wanted one night to please myself. One night to have fun and pretend I wasn't the suburban soccer mom. The dress was my "costume."

Chapter 2

Once en route to the Midtown hotel on West 46th Street, I called Matt to let him know I'd arrived safely in New York. He didn't pick up so I left a message. "Hi, honey. I'm in the cab on my way to the Muse. *Please*, remember vegetables with dinner. *Thank you.* I'll call you later. Kiss the boys for me. Love you."

Mom duties out of the way, I leaned back and enjoyed the sights. I loved New York. I loved the vigor of the crowds. I loved the muggy heat. I even loved the sweaty smells and the noise. Matt and I had planned to move here after graduate school. I'd had some decent theater contacts and a potential agent, but Matt trumped me with his once-in-a-lifetime research opportunity in Silicon Valley. Then, life kept us there. After Micah was born, I gave up theater entirely. Matt loved his job. I'd started getting promotions. We'd bought a house not far from where Matt had grown up, and the New York dream slowly had faded.

As soon as I got to my room, I showered off the clammy, grimy feeling I had whenever I traveled cross-country. Then I sprinkled baby powder over my body; it cooled and refreshed me. I put on my new panties and matching miracle bra. I felt young and sexy slipping on my wrap dress and strappy heels. I looked good—better than good. I looked great. A thrill of impending adventure raced through me. No way was I going to spend the evening in my room watching pay-per-view and reviewing reports for tomorrow's meeting.

Without a plan or any idea where to go, I ventured into the throngs of Manhattan and walked a few blocks invigorated by the vibrations of humanity en masse pulsing through me. I walked a few more blocks and my feet pinched. I wandered aimlessly two more blocks, and my dress started sticking uncomfortably to my sweaty breasts. What was I doing? I should just order room service and work. I turned back, but a block from the hotel a swanky wine bar caught my attention. It was ultra-sophisticated, ultra-hip, with black leather bar stools and brushed chrome walls. My mouth moistened as I surged with reckless courage.

I chose a character: the fearless New Yorker a la *Sex in the City*. Strutting into the bar, I did something I never did. I sat at the bar itself and ordered a glass of wine. My mother had taught me that real ladies never sat at the bar. I let my dress tumble open, revealing my tan legs. Tonight I didn't care and smiled at my daring.

Urban sophistication surrounded me as well-dressed New Yorkers mingled and sipped twenty-dollar glasses of wine. Funky blue lights hung from the ceiling, and jazz music was barely discernable above the din of conversation. This was what I needed to ease my tension.

Sipping my wine, I surveyed the room, assessing the men. *He's cute, but too young. Is he old enough to drink? That one is too short. There's a looker. Oh, he smiled at me. Damn, too bad his teeth are crooked. Where are the truly great looking men? So picky, Goldilocks.* I chuckled to myself. This was fun. I wasn't going to talk to any of these men. I may have been married for thirteen years, but I was still a woman. I wasn't dead yet. What was the harm? Why feel guilty? It was a victimless crime, just a little innocuous entertainment for the soccer mom from California. Even so, a nagging voice in my head told me Matt wouldn't approve. Besides, I had an all-day meeting the next morning and couldn't be completely irresponsible.

I tipped my head and drained my glass.

As if being cued, the bartender walked over and handed me another round. He gestured towards the other end of the bar. "The wine's on him."

My eyes darted in the direction the bartender had pointed. *Oh, my, my, my.* My heart skipped a beat and I almost dropped the glass. The man had Mediterranean good looks with black hair and startling blue eyes … sensuous mouth and a seductive look in his eyes. He smiled, clearly amused, and gratified, by my flustered reaction. I didn't want to rebuff him, but at the same time, I was too much of a coward to accept the drink.

I turned back to the bartender. "I'm sorry, but I have to leave." He shrugged with a little smirk. "Please, thank the gentleman for me."

As I headed to the door, I felt those startling blue eyes following me and couldn't resist looking back. His eyes met mine for what was probably only the briefest moment, but in that moment, a dozen images flashed through my mind: all of them involving this stranger touching me. It was unnerving and my stomach did a back flip. I hesitated. He took a step my direction. Okay, this was dangerous and too reckless. I bolted for the door and didn't slow down until I walked into the lobby of my hotel.

How mortifying. I cringed as I unlocked the door to my room. I'd acted like a sixteen-year-old girl being checked out for the first time, far from a sophisticated thirty-six year old woman. What had I been thinking? Why did I even buy this stupid dress or go into that bar?

I untied the dress, kicked off my heels and put on my comfortable mom pajamas. The responsible, suburban mother was back. Needing to hear my boys' voices, needing Matt to ground me, I called home, but no one answered. They must have been out to dinner or a movie.

I turned on the television and started flipping channels. Nothing caught my attention. I kept thinking about what would have happened if I had accepted the drink. Would his lips be seeking mine in a dark corner of the bar right now? Forget kissing. Would he be between my thighs? If I knew Matt would never know, could I do it?

My imagination was out of control. I turned off the television determined to put him out of my mind and get a good night's sleep. I slept, but he was the star of my dreams that night.

Him—the unknown him— cupping my breasts and teasing my nipple with his tongue ... My senses filled with his taste, his scent, his hard body moving urgently with mine ... He arches dolphin-like above me, the sight of his contoured chest and the line of his jaw make me dizzy with exaltation. He becomes a God cresting on a wave, his waters rushing into me.

"Brrring ... Brrring ..." Crap! My eyes popped open.

"Hello?" I answered more asleep than awake.

"This is your wake up call," the recorded voice at the other end announced.

I needed a shower, preferably a cold one. A god cresting on a wave? Waters rushing into me? No way would I ever have a one-night stand, or cheat on Matt.

Putting the prior night behind me, I began to focus on my meeting. For the last couple years, I had managed a team who sold data security services to financial institutions on the West Coast, but as Senior Vice President of Sales, Mobile Banking, I would be covering the entire country. Mobile Banking was a new product line and a new division for my company—very cutting edge. It was a much higher profile position, and although exciting, came with increased pressure; consequently, I couldn't help being nervous about meeting my new boss. Reese Kirkpatrick was a hot shot Harvard

M.B.A. with a reputation for being a *Rainmaker*. I imagined him with bald-
ing hair and a stern demeanor, just like the other senior executives.

I showered and took particular care with my hair and make-up,
wanting to be attractive in a business way, nothing sexual. I put on my
new Burberry banker blue suit, which was stylish without being trendy,
starched white shirt, and Stewart Weitzman pumps. A quick perusal in the
mirror assured me I projected the image of a no-nonsense, successful businesswoman straight out of central casting. I smiled, thinking about how
different I looked from last night.

Desperate for coffee, I just had time to stop at the espresso bar in the lobby
of our office building. It may have been 8 a.m. in New York, but my internal
clock insisted it was five. I checked my watch again. It was taking longer
than I had anticipated, and I debated my need for a jolt of caffeine versus
not being late.

"You look like you're in a hurry. Would you like to go ahead of me?"

"I …." A chiseled face with perfectly shaped lips stared down at me. "I,
uh … I couldn't possibly."

"I insist, ladies first."

"Well, if you insist, thank you," I mumbled and stepped in front of him.
I'd always preferred blue-eyed blondes, but his fair skin contrasting with
the darkness of his hair and deep brown eyes took my breath away. He was
very urbane with his wavy, gelled hair and GQ attire.

I could feel the heat of his body behind me and inched forward as
much as possible. I could still feel him and turned to check just how closely
he stood. He caught me and winked. *Embarrassing.*

My turn came and I ordered a skinny latte. I dug for my wallet, but
there was too much crap in my bag between my laptop, files, and personal

items. Needles pricked my neck. I knew I should have carried a separate purse.

"For the lady's coffee." I opened my mouth to object, but the cashier already took the twenty from his hand. He ordered a large black coffee for himself.

The man must think I'm an idiot. "That wasn't necessary, but truly, thank you."

"*Truly,* you're welcome. I actually have an ulterior motive," he said with the most disarming mixture of confidence and sheepishness. He was rather adorable.

"Oh?"

"I figured if I bought you coffee, you'd have to talk to me." My lips lifted up involuntarily and his grin widened. "So, do you work in the building?"

"No. I'm only here for a meeting."

"Large skinny," the barista called. I grabbed my coffee and started to go.

"Hey, wait a second." He took a few steps toward me and I stopped. "How about a drink after work? I promise, I'm quite normal."

"Oh, well … okay." I felt exquisitely flattered. *Wait. If a cup of coffee obligated me to talk to him, what would he expect if I accepted a cocktail?* My cheeks burned. "Actually, I'm sorry, but I'm only in town for business." *And, I'm married.* "Thanks again for the coffee."

I turned and zipped out before he could respond. I'd have to think about the vibes I was sending. The hottie in the wine bar was understandable, but this morning I wasn't dressed for attention, nor did I want it.

Focus. I had a meeting and needed to focus.

By the time I slipped into the executive conference room, all the other senior managers had arrived. The glistening mahogany table and plush leather chairs made a statement. After the hand-shaking ritual, I took one of the two seats left in the back. No surprise, I was the only woman in the room. When other women joined our meetings, they generally represented HR or one of the other support areas. My company was progressive, but sales, and more specifically sales management, was still dominated by men. It was old school in many ways. I was invited to the table, but wasn't part of the club. I knew the game and how to play my part.

I recognized everyone and wondered where the mysterious Reese Kirkpatrick was. Joe Benedetti, the President of our division, called the meeting to order. Just as he finished reviewing the agenda for the day, the door opened, and my eyes widened.

"Ah, there you are, Reese," Joe greeted.

I almost spewed the coffee I had just sipped … the coffee *he* had just bought me. *Holy crap!* It would be funny if it weren't so damned awkward.

"Sorry I'm late." He focused all of his attention on Joe. "H.R. held me up." He turned and gave us all a dazzling smile.

Reese Kirkpatrick hadn't noticed me yet. Certain my game face was back on, I studied him. His most striking feature was his eyes, big chocolate orbs framed by thick lashes. Any woman would kill to have those eyes. I gazed a little too intently and our eyes locked. A flicker of acknowledgement passed between us.

As each executive introduced himself, Reese politely nodded or made a, "It's nice to meet you," type of comment. My turn came, and he looked at me with a blank expression.

"I'm Susan Sinclair, SVP Mobile Banking. I've been with Global for eight years."

He gave me a tight little smile and a curious gaze that made my heart pound. "I understand you and I will be working very closely."

"That's correct."

When the introductions were over, Reese took the only seat left, right next to me. I wished I knew what he was thinking. His close proximity made it hard to concentrate. I shifted positions and accidently bumped his leg. Tingles raced up my thigh. This was bad.

I whispered, "I'm so sorry."

"Don't be," he whispered back.

Each VP took their turn presenting overviews, responding to questions, and receiving feedback from Joe. When my turn came, thank God, my voice came out normal. At the conclusion, Joe nodded his approval. "Excellent work. Reese, you're fortunate to have Susan on your team."

"I couldn't be more pleased," Reese responded and smiled at me. *What did that mean?*

After the meeting, Reese barely acknowledged me before leaving, but he ambushed me in the hallway. "Excuse me, Susan. If you have a minute, I'd like a private word."

I had a good idea what the *private word* was about. I followed him down the hall and out of hearing range of the others. He lowered his head and his voice. "About this morning. I obviously had no idea who you were."

"There was no way for you to have known. Don't worry. It's forgotten."

He nodded and his demeanor relaxed. "Thank you. I'll see you tomorrow."

The next morning I was in Reese's office at 8 a.m. sharp. He'd managed to score a big corner office with a view. I speculated it had been part of the negotiation when he was hired. We shook hands and he asked me to have a seat.

"So, Susan, before we start, I thought we could get to know each other a bit."

It seemed a reasonable request, but there was something about him I didn't trust. He had used a tried and true sales technique when he'd bought me the coffee. The theory was if you give a prospect something of value, they'd feel an unconscious obligation to hear your pitch, or even better, buy your product. I should've spotted him as a salesman.

"What would you like to know?"

"Tell me about yourself ... Are you married? Do you have pets?" He leaned back in his chair with his hands cupped behind his head and waited with a confident smile.

First question, are you married? Hmmmm. "Yes, I'm married, and I have two boys, who are ten and eight. No pets, unless you count goldfish. Anything else?"

He chuckled and switched tactics. "How long have you been in sales?"

"Since I was old enough to have a job." I enjoyed making this difficult for him.

He sat up and tried the "open-ended" question. "Tell me what you like about sales?"

"Winning and uncapped bonus potential."

He crossed his arms. Most sales people were like actors; they loved the sound of their own voice. He studied me, waiting for me to speak. I didn't. He uncrossed his arms and gave up the subtle approach. "Are you uncomfortable working for me after yesterday morning?"

"Not at all. I told you, it's forgotten." I smiled in attempt to emulate his earlier confidence. "I simply have a noon flight, and we have a lot to cover."

"Fair enough. Joe warned me you were a spitfire."

"I'll have to thank him next time I see him."

He laughed and switched gears to business. His strategy was sound, and we only had one heated debate. Reese wanted to target the largest bank in Global's portfolio for our first sale.

"Susan, if one of the largest financial institutions in the world signs with us, smaller banks will follow. We'll be the market leader by default."

"Yes, but big banks are like dealing with the government. You know how much more nimble smaller banks are. Think about it. We can be closing deals by the end of the year."

He paced while he weighed my argument. "I don't know … it makes me nervous. We could lose market share overnight if it fails." He turned and started pacing again.

I rolled my eyes at his back and whispered under my breath, "*But screw your courage to the sticking place and we'll not fail.*"

"What did you say?" He turned and looked at me straight on.

"Nothing." I tried to make my eyes as wide and innocent as possible.

"Susan, are you a risk taker?"

"Calculated and only when it's worth it," I said, challenging him.

"Okay, we'll try it your way. We're still gunning for the big guys, but it makes sense to balance with some quicker sales first … that work for you, Lady Macbeth?"

No one at work ever caught the little quotes I occasionally threw out. It was my private joke, and I was impressed he'd caught it. "At least I don't want you to assassinate a king."

"Lucky me. I'm sure you'd find a way to persuade me it was a good idea."

His eyes were playful, and he had such an attractive smile. My stomach fluttered. "Well, I should get to the airport. I'll have the finalized plan to you Monday, end of day."

"Make it *beginning* of day. Our first meeting is next week in Boston."

Crap, I'll have to work over the weekend. I nodded and nabbed up my things before I was given any more assignments. I almost made it out the door when he stopped me.

"By the way, when we're in Boston, plan on dinner after the meeting."

I frowned. "Dinner?"

He mock frowned back. "Yes, with our Bank of Boston contact. That a problem?"

Of course with a client. What was I thinking? "No, I haven't booked my flight yet."

"Good. And next time we meet, I expect you to be pleasant and tell me about yourself."

His tone was crisp and business-like, but it still felt flirtatious. I stared at him for a moment, trying to get a better read of him. "I promise … to think about it." I left with my hips swaying of their own accord.

I could hear him laughing in his office.

He was smooth, way too smooth. I needed to keep him at a distance until I became desensitized to him, until he became a real asshole boss, and then I would probably wonder why I ever found him attractive.

Chapter 3

I finished the week working out of my home office and buzzing with energy, exhilarated by my new position. Reese and I had spent hours on the phone collaborating on various projects, and seemed to be working well together. I already was used to him, and doubted he would make my knees weak the next I time I saw him.

The weight on my chest was lighter. This was what I needed to be myself again—a challenge, a new adventure. As an actress, I had been accustomed to starting a new play about every three months. Every few months I'd be researching a new character, meeting a new cast, pretending to be someone else. I got restless if I did the same thing too long.

In a heartbeat, it was Saturday morning again. I did a quick inventory of what needed doing. Laundry and grocery shopping were a given. I'd hoped to get away with not mopping, but the floors needed it. I checked the boys' bathroom. It required a thorough cleaning. I wished Matt would teach the boys how to aim better. I felt like Cinderella before the ball. If I hustled and finished the housework and my Global Security reports today, then maybe, just maybe, I could have a little down time on Sunday.

I couldn't expect any help from Matt. He and Micah had escaped to a birthday party and left Jason home with me. My little guy trailed behind me, moping from one room to the other while I gathered laundry and started in on the dusting.

He kept uttering something between a moan and a sigh.

I finally asked, "Jason, what is it?"

"I wish you didn't have to work all the time," he said with his head hanging.

God, it pinched my heart to hear him say that. It was so hard to know how to be a good mother. I didn't have a great example. My mother was young when she had me, and my father hadn't stuck around. For most of my youth, she had worked as a cocktail waitress while I stayed home by myself. Even when she had been home, she'd had little interest in being a mother.

I wanted to be the mother she hadn't been. I wanted my boys to live in a nice neighborhood and go to good schools, and for them to take a clean house and well-prepared, nutritious meals for granted. I didn't want them to have to wait for payday for something they needed today. The effort to give them those things took time, sometimes too much time. Matt thought we should get a housekeeper. There were times I agreed, but I couldn't bring myself to outsource. I knew it was irrational, but I liked knowing I was the one who took care of them.

"Honey, I have a lot of work to do, but guess what?"

He exhaled with great drama, "What?" He looked like Matt, but there was so much of me in him.

"I'm not going to do it. I'm hanging out with you. So what's it going to be?"

He shrugged his little shoulders. "I don't know."

"Jason, is something else bothering you?"

"Mike's parents are getting divorced."

Mike Carter and Jason had been best friends since pre-school. Although Matt and I weren't close with Mike's parents, we knew them fairly well because of the boys. Jack was majority owner of a successful software company, and Denise stayed home. Her main function was to be beautiful. She had a housekeeper and a nanny. It was sad, but not surprising. Jack was a good looking guy with a wandering eye and a fat bank account.

"I'm sorry to hear it. Is Mike sad?"

"Yeah."

"It's sad when these things happen. I'm sure he could use a good friend right now."

"Yeah."

"What's worrying you?"

"You and Dad won't get divorced, will you?"

"Why would you ask that?"

He shrugged again. "I dunno."

"No, bud. Daddy and I love each other. We'll never get divorced. Okay?"

"Okay." He smiled, satisfied with my assurance. "Will you read to me? You read Micah *Harry Potter* when he was my age. Will you read it to me?"

I remembered the hours Micah and I had curled up on the couch, getting lost in the magical world together. It had created a special bond between us. I wanted the same bond with Jason. The next two hours, we sat together and read. Having my little guy cuddled up next to me made me wish I never had to work. Plus, it was fun stretching my acting muscles with interpretive reading.

"Mom, you do really good accents," Jason said.

"Thanks, buddy. Want me to teach you how?"

A big smile lit his face. "Okay."

Just then, Matt and Micah walked in the door. Jason jumped up and ran after his brother, *Harry Potter* and the dialect lesson forgotten. A chill seeped under my skin at the loss of Jason's body next to me. For the first time in a long time, I missed having a baby. Not the diapers and midnight feedings, but having a baby against my chest, that lovely baby shampoo smell and soft fuzzy head warming my skin, holding him until my arms ached.

I asked Matt, "How was the party?"

"Great. The boys and I were invited to a pick up baseball game. We don't have anything else on the agenda today, do we?"

A part of me wanted to tell him he couldn't take the boys. More and more frequently, the three of them were running off together, while I kept the house functioning. I wanted them home, but another part of me said let them go. Let them have fun. Besides, I had a ton of work.

I stood and picked up the dust rag. "Day's clear. Hit a homer for me."

Matt shoved his hands in his pockets. "That's not why I was asking."

"I give, why are you asking?"

"We've been invited to dinner."

"By whom?"

"Todd and Sara Daniels."

"Did you accept?"

"Yes."

Sometimes dealing with Matt was like a game of twenty questions. It drove me crazy. "Oh come on, Matt. Seriously? You know Sara works my nerves. Couldn't you have come up with an excuse?"

"Honey, I work with Todd. We have boys the same age." He shrugged. "I like Sara."

"She's always trying to get me to join her Craft Club."

"So, you're crafty. What's so bad about that?"

I stared at him. I hated him making plans without discussing it with me. "Anything else I should know?"

"I told Todd we'd bring dessert. Don't worry, ice cream will be fine."

Matt knew I would never let us show up with a squirt bottle of chocolate syrup and a half-gallon of vanilla in a paper bag. I heaped dessert on my "to do" list.

There was a scramble getting them out the door with gloves, bats, hats, and water bottles. Once they were gone, the quiet left in their wake was oppressive. The weight was on my chest again, and the old tired restlessness crept over me. It stayed with me while I did laundry and cleaned the house. It distracted me when I made caramel sauce. I noticed when I powered up my laptop, my energy powered up with it. I guess work was more interesting than laundry.

I chuckled quietly and told myself that I was probably just suffering from *ennui*, that *my bourgeois life was suffocating my soul.* I was tired of the sight of minivans. I was tired of shopping at Safeway every week. I was tired of the generic middle-class families, and having generic conversations. *My life is achromatic!* I craved color.

I laughed at myself. I was probably just dreading dinner with Todd and Sara.

Late afternoon, the phone rang. It was the minister from our church. Even though we were haphazard with our attendance, Matt and I wanted to give the boys a sense of community. Our parish was low-key, and our minister was happy to have us whenever the spirit moved us.

"Susan, this is Reverend Jim," he sounded cheerful. I never heard him not cheerful. I think the man was perpetually happy. "Hope I'm not interrupting?" He was always very careful not to intrude. I liked that about him.

"No, not at all. What can I do for you today?"

"Tomorrow we're having a special children's service in Sunday school to kick off summer break, and I thought the boys might like to be there."

The heaviness in my chest made it hard for me to want to do anything, but maybe church would be a good idea. Hopefully, it would give me the lift I needed.

"We'll definitely be there," I replied, matching his upbeat tone.

I hung up thinking whatever sins I had committed by having unfaithful thoughts in New York last week, I was making up for with all of my good deeds this weekend.

Later that night, Todd, Sara, their two boys, and our family all sat together for dinner at the same table, eating some sort of baked pasta that reminded me of the tuna casserole my mother used to make. Sara's dish even had the mashed up potato chips on top. My mother would make it on Sunday afternoons and expect me to reheat it for dinner the nights she'd be gone. I had a gag reflex just looking at it. In fairness to Sara, it was better than my mother's concoction. Sara used chicken, and the pasta wasn't cooked to mush.

Matt praised the dish, giving little rhapsodic "*yums*" and "*so goods*" throughout the meal. He even requested seconds. He finished with, "Sara, this was really great. You have to give Susan the recipe."

Sara beamed. "I'd be happy to, but it's time consuming. I know Susan works."

Sara didn't work. I glanced at my boys' plates. They had pushed their food around, but hadn't eaten. I smiled, determined to be nice. "I would love the recipe."

We finally made it to my contribution to the meal, a chocolate ganache bread pudding with caramel port sauce. Being the gracious hostess, Sara said, "Susan, this is wonderful. Where did you buy it?"

"I didn't. It's a recipe from *Bon Appetit*."

"I don't like it," Sara's youngest complained.

"Well, it's more of an adult dessert," Todd said.

My boys scraped their plates in an attempt to get every bite, and Matt defended me. "Susan knows it's my favorite." I squeezed his hand under the table. He squeezed it back.

"What do you guys say to a game of poker?" Todd asked, pushing away from the table.

"Matt …." It was one thing for Matt occasionally to have a poker night with buddies from work. It was another to teach little boys how to gamble. Matt's eyes begged me not to put my foot down. "I'll help Sara with the dishes."

While we washed up, Sara explained her shopping methodology. "The grocery ads come out on Wednesday, so I plan our meals for the week Wednesday night. I usually start with meat and decide on the entrée. Sometimes I go to four different stores to get the best prices, but it's worth it. Did you know Lynardi's has the best prices for meat?"

"No, I didn't."

"Most people think Safeway does, but they don't. Lynardi's has the best. Have you ever shopped at Lynardi's?"

"No."

"You should."

I tried to think of something to say. I didn't care which store had what on sale. I didn't have time *and I didn't care.* I *had* to think of something to say. "Ever shop at Mollie Stone's?"

"Oh, no. Mollie Stone's is way overpriced."

"Ah."

The pause in the conversation grew to the uncomfortable zone. Sara handed me a towel and I started drying dishes. She said, "I was sorry not see you at the game last week."

"Game?"

"The company sponsored A's game. They went all out and reserved a barbeque area. Must have been at least a hundred of us there. Matt said you had to work."

In a nanosecond tears rushed to the edges of my eye lids, and I blinked them back. *Why would Matt not invite me? Was it supposed to be some sort of punishment?* I didn't know Sara well enough to share what I was feeling. It would be humiliating for her to know the truth.

I smiled. "It was disappointing not to be there, but I had no choice." I turned and kept drying and stacking plates and heard the guys laugh in the next room.

As much as I dreaded it, I asked, "So, do you have a Craft Night coming up soon?"

"I do. I'm hosting next week. We're making candles. Do you want to see what I have planned?" she asked, sparking with excitement.

"Love to," I answered.

It did the trick. A babbling monologue on the nuances of candle making ensued. I nodded and smiled sweetly the rest of the evening. By the end of the night, I was dazed, and not paying attention when she asked as we were leaving, "You'll come to the meeting next week?"

"Absolutely," I replied. *Crap.*

As we were undressing for bed later that night, Matt said, "I was happy to hear you're going to Craft Night. It would be good for you to have a friend like Sara."

What did that mean? I wasn't a deviant child in need of the influence of a *nice* friend. "Matt, please, she's a nice lady, but I don't see us being friends."

"Fine, but please don't be rude to her next week."

"What are you talking about?"

"Showing her up with *Bon Appetit*. I told you ice cream would be fine."

Responding without screaming would be impossible. I'd spent a couple hours making that damn bread pudding because it *was* Matt's favorite. I thought he would appreciate me making an effort for his friends. I pulled on my nightgown, and grabbed my pillow.

"Where are you going?" he asked.

"Family room to watch a movie."

"Maybe I'll join you. What are you in the mood for?"

"*Pride and Prejudice.*"

Matt went to bed, and I had the family room to myself.

I dutifully brought the boys to church the next morning and paid as much attention as I could. I have to admit I wasn't quite sure where Reverend Jim was going with the sermon. He lectured on the Ten Commandments and attempted to put them in the context of our modern world. I prepared to be chastised for my unchaste thoughts and expected to be reminded that adultery, whether taking place in the mind or the flesh, was a sin.

Reverend Jim had other ideas. He contended the commandments were more or less a moral guide God gave us to follow. The Ten Commandments were not so much God's laws, as they were his Ten Requests. God created us as imperfect beings, and he would forgive us if we failed always to obey. God's forgiveness would give us the ability to forgive ourselves.

I questioned the underlying message: sin away in the comfort God will forgive you? By the way, forget the guilt! Forgive yourself … it's what God wants. I doubted it was the message the good Reverend had intended.

Sunday night I cooked Micah's favorite dinner: rosemary pork roast with roasted herb vegetables, a fresh salad, and crunchy sourdough bread. Micah was happy.

After dinner, I read a couple chapters of *Harry Potter* to Jason. Jason was happy.

After the boys went to bed, I had sex with Matt. Matt was very happy.

I had muddled through the weekend trying to be a good mother, trying to be a good wife, and trying not to look forward to Monday and work. I couldn't help it. Work was my refuge.

Chapter 4

Settling into my window seat, I sighed with satisfaction. I was off to Boston where I'd be joining Reese for our first client meeting. I loved getting on an airplane and just going somewhere, anywhere. No cell phones, Blackberries, or e-mail. No one could pull on me. With a copy of *The Golden Bowl* on my lap, the middle seat empty, and the man sprawled in the aisle seat already dozing, I was free for a few blessed hours.

When I was a little girl, I used to make up stories about traveling all over the world. My mother had been a waitress at the Burbank airport lounge. Back then, you could walk up to the gate without a boarding pass. The summer I'd turned ten, my mother had wanted to save on babysitting and suggested I accompany her. It had seemed like a grand adventure.

She bought me a special orange-flowered tote bag, a sort of prop to give me the appearance of being a traveler, and instructed, "When we're at the airport, don't call me Mom. Call me Lana and find a corner where no one will notice you."

I did as told, but one day while I sat reading at a closed gate, a man sat next to me. I didn't look up, but I could see he was wearing blue polyester pants and scuffed black shoes.

"*Johnny Tremain*," he noted. "I read that book. You like it?"

I nodded, wishing he would go away.

"You don't need to be afraid of me. I won't hurt you."

I looked up at him. He was probably in his mid-thirties and creepy. He smiled and said, "You're a very pretty girl. What's a pretty girl like you doing traveling by yourself?"

Snatching up my bag, I ran to my mother. I could still see her in her waitress outfit of hot pants, billowy peasant blouse and knee high boots, her hair blown and curled just like Jacquelyn Smith. Lana laughed with a dark haired man in a gray suit who had a glass of beer sweating in his hand. I raced up to her.

"Mom …" She gave me a chilly, vacant stare. "Lana—"

Grabbing my arm, she tugged me aside. "You can't bother me while I'm working."

"But a man called me pretty and asked why I was by myself."

"Well, you are pretty. You're going to have to get used to attention."

"But I didn't know what to tell him."

Out of patience, she hissed scooting me along, "Make something up. You read enough books. Think up a story."

I did think of a story. I thought of a lot of stories. I invented a father who lived in New

York and had an apartment on the 27th floor. Other times, I was on my way to meet up with my parents who were photographers for *National Geographic*. They went to many exotic places.

Lana made it a sort of game. On the way to the airport, she would ask, "And where are you flying today, young lady?"

"I'm meeting my father in Seattle. He has business with Boeing."

"Oh yeah? What does your father do?"

"He's an aerospace engineer. He's going to take me to the Space Needle."

It was easier to talk to people when I pretended, but pangs of con-science hit me every now and then. I tried talking to Lana about it and asked her, "Does God punish liars?"

"Sure. He sends them to hell." She looked at me with a semi-stern glare. "Especially little girls who lie to their mothers. Why?"

"At the airport, I lie all the time. Do you think God's going to send me to hell?"

Lana laughed. "You're not lying. You're acting."

"What's the difference?"

"You're pretending to be someone else. It's not the same thing."

I supposed she was right, but it still felt like lying.

I especially had liked watching the businessmen, so important looking with their briefcases swinging at their sides. The only memory I had of my father was of a handsome, blue-eyed man giving me a shiny red tricycle for my third birthday. Watching those men, I dreamt about what it'd be like to have one of them as a father. I just knew he'd smell like Old Spice and would do things like fix my bike and play Monopoly with me while my mom made popcorn. We'd drink Coca Cola and laugh together. When I'd fall asleep on the couch, his strong arms would carry me to bed.

Sometimes, I'd watch my mother while she worked. Lana liked men. Some of them would touch her bottom or brush against her. Occasionally, she'd be offended, but most of the time, she loved it. She claimed being nice earned her bigger tips, which paid for my macaroni and cheese, thank you very much.

I decided to be a businesswoman when I grew up. I didn't want to be like Lana and have men fondling me just so I could afford macaroni and cheese, thank you very much.

Luckily, I excelled academically and tested into the Gifted Program. My mother wasn't thrilled, as one would expect. She resented my accomplishments and the camaraderie we had shared had been supplanted by an odd competitiveness, which intensified the older I became.

"Put that book down and watch a show with me," she would say. "Just because you're in that special program doesn't mean you're smarter than me."

"I don't think I'm smarter than you. I'm only as smart as you made me."

She married her auto mechanic about the time I turned sixteen; the same year my English teacher had encouraged me to audition for the school production of *Romeo and Juliet*. Having honed my skills before ever walking on stage, acting was second nature.

A hand touched my arm, jolting me back to the present, and I turned to big teeth leaning toward me. "Excuse me, Miss?" The flight attendant was taking drink orders. I ordered coffee with cream. The man next to me requested the same.

He asked, "You traveling for business or pleasure?"

"Business. I have a meeting in Boston."

I really didn't want to chat. Turning my head, I looked out the window and watched clouds wisp by. Life with Matt and our boys was a world apart from that of my childhood. Matt was never coarse or loud, and he was a devoted father. As a family, we valued education and polite behavior. We were steady and reliable, the type of family I'd coveted as a child.

My throat constricted and my chest weighed heavy again. *Breathe … deep breath, just breathe.* What the hell was my problem? I had a nice husband, two great boys, a beautiful home, and a successful career. My life was perfect.

I picked up my book, looking to escape my perfect life for a while.

After the first chapter, I was blissfully sucked into the world of Henry James. Having to switch flights in New York came as an unwelcome interlude. I trudged to the next gate, claimed a seat, and whipped out my book. Before I finished a single paragraph, a man sat next to me.

Impeccably polished black Gucci loafers. Charcoal grey, summer-weight—no doubt Italian wool—trousers. "Hello, Susan."

Reese. *Crap.* Levis and a snug-fitting V-neck t-shirt from Gap. I'd worn a sweater earlier, but had taken it off. I hoped my breasts weren't screaming, *"Look at me!"*

"Reese, I had no idea you were on this flight. I thought you weren't getting into Boston until tomorrow." I was proud of how quickly I'd composed myself.

"I went to school in Boston and have some college friends who still live there. I'm meeting them for dinner." That accounted for his GQ casual attire. "I'd invite you to join us, but it's a boys' only night."

Of course, but in his case, I didn't care. "No worries." I smiled, truly relieved not to be obligated to spend the evening with him.

His lips parted, as if he was going to say something, and I realized his eyes were fixated on my breasts. His jaw dropped a fraction. He looked back up, knowing he'd been caught, and shrugged. "Well," he said and stood, "I'll let you get back to your book." Then he walked away without a backward glance.

The sensations coursing through my body were inappropriate, but far from unpleasant. I caught myself wondering what it'd be like to kiss him, wondering if he'd known I'd be on this flight. Shaking a bit, I put on my sweater and buttoned it to my neck even though I wasn't cold.

I didn't see Reese again until I made my way down the aisle to the coach section of the plane. He sat in First Class, absorbed with his Blackberry. As luck would have it, the line halted just as I approached his seat. He glanced up at me, and I said, "Hi."

He barely nodded and kept typing.

I must've imagined him looking like he wanted to lick my breasts. I took my seat, amused by the wild fabrications of my ego. As my mother used to say, "That girl has some imagination."

I came by it honestly. Lana had had quite the imagination too. She'd convinced herself that one day some rich, successful man would order a beer and fall in love with her before he finished his pint. Occasionally, a customer would ask her out. She would be excited about the possibility of landing him as a permanent fix for our financial woes. Late at night I would hear them and think *he's not going to marry you.* Mrs. Fowler had told me if you want a nice husband, you had to be a nice girl. Mrs. Fowler had been my Sunday school teacher, and she had a nice husband who was a doctor.

For a little over a year, Mrs. Fowler would pick me up on Sunday mornings and take me to church while my mother slept. She'd discreetly warn me my mother's behavior with men wasn't nice. I think she believed it was her moral obligation to point out my mother's sins, lest the apple fall close to the tree.

She taught me Romans 8:7-8: ... *because the mind of the flesh is hostile to God; for it is not subject to God's law, neither indeed can it be. Those who are in the flesh cannot please God.*

One day I attempted to save my mother from her wanton ways by repeating some of Mrs. Fowler's wisdom. I never knew exactly what transpired between Lana and Mrs. Fowler, but Mrs. Fowler no longer took me to Sunday school.

I didn't forget Mrs. Fowler's warning about being a nice girl, but like my mother, I didn't lack for male attention. Unlike her, I was wary of it. I became very adept at making friends out of my would-be-suitors. For some reason, it's always been easier for me to be friends with men.

After Matt and I were engaged, I was greatly bothered if a man looked at me too fondly or complimented my appearance. Even Matt noticed and found it amusing.

"Why does it bother you when an attractive man talks to you? Are you tempted?"

"Of course not, I love you."

He chuckled. "Then relax."

But I couldn't relax because deep down a part of me enjoyed the attention, and was ashamed of enjoying it. Matt had adored me, and I'd felt so incredibly lucky to have him. I feared doing something that would jeopardize his love, but he'd stopped adoring me anyway. Early in our marriage, he'd said, "Grow up, Susan. Stop being so narcissistic. You have no idea how exhausting being with you is. I have serious work to do and don't have time for this."

I remember his words wounding me, shaming me, making me feel petty and small. After I had cried myself dry, I'd thought about my experience with Mrs. Fowler. My conclusion had been that Mrs. Fowler must have detected an unnatural hunger for male attention in me, and maybe she'd been right, but after I married, I only had wanted Matt's attention.

I grew up. I worked on being content with less, dialed down my personality, but sometimes my weaker nature got the better of me. Maybe that was why I was so restless.

I shook my head, internally chuckling. I over-think sometimes. What was unnatural about being flattered by a little notice? Wasn't that why women spent billions every year on cosmetics?

I reached for my bag under the seat and took out my book. My restlessness probably had more to do with the fact that I drank too much coffee than Mrs. Fowler's amateur psychology. When I got married, I had been an immature drama queen. Matt was a good husband, I was nothing like

Lana, and Reese was just a man who'd had a natural reaction to seeing cleavage. I didn't want to think about any of it anymore. I opened my book, longing for a mental escape, but the plane was already landing.

Chapter 5

The next evening, I arrived at the restaurant promptly at seven. Even though Reese and I had spent the day without any obvious awkwardness, I didn't change into the dress I'd brought. It was far from risqué, but I was more comfortable with my breasts well covered. Reese arrived ahead of me and was talking on his phone with a grim face. He gave me an abbreviated wave.

All day, he had fascinated me as he seamlessly directed dialogue and opinions. He oozed charisma and possessed a talent for putting people at ease by giving his full attention to whomever was speaking. As it turned out, we made a great tag team, knowing exactly when to jump in the conversation and when to defer to the other. The result being, we'd won a "next step" meeting. We were both looking forward to hearing an insider's view over dinner.

Reese clicked off his phone and shoved it in his pocket. "Bad news. That was John Frazier's assistant." John was our Bank of Boston contact. "His wife was in a car accident. She's fine, but he won't be able to join us."

"Oh jeeze, sorry to hear it." The hostess glanced our way, probably checking if Reese's entire party had arrived. "Guess we should cancel the reservation."

"Why? Do you doubt my ability to provide witty repartee?"

I tried to suppress a smile. "Honestly, please don't feel obligated to entertain me."

"I don't. You'll be entertaining me." I raised my brows, and he added, "You promised to be *pleasant*."

"I promised to *think about it*."

He laughed, not easily put off. "Come on, I'm starving, and I was looking forward to a good meal. Dinner for one would be a bit awkward in this fine establishment."

After clarifying only two of us would be dining, the Maître'd must have thought we were looking for a romantic evening because he ushered us to a dimly lit table in a secluded corner. I immediately noticed the tablecloths and velvet chairs. As I suspected, entrees started at thirty-five dollars. The prices weren't outrageous if we were entertaining a client but were well above company guidelines for just us. Reese would be paying out of pocket.

Being alone with him in a romantic setting made me increasingly self-conscious. It didn't feel like a business dinner anymore. I should have insisted he cancel the reservation.

He set his menu down, while I continued to feign great interest in the selections. "Have you decided on anything?"

I set my menu down too. "Yes, I have."

"Good." He paused, tilted his head, and contemplated me. "So, you read Henry James?"

"Is that against corporate policy?"

"Funny girl … I'm just surprised."

"Why? I can read, you know."

"Okay Sparky, can you work with me here?" he requested with a little chuckle. "May I be honest with you?"

No! I wasn't sure I liked being called Sparky. I tried to sound Lauren Bacall cool. "I hope you'll always be honest with me."

"I'll rephrase. May I be candid?" He focused those magnetic eyes of his on mine. "You intrigue me. You're always so cool and composed, wearing your game face. Only once have I seen you without it," he said, hinting at our espresso bar encounter. "But I've observed some things that tell me someone else is hiding behind the banker suit. I want to know *her.*"

I had to look away. I didn't know how well I wanted him to know me.

His voice dropped to just above a whisper. "I just want to get to know you. Will you let me?" He looked uneasy, as if he'd tipped his hand more than he'd intended.

I took a deep breath. *Matt would disapprove.* I exhaled slowly. *What was there for Matt to be upset about?* I read too much into things. "As long as it's not against corporate policy."

He smiled. He had won. "I think we're safe."

The waiter arrived to take our order. Reese selected a Silver Oak cabernet. Since he'd set the precedence with an expensive wine, I didn't feel badly about ordering a pricey steak.

Reese popped his eyes at me. "Ah, the lady has an appetite."

"Yes, the lady likes her meat products."

"All meat products?"

"Big and juicy are my favorite."

He raised his eyebrows and made a poor attempt not to laugh.

My cheeks instantly blazed. Oh, my God, it had been a long time since I had to worry about such things having more than one meaning. "Uh, I didn't mean it like that."

We both laughed. The mood definitely lightened. He let it pass and went back to his original question. "So, you like Henry James?"

"Yes, he's one of my favorite authors."

"Really? What do you like about him?"

"I find it interesting that the characters have public faces of propriety and manners. They behave according to the social constraints of the day, but underneath there's heightened emotions, passion. The characters are like boiling pots of water: the longer they repress, the steamier things get. And it's all subtext, subtext, subtext … I just like it." It was rather embarrassing to admit. I wished I had some brilliant explanation involving literary theory.

"That actually makes sense. Maybe I'll give James another try."

The waiter brought our wine. Reese skipped the requisite swirling, smelling, and tasting and indicated the waiter should pour without ceremony.

I took a sip. "This is yummy. Thanks for the treat."

"My pleasure. Wine is a little hobby of mine. I'm a minor collector. How about you?"

"I have a glass or two almost every night, but I'm strictly amateur, less than $20 a bottle is my speed." I continued with a question of my own. "So which Henry James have you read?"

"*Portrait of a Lady* is the only one I finished. Required reading." He rolled his eyes.

"Don't tell me. You had to take an English class to graduate. Business or Econ major?"

"No, actually my major was English. I'd had dreams of becoming the next great American novelist, but after I graduated, business school seemed more practical. The idea of being a starving artist didn't appeal to me. I like my luxuries," he said, lifting his glass.

"Wait a second. How could you dream of being the next great American novelist and not love Henry James?" I asked with mock outrage.

"Too much … *subtext*," he joked.

"English major? Writer? I never would have guessed." Now I was intrigued.

"Why would you? Most of our colleagues were Business or Econ majors. I doubt very many of them even know who Henry James is."

"Very true." Global Security employed very bright people, but it was a wasteland when it came to cultural conversation. Maybe we could be friends. We could be comrades in books.

He looked puzzled, probably wondering why I was smiling, but asked, "Who else do you like? Jane Austen?"

"Too obvious. Being a woman, I have no choice but to love Jane."

"Which book is your favorite, *Pride and Prejudice* or *Sense and Sensibility*?"

"Aren't you really asking if I prefer Colin Firth or Hugh Grant?"

"Okay?"`

"Have you read any of her novels or just seen the movies?"

"Hey, I've read Jane Austen."

"Required reading?" I teased.

He rolled his eyes at me again. "Just because I'm a man doesn't mean I can't enjoy Jane Austen. And just so you don't get the wrong impression, I'm also a serious hockey fan."

"Okay, Mr. Manly Man—"

"Okay, Ms. Smarty Pants, just answer the question."

We were both grinning and snickering.

"Alright. I love Hugh's boyish charm and the way his eyes crinkle up, but Mr. Darcy's love for Elizabeth and Colin's big brown eyes … well …." I couldn't help sighing.

"Ah, you're a romantic," he accused good-naturedly.

"Guilty," I admitted, wishing I hadn't.

Our conversation was interrupted by the waiter serving our salads. We chatted about business until we finished our meal. Then Reese turned the conversation back to "getting to know you" as we lingered, sipping the last of the wine.

"Mind if I try to guess what your major was in college?" he asked amused.

"Sure, go ahead." I maintained a poker face, certain he'd guess incorrectly.

"Well, let's see … this morning I would have guessed Business Administration or Econ, but since I know you better, I'm going with … Art History."

"You got part of it right."

"History?"

"Wrong half." I showed him some pity. "*Dramatic* Art. I have an MFA in Acting."

"Hmmm, that explains a lot," he said chuckling. "Ever perform Shakespeare?"

"Yes, Shakespeare was my favorite to act."

"Bet you played Juliet." His eyes twinkled flirtatiously.

"As a matter of fact, I did. Twice." I smiled back.

He quoted:

"But soft! What light through yonder window breaks?

It is the east, and Juliet is the sun.

Arise, fair sun, and kill the envious moon,

Who is already sick and pale with grief

That thou, her maid, art far more fair than she."

"Very good." He was good. He said the line beautifully, a musical cadence in his voice.

"English major," he said quite pleased with himself. "What was your favorite line?"

I quoted with feeling,

"My bounty is as boundless as the sea,

My love as deep: the more I give thee,

The more I have: for both are infinite."

Reese's expression softened. He looked straight into my eyes. "I'm sure you were a beautiful, enchanting Juliet. I would have loved to have seen you play her."

I giggled, buzzing from too much wine. "We should go. It's getting late."

He asked for the check and paid the bill. It was a nice evening, so we walked the ten or so blocks back to the hotel. Reese stayed very close to me; close enough that we could have held hands, close enough that he occasionally bumped me with his arm. We walked in silence, and I was struck by how surprisingly tranquil I felt. Being around him was easy.

When we got to the lobby, he spoke first. "Would you care for a nightcap?"

Matt wouldn't like it. The good girl in me said, "Sorry, I have an early flight. Best not."

"Of course, I understand." His half smile didn't conceal his disappointment.

"Thank you for dinner, and the wine, and the company. I really enjoyed myself."

"Me too." He grinned and gave me a wink.

"Well, good night," I said and thrust my hand out.

He took my hand but didn't shake it. He held it and leaned toward me. For a second I thought he was going to try to kiss me, but he didn't. He whispered, *"Sleep dwell upon thine eyes, peace in thy breast."* Reese didn't finish the line. He squeezed my hand and grazed his thumb over my palm as he pulled away. Then he sauntered in the direction of the hotel bar, leaving me stunned with his breath still warm in my ear.

He had to know I knew the second half of the line. *Would I were sleep and peace so sweet to rest.* An image of Reese lying naked on top of me blurred my vision, and I struggled to wrestle it out of my head. My wedding ring and corporate policies were thick, insurmountable barriers. His flirtatiousness had safe limits, and he'd never do something that would jeopardize his position. His parting line had been nothing more than being a show off.

The following Monday morning, I woke especially early, unable to sleep. I was wide-awake, and the house quiet. I thought about going straight into my office, but my staff would think I was nuts if they got e-mails from me at that hour. Instead, I made coffee and sat down with *The Awakening*, but was too restless to read. My only other option was an early morning workout, so that's what I did. After I finished and showered, it was almost six. Since arriving home from Boston late Friday, I had stayed away from my laptop. My penance was over.

It didn't take long to zip through the hundred or so e-mails that hit my Inbox while traveling and over the weekend. Most were redundant. My staff tended to copy me on conversations, which meant I would receive ten e-mails on the same subject, but really only needed to read the last one.

An e-mail from Reese popped up: *Thanks for having dinner with me and being pleasant.*

I responded: *The pleasure was all mine. Your witty repartee did not disappoint.*

My phone rang less than a minute after I hit the send button. I checked the caller id.

"Good morning, Reese," I answered.

"Morning. You always start this early?"

"Most days. I like to get in a workout and clear my first round of East Coast e-mails before the West Coast starts pinging me."

"I love a woman who wakes up with energy."

I tried not to laugh, but couldn't help it.

"What?" He paused to think about why I was laughing. "*That's* not what I meant."

I love a man who is quick in the morning. "I think we're even now."

"Fair enough. How was your weekend?"

"It was okay."

"Just okay? What did you do?"

Did I really want to tell him? What the heck. "I spent a lovely Saturday evening with the wife of my husband's colleague and her friends who chatted about what's on sale at the grocery store and Handy Household Hints from Heloise."

Reese chuckled. "I take it the conversation was less than witty."

"You are correct. The conversation was decidedly waxen."

"Waxen? What do you mean?"

"It was Craft Night. We made candles."

Reese laughed. "I can't see you at a Craft Night. How did you get through it?"

"With plenty of cheap wine." We both laughed. "What did you do this weekend?"

"I saw *Wicked.*"

"Ah, you had a date." I cringed. Why did I say that? It was none of my business.

"Yes, but sadly, the conversation was waxen compared to your company."

My cheeks burned. "How was the show?"

"Wickedly entertaining."

"Were you bewitched?"

"Spellbound." He chuckled again.

There was a pause, and I redirected the conversation before I said something I would later regret. I already regretted what I was thinking and feeling. "Well, if you don't mind, I have a question about the report due this afternoon."

We flipped into business mode and sorted through concerns I had about the data he'd asked me to analyze. Before we hung up, Reese turned the conversation back to personal.

"I really did enjoy having dinner with you."

"I enjoyed it, too."

"Does this mean you'll answer more of my 'getting to know you' questions?"

I laughed and asked, "How many more do you have?"

"Only a few dozen."

After talking to Reese, I bubbled with energy and was in a better mood than I'd been all weekend. It was nice that we could joke together and get work done. That conversation established our morning routine. Unless we were traveling, Reese called me every morning.

I wasn't surprised to learn that *Romeo and Juliet* was his favorite Shakespeare and accused him of having adolescent tastes. I preferred *Antony and Cleopatra*: epic, power couple, a more adult romance. I visualized Reese when I thought of Cleopatra's line:

His face was as the heavens, and therein stuck

A sun and moon, which kept their course and lighted

The little O, the earth.

His favorite season was autumn, just like me. We both liked the crispness in the air and hearty comfort food that came with it. Assuming I'd prefer something exotic, he was surprised yellow roses were my favorite flowers. He'd been an only child and had grown up in New York. We both had gone to college on scholarships. On and on it went.

He became my mood elevator. I looked forward to his calls like a druggie looking forward to her next fix. Each night I went through the motions of living: cooking dinner, watching the boys play catch, or kicking a soccer ball around in our backyard. I read to them, tucked them into bed, and kissed them goodnight. I visited with Matt before turning off the lights. As the night wore on, it'd be as if I was holding my breath. I couldn't sleep and was in a constant state of anticipation. As soon as I'd hear his voice, I'd relax and could breathe again.

Why shouldn't I look forward to talking with him? Work was exciting and engrossing. He was an integral part of it. Besides, we never discussed anything inappropriate. Not to say Reese wasn't a flirt—he was, but so were a lot of men in sales. It didn't mean anything. We were buddies. Good buddies.

Chapter 6

Matt planned for us to abandon civilization early Thursday morning Fourth of July weekend and return to the land of air conditioning, soft beds, and lattes late Sunday. Just after ten Wednesday night, I finally finished an overview of existing client relations for Reese. I sent the report, set my out-of-office message, and was about to shut down my laptop for the next four days, when I received an email from Reese: *May I call you?*

I replied: *Yes. Home office. Thanks*

Seconds later, Reese's number lit up my phone. I grabbed it before it rang. "Jeeze Reese, it's one in the morning in New York. What are you doing up?"

"Same thing you're doing: working. Thanks for taking my call."

"Sure. What's up?"

"May I borrow you from your family a few hours Friday? I really want to review this presentation deck with you and need some help with a few other things."

Matt would kill me. I'd have to leave the campsite and go to the nearest town for wireless connectivity. "Can it wait for Monday?"

"I'd rather it not. Honestly, I don't trust anyone else in this company yet. You can call me any time it's convenient … *please?*"

The vulnerability in his voice tugged on me, and I glanced at the clock. How could I say no to a boss who 'trusts' me and was still working at one in the morning? The man was going to kill himself if he kept going at this pace. By comparison, I was a slacker.

"Okay, but only if you promise you'll power down your laptop and go to bed."

He chuckled and his voice dropped low and intimate. "I promise, and I'll even sleep in tomorrow if it'll make you feel better."

"It does. Now go to bed."

"You say that as if you're giving a corporate directive."

"I am," I ordered.

"Well, in that case," he paused and then whispered like a caress, like a lover's breath on my ear, "sweet dreams."

Of course, he was tired, and I probably imagined unintentional intimacy. I sighed and shut down my own laptop. I thought I was a driven type A. I was a type C in comparison.

Matt was still awake when I crawled into bed. His expression warned me he was disgruntled about something. "Are you finally done?" he asked.

"Yes." Now was not the time to tell him I had committed to working a few hours on Friday. "Are we all set for tomorrow?"

"All packed. Just have to load the ice chest."

And my laptop. I have to find room for my laptop bag. I leaned over, kissed him goodnight, and turned off the light.

He asked in the dark, "Who were you talking to?"

"When?" I knew when.

"Just now … in your office."

"My boss. He had a few questions."

"You've got to establish boundaries with him. He's taking advantage of you."

"I can handle Reese." Now was definitely not the time.

I was up at five to fix snacks for the road, and Matt had us cruising up 101 North by six. We made it over the Bay Bridge before it clogged up with holiday travelers and sailed up I-80 towards Truckee with clear roads. The boys went immediately back to sleep and Matt and I enjoyed an hour of quiet.

He seemed perfectly placid, until he said, "I noticed your laptop bag made its way into the van." His tone wasn't confrontational. It was blasé, and he kept his eyes on the road.

"I wasn't able to wrap everything up. I'll have to work a few hours tomorrow."

"You won't have power or connectivity at the campsite."

"I figured that would be the case."

"You promised you wouldn't work."

He said it with no more importance than commenting about the weather, but there it was. He was pissed. His knuckles were white from tightly gripping the wheel.

"I know. I'm sorry." Mom guilt crept into my heart. My family deserved four days of my undivided attention, but I had already promised Reese.

Micah piped up from the backseat. "Are we close? I'm hungry."

Matt dropped the work subject. "We'll stop for something to eat in Sacramento."

Micah groaned. "How far is Sacramento?"

I handed him a baggie of sliced apples. "These should hold you."

The rest of the drive passed in relative peace and with only one major squabble between Micah and Jason. Micah was very sensitive about Jason touching him, but Jason kept taunting Micah with his finger a hair away from Micah's arm.

"Jason, stop now!" I ordered.

Less than a minute later, Micah screamed, "JASON." Then he punched Jason in the arm.

"I didn't do anything."

"You BREATHED on me."

"Boys, if I have to pull this van over, you're both going to be *very sorry*. Neither of you are too big for a spanking." Matt had never once actually spanked the boys, but the mere threat was enough to make them settle down.

I don't know how the guys could sleep on the hard ground. I intended to invest in a blow up mattress before agreeing to another camping trip. Why go through the hassle of erecting a tent when there were perfectly good motels within half an hour of the campsite? Matt's explanation had been, "It's a completely different experience." Yep, my point exactly.

It didn't help that Jason had announced he had to go to the bathroom after we'd settled into our sleeping bags for the night. Matt had been asleep so I had to walk Jason to the bathroom. I told him to go behind the tent, but he'd said he had to go number two. Walking back in pitch black with the flashlight providing the only light, every noise seemed a prelude to an ax-wielding psycho killer leaping out of the woods or a rabid raccoon dropping on our heads.

I couldn't sleep the rest of the night, and as soon as the sun made the world semi-visible, I dressed. I planned to drive into town and be back before the guys hit the trail for the day. I couldn't find the van keys and had to wake Matt.

"Where are you going?" he asked.

"Into town. I have some work to do."

He reached under his pillow and handed me the keys. I thought that was the end of it, but before I could start the engine, Matt was standing in front of the van. I stepped back out.

"Is there something you want me to pick up?"

"No." He crossed his arms. "I want to know why you're going."

"Matt, you know why. I promise I won't be gone more than a couple hours."

"You promised to turn off work."

"I know and I'm sorry. I'm in the middle of a project … I don't have a choice."

"It's a holiday weekend! Who the hell is working other than you?"

"My boss for one. You knew when I took this promotion it would be more demanding of my time. We discussed it and agreed it would be worth it." Matt shook his head. "No. I agreed because I knew how much you wanted the job. If I had any idea you'd be taking calls at night and working holidays, I wouldn't have agreed. We don't need the money that badly."

"You're being *so* not fair. This is an important career move for me, and we did talk about it. We talked about the money and the difference it would make to our lives."

"Yes, but we don't have to drive $50,000 cars and shop at Neiman Marcus. Look at Todd and Sara. She doesn't work, and they manage just fine. I swear, Susan, I don't know where you've developed your champagne tastes."

He hit so many nerves I didn't even know where to start with a response. "Is that what you want? You want me to stay home and be like Sara?"

"You know that's not what I meant."

"Then, I don't know what you meant. The money I make allows the boys to go to private school and riding camp. It allows you to go on ski trips and buy all this expensive camping crap. Don't make it sound like it's just for me."

"Just because you make more money than me, doesn't mean your job should dictate our lives. You don't have to let your company take so much out of you. It's just a job."

"It's not just a *job*. It's my career. It's as important to me as your research is to you."

"It's not the same. What I do is important—"

"And what I do isn't?"

"Quite frankly, no. I don't think selling services so people can access bank accounts from cell phones is very important. As far as I can tell, you spend your day on the phone. I don't know what you actually do."

Shaking, I didn't know if I was more hurt or flat out angry.

"Dad, Mom …" Micah walked up to us. "We can hear you fighting. Jason's crying."

"I'll talk him," I announced, forcing myself calm. "Give me a minute, please."

Micah and Matt waited while I went into the tent to talk to Jason. I found him curled up in his sleeping bag with his head buried in his pillow and his little shoulders trembling. I crouched next to him and ran my fingers through his hair.

"Hey, buddy. Why the tears?"

"I heard you and Dad fighting," he answered in between hiccups.

"We weren't fighting. We were talking. Sometimes adults have to talk to each other."

"Sounded like fighting to me. Mike told me about his parents fighting."

I had forgotten about Jack and Denise Carter splitting up. "We had a heated discussion. It's not the same as fighting."

"Okay. Mike's dad doesn't live with him anymore. You won't make Dad leave, will you?"

"Of course not, Jason. Dad and I disagree sometimes, but it doesn't mean that we don't want to stay a family." I hugged him and he wrapped his little arms around me. "Feel better?"

"Yeah."

I walked outside and Micah went into the tent. Matt sat in the passenger's seat of the van waiting for me. I geared for another round and got into the driver's seat.

Matt turned to me, and the fight was over. "I'm sorry for what I said. I know your work is important to you, and if you ever make Sara's casserole, I'll consider it grounds for divorce." He reached over and took my hand. "I don't want you to be like Sara."

"Thank you. I'm sorry I committed to working this morning."

"I understand. Should we wait for you?"

"Please. I'll be back as fast as I can."

He pecked my lips before he got out of the van. I appreciated Matt's apology, but I wasn't sure what it encompassed. Was he sorry for trivializing my work? For slamming me for buying a car? I thought he approved of the car. I needed to dress well for work. I thought he liked that I dressed well. Was he truly sorry or was he simply weary of the fight?

I did agree with Matt about one thing; it was ridiculous Reese couldn't wait until Monday. No one was working. It didn't take long before Reese irritated me, too.

Our work discussion kept sidetracking. Reese wasn't focused. After fifteen minutes of idle chat, I finally said, "Well, if there isn't anything else …."

"I'm sorry. I'm keeping you from your family."

"I'm sure you have things to do, too."

"Not really. The office is empty. The whole island of Manhattan is empty. They've all gone to the Hamptons. I could be there, too. I have an open invitation to join friends who have a house on the beach. They want me to meet a woman who's staying with them."

"Then what are you doing in the office?"

"I'm talking to you," he said with far too many undercurrents.

And getting me in trouble with my husband. "Well, I'm out of time."

"I see. Maybe I will go to the Hamptons." Was he trying to make me jealous?

"Good." Why should I care if he met some woman in the Hamptons?

"Susan, are you mad at me?"

"I really have to go."

Part of me was jealous and a part of me was just plain pissed off. I let Reese flirt and flatter me to a point where I'd do almost anything he asked. This was my vacation for heaven's sake. Reese needed boundaries. I didn't want to hear about his personal life.

I returned to the campsite contrite and ready to be a good sport. Despite the heat, the flies, and the mosquitoes, I was glad to be there. The best part was at night when we sat around our campfire toasting marshmallows and making s'mores. The heat earlier in the day had been replaced with fresh, cool air scented by the surrounding pine. Without televisions, video games, or computers, there was only one thing left to do. Wonder of wonders, we talked.

Jason surprised me the last night when he asked, "Mom, was I adopted?"

Micah snorted. I knew the source of the question. "No, buddy, you were not adopted."

"I was just teasing, but how come Jason has blue eyes? He should have brown like me," Micah stated logically. "Dad told us brown eyes are dominant. The only way for Jason to have blue is if you have a blue gene, but everyone in your family has brown."

Matt met my eyes and said, "Tell them. They're old enough."

I took a breath first. "Well, the reason Jason's are blue is because Grandpa Rich isn't my birth father. My biological father has blue eyes."

"Grandpa Rich isn't your dad?" Jason asked with disbelief.

"No, honey. He's my stepfather, but he thinks of you as his grandsons. It doesn't change anything for you."

"What happened to your dad?" Micah asked.

"He left Grandma Lana and me when I was three. I don't know what happened to him."

"Didn't he want you?" Jason asked, on the verge of tears.

He wanted his new wife more. My chest clenched with an old ache, but I kept my voice steady. "It's complicated, and it was a long time ago."

Matt handed me a s'more. I bit into gooey chocolate and marshmallow, so decadently comforting, but Matt's arm around me was even more so. I leaned against him.

"We're Mom's family now. Micah, when you were born, I couldn't believe how much you looked like Mom. Then Jason was born …"

"And he looked just like Dad," I added.

"The day Jason came home from the hospital, I thought, 'now we're a real family.' We weren't just a couple anymore or a couple with a baby. We were a family."

I smiled at my boy's chocolate covered faces. *We are a family.*

"When did you decide you wanted to marry Mom?" Micah asked.

"The first day I met her. I'd seen her around campus for about a year, but she never noticed me. Then one day I saw her in the cafeteria. I kept the chair at my table open, hoping she'd take it. Like magic, she did. I thought Mom was the most beautiful girl I'd ever seen."

"You've never told me that before." I kissed his cheek, touched by his admission.

Shrugging, Matt got up to put more wood on the fire. He was a funny guy sometimes.

Matt and I didn't discuss our disagreement at the campsite again. He didn't hint in any way that he was unhappy with me until my birthday the first week in August. Earlier in the day, I had received a dozen yellow roses. The note was simple, nothing cryptic: *Juliet, Happy Birthday.* No signature, as if I wouldn't know who sent them. I set the flowers on the kitchen table and tore the note into little pieces before tossing it into the garbage.

When Matt came home from work, he asked, "Who sent the flowers?"

I didn't like the idea of lying to Matt, but I didn't want to tell him they were from Reese either. Of course, Reese represented Global Security. "Global Security."

"They've never sent you flowers before."

That's because Reese wasn't my boss before. "I wasn't a Sr. Vice President before."

"As hard as you've been working, they owe you more than flowers."

I couldn't have agreed more. I'd been working my tail off.

I cooked dinner just as if it were an ordinary night. I was beginning to doubt Matt would do anything special for my birthday. Just before dinner, his mother had dropped off a cake she and my boys had made, but Matt had done nothing.

After dinner, the boys gave me a card and framed photos from our camping trip. Based on the style of the frames, I was sure Matt's mother selected them. Then Matt handed me a small package. My heart softened at the idea of Matt buying me a piece of jewelry. He'd never bought me jewelry. I opened the box and looked down at a cheap BMW key chain, the kind sold at novelty stores. I picked it up and stared at it in my hand, expecting it to morph into something special, something symbolic of how much Matt loved and esteemed me.

Matt explained when he saw me looking puzzled, "The car was your gift, remember?"

Chapter 7

I wasn't quite sure if it was planned on his part or mine, but Reese and I were never alone. I kept my travel schedule tight to minimize time away from home. If we had an overnight together, he'd invite a client or another colleague to join us for dinner. I avoided staying in the same hotel with him. Our friendship safely blossomed, but after my birthday, things started to change. Our conversations became more personal, and then one night we were at the New York office working late in a small conference room. Curtis Pope, a young attorney from the legal team, was helping us with contract templates.

I didn't realize how late it was until Curtis said, "Hey, guys. Sorry, it's almost eight and my wife will kill me if I don't get home. It's our date night."

"I appreciate you staying as late as you did. Enjoy your date," Reese said graciously, but as soon as Curtis left, he grunted, "*Fuck*. This should've been finished yesterday."

"Tonight or tomorrow morning doesn't matter."

"It matters. Look, I was hired with high expectations."

"You're doing an impressive job. Everyone thinks so."

"Even you?"

"Especially me. I think you're rather brilliant with all of this."

His lips pressed together, but they were turned up at the corners. "Thank you. I appreciate you being my little cheerleader. I shouldn't dump on you though. You can take off."

I couldn't walk out on him. I just couldn't. In front of everyone else, Reese maintained an unflappable demeanor, but he dropped the mask with me. We had an important project to finish. No rule stated we couldn't be alone together, and no one was waiting for me. I could work in the office or in the hotel room.

"Let's get it done," I said.

Reese ordered Chinese food and we kept working. Exhausted and blurry eyed, we had to stop just before midnight. We couldn't do any more until Curtis reviewed the documents in the morning. I stood up, stretching and twisting, trying to work out my kinks.

"Poor thing," he said. "On a plane all day yesterday and now I've kept you late. You need to tell me when I'm overworking you."

I smiled at him. Acknowledging how hard he pushed me was rare. "I'm holding up."

He grinned back. "You've earned a shoulder rub."

If it hadn't been so late, and I wasn't so tired, I wouldn't have agreed. He sat me in a chair and started on my shoulders. His fingers applied the perfect amount of pressure, and I groaned with pleasure.

"You have a big knot right there," he said, digging his thumb into my shoulder blade.

"Ah, that's heavenly. I may not move for the rest of the night."

He chuckled and kept rubbing me while we talked. "I owe you an all-night massage. Honestly, I don't know what I would've done without you these last couple months."

"You know what you're doing."

"But I don't know Global Security and you do. You're my walking atlas. If I didn't have you by my side, navigating this company would be a nightmare. I want you to know how much I value your help. Thank you."

To be indispensable to someone like Reese was a huge compliment. He couldn't see me grinning stupidly. "This mean you're going to remember me when you're CEO?"

"Are you kidding? I plan to keep you by my side each step of the way." He shifted from my shoulders to my head and asked, "Feel good?"

I moaned. "Uh huh, really good."

"You've never told me how you went from being an actress to an SVP of this corporate behemoth. What's your story?"

"Well, when we finished school, Matt wanted to move back to the Bay Area. It's not exactly a theater Mecca. He didn't want me to work, but I hated being the little wife."

"Staying home wasn't for you?"

"It wasn't just that …."

"What was it?"

"I hated that he was so … condescending."

"How so?"

"Little ways. He assumed he was smarter because he had the academic degree, and I was just this cute little actress. He talked about my acting as if it were a hobby."

"Like a Craft Club?"

I snickered. "Yeah, like a Craft Club. I took my acting career seriously. When he didn't, it was as though …"

"He didn't take you seriously?"

"Exactly. Can you believe he actually gave me an allowance?"

"I'm sure that went over well." He chuckled. "So you decided to get a regular job?"

"Uh huh. I refused to do the actor thing and wait tables. I always had sales jobs. Given my experience, getting into outside sales was easy. I decided I'd show him."

"And you did?"

"I did. I made more money than Matt my very first year."

"How'd he take it?"

"I don't know. My income took some pressure off, but it bothered him. It's still a sore spot. I think he sees it as a scam that he does 'serious' work, but I make more. I didn't set out to bruise his ego. I just wanted him to respect me." I paused and Reese's hands rested idly on my shoulders. He studied my reflection in the window. It was wrong of me to discuss my marriage with him. "I don't know why I'm telling you this." I moved to get up, but his hands held me in place.

"We're kindred spirits. You trust me, just like I trust you ... Is it hard for you?"

I knew he was referring to being married to Matt. "No, sales is a lot like acting."

His hands started moving again and glided to my lower back. I bent over, unintentionally pulling up my blouse. He made brief contact with my skin. I straightened and his touch became caressing. "How's that?"

"Heavenly, but you can stop if you want."

He didn't, but clarified, "I meant how is sales like acting?"

"Oh, sorry. Good acting requires being a good listener. In a scene, each character has an objective. Actors listen, read the body language of the scene partner, and then react to achieve their objective. Sales is no different. Listen to the customer, watch body language for buying signs, give them what they want so you get what you want, a close ... you do it all the time."

"Really? Hmmm. Sounds borderline manipulative."

"No, it's figuring out what the customer really wants or needs, even when they don't know what they want or need, and then meeting that need or want. It's not manipulative. But I have seen you be manipulative."

"Nope, I'm persuasive. There's a difference."

I laughed. It was a fine line, just like "lying and pretending" was a fine line to my mother when I was a little girl. "What's the difference?"

"Choice. With persuasion, a choice is given to the decision maker. With manipulation, the choice is taken away."

"But you know the choice you want the prospect to make."

He laughed. "Absolutely."

I laughed with him. "The ethical splitting of hairs."

He worked his fingers under my hair into the base of my neck. I tilted my head to give him easier access. He said, "I've been listening and watching your body language. Am I giving you what you want?"

"You are."

"Am I being persuasive or manipulative?"

"Neither. You're being nice."

He pulled my hair back, gingerly kissed my neck, and then whispered, "Am I still giving you what you want?"

He pressed his lips against me again, sending waves of heat scalding through me. God, how I wanted to turn around and crush against him, but Matt's face flashed in front of me. I held perfectly still and made my voice icy. "And what is it you want, Reese?"

He shot upright. "I want you to forget that just happened. I'm sorry. I shouldn't have done it. Please, forgive me."

"It's late. I need to go."

I packed up my things, but Reese stayed. He called a security guard to escort me out of the building and hail a cab for me.

Alone in the hotel room later that night, I couldn't sleep. I couldn't stop thinking about what happened. I blamed myself. I shouldn't have let him touch me. It was completely inappropriate. I wouldn't want another woman's hands running over Matt's body. Reese had accurately read my voice and my body language. He was a man, not a saint. As a little girl, I'd been ashamed of my mother. She had been beautiful and no poorer than our acquaintances, but she had lacked judgment. I was more like her than I cared to admit.

The next morning, Reese called me into his office. He sat barricaded behind his heavy mahogany desk with his face creased and his eyes avoiding mine.

"About last night …," he started.

"It was late. We were both tired. It didn't mean anything."

He locked eyes with me. "Is that what you really think?"

I wasn't sure. I wasn't sure about anything but held steady. "Of course. Don't you?"

A flicker of anger, or possible hurt, marred his handsome features. I averted my eyes, not wanting to see either. When I looked back, his face was smooth, making me think I'd imagined emotions that didn't exist. He asked, "Can we still be friends?"

The thought of losing his friendship made my insides twist and my chest tight. I had come to rely upon it more than I'd realized. "I treasure your friendship. You are my friend."

"*Good* friend?"

"Good *friend*."

We went back to work. It took a few days before the awkwardness dissipated. After a week, I could almost pretend it had never happened.

Chapter 8

I arrived home late August, after yet another business trip, to an empty house and a note on the kitchen table stating Matt had taken the boys to a ball game. I had wanted them home greeting me when I walked in the door. The fact that their lives hummed along without me left me feeling obsolete. Admittedly, it was an emotional response after a tiring trip, selfish of me to expect their lives to revolve around my schedule.

When they got home an hour later, Micah and Jason were all hugs and smiles. Matt said hello, but didn't reach for me. I disentangled from the boys and put my arms around him. He gave me a perfunctory squeeze and released me. I tried to ignore the pang zinging me and gave my full attention to Micah and Jason. They'd received news in the mail for the new school year.

"Jason got Mrs. Jacobson, and he started crying," Micah volunteered.

Jason's face reddened. "Well, everyone says she yells and gives lots of homework."

"Don't be a wuss, Jason."

I hated that word. "Micah, I've told you."

"All the guys say it, Mom."

"Matt?" I looked to him for reinforcement.

Matt sighed. "Micah, listen to your mother."

I turned to Jason, still teary-eyed, and put my arms around him. "You were scared of Mrs. Bates last year, and then you had a great year."

"Will you take me to school the first day?"

He looked so much like Matt—blond hair, wide blue eyes—I gave him a squeeze. "You bet. I'm sure everything will be fine." I turned to Micah. "Who did you get?"

"Mr. Stewart. He's cool. He has pizza parties when the class does really well on tests."

I missed hearing their chatter. They continued to give me a rundown on what happened in their lives while I was gone. It was funny how many insignificant things they wanted to share once I was home. When I called from the road, the most I could get out of them were a few grunts and 'yeah' or 'no.' Matt wasn't much better.

School and fall just around the corner meant soccer would be starting soon. After I sent the boys off to get ready for bed, I asked Matt, "Any word about soccer?"

"Micah has his first practice tomorrow morning."

"Who's his coach?"

"John Roberts."

John had been his coach a couple years ago. I liked John and his wife, Tracy. She was fun to chat with during the games. "That's great. I can't commit to anything weekly, but I'll sign up for the end of season party."

He smiled. "I already volunteered you."

"Thanks. What about you and Jason?"

Matt was coaching Jason's team this year, and he'd been playing in the same men's league for years and loved it. Our house would be soccer crazed in a few weeks. It wasn't my thing, but I went to the games anyway. At least Matt didn't expect me at all of his matches.

"Men's league starts next week, and I'm having the first parent meeting for Jason's team on Monday. Will you be home?"

"All week. Want me to go with you to the meeting?"

"It's not necessary." He got up and stretched. "Think I'll go to bed. Can you take care of the boys?"

"Sure. I'll tuck them in." Matt started to walk out of the room. He didn't ask about my trip. He didn't tell me he missed me. "Matt, anything wrong?"

He looked at me with a blank expression. "No, why?"

"No reason. Guess I just missed you."

"Missed you, too," he said and went into the bedroom.

I wondered if he really did miss me. Maybe I *was* becoming obsolete to him. The heaviness crept back on my chest. I felt unmoored with Matt drifting away from me, and it scared me. Good thing I'd be home for the week.

The next day Matt told me he'd planned another camping trip for Labor Day weekend. I didn't object. "Great idea. It'll be nice to get away a few days."

"I don't expect you to go," he offered.

"Don't you want me to go?"

"Not if you'll be spending half the time working."

"I'll leave my laptop at home. Promise." I kissed him. "I want to come with you."

"Then come."

We took the boys to their first day of school the following week. Matt had had a much more affluent upbringing; not that his family was rich, but for him, private school was a given. Peninsula Day School was expensive and, consequently, exclusive. As a family, we'd endured an extensive interview process before Micah, and then Jason, were accepted. The first couple of years, we barely had been able to scrape together the tuition payments.

At the boys' school, polite behavior was a rule. Cell phones, iPods, and the like were strictly prohibited. It was a nice environment with nice children, who came from nice families. We were all extremely damn nice to each other.

As soon as we walked on campus, Micah wanted to race off to join his friends on the playground. I tried to hug and kiss him goodbye, but he said, "Mom stop, that's embarrassing." He was growing up so fast. He'd had no problem kissing me goodbye last year.

Matt and I then walked Jason to class and met the terrifying Mrs. Jacobson. She seemed like a kind grandmother. She smiled affectionately at my little guy. He smiled shyly back. He would be fine. Jason hugged me and let me kiss him on the cheek before I left.

We finished our back-to-school ritual in the multipurpose room for the annual welcome back coffee hour hosted by the PTA. No home baked goods or weak Folgers for this crowd. The event was catered by *Patisserie Bleu*. On the walls, the best of last year's art projects were displayed like pieces of fine art. Micah's scribble jobs were nowhere to be seen, but Jason's purple witch and Beluga whale had places of honor.

As I chatted with other parents, Matt at my side, I wondered what they thought of us. Matt was his usual reticent self. He wasn't unfriendly, just quiet. He wore jeans, a polo shirt, and sneakers, his standard work ensemble. I was the queen of cocktail, or in this case coffee, conversation in my cashmere sweater set, dress pants, and heels. It occurred to me that we must seem like an unlikely pair. I don't know why it bothered me that morning. It never had before.

I spotted Jack and Denise Carter standing together across the room. If Jason hadn't told me, I wouldn't have known they were already separated and headed to divorce court. Denise smiled and chatted, and Jack did the same. I couldn't tell if either was unhappy. Jack caught me looking at him, winked, and started walking toward us. *Damn.*

"Matt, good to see you again," Jack said, shaking Matt's hand. "Susan, you look great as always." He placed his hand on the small of my back and kissed my cheek.

I took a step back. With a smile pasted on my face, I asked, "How've you been, Jack?"

"Good. Busy. I was hoping to see you today. My company has an opening that would be a great fit for you. How about getting together over lunch sometime this week and talk about it?" He eyed me as if he had more than business on his mind.

"Sorry, my schedule is packed."

"I don't mind meeting you in the evening."

"Thanks for thinking of me, but I just got a promotion and am really happy with Global Security. Speaking of which, I need to get back to work. *Matt*, ready?"

"Yes, I'm ready." Matt looked amused.

I grabbed Matt's hand. "See you later, Jack."

I couldn't believe Matt had watched the whole exchange and hadn't said or done anything. I refrained from commenting until we got into the car. "Can you believe Jack?"

Matt sniggered. "He's a good looking guy."

"You know, you could be a little jealous."

"Why? You're not interested in him."

"God, no."

"Then why should I be jealous?"

"You could have at least been a little protective."

"You were handling him. You didn't need me to protect you."

"I *am* your wife."

"Susan, if you don't want attention, then why ask for it?"

"What are you talking about? What did I do?"

"You did that actress thing, walking in a room like you expect to be the center of attention. Most of the women were in jeans, and look at you."

I wanted to say, "*Yes, their oh-so-casual-I don't-care-how-I-look $200 a pair jeans from Bloomingdales.*"

I dropped it. Matt was never going to understand I'd taken care with my appearance for Micah and Jason. I didn't want to embarrass them. I hadn't been looking to be the center of anything. Nothing I did was right. He was never going to understand that even if I didn't need protection, I wanted it. In any case, Matt didn't seem to care.

I sat in my home office the Friday before Labor Day talking to Reese while I gazed at pictures of Matt and the boys pinned to my corkboard. I told him I absolutely had to turn off work Labor Day weekend—no calls, no e-mail.

"Can I text you?" he asked.

"You can, but I won't answer. I'm leaving civilization behind."

"Poor thing," he said, "I know how much you love camping."

"Oh, I do. Sleeping in a tent and cooking over a campfire while swatting flies away from my food is a great time."

He laughed. "I can't see you roughing it. You're more like a five-star hotel kind of girl."

"I am, but my husband prefers a tent. During the winter, he skis cross-country and snow camps. Can you imagine?"

"Not really. I take it you pass on snow camping?"

"Absolutely, but this trip won't be so bad. I need bonding time with the boys." The heaviness in my chest had been intensifying, and the odd distant feeling I had from Matt now included Micah and Jason. I was hopeful three days of isolation with them would reconnect me.

"You're a good sport. I'm sure your family appreciates it."

I tried to be a good sport. It meant a lot to my boys, and I really did try. I hiked. I fished. I slept in a tent and cooked over a campfire. Strangely, the more time I spent with them, the more distant I became, and the weekend passed like a surreal dream. I was with them, but I wasn't. I observed myself going through the motions of smiling and chatting as if I were watching someone else. It reminded me of being in a play. I interacted with actors on stage. I would say lines and they would respond, but I always knew it was just the characters' words and feelings, not my own. The real me was somewhere else.

My head was foggy all weekend. I couldn't wake up. I blamed it on not having a decent cup of coffee, but deep down I knew the answer wasn't that simple. I felt heavy, as if I had an extra fifty pounds strapped to my body. I just didn't know why. It was very important to me to hide my melancholy. I didn't want to spoil everyone's weekend.

I caught myself missing Reese, wanting to talk to him, thinking about him kissing my neck. The last morning of the trip, I dreamed about him.

"You smell like baby powder," he murmured in my ear.

"Mmmm." I traced his jaw-line with my tongue.

"Want me to turn off the light?" he whispered.

"No," I answered barely containing my desire for him. "I want to see you. I want to feel you. I want to smell you. I want to taste you. I want you to fill my senses."

I woke damp and tingling, wanting it to be real. My body quivered at the memory, so vivid I could taste his salty skin on my tongue. I looked at my dozing husband in his sleeping bag. His hairline was slightly receding.

His muscles had slightly softened. A second chin was slightly discernable. Still, he was an attractive man. I loved him. *It was just a stupid dream.*

By the time we got home, I was drained. I couldn't wait for Matt to go to work and the boys to go to school. I needed some space. It was easier to be alone than to be with them physically, but not mentally. I couldn't wait to get back to work Tuesday morning. If I could just work, I could wake up. I would be normal again.

I had a meeting in Chicago, sans Reese, on Wednesday. I was looking forward to it. I hoped to sneak off to the theater and planned to order room service with two glasses of wine. It would be my indulgence. On Tuesday morning, the client rescheduled. We were pushed out another three weeks. Reese called me himself to rework the schedule.

"It's disappointing, but …" he paused, "it means we'll be in Chicago the same week."

"Oh?"

"I thought you'd be pleased."

"About what?"

"Nothing. Forget it. I'll let you go." He hung up.

Like an out of body experience, I watched my finger hit redial. "Reese, would you like to have dinner when we're in Phoenix next week?" My heart pounded waiting for his answer.

"Aren't you flying out right after the meeting?"

"I was thinking of staying and lining up a second day of appointments."

"Do it. I hate eating alone."

It wasn't wise, but for some reason I felt I had to do it to keep breathing. His friendship was my salvation, my haven against the dread I felt at home. I didn't even know what I dreaded. In my heart, I knew I loved Matt and my boys. I couldn't explain why I didn't want to be home, why I felt so much better away from the people I loved most in the world.

Chapter 9

Reese had a talent for finding the best restaurants in any city. Phoenix was no exception. *The Garden* was known for its use of fresh, organic ingredients and had a low key, relaxed atmosphere. We were seated on an outdoor patio which was cooled by misters and decorated with an explosion of plants, giving the sense of being in an oasis. It exactly fit my mood. This time I changed out of my suit for dinner and wore a sundress.

Reese's smile expressed unmistakable admiration. "You look lovely," he said.

"Well, thank you, Mr. Kirkpatrick."

"It's nice to see you out of a business suit."

"It's nice not to be wearing a business suit."

After the day's meetings and the weeklong anticipation of being alone with Reese, I desperately needed a glass of wine. I could finally relax. Reese must have been of the same mind. We exhaled simultaneously, looked at each other, and grinned, his beautiful brown eyes warm and inviting.

No weight on my chest, no anxiety grinding my stomach. I could breathe. My lungs stretched to take in the balmy Phoenix air.

"So, how's my friend?" he asked.

"Good, but you already know that. I've been with you all day."

"That was work—you're different when you're in work mode. I want to spend tonight with *you*. No work, just friends."

A part of me wanted to be more than friends, but friends was good. Being *just* friends was appropriate. I chuckled. "Absolutely. No business ... and to answer your question, I'm great. I should be tired, but I'm not."

"Excellent. By the way, your presentation today was impressive."

"What?" I interrupted. "Already breaking the no work rule?"

"Patience—it leads to a friend question." He waited for me to object. I didn't. "You shine in front of a crowd. You're in your element. Do you miss acting?"

Before I could answer, the waitress came to take our drink order. I let Reese select for me. Whatever he chose would be delicious. He waited, making small talk, until the waitress returned with a bottle of wine and poured, before returning to the subject.

"So, tell me about being an actress. Did you love it?"

"At the time, yes, I loved it. I'm not sorry to have given it up, but there were some things I truly loved." I hoped he wasn't going to encourage me to start acting again.

He leaned toward me. "Tell me what you loved about it."

"It's funny. I enjoy being in front of people when I'm making business presentations; but when I was an actress, the actual performances were my least favorite part. What I really loved was being someone else, being free to say things I'd never dare in real life. Things I could never articulate the way I could in a play."

"Give me an example."

Apparently, I wasn't *articulating* very well. "Let's see ... there's a line in Henry IV, '*For where thou art, there is the world itself, And where thou art not, desolation.*' Who talks like that? With that emotional depth?"

"I don't know, but maybe when two people are in love, they should."

Matt had never said anything more than a cursory *I love you* to me. I'm not sure he felt anything deeper. For him, emotions were simple, but there had been a time when I thought maybe he had felt more and wished he'd said more. I'd tried. One time I'd said to him, *"I love you so much, I want to crawl inside you and be with you forever."* I had overwhelmed him. He couldn't reciprocate the sentiment, and I'd been left hurt and embarrassed.

I didn't want to think about Matt with Reese sitting in front of me with rapt attention. I smiled. "Maybe they should."

"Was it saying the words, or the emotion that appealed to you?"

As he so often did, Reese made me feel as if my answer was extremely important to him. "Both, I guess. In real life it's frightening to go to those places." I couldn't have felt more exposed if I were standing naked in front of him. I took a breath. I wanted to get this right. I wanted him to understand. "In a play, your heart and mind are only there for a finite time. You can completely commit, knowing in two hours it will be over. It's just pretend. In real life, *'momentary joy breeds months of pain.'*"

"Joy doesn't necessarily bring pain in real life." He chuckled at me, snapping me out of my heavy thoughts.

"See what happens when you get me talking about acting? I get all melodramatic." We both laughed, and I asked, "Can we change the subject now?"

"Sure, what do you want to talk about?"

"I want to know more about you." I smiled my encouragement.

"You already know a lot about me. What else would you like to know?"

Everything. "Tell me what you were like in high school."

"That's rather embarrassing." He grimaced, but I knew he was amused by the request.

We were interrupted by the waitress bringing our appetizer. She couldn't keep her eyes off Reese. She was quite attractive, but Reese didn't seem to notice. His eyes stayed on me. I waited until she left before I asked, "So, were you the captain of your football team? Prom King?" I saw him as the golden boy. Every girl in school probably had had a crush on him.

He laughed. "The opposite, skinny and bookish. I was on the Debate Team and president of Math Club. A classic geek."

Although he was well built, he was slim so I could imagine him being a lanky teenager. "I can see you being the brainamaniac, and can definitely picture you debating, but I can't imagine you ever being a geek. Nope." I shook my head. "You're too good looking to be a geek." I couldn't believe I'd said it. I blamed the wine.

Obviously pleased by my assessment, he grinned quite adorably. "Trust me. In high school, I wasn't the manly specimen I am today."

Okay, there was something geeky about him, but I found him more attractive because of it. "So what was responsible for your transformation?"

He hesitated and then admitted, "A stylist and a personal trainer."

"Seriously?" I laughed.

"I don't use them anymore, but yes. Told you I was a geek." He joined in my laughter. "You know, you're doing wonders for my self-esteem."

I tried to control my giggles. "Okay, I'll stop … Did you have any girlfriends?"

"No, no girlfriends. I didn't even kiss a girl until college."

"Are you serious? Not until college?"

"Hey, give me a break! I was six feet and weighed about one thirty. I wasn't exactly a babe magnet, and I went to an all boys' Catholic prep school. My opportunities were limited."

"Bet you've kissed a few since then." I thoroughly enjoyed making him blush.

"You could say that."

Bet he made up for lost time. Tempted to ask how many girls he had kissed, I dismissed the thought and moved on to a bolder question. "Have you ever been in love?"

I don't know why I asked or why it was important for me to know, but it was.

His body shifted, and he slid back in his chair. I didn't think he was going to answer, but then he said, "Depends on the definition. If you mean having strong feelings for someone, then sure, I've been in love. I've said the words. If you mean the 'if you cease to be, then I cease to be' love, then no, I've never been in love."

I saw it clearly, no doubt in my mind. Reese Kirkpatrick longed for an all-consuming and exquisitely painful kind of love. I asked, "Is that why you're not married?"

"Exactly why. I was engaged once, but I backed out at the last minute."

"What happened?"

"I was twenty-nine. I had just hit my first jackpot when the company I worked for went public. My friends were all married or engaged; I thought it was time. Then, I was introduced to Angelique. She seemed ideal, beautiful and poised … her family had money and were well connected. We made the perfect Manhattan couple." He shrugged. "I thought I loved her."

"If you loved her, why back out?"

"Everyone said how great we looked together, but that was just it. We only fit surface deep. We lacked real intimacy. There just wasn't … passion. I woke up next to her one morning and realized I was about to marry a stranger. She didn't know me either. I should have been able to talk to her about anything and everything, but I couldn't. I had to be this perfect person for her. I couldn't see spending the rest of my life keeping up the façade. She didn't really love me. How could she if she didn't really know me? I called it off."

"How did she take it?"

He snorted. "She was more upset about not getting her wedding than she was about losing me." He paused. "I love my freedom—I can't deny it—but I don't necessarily like being alone. I've thought a lot about it. I won't compromise. I'll wait for someone it would devastate me to lose, who I can be completely myself with." He met my eyes before continuing, "A woman who loves me just as deeply." He looked away. "I'm not a commitment phobe."

"I believe you, and I admire your standards. I think a lot of people settle for less. Whoever wins your heart will be one lucky woman." I hoped I sounded sisterly, knowing my heart ached for him in a decidedly non-sisterly way.

He chuckled. Then he looked at me and said quietly, almost as a question, "Obviously, you've been in love. You're married."

"Yes, but not to your standards."

Surprised by my honesty, I wished I could take it back. It was too late, and our eyes locked together in mutual understanding.

The waitress cleared her throat. I looked up, and the poor thing hesitated with our entrees in her hands, unsure what to do. I slid back in my seat. I hadn't realized how closely we were leaning towards each other.

The conversation stayed on lighter topics for the rest of the meal. We talked about books, movies, corporate gossip, and the like. The restaurant was practically empty by the time the waitress brought our bill. Reese gave her an apologetic smile and a generous tip.

When we got back to the hotel, he suggested a nightcap. I agreed, and we continued our evening in the bar. He ordered scotch, and I ordered diet coke.

"Diet coke?" He laughed at me. "At least have a glass of wine."

"No, I've had plenty. You don't want me dancing on tables, do you?"

"I'd love it. Can I interest you in a shot of tequila?"

"Oh no, tequila makes me howl at the moon. Diet Coke." Reese's smile lit up his whole face. He gazed at me without saying anything. I asked, "What?"

"I love talking and being with you like this. You've become my favorite person."

I could barely look at him. I wish he hadn't told me. I didn't want to know. The cocktail waitress saved me from having to respond.

When she left, Reese's eyes twinkled playfully. "I shared some of my secrets. Turnabout is fair play. Tell me about your first kiss," he requested.

I snickered. "You'll think I'm a little hussy."

He leaned closer towards me. "Now I really am curious."

"Alright, his name was Frank Delgado. He had wavy black hair and full red lips. He was my first serious crush. There was only one problem."

"What was that?"

"He was an older man. I was in sixth grade, and he was in seventh. I would sit on my front porch and watch him ride by on his yellow mountain bike. I thought I was destined to live with catching glimpses of him zooming past. Then one day, he smiled at me when he rode by."

"Bet you were a little cutie."

"I don't know, but I sure thought he was. Anyway, the next day I was in my front yard watching for him, hoping he would smile at me again."

"Did he?"

"Actually, he stopped right in front of my house … I panicked and ran inside."

"Poor Frank Delgado."

"He was persistent. The next day he stopped again, and said to me, 'Don't be afraid.'"

"Were you?"

"I was terrified, but I didn't run away. He became my first official boy-friend a year later. He asked me if I would 'Go Steady'. Of course, I said yes."

"What does that mean at that age?"

"Not much. Basically, he walked me home from school."

"And the kiss?"

"One afternoon we were watching a rerun of the Brady Bunch. He turned to me without warning and tried to kiss me. I pushed him away, but then he said, 'Don't be afraid.' So I let him kiss me. He actually frenched me." I smiled at the memory and laughed. "I liked it."

Reese laughed, too. "How old were you?"

"Just shy of thirteen."

He hooted. "You were a little hussy."

"Told you," I giggled.

"*Don't be afraid.* Good line. So what happened with you and little Frankie?"

"He bragged to his friends about having his nasty little tongue in my mouth. I was so ashamed that I broke up with him."

"Poor kid. Bet you broke his heart."

"He broke mine first."

"I'm sure that taught him not to kiss and tell."

"Let's hope. It's a lesson all men should learn."

He gave me an enigmatic smile. I wondered what the *subtext* was. I'd never told Matt the story. I always had worried he would think I wasn't a *nice girl*. I'm not sure why it didn't bother me to tell Reese.

A little before midnight, I was ready to leave him in the lounge, but he stood, too. He walked with me to the elevator and stepped inside. I'd just spent the evening with the man, but now I couldn't get my tongue to func-tion. I pushed the fourth floor button. Reese didn't push a button. Neither of us uttered a word as the elevator jerked upward.

I looked down at his Gucci loafers. Then my eyes fixated on his waist, the way his dress shirt tucked smartly into his pants. He had no hint of a softening middle, and I imagined how hard and defined he must be underneath that shirt, what it would feel like to wrap my arms around his waist, what it would be like to tug his shirt out of his pants and slip my hand underneath it.

The doors opened, and he followed me out. I stopped and turned to him. Despite my little fantasies, I hadn't intended the dinner invitation to be code for inviting him to my bed. It had been naïve of me to think he wouldn't expect more. I wasn't sure what to do.

"I'll leave you here," he said, smiling as if he knew what I was thinking. "May I hug my *friend* goodnight?"

I was being ridiculous. We were *just friends*. I smiled back. "Yes."

Our eyes met and we both stopped smiling. He stepped closer, so close I could feel the heat of his body and smell the scotch on his breath. One of his hands flattened on the small of my back and the other cupped the back of my head as he pulled me tight. The entire hard length of him pressed against me. I let him hold me as desire coursed through my body, extinguishing my reason with a flood of hormones, and eventually pooling hot between my legs.

"Susan ..." he whispered.

I dug deep to muster self-control and stepped out of his embrace. His eyes bored into me half crazed. It would be so easy to take his hand and lead him to my room. He wanted it. I wanted it. *Matt. I'm married. I'm married to Matt.* I flipped into business mode.

"Thank you for a delightful evening."

Catching the mood shift, he looked confused and then wounded. "You're welcome."

"Well goodnight then," I said, concluding the evening.

"Goodnight," he murmured.

I walked toward my room with jolts of guilt shooting through my stomach. If he had kissed me, I would have had sex with him, no doubt about it.

Tonight had been too close … too reckless. I enjoyed being with him too much. I had been riding a high, buzzing on the euphoria of my crush for months. I was jeopardizing my career and my marriage by being so emotionally intimate with him.

I remembered a reader's theater I had once watched in church. It was a story warning couples of the dangers of temptation. In the play, a man started having coffee with another woman. "What's the harm in a cup of coffee?" he rationalized. He started talking to the other woman on the phone. "What's the harm in talking?" he rationalized more. The harm had been with each little conversation, he'd distanced himself from his wife until he felt more strongly connected to the other woman than his wife.

At the time, I had been dismissive of the sermon. How ridiculous that a man and a woman couldn't be friends? I had male friends. Wasn't that proof? Being in sales, I interacted closely with men on a daily basis. Hell, as part of our corporate bonding, I had been out drinking with men from work on numerous occasions without anything inappropriate ever happening.

I'd obtusely missed the point. The harm was not in having coffee with another man. The harm was having coffee with *the* man who had the power to tempt me. I had already progressed past the first two acts. I was in Act III, fighting temptation.

Only this wasn't a play. It was my life. I wasn't innocently sharing morning coffee. I was having dinner and drinks and staying in the same hotel with *the man* who made me want to forget my marriage vows; the man for whom I achingly lusted … the man who'd kissed my neck. How long could my marriage and his position in the company remain insurmountable barriers?

I remembered the sermon Reverend Jim gave at the beginning of summer. What if the Ten Commandments weren't commandments, but merely requests? What if I failed and broke one particular request? Would God forgive me? Could I forgive myself? If I called Reese, would he come to my room, right now, at this moment? Was he lying in bed thinking of me?

I knew right from wrong. *Shame.* Shame on me for considering some New Age interpretation of the Bible as justification for doing something that was wrong. Breaking faith with Matt was wrong. God might forgive me, but I didn't think I could forgive myself.

I would try harder with Matt. He and I needed time without the boys. I would propose going to Carmel for the weekend, just the two of us. This weekend. The sooner, the better. If we had more time as a couple, I would rediscover why I loved Matt, why I married him. We just needed to reconnect as lovers. With that thought, I finally fell asleep.

Chapter 10

I had my Carmel plan all worked out by the time I got home. I waited for the boys to go to bed before I approached Matt. It was stupid to be nervous. Why wouldn't he jump at a romantic weekend in Carmel? Good wine, food, and sex. What was objectionable about that? I found him in the family room watching a movie.

"Matt, can I talk to you for a minute?"

"Sure," he said not turning his head from the screen.

"Do you mind turning off the television?"

Matt sighed and hit pause on the remote. "Something wrong?"

"No, not really … I've … I've missed you."

"Honey, I missed you too when you were in Phoenix. Come here." He reached his arm out to me. I sat next to him, wrapped my arms around his waist, and leaned against him.

"I don't mean that I only missed you the last couple days, but we haven't spent much time together in a long time."

"What do you mean? We went camping last week and you were only gone two days."

"I mean it's been a long time since we've had couple time, just the two of us. I was thinking it would be nice if we could go to Carmel this weekend.

I'm sure your parents will watch the boys. We could drive down Saturday morning and come home Sunday afternoon. What do you think?"

His brows creased and he let go of me. "We'll miss the boys' soccer games."

I sat all the way up. I'd had a feeling he would use that argument. "Matt, they have plenty of games. We can miss one."

"I'm Jason's coach."

"They're eight-year olds and you have an assistant coach."

He paused and then suggested, "Let's bring the boys. We can take them to the aquarium. They'd love it."

What did he not get about *just the two of us*? He didn't want to be alone with me. *Why didn't he want to be alone with me?* Tears welled up in my eyes. I tried to turn away before he noticed. I gave up, choking on my words, "Never mind."

"What's wrong? Are you crying?"

"I don't know what's wrong," I said, fighting against the tears.

"You win." He hit play on the remote. "I'll call my mom about watching the boys."

I made it to our bedroom before I let another tear fall. Matt hated it when I cried and hated scenes. He'd rather agree than risk either. In the early years of our marriage, he'd dismiss me as being "melodramatic" whenever I cried. I stopped crying in front of him and tried not to be overly emotional. It didn't matter if he wasn't excited; he'd agreed to the weekend.

In preparation, I made a discreet stop at Victoria's Secret. It had been a long time since I had worn anything sexy to bed. Rallying my courage, I tried on a handful of over-the-top lingerie ensembles: bustiers with matching garters, see-through teddies, and animal print bras with matching thong underwear. My intent was to excite him, not scare him. The black satin negligee I found was perfect. It gracefully draped my rounded curves and showed plenty of skin.

My next stop was our local bookstore. I found the section where they sold sex books. I wasn't looking for pornography. I sought advice. I couldn't believe how many books were dedicated to sex. My eyes ran by titles like *What Every Good Call Girl Knows, Going Down,* and my personal favorite, *Hump!* It was rather intimidating. I couldn't bring myself to walk to the counter and actually buy one of the many books explaining the erogenous zones and 180 possible positions. Instead, I grabbed a Van Gough picture book, slipped books one at a time between the covers, and hid in the back of the store educating myself on how to be more pleasing for my husband.

I wanted our night alone together to be special. I imagined awakening Matt's hidden passion, staring into his eyes and fusing a deep connection, exciting him in ways I never had. I was focused on re-energizing our marriage.

The next morning we finalized our plans. After dropping the boys with Matt's parents, we would have a leisurely drive down Highway 1, which hugged the coastline, and then spend the night in Carmel. Matt wanted to go to the Monterey Aquarium. I would have preferred wine tasting or strolling through boutiques, but I agreed as long as I got my romantic evening.

On Saturday morning, Matt dropped the boys at his mother's house while I finished packing. Smiling to myself, I packed the new negligee in my bag and reviewed my newly acquired knowledge. Matt wouldn't know what hit him. By the time the weekend was over, we would be closer than ever, and Reese would no longer be a temptation.

As soon as Matt walked in the door, I threw my arms around him. *Why not try for a quickie before we hit the road?* I kissed him and purposely wiggled against him.

"What are you doing?"

"Seducing my husband," I answered kissing him on the neck.

"Susan, flattered as I am, we should go."

It doesn't matter. I will not cry. I'll save my energy for tonight. It's just Matt's way of telling me he isn't happy being forced into a weekend get-away. He'll loosen up later.

I followed Matt out the door. He started to put our bags in the minivan.

"Matt please, let's take the BMW." He glared at me. "I'll let you drive."

"Fine."

We rode in silence for the first half of the drive. I wanted to talk but I didn't know what to say to my own husband. I thought about asking him what his favorite season was. I really didn't know, but he already thought I was acting oddly. I didn't want to freak him out.

"How do you like driving the car?" Matt had never driven it on the freeway before today.

"Love it. It handles really well."

"Why don't you test it out a bit?"

"You don't mind?"

"No, go for it."

Matt grinned and gunned the gas. When we were younger, Matt loved to drive fast and a little recklessly. Once Micah was born, Matt drove the speed limit and cringed whenever I went more than five miles over. I looked at the speedometer. Matt zoomed us along at eighty miles an hour. He seemed happier and more relaxed for the remainder of the drive.

After a quick bite to eat, we went straight to the Monterey Aquarium. I took Matt's hand and held it as we wandered through. He didn't object or pull away.

This is better. It's going to be a good weekend.

Matt knew the names of all the fish and sea creatures. As a boy, he'd devoured books about ocean life. He originally had wanted to be a marine biologist, but ended up in high tech bioresearch. Funny how life takes little turns when you least expect it. He'd had a professor that suggested an internship in his current field. By the time the internship was over, Matt had given up the idea of becoming a marine biologist.

Matt talked much more than usual and was my own personal tour guide. I didn't mind looking at the exhibits, but I really wasn't that interested in the details. After a while, I caught myself zoning out as he pontificated and had to force myself to remain attentive. If Matt and I were going to be closer, I had to do my part by showing some interest in what he enjoyed.

After seeing the aquarium, we drove down the road to Carmel to check into our room and change for dinner. I had carefully researched restaurants and found one celebrated for their inventive preparation of seafood and extensive selection of wine. On the website, it looked cozy and perfect for gazing into each other's eyes.

Matt wore a sports jacket for dinner. The jacket made his shoulders appear a little broader and the blue dress shirt brought out his eyes. I was so accustomed to seeing him in jeans that I'd forgotten how well he cleaned up. I kissed him before putting on my lipstick and was pleasantly rewarded with an "I love you," whispered in my ear. Then he pulled me close. This time, I put on the brakes. I didn't want to be late or we would lose our reservation. The sexual tension started to crackle between us, and I smiled to myself.

The restaurant was exactly what I'd hoped for. The dimly lit dining room was cozy and romantic with soft music playing the background, and we were lucky enough to be seated by the wood burning fireplace. Once our order was taken and our wine poured, I looked intently at Matt, trying to draw his eyes to mine. If he would let me, I would dive into his clear blue pools.

He smiled. I always loved the way his eyes crinkled when he smiled. He asked, "Is something on my face?"

"No. Why do you ask?"

"It feels like you were staring at something."

"I am. I'm staring at your handsome face."

"Oh." He took my hand and kissed it. Not exactly body heating eye contact, but still nice. "Getting away was a great idea. Sorry I've been difficult."

"I'm just happy that you're happy about it now."

We weren't any more romantic through the rest of dinner. We talked about our boys and speculated on what they were doing. We talked about the weather.

"It sure gets cool in the evenings here. I wish I'd brought a coat," I said.

"I almost suggested it. It'll be warm again tomorrow."

"You think?"

"Guaranteed."

As mundane as our conversation was, I was grateful for it. At least we were conversing. At least he appeared to be happy being with me.

When we got back to the hotel, I felt like a schoolgirl looking forward to losing her virginity on Prom night. I asked Matt to wait for me on the bed while I stepped into the bathroom to change. I brushed my teeth and sprinkled baby powder on my body. I wanted my skin to feel silky smooth for him. Then I slipped on the black negligee, tousled my hair, and made my entrance.

Matt released an audible gasp. "You look beautiful."

"Thank you," I said as I slithered my way toward him.

He started to get undressed. "Let me," I murmured. He stopped pulling on his tie. As I undressed him, I used my hands and my tongue to tantalize him as the books had instructed. His body tensed and his eyes dazed. After he was undressed, I placed his hand on my breast and guided his thumb over my nipple. Then, I pushed him back on the bed and crawled on top of him, preparing for my next phase of seduction.

He grabbed me and thrust his tongue in my mouth as he rolled me on my back. Then he entered me roughly and peaked before I caught up. Heavy lidded and panting, he rolled off me.

"I'm sorry, Susan. Did you …?"

"No."

"Would you like me to …?"

"No, it's okay."

"It's your own fault. You got me so excited I couldn't control myself. My god, you're sexy tonight. I like the nightgown."

"Thank you. I bought it for you."

"Well then, *thank you*," he said pulling me into the crook of his arm.

I laid my head on his chest and whispered, "Love you, too."

We laid in silence a few minutes before he began snoring. The drive, the wine, and the sex wore him out. It was just like the night I lost my virginity—disappointing, like having sex with an over-eager youth who has not yet mastered self-control. When I was sixteen, my teenage boyfriend knew more about how to touch me than my husband of thirteen years.

After the bitterness passed, sadness crept in. It had nothing to do with not having an orgasm. I wanted to excite him sexually, and I had succeeded, but what I really had wanted was to connect, to feel our love-making meant something. The weight on my chest became oppressive. I focused on getting air to my lungs as I cried silently next to my sleeping husband.

The next morning, Matt woke up glowing and eager for another quick round. Not wanting to burst his bubble, I played along. Afterwards he was very sweet, and offered to take me window-shopping. I could always count on shopping giving me a temporary high.

As we meandered around downtown Carmel, my mind wandered back to Reese. I had kept him at arms distance since Phoenix. I hadn't always picked up when he'd called. I'd made excuses to keep conversations brief, and I'd cut off on-line chats.

We had a conference in Atlanta next week, and Friday morning he had called to confirm our schedule.

"Plan on dinner with me Wednesday night," he'd said.

"Sorry, can't."

"Why's that?"

"I don't get in until after ten," I'd explained.

"Then have dinner with me after the cocktail party Thursday night."

"Can't. I'm flying home right after the party."

"I see. Well, what if there was a corporate directive that you had to stay?" His tone had been teasing and light, but underneath, there'd been steely determination.

"Reese, please ...," I'd begged.

The light teasing had left his voice. "Why are you avoiding me?"

"I'm not. I have a lot going on and have to get home."

"Come on, Susan, we need to—"

"I gotta go. I'm late for a call," I'd said, cutting him off.

Just thinking about it made me wince. I missed him.

Thinking about Reese got me thinking about the cocktail party. I had a sudden, capricious desire to look good for Reese. I wanted him to gasp when he saw me the way Matt had when he saw me in the negligee. Matt poked through a bookstore while I picked out the perfect little black dress at one of the chic little boutiques dotting downtown Carmel.

Chapter 11

My decision to put distance between Reese and myself was morally the right thing to do, the right thing for my marriage. Once in Atlanta and the closer the taxi got to the hotel, the more I wished I had arrived early enough to have dinner with him. Between the conference and the cocktail party our company would be hosting for major clients and prospects, the schedule was too tight for any time alone with him.

When I arrived at the hotel, I scoped out the lobby with an irrational hope he would be waiting for me, but he wasn't. I couldn't believe I'd actually applied lipstick and changed my clothes in the airport ladies' room before getting in a cab to go to the hotel. I went to my room, annoyed with myself and filled with unjustifiable disappointment, literally stomping, the same way Micah stomped when he didn't get his way, and dragging my bag behind me.

I flipped on the lights, dumped my bag, took out my cosmetic case, and went to the bathroom to take off my make-up. I was sloppy and got my hair wet in the process. I brushed my teeth and went into the bedroom area to change into my pajamas. That's when I saw it, a bouquet of yellow roses lying on the bed. I don't know how I missed it when I came in. My heart soared as I raced over and grabbed the card.

Reading it my heart thudded,

"Thank you for the weekend."

-Love, Matt

Damn! I hated men! I hated Matt for being so, so … inconsistent? He frustrated me. Just when I was about to retract my "keep a distance from Reese policy" Matt does a grand romantic gesture? Well, maybe not *grand,* but unusually romantic for Matt. I couldn't remember the last time he'd given me flowers.

I hated Reese for making my heart skip. Why would the flowers possibly be from him?

My Blackberry rang. Reese's name lit the screen, and I hit the answer button.

"Hi, it's me," he said.

"Hi. What can I do with … I mean for you, Reese?" I was definitely rattled.

He chuckled. "For starters have a drink with me. I'm in the bar."

"I would, but—"

"Susan, please. I'm sorry if I did something to offend you. I just want to talk."

His tone tugged on my heart. I looked in the mirror. It would only take a few minutes to dab on a little make-up and fix my hair. Then, I looked at the flowers.

"I'm exhausted and I've just gotten ready for bed. Now isn't a good time." I didn't want to hurt him, but the last thing I needed was alcohol blurring my judgment when my feelings for him were so confused.

"I understand. Call me when you're ready to talk."

"I will. Thanks for understanding."

"Sleep well, Juliet."

He hung up the phone. I'd had enough for one day and took two Sominex. I *did* want to sleep well. Before I crashed, I called Matt and thanked him for the flowers.

The downside of sleeping pills was waking up groggy, but the upside was waking up rational. I wasn't going to cross any lines with Reese, but I had to make things right. He was my friend and my boss. We needed to be able to work together without the tension. It was early, but I called him anyway.

"Hi, it's me."

"Morning. How'd you sleep?"

"Well enough, but I could use some coffee. Care to join me?"

"I'm meeting Bill in ten minutes." Bill Warren was the Executive Vice President of Operations for our Atlanta facility. He and Reese were technically at the same level, but Reese's position carried more clout in New York. "I'll save you a seat at lunch," he offered.

"I'd love that but, I'm sitting with a group from Greater South Bank and Trust."

"Good job, they'd be a great score. At the very least I'll see you at the party tonight."

"Sure," I said, yet again disappointed. There would be a hundred clients and potential clients at the party.

"How are you getting to the airport?"

"I've arranged for a car."

"Cancel it. I have a rental. I'll drive you." I could hear him rushing to get his things together. "I can't let you blow our expense budget."

His joking made me feel better, and I was guaranteed at least twenty-five safe minutes alone with him.

The morning was divided into breakout sessions covering various technological changes in the banking industry. Our strategy was to divide and conquer. We selected different sessions to ensure maximum exposure. There would be a break for lunch and then everyone would congregate in the grand ballroom for general addresses. Reese, as the keynote speaker, would be seated in front with the other presenters, and I'd have to scramble for a chair wherever I could.

The sessions were dry, but my adrenaline surged when I secured a meeting with Greater South Bank and Trust over lunch. Reese would be impressed, and I couldn't wait to tell him. I looked for him when I entered the ballroom, but luck wasn't with me this trip. I spotted him up front and surrounded by a crowd. I sighed and took a seat.

Although security and fraud can be an interesting topic, three hours of non-stop droning about changes in the banking industry in a dimly lit room made it difficult to stay awake. Even with the air conditioning blasting, I had to pinch myself to keep from nodding off. Finally, Reese was introduced. I perked up. I'd never seen him do a full-on public speaking event.

He strode center stage and gave the audience a dazzling smile. I saw a few women around me instantly perk up, too. Just as he opened his mouth to speak, his Blackberry started ringing. It must have been in the inside breast pocket of his jacket because it blared out over the microphone clipped to his lapel. I cringed for him, but he just laughed. He took the phone out of his pocket and held it up to the crowd. "Does anyone have one of these?" he asked rhetorically. The entire audience raised their hands. "That's right. We all do. Worldwide three billion people have a hand held communication device …." It was a set up. He wanted to catch everyone's attention, and he did.

He went on to explain how today people bank in retail locations or on their computers. In the future, they would be banking from smart phones. Imagine depositing a check from your phone. The future mode would attract a new generation of customers for the bank. It would be a solution for the less affluent, who have cell phones, but not home computers. It would reduce the number of calls to call centers by fifty percent. How many calls are taken today? What's the cost per call? Do the math. Mobile Banking makes economic sense. What is necessary for consumers to transition to the new way of banking? Simple: Trust. Trust that their financial data is secure. Trust in their financial institution. Trust in you, the banking community. He finished by asking where bank relationships were held today. The answer: in brick and mortar branches. Where was the future? In his pocket, next to his heart. Corny, but the audience ate it up.

Reese had been eloquent, concise, and he timed jokes well. But more than all of that, he had charisma. He could be a politician. The room had been energized and alive when he spoke. I thought I was good in front of a crowd, but he had been amazing. He must have won a lot of trophies for his high school debate team. I couldn't stop a huge smile from spreading across my face. I was proud of him, of my Reese. I had no right to claim him as mine, but I did anyway.

Afterwards I still couldn't make my way to him through the crowd, but I caught his eye. I gave him a congratulations-I-adore-you smile. He smiled back and winked, clearly exhilarated by his triumph. I couldn't have been happier for him, and he had never been more attractive to me. I left to change into my new dress with Reese fantasies dancing in my head. Still, I was fully aware of the boundaries neither one of us could cross. Corporate policy was clear about fraternization with subordinates, and my marriage vows were crystal clear.

Entering the party in my *perfect little black dress*, I knew I looked good. The dress didn't show cleavage, but the scoop neckline was flattering. Better yet it hugged my body emphasizing my well-proportioned curves. Three-inch heels helped, making my legs look longer and leaner than they actually were.

As soon as I walked in the room, my eyes found Reese, and he had some Georgia peach hanging on his arm. A tall blond, not much older than twenty-six or seven, she displayed ample cleavage and gazed adoringly up at him with big blue eyes. My heart sped up and my lungs froze. I fought an impulse to excuse myself as jealousy growled in my stomach. I hushed it before it showed in my demeanor. He saw me and ushered her over to introduce us.

What did it matter if he saw me looking my corporate best? My boss was all he could ever be to me. It was time to smile and schmooze; my business mode flipped into gear.

"Susan, there you are. I've been looking for you," he said, seemingly pleased to see me.

"I just got here."

"Please, allow me to introduce you. Susan, this is Cynthia Warren, Bill Warren's daughter. Cynthia, this is our Senior Vice President for Mobile Banking, Susan Sinclair."

"It's nice to meet you," I said with my professional smile in place.

"Nice to meet you as well," she drawled in a charming Southern dialect.

"What brings you to our little soiree this evening? I'm afraid you'll be bored to tears with all of our shop talk."

"Not at all, I'm enjoying myself immensely. Reese has been kind enough to introduce me to everyone. My mother couldn't be here this evening, so Daddy asked me to be his date." I wondered why she wasn't with "Daddy" instead of hanging on Reese's arm.

"That's very generous of you."

"Excuse me, would you ladies care for a drink?" Reese asked like a perfect gentlemen.

"I'd just love a glass of white wine," she actually purred at him.

"I'll take red, please."

"Be back in a minute." He smiled at both of us.

When Reese walked away, Cynthia whispered to me as if we were sorority sisters, "Actually, my father wanted me to meet Reese." She giggled like a schoolgirl. "Lordy, he's hot and not married, right?"

"I guess you could say he's attractive and no, not married."

"Does he have a girlfriend?"

"Not that I'm aware of." I kept up my corporate smile, pretending to enjoy the girl talk.

Reese returned with our drinks. It was time to split up and start making the rounds. Cynthia was intent on sticking with Reese.

"Cynthia, it has been a pleasure meeting you. Good luck with your *endeavors*," I said with a small wink. I hoped she'd choke on her wine.

"Well, thank you." She giggled.

I don't think anyone knew how distracted I was. I laughed at bad jokes and had smiles for everyone, playing my part to perfection. Every now and then, I caught a glimpse of Reese and Cynthia. I couldn't deny they looked great together. Reese was well dressed, tall and had model good looks. While not knockout gorgeous, Cynthia was more than reasonably attractive. She would meet the criteria of a Trophy Wife and would be the ideal corporate wife. She already knew how to work a room. They'd be very happy together.

What had I been thinking? Buying a dress with the intent of attracting him … wearing three-inch heels, which were killing my feet, in an attempt to make my legs sexier. Stupid. So adolescently stupid. Obviously, humiliatingly, I'd misread so many things in order to feed my inner fantasies. He wasn't pursuing me. I was pathetically pursuing *him*: trying to impress him with my knowledge of Shakespeare, encouraging him to massage my back, and inviting him to dinner. He didn't care about me romantically. I was married. Someday he would be married, and it wouldn't be to someone like me. It would be to some country-club-bred, blond and blue-eyed tall beauty. She would give him perfect children and be the perfect hostess, helping him to advance his perfect career. They would live a perfect life and be perfectly happy.

Finally, the party began to wind down. Certain he'd prefer to continue his evening with Cynthia, I walked up to him, ready to release him from his offer to drive me to the airport.

"Ready to go?" he asked.

"Yes, but look, it's completely unnecessary for you to drive me. I can grab a cab."

"What's wrong?"

"Nothing, I'm just tired with the time change and all."

"I'm driving you and that's a corporate directive." He smiled at me. I tried to smile back, but it wasn't very convincing. "Give me a minute to say goodbye to Bill and Cynthia."

Cynthia's face drooped, crushed at the announcement of Reese's imminent departure. She brightened when Reese pecked her cheek. My spirits sank a little lower if that was possible.

I stopped at the bellhop desk to pick up my luggage while Reese had the valet bring around the car. We didn't really say much until he had maneuvered onto the freeway.

"You're awfully quiet. Didn't you enjoy the party?"

"It was bearable." I answered more crisply than I'd intended.

"Every time I looked at you, you were smiling or laughing. You must've been an exceptional actress." He winked, trying to coax a smile out of me.

I only gave him a half smile, wishing I'd taken a cab. "How about you? You enjoy the party?" I asked trying to sound casual.

"It was … tolerable."

"It looked like it was more than tolerably enjoyable for you." I paused and then asked my burning question, keeping my tone light, "Was Cynthia interesting?"

He took his time answering by drawing out his one word answer, "Tolerably." He took a breath and then asked quite seriously, no hint of teasing, "Were you jealous?"

"No! Good, God no. Why would I possibly be jealous?" He flipped on the blinkers and shifted lanes to exit the freeway. "What are you doing? This isn't the airport exit."

"Pulling over so we can talk."

"This is completely unnecessary."

"No, this is completely *necessary*. I'm tired of the game playing. I'm not doing it anymore."

Oh God, please, don't let this happen. I didn't want to have to admit I had a schoolgirl crush on him. I didn't want to listen to why things could go no further, or how much he regretted our flirtation. Mortified, I cringed in my seat.

He pulled into an empty parking lot, killed the engine, and angled his body towards me. "Let's be clear. This discussion will never leave this car. It's just between you and me." His eyes bored into me. "Were you jealous?"

I didn't see an out. "Yes." Hot tears welled, stinging my eyes. I blinked to keep them there while I watched elation light his eyes and spread across his face. "That makes you happy?"

"How can you even ask? I've wanted you from the moment I saw you. You walked into that espresso bar and took my breath away. I could tell you thought your little business suit hid your sensuality. It made me smile and want to know you." He paused and his voice lowered seductively. "You can't deny we've grown exceptionally close."

"I know we have."

"I thought you wanted me as much as I wanted you in New York and then again in Phoenix, but you shut me down both times." He stopped to take a breath. "I can't stop thinking about you. I even dream about you."

I couldn't speak. I couldn't breathe. I couldn't believe this conversation was really happening. It shouldn't. It was wrong. But it did things to my heart, oh God my heart ….

"I didn't know," I finally said.

"Well, now you do and I'm happy because now I know I'm not crazy. You like me, too."

I cracked a smile. He was so boyish sometimes. "You've known that I like you for a while now. We've been friends."

He laughed, grinning happily, playfully. "But now I know you *like me, like me.*"

"Yes, I *like you, like you.* Are you going to give me a Cracker Jacks ring next?"

"No," he mouthed silently, looking into my eyes. His eyes, my God, his eyes had a way of drawing me in that was hypnotic. He leaned over the car console and his lips touched mine.

At first, I was only aware of our lips moving together and thinking *I'm crossing a line … I can never go back to the other side. I'm kissing a man who is not my husband. I'm kissing my boss. I'm kissing Reese.* Then, I couldn't think. All my senses focused on his soft lips. I wanted him closer. He wanted me closer. I opened my mouth for him, and he pulled my body against his chest. His tongue caressing mine was magical—all weight and heaviness gone—only intoxicating warmth, lightness, and a sense of immense relief. Then, he groaned, and something between us exploded, becoming a feeding frenzy of hands and lips and tongues. He unbuckled my seatbelt and lifted me onto his lap.

In our scramble, one of us hit the car horn. That snapped me back to the rational world, and I wrestled away from him gasping. "You should take me to the airport." I was shaking. I'd done something irreversible, but it had to stop there.

His eyes opened, unfocused, and he breathed hard. "You're right."

He started the engine and in minutes, we were back on the freeway.

"By the way," he said. "I never got a chance to tell you how beautiful you look this evening. I like the dress."

"Thank you. It's nice you noticed."

"Noticed? It was all I could do not to touch you. It was actually a good thing I couldn't shake Cynthia Warren. It kept you safe. You've no idea how desirable you look tonight."

"Why did you peck her on the cheek then?"

"To make you jealous," he said chuckling.

He sounded deliriously happy. I was glad he couldn't see me blush. I was ashamed—ashamed of dressing to allure him, ashamed of desiring him, and ashamed of kissing him.

He took my hand and brought it to his lips as he drove. I stiffened. He glanced over and saw I was crying. "Hey, what's wrong?"

Everything. "I should not be doing this. We shouldn't be doing this."

"I'm not going to argue with you tonight. Promise you won't do anything rash."

I was too tired and too confused to answer.

"Promise me," he insisted.

"I promise," I mumbled.

When we arrived at the airport, he set my bags on the curb, and pulled me tightly against him. "Please, don't panic … don't run away from me," he whispered in my ear. Then he took my face in his hands and made me look at him. His eyes, lovely warm loving eyes, gazed into mine. For a moment, I thought he was going to tell me he loved me. Instead, he kissed me lightly on the lips and said, "I'll call you tomorrow."

Chapter 12

During the long flight home, our kiss replayed over and over in my mind, torturing me with equal part desire and gut-sinking guilt. It had been the most intense kiss I had ever experienced. It had felt like he loved me. He'd gazed at me as if he loved me.

The plane was dark and practically empty. I was free from casual chatter and left in peace with my inner turmoil. I remembered the yellow roses and Matt, and vomit rose in my throat. I had created a mess and had to fix it. Rational, moral judgment dictated I should make a clean break with Reese before anything serious happened. It would be an easy plan to execute if my heart wasn't so involved.

When I got home, everyone was asleep. I tiptoed to the boy's rooms and kissed each of them on the cheek. They looked like little angels. Then I went to my room, slipped on my nightgown and laid down next to Matt. I studied his face. I could see the young man I'd fallen in love with. It may not have been devastating love, but it was love all the same. He looked peaceful, so unaware I was teetering on a precipice that could destroy our life.

I couldn't sleep despite my mental and physical exhaustion. I got up and sent an e-mail to Reese's administrative assistant, Anne.

I came home with a raging temperature and won't be working tomorrow.

Since the next day was Friday, Matt and the boys would be out of the house. It bought me a long weekend and the quiet time I needed to think. Besides, I had twelve weeks of accumulated sick time and nothing major going on the next day. After taking a couple of Sominex, I crawled into bed and kissed Matt lightly on the lips. He rolled over with his back to me. I laid my head on the pillow, longing for dreamless sleep.

The next morning I didn't look at my cell phone until after I'd dropped the boys at school and made a stop at Starbucks. There were four missed calls from Reese and two messages.

I played the first message:

"Hi, I want you to know I really do care about you. We'll figure this out. I'll call you in the morning."

I deleted the first message and played the second:

"You're not sick. Don't do this to me. Please, call me."

He sounded in pain, which made me feel like crap. I stared indecisively at my cell phone. It beeped a text from Reese: *We have to talk.*

I stopped being a coward and dialed his number. He picked up on the first ring and whispered, "I'm in the office. I'll call you in five. Promise you'll answer."

I promised. It was a long five minutes, during which my stomach twisted into knots. When he called back, I could hear traffic in the background.

"Thank you for talking to me," he started.

"Reese, I don't know what to say …."

Apparently he didn't either because there was a long pause before he said, "I care deeply for you. I wouldn't be doing this for something trivial. I wouldn't be doing this if I didn't … if I didn't believe you cared just as deeply about me. I know I'm asking for something I shouldn't, something I have no right to ask, but I want more than friendship." I couldn't answer.

My muscles had frozen. "Please, say something … tell me what you're thinking."

"I care more about you than I should, and I'm very confused."

"I have a proposal. We're both due in Chicago a week from Monday. Meet me early. Come in on Saturday. I know a great resort north of Chicago that sits right on the edge of Lake Michigan. It's beautiful this time of year. We can talk and sort things out."

"I don't know if that's a good idea."

"I promise nothing will happen that you don't want to happen."

"That's the problem. When I'm with you, I want *things* to happen."

"Is that a yes?" He sounded happier and optimistic.

"It's a maybe. Can you give me until Monday?"

"Of course, but if you decide sooner or want to talk, call me. I'll have my cell with me all weekend."

"Thank you. Thank you for understanding and being patient."

"I'd do anything for you. Unfortunately, I was due on a call five minutes ago."

"Oh jeez, I'm sorry. Go! Have a good meeting."

"I always do."

"Cocky."

He chuckled. "Talk to you soon."

I hung up and realized I was smiling. I couldn't help it. Just hearing his voice had me glowing inside. Thankfully, I had three days to get my head together. I had to be rational now that Reese's wants were irrefutable, and I was glad I had the day to myself.

Conversations were on repeat in my head:

He thought about me all the time.

He'd been in love, but never 'if you cease to be, I cease to be' sort of love.

He *liked me, liked me.*

Images of his eyes locking on mine, his lips a breath away, his hard body pressed against me, and our electrifying kiss replayed over and over in my head, making me dizzy.

I kept hearing Reese say, "Please, don't panic … don't run away from me."

I analyzed, and I guess rationalized, why I was so consumed by him. Granted he was highly intelligent, attractive, and successful, but I'd met men like him before and not been tempted. It was more than his surface appeal. *It was the way he paid attention to me.*

I had an epiphany. I had a family. I was with people every day, but deep down, in the center of my being, I was lonely, deeply … painfully lonely. I had been for quite some time. There were parts of myself I was afraid to explore. I'd always kept a protective shield against the depth of my emotions. My defense mechanism was to pull back if anyone got too close.

I wondered if this was why I'd had so few female friends, or why I chose a husband who was naturally private, or why I'd been drawn to acting. Acting had given me the sensation of being intimate without really having to risk anything. Reese had given me the courage to understand myself. I wanted to for him. He wanted to know me, not just the business me, or the intellectual me, or any other segment. He wanted to know all of me. No one had ever wanted to know me that completely, ever.

Matt and I talked about our boys, bills, or which plumber we should use. Day in and day out mundane concerns filled our life together. We didn't read the same books or enjoy the same movies. We shared no hobbies. We didn't discuss anything on a deeper level. We didn't even fight very often. There just wasn't much of anything.

I called people friends, but they really weren't anything more than social acquaintances. I chatted with other moms on the sidelines during soccer games and school functions. We had superficial conversations about our children, teachers, or brands of laundry detergent. We gossiped about the soccer coach, occasionally giggled about *Sex in the City* episodes, but I didn't have a single friend I felt comfortable inviting to a movie or a day of shopping.

I had stopped sharing the inner me with anyone else years ago. God, I was lonely. The realization shook me to my core. It was the reason for the oppressive weight on my chest. It wasn't restlessness or boredom. It was loneliness. Reese burst into my life, and I started to breathe again. He awoke a dormant part of me. Now that I was awake, fully aware of myself, I desperately didn't want to be alone again.

Without a doubt, I was in love with him. It'd been a long time since I'd recognized the sensation and forgot how confusing and painful it could be. How much in love, I didn't know, and I didn't know how far I could trust him.

Why was he interested in me? He was thirty-six, very eligible, and yet still single. His explanation had been he had never fallen in love deeply enough to justify marriage.

Maybe he was just one of those men who loved the chase. Once he got what he wanted, he lost interest. I was married. I lived 3,000 miles across the country. He was my boss, and I had not completely succumbed. All those things would be a challenge for a man who could walk into any room and have half the women panting for him.

On the other hand, in some respects, I was an easy target. No fuss, no muss, married, three thousand miles away; I was the perfect dalliance. How could I make any demands on him? Marriage would be out of the question. He was safe. I'd never know if he was sleeping with other women. I certainly would have no right to object. What was hugely complicated for me might be pleasingly uncomplicated for him.

I was still attractive. I still had a good figure, but I was thirty-seven and no Super Model. Nothing added up. It came down to two possibilities.

Option 1: He was dallying with me, just having fun flirting with the married lady. He might even have convinced himself there was more to it than sport.

Option 2: We connected on a deeper level. Even to me it sounded ridiculously dramatic, like I was fricken Jane Eyre or something, but what if he truly was my soul mate?

Option 1 was humiliating and hurtful. I saw myself as a pathetic middle-aged woman losing her head to a younger, well, slightly younger, better looking man. If that was the case, I was strong enough to put a stop to this nonsense. I might be lonely, but my ego was still healthy.

Option 2 was even harder to consider. It was spine-tingling to believe he was in love with me, just as I was with him, but what could the end-result be?

Regardless of the current listless state of our marriage, Matt was a good, decent man. I loved him, and had to believe he still loved me. It might not be the passionate, depth-of-your-soul love that inspires poets, but it was love. I could never leave him. I could never do that to my boys. I'd promised Jason that Matt and I would never divorce.

I was getting ahead of myself. Reese had kissed me. He'd said he cared about me. He hadn't used the word *love*. He wanted *more than friendship*. He wanted sex, that was very clear, but how much more he wanted was murky. What I wanted was just as hazy. His true feelings frightened me. I didn't want to face shallow affection, which was worse than rejection, nor did I want to deal with the consequences of loving him and him loving me.

Saturday passed in a blur of morning cartoons, soccer games, and laundry.

On Sunday, I went to church. I dragged my sleepy children out of bed with me, but let Matt sleep. Reverend Jim gave an upbeat sermon about our duty to God. According to Reverend Jim, our first duty to God was to be happy. He didn't advise what we should do if, in the pursuit of bliss, we destroyed the happiness of others. The reverend was an honorable person. His joy came from being good. Couldn't he understand that not all of us were as unselfishly virtuous as he was?

I knew what Reverend Jim meant when he said we were the creators of our own happiness. He meant we should be gratified with the gifts God gave us on a daily basis. He wanted us to find contentment in the simple things of life. Even so, the overriding theme was I would be failing God if I allowed myself to remain unhappy.

I wasn't happy. I hadn't experienced pure joy in a long time. I tried to find happiness at home with my husband and children. I experienced moments that gave me hope, but holding on to it was like trying to hold water. It slipped maddeningly away before I could bring it to my lips and quench my thirst.

On the way out of church, Reverend Jim hugged me and said, "It's so good you joined us this morning."

"Thank you. I enjoyed the sermon. It's given me a lot to think about."

"Well, you probably don't need to work too hard at being happy. You're so blessed with your beautiful family." He smiled and moved on to the next parishioner.

The man was a simpleton. How easy life must be for him.

Shame washed over me. I had no business muddying our lives. Reese wasn't a viable fix. I had to try harder with Matt. I drove home from church resolved.

Later that afternoon, I opened Matt's top dresser drawer to put his socks away. While shifting a few things to make everything fit, I noticed an unused A's baseball ticket at the bottom. I picked it up and looked at it. Then, I took it to my office and compared the date on the ticket to my calendar.

It was for the day Matt had taken the boys and told me he didn't have a ticket for me.

The next morning at 6 a.m., I revved up my laptop, opened Outlook, and typed in Reese's e-mail address. In the subject line, I typed, "YES."

At 6:02, my phone rang.

No greeting, he said, "I about lost my mind waiting to hear from you."

"Sorry I did that to you." My voice shook.

"It's okay, you needed time."

I heard someone using the bathroom. "I can't talk right now."

"I understand. Let me know when your flight arrives. I'll arrange everything."

I hung up believing he loved me. I imagined what he would say and what I would say when we actually said the words. I rewound, rewrote, and edited my little screenplay multiple times during the next five days.

I don't know how I got through the week. Reese and I didn't talk or exchange e-mails as we had done. Our conversations were awkward, and we stuck to business. I was cautious of being too familiar. I think he was cautious of my coolness. I wish I could say I almost cancelled our assignation half a dozen times due to my consuming guilt, but I can't.

Maybe it was my acting skills, or it could have been my childhood, engrained desire never to be caught being naughty, but I lied smoothly. I told Matt I was required to be in Chicago for a weekend of teambuilding activities. Matt didn't question it.

To assuage my guilt, or more precisely, guilt for not feeling guilty, on Friday night I did laundry, made a batch of chicken enchiladas for Matt and the boys to eat over the weekend, and had sex with Matt.

Chapter 13

Despite my evening's exertion, I didn't need an alarm clock to be up and at the airport in time to catch my 6 a.m. flight to Chicago. It felt no different than any other routine business trip until the plane landed; then, my nerves woke with a vengeance. I made my way to the baggage claim area with sweaty palms and butterflies flapping wildly in my stomach. I didn't see Reese. His flight arrived thirty minutes prior to mine, and he was supposed to be waiting for me. *Please, don't bail on me.* Then, I spied him leaning against a pillar.

He could have been a Calvin Klein advertisement with his jeans hanging loosely on his hips and a casual V-neck sweater over a partially unbuttoned shirt, hinting at a well-built chest. It was the first time I'd seen him in jeans, and he'd never looked sexier.

Reese smiled when he saw me. I walked toward him, unsure how to greet him. Shaking hands was out. Throwing my arms around him and planting a smacking wet one on his lips would be inappropriate. He made our reunion easy by gliding smoothly to my side. He wrapped his arm around my waist and pecked me on the cheek.

"It's good to see you," he said.

Reese had arranged for a limo to take us from O'Hare to the resort. The limo wasn't a romantic gesture. It was simply the way he was accustomed to traveling.

We rode, holding hands and making small talk for the first few miles of the drive. Too nervous to look at his face or his eyes, I studied his graceful, callus-free hands. He worked with his mind, not his hands. Imagining those hands touching me made me shiver.

"Are you cold?" he asked.

"No." On the contrary, I was sweating.

Reese angled my face to look at him. Then, he took my hand, brought it to his lips, and inadvertently kissed my wedding ring. We both colored, and he dropped my hand. He put his arm around me, and I leaned against him.

I just started to relax when Matt called. I instinctively pulled away from Reese and turned my back to him. "Matt, I can't talk right now."

"Micah can't find his cleats."

"They're on the back porch."

"I already looked there."

"Oh, that's right. I cleaned them. They're next to the wash basin in the laundry room."

"Thanks."

"I'll call you tonight."

I hung up and glanced at Reese. "Sorry."

"It's fine."

Then I glanced at the limo driver. I could see his eyes in the rearview mirror. He seemed to be looking at me. Reese guessed my thoughts and squeezed my hand. "He doesn't know. Even if he did, he doesn't care."

When we got to the resort, Reese checked us in while I waited in the lobby. He wore the boyish grin that I loved when he returned to walk me to our room. He knew I would find it enchanting. A four-poster bed with a fluffy down comforter, wood burning fireplace, and a view of Lake Michigan. I could see a path leading around the lake from the window. He had chosen the setting for our big weekend well.

I looked at the fireplace and the bed again, and started to shake as a wave of unacknowledged guilt crashed over me.

"Something wrong? Don't you like the room?"

"The room is fabulous. I …well …" I couldn't control my shaking.

His arms were around me in seconds, and he held me securely against him. While he held me, his hand ran up and down my back, soothing me. His strong body pressed against mine calmed me, like slipping into a warm bath. I felt safe and much loved. My body relaxed and molded to his embrace.

"Don't be afraid … I love you," he whispered in my ear.

How many times had I fantasized about this moment? Instinctively, I pulled back. Option 1 flashed through my head. Was that supposed to be a joke? *Don't be afraid?* He wasn't my seventh-grade boyfriend trying to French kiss me.

I fully acknowledged having a tendency towards drama, but I was afraid. I was afraid of the pain I'd endure if I gave him that part of me. It would start as a dull ache and eventually that part of my heart would separate from my body, dead and lifeless. There would be a black hole where it had been. The only thing to fill it would be pain, but it would never be filled. It would be a black hole. I would be alone again. Loneliness would once again be my only companion.

"You don't love me."

Grabbing my shoulders, he bent down so we were eye level. "Don't tell me what I feel."

I jerked away. "I shouldn't be here. We need to stop before people get hurt."

He stared at me with watery eyes. "Too late. You're hurting me."

"I'm so sorry." I couldn't get air in my lungs. I had to get away from him before my floodgate broke, but before I could think what to do, bile pushed into my throat. I jetted to the bathroom, locked the door, and let go of a low moan. My stomach erupted, heaving until nothing was left.

With my head hanging in the toilet, I heard Reese knock. "Are you okay?" When I didn't answer, he tried to open the door. "Susan, open the door."

"I'm fine," I groaned. "Give me a minute."

Slowly, I pulled my head together. It wasn't too late to back out. A ripping feeling split down my chest, but knowing someday it would just be a dull throb, gave me hope. No one had to know how close I'd come to falling off the precipice. Matt hadn't noticed a difference in me up until now, and he never would. Despite the guilt, I'd never tell him. It would be the worst kind of selfishness to confess just to ease my conscience.

I splashed water on my face and washed the sour vomit taste out my mouth. When I opened the door, Reese was sitting in the chair by the window.

"I'm sorry," I choked. I couldn't hold back my tears.

He silently got up, led me to the chair, and cradled me in his lap. He held me and gently rocked me, occasionally kissing my hair or my forehead. I listened to his heartbeat and our breathing synchronized. He felt right. I was such a mess.

He held me for a long time before he quietly said, "Susan, I—"

"No, please, I don't want to talk." I hadn't been held like this for years. The physical closeness of a man, the comforting warmth of his body, the soft caresses, and the sound of his heartbeat thrumming rhythmically lulled me into a state of nirvana. I didn't want to talk. I didn't want to think. I just wanted him to hold me and let time stand still.

"All you have to do is listen."

How could I not?

"I thought it would be easier for you if you knew how I felt, but I scared you. I think there are two reasons. First, you have no idea what to expect, so I'll make you a promise. You'll never have to choose between your family and me. They're on the West Coast. I'm on the East. I'll maintain a 3,000-mile distance if that's what you want.

"The second reason is you don't completely trust me yet. I wasn't trying to imitate your old boyfriend when I said, 'Don't be afraid.' I swear I didn't even think about it until you ran into the bathroom. All I meant was that I don't want you to be afraid of me hurting you."

He was right on all counts. My nerves were too raw and I didn't think I could handle much more. I tried to get up, but he pulled me back onto his lap.

"Please, just listen," he whispered in my ear. "I love you." He said each word slowly and distinctly. "I feel very connected to you. I know I love you … hey, look at me." He gently lifted my chin and made me look into his mesmerizing eyes. They were soft and oh so loving, inviting me into his soul. "Can't you see—no, can't you feel how much I love you? Please, trust me … stop thinking and let yourself feel."

Staring into his eyes, I did see. I did *feel* and for reasons I couldn't define, I trusted him. I wanted him to know me, all of me. I wanted him to see inside me, and in that moment, my soul left my body and joined with his. The bond wasn't just spiritual. It was physical. We became one—not soul mates, one soul, a completely out of body experience. It was beautiful and wondrous, and Godly. How could I feel guilty about it? How could it be wrong?

"I love you," I murmured.

He kissed me softly, ever so tenderly, our lips parting and carried me to the bed.

"I need to make love to you," he whispered.

He took his time unbuttoning my blouse, stopping to rest his head on my breasts, listening to my heartbeat, caressing my waist, inhaling the scent of me. In turn, I slowing pulled off his sweater and unbuttoned his shirt. I took a moment to savor the sight of his bare chest. It was as hard and defined as I had imagined. My touch made him quiver as I glided my fingertips down his chest and through his course curly hair, trailing to where I wanted to touch him most. I moaned when he put one of my nipples in his mouth.

After we explored each other's body with our hands, our lips, and our tongues, he entered me. Sighing with utter completeness, we became one soul and one body. We moved as one, and as one exploded in a burst of pleasure. I shattered as blinding white light gave way to vivid colors—dazzlingly bright colors—that suffused my vision. Consumed by fire and reduced to ash, I was reborn through the power of his love.

Afterwards, he continued to touch and kiss me. His skin was caress every time he moved, and I'd never felt so loved, so desired. How could I not want him? I knew I had a lot to consider, that I fell—no, jumped with my arms spread wide—off the precipice. I was still soaring and didn't want to think about what would happen when I hit the ground.

My rumbling stomach temporarily pulled me down from the clouds.

He asked, "Is my love hungry?"

Hearing him call me his "love" made me ravenous. I sought his mouth and kissed him hungrily. Our arms and legs twisted together and our bodies roared with life. Nothing slow about it, we made love wildly. Reese teased and tantalized me, making me crazy with delicious agony until I couldn't take it another second. I screamed, "Now! For the love of God, now." He rolled us, letting me take control, and we exploded together a second time.

Collapsing on his chest, I panted, "You are an incredible lover."

"I aim to please."

"Oh, you pleased alright. I've never had that intense of—"

"An orgasm," he finished for me chuckling.

"Yes," I admitted with a giggle. "But I was going to say 'of a physical experience.'"

"Much more lady-like." He beamed. "That was damn intense for me, too. As much as I'd like to take all the credit, I think we're pretty incredible together."

"I think you're right." I kissed his chest. "By the way, your love is still ravenous."

"Wasn't I *big and juicy* enough for you?"

"Nope."

He looked at me incredulously.

I laughed. "You are a delectable piece of meat, but I'm starving. I need food."

He laughed, too. "Want to get dressed and go somewhere special?"

"No, I'm enjoying the view too much." I guessed he was in a gym on a daily basis. He couldn't get that physique sitting at a desk. "How's the room service here?"

"Supposed to be pretty good. It's one reason I chose this resort; I was hoping to keep you locked up here all weekend. And by the way, I'm enjoying the view, too. I love your curves."

While we waited for room-service, he built a fire. We spent the evening cuddling in front of the fireplace, feeding each other dinner and drinking the wine he'd brought until our stomachs were full and our heads buzzed with wine.

He made me smile. He seemed so unabashedly happy. I asked, "Happy?"

"Insanely happy. I've wanted to be with you like this for months, but you're even more beautiful than I'd imagined, being with you is more amazing than I'd imagined."

Staring into each other's eyes, we made love again. When we were done, we fell asleep in each other's arms.

Chapter 14

I woke up peaceful and warm with the sun streaming on my face and a soft sheet caressing my body. It took me a moment to remember where I was and why I was naked. I rolled over to find Reese lying on his side gazing at me with a deep crease marring his brow.

He murmured, "Good morning."

I frowned at him. "What's wrong?" I couldn't imagine what could be wrong. Last night had been perfection.

"I know you can't stay with me, but I'm worried you'll go home and never come back."

"Don't be afraid," I teased and smiled at him. I brushed his forehead lightly with my fingertips, trying to erase his worry lines. "I love you," I said softly.

He pulled me to his side and held me as if he never intended to let go. His muscles were tense and his grip like iron. I glanced at the clock. We'd been up late and consequently, had slept late. I didn't say anything until his muscles relaxed and his grip loosened.

"Let's have brunch and then take a walk along the lake."

He agreed and let me shower first. He kissed me when I came out and then took his turn. I started to get my clothes out of my bag when it hit me that I hadn't called home. *Crap.* I found my purse underneath discarded clothes and retrieved my phone. It seemed a bit indecent calling with only a towel draped around me, but I wanted to finish before Reese got out of the shower.

Micah answered, "Hello?"

"Hi, Micah. It's Mom."

"Oh, hi."

"Did you win your game yesterday?"

"No, we lost by one goal."

"That's too bad, but you were up against a really good team."

"Yeah. Do you want to talk to Jason?"

"Sure."

I could hear Micah yelling for Jason.

"Hi, Mom."

"How's my baby boy?"

"I'm not a baby."

"You're my baby."

"Not any more. I'm in the third grade."

"Okay. What're you doing?"

"Watching cartoons. When are you coming home?"

"Wednesday."

"Oh. Do you want to talk to Dad?"

"You bet."

Matt got on the phone. "Hi, Honey. Why didn't you call last night?"

Guilt rippled through my chest. *I didn't call because I was in the arms of my lover and forgot.* "Sorry. I had to go out with colleagues, and it seemed too late when I got back."

"I understand. How's the teambuilding? Are you bonding?"

My stomach twisted. "As much as can be expected. How are you and the boys?"

"We're fine. Don't worry about us. We're just leaving for breakfast with my folks."

"Well, I won't keep you, then. Please make sure the boys have milk with breakfast and that they eat some vegetables today."

"Does ketchup count?"

"No, ketchup doesn't count as a vegetable."

We both chuckled, and Matt said, "Well, I need to get going."

"I understand. Love you and kiss the boys for me."

"Sure. Talk to you tomorrow."

He hung up without telling me he loved me, too. Guilty disappointment settled heavily on my chest. I shut off my phone and looked up. Reese stood with a towel wrapped around his waist staring down at me, his pained expression back. Without saying a word, he dropped to his knees and pushed his head between my thighs.

After brunch, we strolled along the path winding around the lake. A few clouds whispered about, but otherwise the sky was the most beautiful blue I'd ever seen. I loved the crisp air—cool enough for a sweater, but not quite jacket weather. It made me think of savory rich stews, crusty bread, and hearty wine. My favorite kind of day made better having Reese beside me. I smiled. Being with him made me feel so happy.

"What are you thinking?" he asked.

"I'd like to cook for you."

"Nice thought. Bet you're sexy with a little sweat on your brow."

"I usually wear pajama bottoms and a t-shirt when I cook. I doubt you'd think I was sexy." What would he really think of me schlepping around my kitchen without make-up?

"I'd love to find out." He stopped walking and pulled me into a kiss.

I sighed. "I guess we should talk."

We found a dry patch of ground and sat down facing the lake. He took my hand in his, expecting me to start the conversation, but I wasn't sure where to begin.

"You've brought out a side of me that's been dormant for a long time."

He tucked a lock of hair behind my ear. "Your sexuality was never that dormant."

"That's not what I meant. Although you definitely brought out the hedonist in me." I'm sure I had a ridiculous grin on my face. I didn't mind. He had a silly grin too. He was too sexy smiling with the sun shining on his face and made me lose my train of thought.

I took a deep breath and started again. "If it were just you and me, I'd be happy letting things just take their course. But I have a husband and children, an entire life in California. I have to know what you want and expect from whatever this is we're doing."

"Honestly, I want more than I can expect. I've never experienced anything close to what we shared last night. It was as if we fused somehow. I know you felt it too. You can't deny it."

I wanted to believe it was real, but as an actress I'd experienced moments on stage when I'd been *in the moment* and connected with acting partners by looking in their eyes and feeling great love. After the performance, it would be over; it was ephemeral, just passing connections. Moments of great passion happen but it doesn't mean it lasts. We could have had just another fleeting connection, which ultimately means nothing, as transitory as the seasons.

"It was the most visceral experience of my life, but I don't know if it means anything over time."

"It does," he said with absolute certainty. "You and I are meant to be together. I felt it the first time we met. I think I actually fell in love with you the moment I saw you." He quoted, "*Hear my soul speak; the very instant that I saw you, did my heart fly to your service.*"

"*Tempest.*"

"Don't tell me, you played Miranda?"

"A long time ago."

"Damn, I thought I'd stump you with that one."

"Sorry, but nice try."

"You do know your Shakespeare," he said with a small grin.

I had to process what he'd said. "I don't believe in love at first sight."

"So maybe I overstated."

"You think?"

He laughed self-consciously. "Okay, lust at first sight. I started falling in love with you over dinner in Boston. Then we started talking on the phone every morning …."

"It was the highlight of my day."

"Mine too." He squeezed my hand. "I was afraid of what I'd I do if I was ever alone with you and then we were—well, you know what happened."

I smiled up at him. "Oh, I *know.*"

"That night in Phoenix I wanted you so badly I thought I'd explode. It took all of my self-control to get back on that elevator." He hugged his arm around me. "Now that I have you, I don't ever want to let you go."

"I feel the same, but—"

He put his hand over my mouth. "No *buts.* I hate *buts.*" He dropped his hand and turned to stare out at the lake. "Do you love your husband?"

"I wish I could tell you that I don't, but yes, I love him and could never leave him. My boys deserve a family. It's hard to explain, but at the same time, I love you with a depth I've never felt for him."

He turned and looked me in the eyes. "I'll keep my promise. I won't ask you to choose between me and your family. Our relationship can be just between us. No one else has to know what we are to each other."

I'd heard stories of people who'd carried on affairs for years without their spouses knowing. I always had wondered if, deep down, their spouses had known, but chose to ignore the signs. Would Matt notice a difference in me? I wasn't sure how long I could maintain a double life, and I wasn't confident Reese had thought it through either.

"When I'm home, I'll still be Matt's wife in every sense."

I could see him processing the implications. For a moment, I thought it was too much for him, but he said, "I don't like it, but I guess I'll have to live with it."

He was more tolerant than I was. "I know I'm being selfish and one-sided, but I can't stomach the thought of sharing you. I *can't* live with it."

He took my face in his hands and made me look at him. "Hey, I'd be more upset if you didn't want me all to yourself. I promise, only you."

"This isn't some nineteenth century novel. You're a man with real physical needs."

"I only want you," he said with resolve. "My only condition is that when we're together, in our own private world, there's no holding back. We love each other without restraint. Deal?"

"Deal," I whispered.

He shifted me between his legs, and I sat leaning against him with his chin resting on my head and his arms wrapped around me. We watched the waves from the lake crash on the shoreline for most of the afternoon, talking some, but mostly existing quietly together.

I was astounded by how nourishing the simple act of being held could be. Soaking up Reese's warmth, I watched a piece of driftwood swirling in the water. Each time a wave broke on the rocks the wood got a little closer.

How many violent waves could it withstand before hitting the massive, jagged rocks and shattering?

I guess I had landed, but not on solid ground. I swirled in the water, unsure where I would find myself, unsure how much I could withstand. I wished with all of my being that somehow things would work out. If I could only split myself in two, everything would be fine. Half of me could go home to Matt and my boys; half of me could stay with Reese forever, but that was impossible.

I rested my cheek against his chest. "I don't ever want this to end, but I'm not sure I'm strong enough."

"I'm strong enough for both of us. Never doubt that." He held me tighter. He was so strong, so sure, that I believed him. After a minute, he tilted my chin towards his face and kissed me. His kiss was giving; full of love and assurance and asked for nothing in return, only acceptance. I gave myself to him and entwined my fingers in his hair as he rolled me on my back. We both heard footsteps approaching on the path.

Reese pulled away, panting slightly. "Ready to go back?"

"I think so. I'm getting a little hungry."

"In the mood for something *big and juicy?*"

I snickered. "Jeeze, will you stop with the *big and juicy*?"

"Alright, what are you in the mood for?"

"*Hot and spicy.*"

Reese's face lit up with a gleeful grin. He pulled me up and sprinted back to the room with me in tow.

Chapter 15

Monday morning arrived too soon and with it, a pile of work. Although we were meeting with separate clients, Reese and I were both due in the Loop area of Chicago that afternoon. I woke to Reese at the desk clicking away on his laptop. I kissed the top of his head on my way to the shower. He barely looked up, and went back to typing.

When I got out of the shower, he took his turn in the bathroom, and I started working. I spread out my lap top and files on the bed, put on the little reading glasses I wore when I worked, and dug into the presentation I would be doing later in the day.

He walked out with a towel wrapped around his waist and made a little grunting sound.

I looked up. "What?"

"Any room on the bed for me?"

"Sorry. Staff call starts in twenty minutes."

"Which gives us five minutes to spare."

"Reese, I'm already in work mode."

"Alright." He walked to the desk and started to sit in front of his laptop.

"Hey, put some clothes on. I can't concentrate with you only wearing a towel."

He smirked and dropped his towel. Laughing, I threw his boxers at him. He threw them back at me and pushed my laptop aside as he descended on me. We barely made the call.

It was surreal sitting in a hotel room, neither of us dressed, on a staff call. I started to get paranoid some noise would clue people to the fact that Reese and I were in the same room. I participated only when specifically called on. Reese enjoyed my obvious discomfort.

After we hung up, he at least put on his pants and t-shirt before calling Joe.

"Would you like some privacy?" I offered.

"No, you're fine. We're not discussing anything my lover can't hear."

"But what about your direct report?" I asked in attempt to maintain some boundaries.

"No, she can hear too," he invited with a wink.

I tried to concentrate on my work, but couldn't when they started talking about me. Reese said into the phone, "Susan? I've been pleased with everything she's done ... her willingness has exceeded all expectations ... yes; she is very good, very amenable ... she has many unexpected talents. Did you know that she used to be an actress ... hmmm ... I'd say her strength is maintaining contacts ..." He walked over and ran his hand over my thigh as he continued. "She embraces the concept that *Sales is a Contact Sport* ..."

I'd heard enough and wasn't amused. I went into the bathroom to finish getting ready and brought my laptop with me in case the call went long.

It did, and I ended up on a cold tile floor trying to work while my boss/lover talked to the president of our division. The indignity of it was humiliating.

Reese knocked softly on the door after he hung up. I came out a little frazzled and a lot pissed off. I'd had no idea how hard it would be to go back to business as usual.

"Love, you okay?" Reese asked.

"Not funny. I don't appreciate being treated that way."

"What way?"

"Like a dirty little joke."

He looked at me aghast. "I don't think you're a dirty little joke. Honestly, I thought you'd find it amusing. I'm sorry. I really am."

"Well, I didn't, and I guess I'm a little freaked out by how brazen you were. We have to be smart. No one can know about us. No one can even suspect."

"I don't disagree, but two consenting adults can't be fired for being together."

"No, but think of the liability. Do you really think Joe would allow this? We've both been through Harassment Training. There are some very strict rules about fraternization with direct reports. You're more at risk than me."

His arms encircled me, and he reasoned as if he were soothing a child, "The policy highly discourages fraternization between managers and subordinates. It doesn't forbid it."

"*Negative business impact* and *favoritism* are vague terms. You and I both know the policy can be interpreted a number of ways. Reese, please, what if my husband—"

He cut me off, whispering in my ear, "No one is going to find out." Then he patted my butt and said, "Come on, we need to pack up before the limo gets here to take us to the Westin."

"I'm not staying at the Westin."

"What?" he asked puzzled. "You told me you were, so I had Anne book me there."

"I switched to The Whitehall. I wasn't exactly sure what would happen this weekend. If things didn't work out, I didn't want to be in the same hotel. On the other hand, if things did workout I thought it would be more prudent to be in separate hotels."

Reese gave me a disbelieving look.

"Relax. The Westin is literally about a block from Whitehall."

"I never would have guessed you were so devious. I like the Juliet persona better, but I have to admit, Lady M is kind of a turn on."

He grabbed me around the waist, and I pushed away from him. I wasn't in the mood to play. "Will you please focus? We need a plan."

He asked, not pleased, "So Lady M., what's your plan?"

"No public touching. Matt and I have old college friends who still live in Chicago."

"That's reasonable. Anything else?"

"We shouldn't stay in the same hotel again."

He grimaced. "Now you're being paranoid. I understand booking separate rooms, but hotels? For God's sake, there's nothing unusual about colleagues staying in the same hotel."

I decided not to argue. I had to pack and power down my laptop.

When we got into the limo, I was still miffed and slid as far as I could from him. Choosing to let me stew, he retrieved his Blackberry from his pocket and started tapping away. I pulled out my own Blackberry and did the same.

As the limo pulled up to my hotel, he asked, "Ready to forgive? I hate you being mad at me. I'd never do anything intentionally to hurt you. You know that, right?"

"I know. Sorry I'm being so sensitive."

"Does this mean I have your permission to sexually harass you tonight?"

I couldn't stay mad at him. "Yes, Mr. Kirkpatrick, you do." When the driver opened the door, I turned toward Reese, wanting to kiss him good-bye, but instead thrust my hand out. "Good luck with your meetings today."

He took my hand, shook it, and said with a wink, "You, too."

Once settled in my own hotel room, it was difficult not to think about Reese. My love for him was new, and there was so much to consider. The only way to get through the day would be to force myself to compartmentalize my mind. All thoughts of Reese and home, all personal contemplation would have to wait. I had to have my head together for this meeting.

I switched on my Blackberry and rifled through emails. It helped me concentrate. By the time I sat down in the bank's conference room mid-afternoon, my head was all business.

The short time apart was a healthy reality check for both of us. Reese's meeting with Joe brought on a load of work for him. I was behind on reports and proposals I'd normally have done over the weekend. We agreed to delay seeing each other until we both did some catch up, and I made a point to call home first.

It was after eight when we finally met in the dimly lit Whitehall lounge. The little alcoves, which begged for discreet trysts, were almost empty. The concierge told me this had been a favorite rendezvous for Spencer Tracy and Katherine Hepburn. I didn't exactly see us as Kate and Spence, but the incandescent history appealed to my sense of drama.

Reese beat me there and sat in the corner with a drink in his hand. He smiled seductively, and I ached to kiss him. It had been all of eight hours since I'd seen him, but I'd missed him.

"It's unbelievably good to see you, Love," he greeted.

"You too." I couldn't resist touching him any longer. I placed my hand on his leg under the table and ran my fingers up the inside of his thigh. He grabbed my hand.

"Unless you want to skip dinner entirely, stop." His voice was tight with self-control, but his grin said he liked my hand exactly where it was.

The waiter came to take my order. "What may I bring the beautiful lady?" he asked in an indistinct European accent. It was so over the top, I had to bite my lip to keep from laughing. Reese ordered me a glass of wine, and I kept toying with him until the waiter left.

"All play and no work will get us both fired." I held my hands up and scooted away. "Would you be opposed to eating here? We can have a quick dinner and debrief." I was worried he'd want to drop work for the day, but I really did need him to be my boss for a while.

"No fair, but I agree. I've some things to review with you too. Midwestern Security is seriously shopping. I have a list of take-away items you'll have to handle, and we need to decide who from your team is going to work the account."

"That's great. Northern Community is also very interested, and I got a call from Greater South Bank and Trust. They want to set up the first meet before the end of the month."

"Joe will be impressed. I've got another call with him in the morning."

"And Reese, don't take it the wrong way, but we can't decide who covers which prospect based on personal motives. We have to have a solid business justification for everything."

His eyes narrowed, and he snapped, "Give me some fucking credit. I'm not going to do anything that will jeopardize my career. I was hired with the understanding I'll be president of our division by this time next year—that is what motivates my decisions."

I had to remember there were multiple sides to Reese. He was the most ambitious, driven man I'd ever met. He could be playful and romantic with me on personal time, but there was nothing uncalculated or emotional about the way he approached business. He was decisive, demanding of himself and his subordinates, and rightfully commanded respect.

Questioning him had been out of line. "I'm sorry. I don't know why I said it."

His expression softened. "You said it because this morning, I obviously wasn't thinking with my brain, but don't worry about me. I'm not going to do anything foolish."

"Isn't it foolish to be with me? Our relationship does jeopardize your career."

"I knew I could trust you before anything happened. You didn't flinch when you saw me walk in the conference room my first day. I watched you all day. You didn't crack once. It's your turn to trust me."

I smiled my apology. "I trust you completely."

"Good. Now can we please get back to work? I'm in a hurry. I have an appointment to harass my favorite employee."

"Really? Who?" I asked with my best poker face.

He just smirked at me.

After another hour of sitting next to him, even with our minds wrapped around business, the subtext of our interaction bubbled just below the surface. I slid my hand under the table and lightly ran my fingers up his thigh for the second time that evening. Reese didn't stop me. His eyes ignited and he said, "Let's go" in a thick voice.

We scrupulously did not touch on the way to my room. The Whitehall elevator was old and no bigger than a hall closet. A mere sliver of air separated us, but he didn't so much as bump his arm against mine. The hallway was abandoned, but we still did not touch. He was so close his scent was part of the air I breathed, and I could feel the heat of his body.

I slipped the card key into the lock and his breath grazed my cheek as he pushed the door open. Trembling, I stepped into the room feeling him inches behind me. He spun me around.

I thought he was going to kiss me, but he didn't. Taking my wrists in his hands, he held me against the door, keeping his body a breath from mine, and gazed into my eyes. Drawing together like magnets, heat and force pulled from our centers until we became one.

Only then did he kiss me. Nipping and sucking, without using his tongue or letting go of my wrists. His lips journeyed across my cheek to just below my ear. Running his tongue down my neck and into my cleavage, he still wouldn't let me touch him.

"Susan," he groaned, dropping to his knees, wrapping his arms rapturously, longingly around me, burying his face against me. He pushed up my skirt and kissed, with an open mouth, the inside of my thighs. Then he slipped my thong down my legs and helped me step out of it. My legs shook as he ran his mouth back up my thigh, and closed on me, suckling until I shattered. When I cried out, he lifted me, braced me against the door, and made love to me as if his life depended on it.

The next morning Reese left by 6 a.m. and we were on an 8 a.m. conference call with New York. The leisurely pace we'd enjoyed the last few weeks was over. We were buried, and Reese was relentless with deadlines. My day was packed with managing projects, attending conference calls, and scrambling to a second day of appointments.

I loved it. I lived for this kind of pace. It was exhilarating and exhausting simultaneously. The energy was pure Reese—energizing and demanding, but oh, so giving. It was nine o'clock when he and I wrapped up work for the day.

We were both worn out from work and lack of sleep. I still hadn't finished discussing all the ground rules with Reese, but by then it didn't seem necessary. His romantic side didn't bleed into work. He cut me no breaks because I was his lover. When he eventually made it to my room, he headed straight for the bed. I curled up next to him, spent. He wrapped his arms around me and ran his fingers through my hair. It was tenderly soothing after a very long day.

"What time is your flight tomorrow?" he asked.

"Early, six-thirty. What time's yours?"

"Eleven. If you like, I can ride with you to the airport."

"Don't be silly. You sleep."

"I'd argue, but I'm too tired. Sorry about burying you with work. I wanted a romantic dinner." We both had eaten deli sandwiches with laptops in front of us.

"Me too, but don't be sorry. We'll have other nights"

He rolled on his side and propped up on his elbow to look at me. His eyes were droopy and creased. I couldn't tell if he was sad or just exceptionally tired. "Promise me this won't be our last night."

"I promise." I touched his cheek. "What's worrying you?"

He moved my hand from his cheek to his lips. "Same thing that's been worrying me: I'm afraid you'll go home and never come back." He rubbed the backside of my hand against his face. Then he turned it over and kissed the fleshy part of my palm.

"Reese, I should explain something. I think it'll make it easier for you."

"What is it?" He laid down on his side, still holding my hand, facing me, our heads on the same pillow.

"I was so lonely before I met you," I said, trying not to let my voice crack. "Sometimes it's lonelier to be with someone, than it is to be alone." Drops rolled down my cheek. I was tired. Whenever I was tired, I was more susceptible to tears.

"Hey, don't—"

"Please, I want you to understand. I need you. I'm not lonely when I'm with you."

His eyes did their intense focus thing. "Then, don't go back. Stay with me."

I sat up. I couldn't believe what he'd said. "You promised you wouldn't do this."

He ran his hand down my back, kissed my neck, and pulled me back down on the bed. "Sorry, I'll stop. I only want you to be happy. I can't stand seeing you sad."

He had never conceded anything that quickly. Holy crap, he'd said *stay with me* because he knew I wouldn't. He thought hearing it would make me feel better. *Option 1.* "Reese—"

He stopped me with a kiss. "SHHH, I just want to love you. Let me love you."

"Reese, we're going back to real life tomorrow. I don't want any misunderstandings. Be honest. Please?" I rolled away from him and sat up.

"Okay," he sighed and sat up, too. "What do you want to know?"

"Why me? Is it because I'm married and have children?"

Reese blinked at me, absorbing what I'd asked, and then shot off the bed, pacing and shaking, anger vibrating out of him. "How could you ask that? How could you think it?"

"It makes sense. You get an affair without disrupting the rest of your life or losing your freedom."

"I just asked you to stay with me. What the fuck does that tell you?"

"You knew what my answer would be."

"So what if I did? I wanted a different answer. I hate that you're married. I hate not being the only man in your life. I was raised a good Catholic. *'Let marriage be held in honor among all, and let the bed be undefiled'* and all the rest of it. I've never done anything like this, *ever*, and I never thought I would. It's not who I am. I know what I'm doing is wrong on so many levels, and yes, I feel tremendous guilt."

"Then, why?"

"Because, I haven't been able to stop." His voice became low, and he was shaking again. "You're like an addiction; the more I'm with you, the more I have to be with you."

I knew the feeling. "I'm not blaming you, but I had to know for certain."

"If I was using you?"

"Yes," I whispered.

Hurt flickered in his eyes. He came back to the bed, and sat next to me. "I can see why my behavior hasn't inspired a lot of trust. I love you more than I can tell you. It's the only reason I'd be here."

I set my hand on top of his, and he entwined his fingers with mine. If he was lying, he was one hell of an actor. "I believe you."

"I was lonely before I met you, too," he whispered. "I've been with more women than I care to admit, but it's been a long time since I've been with someone I want waking up next to me. I decided a while ago I'd rather go home to an empty apartment."

I looked up at watery, thoughtful eyes. "I understand." And I did. I didn't want him to be lonely.

"You and I fit in so many ways. You are who I've been looking for, waiting for." He pulled me into is arms, and I nestled into him. "See how perfectly you fit in my arms? The fact you're married is definitely a problem."

"Yes, it is … but tonight I won't let you be lonely."

"Yes, tonight I get to love you."

He loved me and loved me for the next few hours. It was heaven to be loved.

Chapter 16

Up at four the next morning to shower and pack, I noticed four perfectly spaced bruises on the inside of my left thigh when I was in the shower. Panic shot through me. Reese must have given them to me. I had no idea he'd been gripping me so tightly. All I thought about was how I wanted him to hold me tighter. If Matt noticed, what would I tell him? I would just have to make sure Matt didn't see them.

Reese slept, dead to the world. It was close to midnight when we nodded off. When I was ready to go, I sat next to him on the bed and touched his cheek. I would see him every week thru October, but it was still hard to leave him. It would be easier if he didn't wake up. I kissed him lightly on the lips and left.

I badly needed sleep, but I also needed thinking time and forced myself to stay awake when I got on the plane. The last few days had been incredibly intense. I was exhausted physically, emotionally, and mentally. I'd never felt as intensely loved as I did the last four days. His way of loving was like a force of nature. He didn't hold back his emotions. He didn't hold back physically either. My body was literally sore from the marathon lovemaking.

Thinking about Matt and our early days together when we first acknowledged our love, my heart tightened. It couldn't have been more different.

Matt and I had been casually dating for a while and had a rare day when I didn't have rehearsal, and he didn't need to be in a lab. It was early October and knowing the cold would be descending on us soon, Matt invited me to have a picnic with him by the lake. When he picked me up for our date, he handed me a single yellow rose. Back then, he could only afford one and I'd worried about him spending the money on it.

We had walked hand in hand to the lake. The sun shined bright, and students were out doors throwing Frisbees, playing touch football, riding bicycles, or just enjoying the day.

I don't remember what we ate or how long it took Matt to work up to what he had to say, but eventually he said, "Thank you for spending the day with me. I know I'm not the most exciting guy in the world. Sometimes I wonder why you spend time with me at all."

I had a surge of affection for him. He'd never seemed so vulnerable. I wanted to wrap my arms around him and assure him he was lovable. "Matt, I love spending time with you. I'd rather be with you than anyone else in the world."

He looked at me incredulously. "But what about all those actors you're always hanging around? You have to prefer them."

"I don't. I prefer you."

He smiled. Obviously, I'd seen him smile before, but this time was different. His eyes crinkled adorably, and it was like watching sunlight burst from the clouds. "I need to tell you something."

"Okay, tell me."

"I love you," he whispered simply, barely meeting my eyes, so afraid of rejection.

My breath caught. I'd had no idea. I looked into his blue eyes, and it was like staring at a calm sea, peaceful and soothing. I could love him. He had an inner strength and inherent decency. He was trustworthy and responsible. I made a conscious decision to love him. I took his hand and declared, "I love you, too."

That was it. No discussion of souls or dramatic declarations. We did nothing more than hold hands. It was a pure and a simple admission of love, but it was powerful. Giving Matt my love changed something inside of me.

Later that day, we had gone to his apartment and made love for the first time. I don't recall any passionate-soul-deep embraces or fireworks, but I remember having had a warm, peaceful feeling and thinking it would be easy to love Matt for the rest of my life.

My sweet, reliable Matt … what have I done to you?

He would be devastated if he knew how I had spent the last four days. Guilt jolted like lightning bolts through my insides. *Do not hyperventilate. Get some sleep.* If I had some sleep, I would be more rational. Closing my eyes, I slept the rest of the flight.

When I got home, Matt was at work, and the boys were at school. Reese was in flight to New York. I could risk a nap without anyone noticing. I woke up an hour later feeling better and decided to unpack before working the remainder of the afternoon.

Opening my suitcase sent the aroma of Reese wafting toward me. His cologne must have rubbed off on my clothes. I pulled one of my sweaters to my face, deeply inhaled, and shuddered. Part of me wanted to put the sweater in a plastic bag to preserve the scent. If I missed him too much, I could pull it out and smell him.

A more rational side was frightened. *What if Matt smelled the cologne?*

I hastily threw some clothes in the washing machine and dropped the rest at the cleaners. It made me nervous thinking about what other evidence might need destroying. I was confused about many things, but I was certain I did not want to get caught.

When I got back from the dry cleaners, Reese called. His plane had landed, and he was in route to the New York office.

"Sweetheart, why didn't you wake me up?"

"You'd barely slept for days. You needed sleep."

"I need you more. I didn't like waking up alone. I already miss you. It's going to be a long six days," he said.

Luckily, Reese had a call he had to take. Having a lover's conversation with him in my family's home had my insides twisting and knotting. Besides, I had to get moving or I'd be working until midnight. I didn't want to think about Reese or Matt; both brought different varieties of anxiety and pain. I threw myself into work until Matt and the boys got home.

As soon as they walked in the door, the boys dropped their backpacks and tackled me with hugs. I really did miss my guys. I had to promise to hear all about their day as soon as I had a chance to say hello to Daddy. I don't know if it was out of guilt, or nostalgia from thinking about our early days, or just knowing I was being pulled another direction, but I needed Matt to put his arms around me and tell me that he loved me, that he missed me.

He pecked my cheek and said, "Welcome home." Then he walked into the bedroom.

Throw your arms around me and tell me how much you missed me! Can't you tell I need more! Why can't you love me more?

Intellectually, I knew I had no right to expect anything from him, but emotionally, my heart craved more. I didn't know if my tears were for Matt, or me, or if I was simply exhausted. Not wanting anyone to see me crying, I retreated to the bathroom.

After I composed myself, I went into the kitchen to start dinner. Matt sat at the table and watched me chop vegetables. I worried he would notice a difference in me.

"How was Chicago?" he asked with polite disinterest.

"Hectic. I made progress with a couple prospects. How were things at home?"

"Fine, but the boys really missed you."

"What about you? Did you miss me?" I couldn't look at him and kept trimming green beans while I waited to hear his answer.

"Of course." He got up and went to watch the news.

His answer angered and frustrated me, but I was angrier with myself. Why bait him with the question? I could have thrown my arms around him and told him I missed him, that I loved him. Another thought had nagged at me for months, but I'd refused to acknowledge it. Maybe Matt didn't love me anymore. Maybe that was the real source of my loneliness and discontent.

I don't know which tore at me more: knowing I'd cheated or thinking Matt ceased to love me. Being home, seeing Matt and my boys, I couldn't believe what I'd done. I felt dirty and disgusted with myself and irrationally angry with Matt, but at the same time, I craved Reese.

Whoever said you can't love two people at the same time was wrong. I loved two men, and at that moment, was in pain because of both. My heart was ripping in two and guilt was a live beast eating me from the pit of my stomach.

Stop thinking about it. Pull yourself together. Appear normal.

Micah and Jason walked into the kitchen with smiles and love in their eyes. If I doubted why I shouldn't give up on Matt, why I shouldn't run away with Reese, their faces told me. My heart wasn't ripping in two; it was ripping in three. I loved my boys. I loved them and wanted to keep them secure and happy, which meant staying with their father.

The boys' prattle during dinner was a welcome distraction. Afterwards, Jason wanted me to continue our reading marathon. After we'd finished the first Harry Potter book last summer, he had decided that I needed to read them all to him. We had just started the fourth book. Micah joined us in the living room. It was comforting to have both boys cuddled around me.

Matt stayed in the family room, watching a baseball game. The playoffs were in full swing. Normally, the boys would have been watching the game with their dad. It was nice to have something that they preferred to do with me. I wished Matt would join us, but it wasn't his thing, just as fishing and baseball weren't mine.

I went to bed, planning to be asleep before Matt joined me. I wasn't, but pretended to be. He crawled in and rolled on his side with his back to me. Less than a minute later, he rolled over again, put his arm around my waist, and spooned his erection against me. My body involuntarily stiffened.

"Did I do something to upset you?" he asked tentatively.

"No … I just wish you missed me. That's all."

It was hard to say without crying. Did he really expect me to have sex with him without so much as a single *I love you* or *I missed you* all night?

"I told you I missed you."

"But I had to ask."

He took a deep breath and said, "You're tired." He rolled back over with his back to me.

It hurt and angered me when he dismissed my feelings. I wanted him to love me. Was that asking too much? *Give me a reason to stay with you that has nothing to do with Micah and Jason. Please, Matt. Please, love me.*

"Matt?"

"Yes?"

"I love you," I whispered.

"Love you, too," he automatically answered, still keeping his back to me.

My husband was inches away but I didn't know how to bridge the gap between us.

Chapter 17

The next morning I skipped my morning workout and slept until almost six. I had been tired and sleep helped my mindset. I was resolved to apologize when Matt woke up.

Walking into my office, I wondered if Reese would call. Sure enough, at 6 a.m. his office number lit up my phone.

I started, "Well, hel—"

"Morning, this is Reese. I'm here with Joe. We have you on speaker."

I sat up straight. "Good morning, Joe."

"Sorry to be calling so early, but Reese assured me you'd be up," Joe explained.

"He's right. I'm already at my desk. What can I do for you?"

"Reese has been updating me on your progress. It sounds like your pipeline is getting full. I wanted to call you myself to congratulate you."

"Thank you. I appreciate it."

"I'd like you to come to New York to review your progress and project calendar. I also think it would be a good idea if the three of us sat down with Legal."

"Of course, how soon would you like me in New York?"

"I understand you're due in Boston on the 20th. Could you extend your trip and be in New York for the remainder of the week?" Joe inquired.

"I'll work it out."

"Thanks, Susan. I'll call you later," Reese said and hung up.

My heart pounded. I easily could have said something intimate not knowing Joe had been listening. *Stupid. Stupid.* Working in data security, I knew how important it was to be discreet. IT routinely monitored e-mails and on-line chats. They could retrieve text messages and trace where we've been with the GPS in our Blackberries. Until recently, our interaction had been relatively innocent, but going forward, we'd have to be extra cautious.

As soon as I heard Matt get up, I left my office to make amends. I poured him a cup of coffee and took it to him in the bedroom.

"Peace offering," I said handing him the cup.

"Thanks." He took a sip and said, "Good coffee. What was that about last night?"

"I was just tired."

"Thought so. Feeling better this morning?"

"A little."

He set the cup down and put his arms around me. "I miss you whenever you're gone," he said quietly. Then he gave me a quick squeeze and went into the bathroom to shower. It wasn't everything I craved, but it was enough.

Reese called about mid-morning, and I could hear street noises in the background.

"Can you talk?" he asked first.

"Yes. No one's home, but I'm due on a conference call in a few minutes."

"I know. I checked your Outlook calendar."

I laughed and asked, "Are you spying on me?"

He laughed too and then explained, "No, I was just looking for a time when I could slip out of the office and catch you."

"Well, you caught me." He did catch me. I loved him.

"I was worried about you last night. How were things when you got home?"

"I can't say it was easy. The boys really missed me."

"What about your husband? Did he miss you?" He sounded strained.

"Yes, I think so ... I don't know."

"Did you make love to him?" I couldn't believe he asked. Tears started to well up. "I'm sorry," he apologized before I could answer. "I don't know why I asked. I don't want to know."

"I love you and miss you. Isn't that enough?"

"It has to be. By the way, we need some kind of 'all clear' signal."

"I thought about that, too. What if we assume all business until after 6 p.m. Eastern? By then, most people will be out of the office, or you'll be home. Matt and the boys don't get home until after 5:30 Pacific."

"I should have known my little schemer would already have a plan."

"Well, I didn't think of it until this morning."

Reese chuckled. "I wasn't sure, but it made me nervous."

"I've got to go. My call is about to start."

"Don't hang up yet. You have one more minute. I don't think you have any idea how deeply in love with you I am. I can't wait to hold you again."

"I can't wait to be with you again, too."

"Okay, now your boss is talking. Go. Don't be late."

I laughed and hung up.

Guilt continued to live in my stomach, but it began to settle and tame. When Matt got home, I greeted him at the door without an excess of emotion. I kissed him lightly on the lips and inquired about his day. We continued on, as if nothing had happened ... nothing worse ... nothing better. We began simply to drift.

Sunday night we had sex. After being with Reese, I expected it to be difficult. It wasn't. Our lovemaking was so predictable we could do it on autopilot, a muscle memory reflex.

Reese and I established a new routine. We no longer chatted about non-work topics at 6 a.m. No flirtatious e-mails or on-line chats. We both understood the risk without having to discuss it. He worked me without favoritism and scrutinized everything client facing. If I didn't love him and respect his drive, I probably would have resented his perfectionist demands.

Reese agreeing to time frames allowed me to segment my life. From 6 a.m. to 6 p.m., I was the SVP of a Fortune 500 Company. I took a break for an hour or so late afternoon to be Reese's lover. In the evening, I was Matt's wife and my boys' mother. As long as I didn't blur the lines, I could maintain the balancing act.

The next week I spent two nights with Reese in Los Angeles. Startlingly, I returned to Matt without the consuming guilt I had experienced after my first adulterous weekend. The following week Reese and I were together in Seattle. Reese made me feel desired and loved. He didn't pressure and seemed content with the time we had together. Leaving him in Seattle wasn't easy, but I was consoled knowing I was due in Boston the following Monday and then would spend the rest of the week with him in New York.

The guilt beast in my stomach growled, but stopped biting. My loneliness didn't evaporate, but it stayed under control, too. I missed Reese when I wasn't with him, and I missed feeling close to Matt when I was with him. I gained confidence that I could sustain both relationships. I tried not to think about Reese when Matt was home; I tried not to think about Matt when I was with Reese. Reese understood discussions about my husband were off limits. Of course, Matt had no knowledge of my relationship with Reese so there was nothing to avoid.

Conventional wisdom dictated I should see a therapist, but I was afraid of diving too deeply into my feelings and forcing decisions I wasn't ready to make. I didn't want to be judged, and I didn't want to give up Reese or my marriage. I opted to do my own research on infidelity in an attempt to sort out what had happened to my life and where I wanted it to go.

The Saturday before my Boston/New York trip, Matt took the boys to an afternoon movie. It was beautiful fall day, my favorite kind of day. Normally around midafternoon, I would have a rich stew or big piece of succulent meat roasting in the oven. Then, I would sit on the back porch and read, enjoying the quiet and the gentle sun caressing my face. That afternoon I powered up my laptop, clicked on the internet, typed "infidelity in marriage" into the search button, and hit enter.

2,750,206 hits. Websites dedicated to every topic imaginable: how to catch cheaters, signs of infidelity, surviving infidelity, how to meet married men, how to meet married women, etc.. The statistics drew my attention. I had to know how many others were out there like me.

My eyes scanned down the screen. It made sense that most people cheat with friends, neighbors, and co-workers. Somewhere around thirty-six percent of people who commit infidelity admitted to workplace affairs. Reese and I weren't that unique after all. According to the website, over fifty percent of adults polled had cheated on their spouse. It was a shocking statistic. I thought about all the couples at the PTA open house: nice, upper middle-class couples. How many of them cheated? Aside from Jack Carter, I couldn't imagine any of them being a cheater, but I couldn't be the only one, could I? Forget the Craft Club. Maybe I could join the Cheating Wives Club. Supposedly, fifty-four percent of us wives either have had emotional affairs or warmed our beds with other men.

I compared my situation to a checklist of the most common denominators. Feelings of Loneliness. *Loneliness was my consort.* Check. Intimate

Emotional Relationship with a Co-worker. *Reese was my 'good' friend.* Check. Pre-existing Physical Attraction. *Espresso Bar.* Check. Trade Up from Spouse. *Reese, well, he was Reese.*

And it added up to what?

I tried another site dedicated specifically to woman committing adultery. The author was a psychologist who purported that female adulterers usually experienced a chemical reaction, which made them addicted to their lovers. What did that mean? Wasn't love an addiction?

The author did write about one thing that gave me guilty comfort. She claimed most women don't get caught. Their husbands don't even suspect. Most men assume if their wives weren't interested in sex with them, they simply weren't interested in sex at all. Therein laid the fallacy. They wanted sex, just not with their husbands.

I only had sex with Matt once since I started sleeping with Reese.

Men also want to believe that their wives are good girls. Good girls don't cheat.

Matt thought I was a good girl.

I got up and paced around my office. I looked out the window and gazed at our backyard. Memories flooded my thoughts: Matt hanging the tire-swing from our tree, the boys splashing around a wading pool, Matt tossing a ball easy enough for five-year old Jason to catch, Matt kissing me on the porch on a warm summer evening after the boys had gone to sleep.

Trying to rationalize my situation from a psychological point of view really didn't help or change anything. I was still an adulterer … a cheater … a sinner … a commandment breaker.

I'd seen a movie years ago with Diane Lane and Richard Gere. Diane Lane's character was married to Richard Gere, and she had an affair with a sexy French book dealer. In the movie, a group of women gossip about another woman who had had an affair. A comment was made that all affairs end badly. Later in the film, the husband kills the lover. I couldn't imagine Matt killing anyone, nor under what circumstances could Reese and Matt find themselves in the same room. Still, I kept thinking about things ending badly. How could they not?

Madame Bovary swallowed arsenic.

Anna Karenina threw herself in front of a train.

What would I do if I got caught? *Please, God, I can't get caught.*

I remembered a radio interview I'd heard with an author pitching a book about how to cheat without the fear of being caught. The interview had ceased being humorous after the author gave her first words of wisdom, "Affairs should take place at least fifty miles from where you live." She had been dead serious. I guess I had the first rule covered.

Going back to my desk, I searched for her book on the internet and found it. After filling out the order form, disgust stopped me from hitting the submit button. I cleared the browsing history from my computer, powered it down, and sat staring at the blank screen.

In my weaker moments, I blamed Matt. I consciously had given him my love. Why couldn't he love me back? The boys were a huge part of why I stayed. Life as I knew it was a factor. Nevertheless, the major reason I stayed was because a part of me wanted my husband.

Reese kept me breathing. Sometimes I thought if I didn't have him, I would suffocate. I needed him now, maybe more than I needed Matt. Ironically, having Reese made staying in my marriage bearable. He kept me from going over the edge.

Not long after Matt and I were married, a friend and I were chatting idly. Somehow or other we started talking about extra-marital affairs. I recall firmly asserting I'd *never* cheat on Matt. If I felt the need to be with another man, I would divorce Matt first.

I had been naïve, not understanding how entwined we would become, how at some point *my* life would cease to exist and be replaced with *our* life, with *our* family traits and eccentricities. At twenty-four, I hadn't understood how easy it would be to go through the mindless motions of life, the habits of living, and not recognize that my marriage—Matt—no longer gave me what I needed as a woman. I had felt it for years, but I couldn't see it. I suppose, in some ways, I didn't want to see it. I wished with all my heart I had recognized it before I met Reese, but I hadn't. I wished my relationship with Reese was only about sex, but it wasn't. I wished I could end the affair, but I couldn't.

Boisterous male energy shattered the silence in the house. It had grown dark, and I hadn't turned on any lights. I hadn't started dinner. No light or comforting smells welcomed my family home. A sense of failure gripped me. I met them in the kitchen.

"How was the movie?" I did my best to sound upbeat.

"Hilarious." Micah looked around for some indication that food would be served soon. "What's for dinner?"

"How about pizza?"

The boys were pleased, but Matt scrutinized my face and raised an eyebrow.

"I'm sorry. I got caught up with work."

"Pizza sounds great." Matt smiled tightly.

Was he happy? I couldn't tell.

The next day, I was up early and heading to the airport once again. Matt offered to drive me, which was unusual. Leaving the boys concerned me, but Matt insisted they would be fine for the short time it would take to make a round trip to SFO on a sleepy Sunday morning. Matt had something on his mind; otherwise, he would have let me drive myself. Not wanting to play twenty questions, I waited in silence for him to say whatever it was he had to say.

Finally, he said, "It's been hard with you gone so much."

Rip went my heart and the beast in the pit of my stomach sprang to life. "I know." I choked, trying not to cry, but couldn't stop. It was such a relief to get things out in the open.

"Please, don't cry."

"I'm trying not to."

"Well, anyway I thought we could go into the city for dinner when you get back."

"I would like that," I said a little more calmly.

"Good. I'll arrange for a babysitter."

When we got to the airport, Matt took my bags out of the trunk and set them on the curb. It reminded me of Reese dropping me in Atlanta, but Matt wasn't Reese. There were no dramatically gazing eyes or bodies pulling together in a meaningful embrace. He squeezed my hand, wished me a good flight, pecked my cheek, got back in the car, and drove away.

A part of me was positively gleeful Matt was making an effort. He did notice all was not well in the Sinclair house. He wanted things to be better. Another part of me worried how much he suspected and if the effort was too little, too late. Our relationship was so damaged I didn't know how long I could hold on.

Chapter 18

As I traveled from the West Coast to the East Coast, relieved to be in the air, my focus drifted from Matt to work and then to Reese. The plan was for me to fly to Boston where I would facilitate a consultation between our product engineers and the bank's IT team for a very technical discussion of servers, protocols, firewalls, encryption requirements, etc. Most of the discussion would be over my head, but I was needed as a point of continuity for the sales process. After the meeting, I'd then fly to New York, where I'd stay with Reese, and be home Friday in time for dinner.

Staying with Reese was risky—reckless even—but he'd used his most seductive voice when he'd asked, "Play house with me, please."

"It'll be too suspicious. I can't."

"Say you're staying with a friend. It wouldn't be a lie."

"You're much more than a friend. You're my lover."

"Exactly why I want to share my home with you. I want to make love to you on my couch and smell you on my sheets after you leave. Say yes … please, say yes."

I caved. Matt never called me at hotels. He called my cell phone and I always used my cell when I called home. Half the time he didn't even know where I was, and my admin wouldn't question my decision to stay with a friend.

At 7:30 on Monday night, a cab dropped me in front of Reese's apartment building. It wasn't what I'd expected. He was always so Mr. GQ at work that I had visualized him living in some chic high rise decorated with sleek leather furniture and glass tables with polished metal accessories. I faced a brownstone walk up. It took a minute to muster my courage before walking up the steps to the entrance. Reese opened the door as I reached the landing.

He wore a silly grin and looked so relaxed in his bare feet, faded jeans, and grey Boston Bruins' t-shirt. Damn, was he sexy in jeans. I preferred the look to his business suits. He wrapped his arms around me and kissed me before escorting me to his apartment.

Stepping back, he let me absorb it all. Hardwood floors and crown molding, large purple velvet couch, but everything else antiques. Two walls lined with bookcases overflowing with a large collection of classic literature and poetry mixed in with business books, biographies, and a smattering of history. An expensive looking stereo system in the corner playing Ella Fitzgerald. A huge flat screen TV, after all, he was a guy.

The overall effect was tasteful and comfortable. He made the room more inviting by having a bouquet of flowers in a crystal vase on the table. The room was Reese. It was who he really was. The GQ Mr. Slick was his persona for work, but it wasn't my Reese.

Being with him, in his home, made our relationship real for the first time. Previously, everything had been our bubble world: mind-blowing sex in resorts and hotel rooms that had room service and maids to clean and change the sheets. I'd only seen what Reese chose to show me, but now he shared his home with me.

He walked behind me and wrapped his arms around me. "What do you think?"

"I love your home. It's so you," I said with a sigh. Even if it weren't true, knowing how important my answer was to him, I would have lied. However, it wasn't a lie. I could see myself living here and not wanting to change a thing.

"I'm glad. By the way, I don't want to hear a single word about work until tomorrow. You can debrief me over breakfast."

"You're the boss."

He nuzzled my neck. "Not tonight. Tonight, I'm your lover and only your lover."

I leaned into him. "That sounds perfect."

"Come on, I'll show you the rest of the apartment." Reese took my hand and led me down the hallway. He showed me his office and black and white kitchen where he had spaghetti sauce bubbling on the stove. He handed me a glass of wine before leading me to the bedroom. Just like the living room, it was comfortable and tasteful. He'd lit candles and the room glowed softly with their light. His wrought iron bed was both masculine and romantic. I couldn't help wondering how many other women had been in this room and in his bed. Not wanting to think about it, I pushed the thought aside.

Leaning against the doorway, Reese grinned and pointed to a wrapped box resting on the bed. "For you." He walked over and handed it to me.

I was sure it'd be skimpy lingerie and laughed when I saw what it contained: a Harvard Business School t-shirt and a pair of pajama bottoms. "Is this your way of romancing me?"

"Well, you told me you like to wear t-shirts and pajama bottoms at home. I want you to feel just as comfortable here." He smiled at me with his eyes full of love, so happy.

"That's very thoughtful. Thank you." I kissed him. "Mind if I change?"

"Please. Meet me in the kitchen. Dinner is almost ready."

I changed into the clothes Reese bought me and looked in the mirror. *Not a flattering look, but comfy.* It was time for him to see another side of me, too. I walked into the kitchen, where Reese was setting a salad on the table, and pirouetted for him.

He whistled. "Very sexy."

"Yeah, right. More like frumpy, but I am comfortable."

"Nope, you're sexy." He pulled me into his arms. "Seeing you look at home is a huge turn on," he whispered as he glided his hand up my shirt.

"Stop." I laughed, pulling away from him. "We should eat first."

"You're right. It'll give you energy for later," he said with a playful laugh.

He was a good cook. Why was I not surprised? Reese had many talents. When we were done eating, I helped him clean up. His idea of cleaning was different from mine. He wasn't even sure if he had any Ajax. Looking around, everything was a bit too clean given what I had seen of Reese's domestic habits. He must have had a cleaning service work their magic just before I arrived. His meticulousness was for work, not home. It made me smile. I filed it away as one more thing I learned about him.

Afterwards, we cuddled on his couch, sipping the last of the wine. I'd never seen him so unwound and content. He wasn't stressing from work or being the ardent lover. I liked this less intense Reese. If possible, I fell even more in love with him.

"Thank you for inviting me. This is much nicer than a hotel room."

He leaned over and kissed me before he jumped up and said, "Time for another present." He went to the bedroom and came back with a small box. I hoped it wasn't something I'd have to refuse. My fingers fumbled with the wrapping. It was a jewelry box. I hesitated.

Reese chuckled. "It's not what you think. Open it."

I flipped the lid and nestled in the middle sat a key. I stared at it.

He explained, "It's a key to my apartment."

I didn't need the clarification, and asked for the answer I wanted, "To use for the week?"

He took my hands and looked into my eyes. "No, for always. I want you to think of my home as your home." He pointed to his door. "You don't ever need an invitation to walk through that door."

"Reese, this is all a little overwhelming. Even if I left Matt, I can't leave my boys. I can't live on another coast." A tear slid down my cheek. This was not the way I envisioned the evening to end. Why did he have to complicate things even more?

"Love, I'd never ask you to leave your boys, but I want more than a series of nights in hotel rooms with you. I want to share my life with you."

"Are you asking me to leave Matt?"

"I'm just making my feelings clear, so there's no misunderstanding. You have options." Despite his calm voice, intense Reese was back. "I won't lie to you—I want you exclusively with me. I'm not playing games."

Vomit rose in my throat, and I wrenched my hands free. How did we get to this point so soon? "I never thought you were toying with me, but you promised. You promised you wouldn't make me choose!"

"No, I said I wouldn't make you choose between me and your children. I never made a promise about your husband."

"You said *my family*. I can't believe you!"

"Damn it, Susan, I'm not giving you an ultimatum. I'm giving you the choice to have a life with me, a real life. We love each other, and I'm ready to give you everything I have to give. People get divorced every day. You've been miserable with him, and I just don't understand why the fuck you stay with him!"

Matt never yelled at me.

"Because I have children and I love him!"

He flinched as if he'd been slapped, and said to himself, "Fuck, I've been such a fucking idiot." I watched him fight tears. "I've been so worried that you would think I'm using you, but you're using me. I'm just a patch for your fucked up marriage."

Things were ending badly. *End it now.* But I couldn't. "No, you're not. I'm sorry … I'm so sorry. I love you, I do, I love you so much," I sobbed, throwing my arms around him and smothering him with kisses, wanting his pain to go away.

He tried to push me away, but I clung to him and kept kissing him until he gave up and kissed me back. Then, he picked me up and carried me to his bed. Our need for each other was urgent, and we made love in a primal and animalistic way. He pounded into me until we were both spent, leaving us out of breath and panting.

Lying on our backs, and not touching, Reese said, "I need to know what's going on before I lose my fucking mind. Do you love him more?"

"No. I've loved him longer, but I love you more. I love you more than I've ever loved him or any other man. You make me feel so alive and happy."

He sat up to look at me. "If I gave you more time, would you be willing to leave him?"

"I don't know." He dropped on his back again. "I want to tell you something, something I've never told anyone, not even Matt. My mother doesn't even know that I know."

"What is it?"

"When my father remarried, his new wife made him choose her or me. He chose her."

"How did you find out?"

"I overheard my mother talking about it, crying actually. She didn't know if she could raise me without his help. I thought she was going to give me away. I was so scared. It's one of my earliest memories."

"I wish I could erase that memory for you."

"Will you hold me?" Reese wrapped his arms around me. "Closer."

He adjusted, molding us together, and said, "I'd never put you in that position. You know that, right?"

"I know, but it's more than that. I swore when I had children, they'd grow up with a mother and father in the same house. I never want them to feel unwanted or unloved."

"I can't imagine what it was like for you, but I know this, you deserve some love and some happiness."

"You live in New York. They live in California. I can't move to New York. And what about Global Security? One of us would have to quit."

He propped up on his elbow. "Look at me." I did and he said, "I don't have an answer for everything yet, but honestly, this is a lot harder than I thought it'd be. I want so badly for us to be a real couple and do normal things, like sit around on a Sunday morning and just read the paper together. I want to hold your hand in public and not worry about who sees us, or take you to a movie—just normal fucking things. You understand?"

I nodded. "I want those things, too. It's not easy for me, either."

"Will you take my key and think about it?"

"Yes."

He eased back on the pillow. "So why marry Matt? What was it about him?"

"I almost didn't. I considered marrying an actor named Trent. He was full of passion and high drama. I envisioned us as the next great acting couple, like the Fabulous Lunts."

"Who?"

"Famous stage actors. Anyway, Trent and I were in the M.F.A. program together, but over the summer, we worked at different theaters. I'd heard rumors he was sleeping with his leading lady so I broke up with him. When we got back to school, he swore he loved me and had been faithful. He asked me to marry him. I almost did, but I'd started seeing Matt. He was a nice boy, and he treated me as if I were a nice girl.

"With Trent, I knew life would never be boring, but Matt would be home every night. He would keep me grounded. I craved the respectable upper-middle class life he represented. I wanted someone to hold me every night and someone I could trust. I chose Matt."

He looked at me as if he didn't recognize the insecure little waif I had just portrayed. "You are a nice girl, despite being a little junior high hussy." He chuckled. "And you didn't need Matt to get you to the other side of the tracks. You did it yourself. You read too much nineteenth century fiction. What you need is a healthy dose of feminist lit."

"I know. I'm pathetic," I half-heartedly joked.

"No, you're not. You're strong and resilient, but I know you have a fragile heart that you protect. So Matt was the safe bet?"

"It wasn't as calculated as it sounds, but yes, I made a choice to love him."

"Did you make a choice to love me?"

I had no constraint when it came to Reese; my moral and logical judgment was overridden by an unbridled yearning to be with him. "No, I can't help loving you."

"But now, you're married, you have children, and Matt doesn't hold you every night." I couldn't answer. All I could do was cry into his chest while he ran his hand up and down my back, soothing me. He whispered in my ear, "Stay with me, and I promise you'll always be loved. I'll guard your heart more than my own."

It was getting late and I needed to call home. I pulled away from him to get out of bed.

"Where are you going?"

"I have to make a call."

He didn't ask whom I was calling. He knew.

We didn't make love again that night, but we slept holding closely to each other. His body remained tense even as he slept. I couldn't sleep well either and woke frequently.

I got up at five a.m. and started rummaging around his kitchen. He'd set his alarm for six and I wanted to be ready for him. As soon as I heard his alarm go off, I poured his coffee and walked into the bedroom with a tray carrying his breakfast, complete with a flower I had snitched from the bouquet in the living room.

"What's all this?" he asked half-awake.

"Breakfast for the man I love." I set the tray on the bed and handed him his coffee.

He took a sip. "Mmmm, good coffee."

I guess there was one thing Matt and Reese had in common. After he finished his breakfast, I removed the tray and the Harvard Business School t-shirt I was wearing.

"What are you doing?" he asked.

Brushing my naked breasts across his stomach, I didn't answer. He grabbed me by the shoulders, but I shook my head. "Just for you."

He groaned and let me slide down his body.

Afterward, I crawled up his chest and wiggled into his arms. "Susan, Susan, Susan, what are you doing to me?"

"Loving you. What do you think?"

"Driving me insane. You can't do that and expect me to be okay when you leave."

I felt tears well up. "I'm sorry. I wanted to make you happy."

"Oh Sweetheart, don't cry. That's not what I meant. Trust me; you made me very, very happy. Hey, look at me," he said pulling my chin up. "I'm sorry I pressured you. My only excuse is that I'm crazy in love with you."

"Does this mean I'm 'your love' again?"

"You are my love, the love of my life, and as much as I'd like to spend the morning in bed with you, we need to move if we're going to make it to the office by eight."

We both jumped up and *moved*. There wasn't enough time to take turns in the bathroom. He urinated while I showered. I plucked a few errant eyebrow hairs and put on make-up while he shaved. I suggested he allow me to pluck a few of his nose hairs and he let me. After that, all of our inhibitions were gone. He stopped shutting the door when he had to pee and I didn't think twice about him watching me do my morning routine. In a matter of weeks, Reese and I had reached a level of familiarity that Matt and I had yet to achieve.

While we got ready, I debriefed Reese on the Boston meeting. We were reliant on Product Development to sort out some complicated technical issues before we could move forward. It would add cost to our proposal, and I worried about staying competitively priced. Some of the issues were going to be problematic for other banks as well. It was always a balance: offering a superior service while keeping our price within market.

We took separate cabs and continued our discussion at the office. Reese had some ideas and wanted to crunch some numbers before our meeting. There was no time for lunch, but we were ready when we sat down with Joe.

Reese proposed offering software applications gratis in exchange for a long-term service contract. We would shift from an upfront revenue plan to a recurring billing model. Over time, it was more profitable, and Reese had the numbers to prove it. By the end of the meeting, one would think it had been Joe's brain-child. The whole interaction was very smooth. I admired Reese's skill and learned much about the nuances of "managing up".

We finished for the day around seven, and I was starving. Joe rode the elevator with us on the way to the front lobby.

"Where are you staying?" Joe asked.

"With a friend. I thought I'd do my part to help with expenses," I joked.

"Would you care for a ride? My driver is bringing my car around."

"No, thanks. I'm meeting my friend for a drink a few blocks from here."

Reese and I automatically split up when we got outside. I left him to chat with Joe and walked a couple blocks before taking a cab to Reese's apartment. I was glad I had a key, or I'd have been stuck waiting outside.

I changed out of my suit, opened a bottle of wine, and started dinner. There was enough food in the refrigerator to feed a family of four very well for a week. It tugged my heart imagining Reese stocking his kitchen in preparation for my visit and knowing how important it was to him for me to be in his home doing normal, everyday things. I had a sudden urge to alphabetize his spices. It was silly, but I wanted to leave some physical evidence I'd been here.

"Susan?" he called when he got home.

"In here."

He walked in the kitchen and a huge smile spread across his face. I kissed him, handed him a glass of wine, and returned to the stove. "I could get used to this," he said still smiling.

"What?"

"Coming home to you."

I could get used to him coming home to me too. I smiled at him. "Why don't you change? I've got everything under control."

That night we didn't argue or discuss the future. We enjoyed simply being together. We ate, washed the dishes, and then sat together on the couch reading. I relished leaning against his hard, loving body while I read. I was warm and at least for the moment, content. It was something I never did with Matt. I set my book down and thought about being Reese's wife.

I couldn't continue working for him. Would I resent giving up my job? I wasn't sure. Without a doubt, I'd be the one quitting, not Reese: he was determined to be a CEO. We'd never discussed Reese wanting children of his own. If we were married, would he want a baby with me? He never actually said he wanted to marry me. If I were free, would he marry me? What would Joe think if I quit and invited him to our wedding? The thought made me laugh.

"What's funny?" Reese asked, setting his book down.

"I was just thinking about what Joe's reaction would have been if I said, 'I'm staying with my lover, Reese'" We both chuckled.

"I'm glad you're a smooth liar, but I wish you didn't have to be."

I had the same wish. I didn't say what was in my heart, not trusting myself and not wanting to make promises I couldn't keep. Instead, I tilted my face up at him. He kissed me slowly and gently and made tender love to me on his purple couch.

We'd gained a new level of intimacy that wouldn't have happened in a hotel room, but the last few days hadn't represented reality either. What kind of life would we really have once children and suburbia were brought into the mix?

Chapter 19

M att picked me up at the airport and kept our date Friday night as planned. We were too tired to go into the city for dinner and ended up at a small family style Italian restaurant not far from our house. The pressure for a "big night" was off, and Matt acted as though nothing was wrong. I thought we were drifting just as we had been. We exchanged pleasantries, but had nothing to say of much importance. Then, Matt announced the real purpose for our night out.

"Susan, I want to talk to you about your job."

My pulse quickened. "What about it?"

"I don't like the way it takes you from us."

Don't panic. He doesn't know. "Matt, you knew there'd be heavy travel. Things will slow down in a couple months."

"It's not the travel. You've been distant. I don't know how else to describe it. I want you to consider quitting."

I knew that voice, quiet but determined. *Consider?* That's not what he meant; he wanted me to quit my job. "What? I can't do that."

"Please keep your voice down."

"Out of the blue, you tell me you want me to quit my job? What do you expect?"

"We should leave."

"I agree."

As soon as we were in the car, I confronted him. "Damn it, Matt, your timing is incredible. Why would you ask me to quit my job in the middle of a restaurant?"

"I thought it would force you stay calm."

I kept control of my voice. "I'll keep quiet until the boys are asleep, but this isn't over."

"No, it's not, but I hope you are capable of a rational discussion."

We rode in silence the rest of the way home. I was capable of a rational discussion. Matt had manipulated my feelings for years. No more. It was time he accepted me as a breathing, feeling woman. If he'd wanted a mousy little wife, then why had he married *me*?

I had a mask of tranquility when we walked in the door. One rule we'd agreed upon years ago was no fighting in front of the boys. An hour later, I tucked them in bed, waited until they were asleep, and then walked into the family room where Matt sat watching television.

"They're asleep," I announced.

Matt hit the remote and the television flicked off. "Are you calm?"

"If you want me to stay calm, then stop goading me."

"Fine … I want you to quit your job."

"Why?"

"I already told you. It's taking you away from the boys and me. You seem to care more about your career than us."

"What do you want? A Stepford wife? All I do outside of work is take care of this family. I cook; I clean; I do laundry; I watch your fucking soccer games every weekend!" I could see Matt shutting down and forced my voice lower. "I don't hang out with friends. I'm not doing any theater work. You and the boys run off every weekend to do your guy thing, while I make sure you come home to a clean house and a decent meal. All I have that's my own is my career and you're asking me to give it up?"

"Yes."

"Well, *fuck you*."

"Nice mouth. I'm glad the boys are asleep."

I cringed. Matt didn't swear. He considered it trashy when I did. Staying rational was the way to persuade him. "My job pays for two-thirds of our family budget."

"I knew you'd throw that in my face."

"I'm only saying it because it's a reality. Our problems have nothing to do with my job." I seethed inside but kept my voice quiet and steady.

"We didn't have problems until you got the promotion."

"That's not true. I've been unhappy for a long time. My job has been my salvation." That *was* the truth. Matt and I didn't talk anymore and had been drifting apart for years. Having a separate life had made our marriage bearable. "Sometimes I feel like there's a weight on my chest, crushing me, and I can't breathe. I'm suffocating. I love you, but I haven't been happy."

"I didn't know." He looked at me as if he didn't know me.

"You haven't known because you haven't wanted to know. I feel like you haven't really loved me for a long time—that you don't even like me." I couldn't stop myself from crying.

"I know I'm not very demonstrative, but it doesn't mean I don't love you. I appreciate everything you do. I don't know how you could think it," he said in a low, hurt voice.

"It's easy. You don't want me to be me."

"Oh, that's ridiculous. Spare me the theatrics."

"You see. I can't even tell you how I feel or you accuse me of being disingenuous. If I express what I want or need, you think I'm self-centered and narcissistic. You don't talk to me. You barely touch me … I feel so alone." I couldn't go on and gasped for air.

"Susan, I …." I wanted him to put his arms around me and say something to make me feel better, but he just stared while I sobbed.

Regaining my composure, I asked, "Aren't you going to say something?"

He looked at me as though concerned for my sanity and said with exaggerated calmness, "I think you're depressed and should see someone professionally."

A scream built deep in my center, ready to erupt, but I clamped it down. "I don't need to see someone. I need you to talk to me. Matt, I need you to love me."

"I don't know how to help you. Your job is stressful. Maybe if you saw a therapist and quit your job, things would be better."

He had already shut down.

"I told you, this has nothing to do with my work." I strove to be as clear and honest as possible. "Nothing can get better unless you give more. I'm so alone … don't ask me to quit."

He physically bristled at my words. "All right, don't quit, but I haven't changed. I'm the same person you married. I don't know where all of this has come from."

His coolness, his lack of emotion, wounded me more than his words. I'd shared my deepest pain, pain that sliced through me like a sharp blade, leaving me bleeding, but he didn't want to help me. He couldn't give me the tiniest bit of love to at least to slow the bleeding.

The truth of my life crashed over me. Matt hadn't changed. He *was* the same person. I thought I'd chosen someone who would love me for the rest of my life. I'd chosen wrong. I was worn out and didn't want to fight any more.

"I'll think about seeing a therapist, but you should think about it, too."

"I'm not the one who has the problem." He reached to grab my hand. "Come on, let's go to bed. You'll feel better after you sleep."

I slapped his hand away. He was emotionally repressed, but I was the one who had the problem? Unbelievable. "I'm sleeping on the couch."

He stared at me. I didn't budge. "Good night." He turned around and left me.

How could he possibly think I was the only one with a problem? My biggest problem was *him*. *He didn't know how to love a woman.* I was depressed. *He made me depressed.*

I poured myself a glass of wine and took a few sips, letting the wine mellow me. I took a few more sips and my pulse evened. I drained the glass, and my rationality returned.

Placing all the blame on Matt had been unfair. He had never been an openly affectionate man. I was the hugger, not him. Even when our relationship had been new, he hadn't been into hanging out and snuggling in bed. He never held me when we slept. Holding hands in public was rare, even when we had been newlyweds.

I don't know when all those things started bothering me. I guess it had crept up on me over the years. The first year of our marriage, we still had been in school. I'd had social interaction independent of Matt. My friends and theater had filled the void.

After we moved to the Bay Area and the boys were born, they took so much of my time that I didn't develop a new set of friends. I had been shocked when Micah started preschool. I'd expected to meet other moms and have this great bonding experience, but I'd been ten years younger than most of them. Matt had been in a silo, consumed with his research. I had tried to mesh with his friends from work and their wives, but I never quite fit in.

My boys had filled the void, but now they were growing up. They didn't want to cuddle the way they used to. They liked doing things with Matt that had nothing to do with me. It was to be expected. They were boys and wanted to do boy things.

Work was a distraction but it didn't give me all I needed, and Matt had never given me all I needed. In the early days of our marriage, I'd been convinced he had a reservoir of passion buried deep inside. If I showered him with affection and kept digging, one day it would blossom and gush at me. But the more I loved him, the more I seemed to push him away. I gave up, accepting we would never take midnight strolls on a beach or make love in the sand. He'd never write love letters or whisper *I love you* just because.

Marriage had been a disappointment from the beginning. Matt had inflicted little injuries without even being aware. Our first apartment had been a little one-bedroom in a sketchy neighborhood on the northern edge of Chicago. It came with one parking space, but we had two cars. Before we married, Matt always saved the spot for me. After we married if Matt came home first, he took the space even if it meant I had to park a block or more away late at night.

He stopped giving me flowers. He stopped picking me up from rehearsal. He stopped going with me to the cast parties. He missed our first anniversary because he wanted to go to a conference. Old hurts piled on my heart. No one thing was a deal breaker, but it added up that once we were married, he stopped giving me much consideration.

Matt wasn't generally unobservant, but he was unobservant about me. He didn't know my dress size, my brand of shampoo, or that I took milk in my coffee. He didn't know my favorite perfume or notice when I cut my hair. Matt spent his life studying minute details. I couldn't understand why he didn't notice details about me. He didn't notice what made me happy or care to go out of his way for me. His attitude and response was no different in bed.

Halfway through our first year in California, I started resenting him and at times, I'd loathed him. I gave up so much and gave him so much, but received so little in return. I'd been willing to give him more if only he'd expressed a little longing for *me*, a little passion for *me*.

Hurt by his indifference, I found myself throwing hissy fits just to see if I could get a reaction. I never got one, but that had been when Matt started accusing me of being a drama queen and dismissed my antics as unworthy of a response. I was narcissistic. I was childish.

At one point, I had decided to leave him. I'd thought we would live in San Francisco proper, but once he'd lured me to California, Matt insisted it was too far of a commute for him. We had ended up in a tiny apartment in Mountain View, closer to San Jose than San Francisco. I had been miserable, and Matt hadn't wanted to hear it. I questioned if I ever really loved him, or if he really ever loved me. We were young and our marriage had been a mistake. We simply weren't compatible. Many of my former classmates had moved to New York. I had wanted to be an actress and New York was where I wanted to be, with or without Matt.

The day I'd planned to tell him I was leaving, I woke up queasy. At first, I thought it was nerves, but my breasts were sore and my period was late. Our sex life had been almost non-existent, but I peed over a stick anyway.

Staring at two increasingly distinct bright pink lines, I went from scared shock to glowing euphoria in a matter of seconds. A baby. My baby. I was already in love. Leaving Matt was out. I wanted my baby to have a father. Matt would be a good father.

Matt was a good father. He had more affection and love for the boys than he'd ever had for me. I wasn't jealous. It made me happy that my boys had a loving father. I wanted it for them more than I wanted love for myself.

Pushing aside my resentment and cutting the drama, I found a way to love Matt for his better qualities and worked on being the wife he wanted.

Now I loved him merely out of habit. This time it wasn't enough. I needed love for myself or I would die. I would suffocate or internally bleed to death. I couldn't go on with this existence. Something had to change. Something already had changed.

Reese loved me. He talked to me and listened. When we were together, he was always touching me. He even slept with his arms around me. He fed my hunger, and my appetite for affection had not been satiated. I wanted more, and he wanted to give more.

I thought I had conquered my daddy issues, that I was strong and independent, but deep down I still needed someone to assure me I was lovable. Reese deserved more than having some sick, needy women begging for his affection every night. I had to figure some things out before seeing him in Atlanta in a few days. He was pressuring, my marriage was crumbling, and I would crash badly if I didn't do something. I needed to regain some control. I couldn't stop seeing him, but I could ask for breathing room.

I considered going to bed, but stayed on the couch.

The next morning I cooked breakfast just as I did every Saturday. We piled into Matt's minivan, joined the sea of minivans, and went to the boys' soccer games as a family. An outsider looking at us would have no idea something was amiss. We looked like a perfectly happy suburban family, the kind of family I'd coveted as a child.

I chatted with the wife of Micah's coach, Tracy Roberts, during Micah's game. She was an executive with Cisco and had two boys, like me. Halloween was only a week away and we compared notes on what our families had planned.

"John loves to dress up. He's like a big kid. This year he's going to be Superman. He wants me to be his Wonder Woman."

"Are you joking?" I laughed.

"Wish I were." Tracy scowled. "I told him there was no way I would wear red leather boots or a skimpy bustier thing in public, and I wasn't going to be seen with him looking ridiculous. I'm staying home and passing out candy," she said jokingly, but underneath there was an edge to her voice.

"So what are you going to wear?'

"Nothing."

"What?"

She laughed. "I mean, I'm not going to wear a costume. I'll leave that to the *kids*."

Was she saying that she thought of her husband as a kid? What was the big deal if the man wanted to dress up on Halloween? Of course, I wasn't Tracy and John wasn't my husband. Who knew what else contributed to her opinion on the matter?

The first line of Anna Karenina haunted me. *Happy families are all alike; every unhappy family is unhappy in its own way.* Was Tracy happy? Did anyone notice how unhappy I was?

Matt and I didn't discuss our argument. We floated through the weekend as if nothing had been said. I slept in our bed Saturday night, but Matt and I did not touch. Sunday night came and went, but we didn't have sex. Reese would be pleased, but I wouldn't tell him. He didn't need to hear the blow-by-blow demise of my marriage. He already put up with enough, and I didn't want to burden him with more.

Tuesday I left for Atlanta. My resolve to slow things down with Reese waned the closer I got to him. All I could think about as I traveled east was being back in his arms. My longing for him throbbed so violently I thought it would burst through my skin.

Chapter 20

Reese was supposed to have arrived in Atlanta ahead of me, but at the last minute, Joe requested he attend a dinner meeting in New York. Consequently, he was delayed until the next day. We had an appointment with Greater South Bank and Trust in the morning and afterwards, more meetings at Global Security's Atlanta facility. It would be a packed, frustrating day of seeing each other without the relief of touching. At least we would get one night together.

After looking forward to being with him the entire flight to Atlanta, I couldn't unwind once at the hotel. I tried to work, but gave up. Reese had said he would call when he got home, but it would be another hour before I'd hear from him. I settled on going to the lounge for a glass of wine to mellow my impatience.

While the bartender poured my drink, I noticed a group of women who appeared to be in their twenties. Surprisingly, Cynthia Warren was with them, all dolled up, laughing and giggling loudly. It had been a long time since I'd had a girl's night, and I envied their camaraderie. I intended to slip out before she saw me, but wasn't quick enough.

She waved. "Hey, there!" I had no choice but to wave back and walk over to say hello. She stood and met me half way. She drawled, "Susan, how nice to see you again."

"You, too. Having a girls' night?"

"Yes, we're old sorority sisters. We get together about once a month. Would you care to join us?" She asked genuinely enough, but I'd be a very intrusive addition to her merry gang.

I smiled. "That's so nice of you to offer, but I've got a pretty full day tomorrow. I just came down to get a glass of wine to take to my room."

"I understand. When does Reese get in?" she asked with a sheepish grin.

How did she know he was coming? And why were her friends at a hotel lounge? There were plenty of bars in Atlanta, but she expected Reese to be here. "He was delayed in New York and won't arrive until tomorrow." I couldn't control my curiosity or the jealousy flaring in my stomach. "How did you know Reese was coming?"

"He told me the last time I talked to him."

"Really? When was that?"

"A couple days ago. We had this amazing connection at the party and then we hooked up when he got back from taking you to the airport. His eyes, well ...." Her dreamy expression finished her sentence. "Anyway, we've stayed in touch."

I knew all about his magnetic eyes, and the thought of him looking at her the way he looked at me was a punch in the gut. It took all my self-control and acting skills to appear pleased for her. "Wow! Good for you."

"We didn't make any plans, but I wanted to surprise him."

I needed to get away from her. I couldn't take hearing any more about her and Reese. It made me sick. It didn't matter that he didn't have a date with her this trip. "I'm sure he'll call you. If you'll excuse me, I really need to get to bed." I smiled sympathetically and started to go, but Cynthia grabbed my arm.

"I'm sorry, but may I ask a favor? Could you, please, not mention this to Reese?"

"My lips are sealed." I squeezed her hand reassuringly. "Good luck."

I couldn't get away from her fast enough. Reese was going to hear about it—damn right, was he going to hear about it. She'd said he hooked up with her; what did that mean? Did he have sex with her? Did he look in her eyes and captivate her just as he had me?

She'd knocked the wind out of me, and I was too pissed off to cry. I wanted to believe in Reese, but I couldn't shut out Cynthia's words. I left him a message, letting him know I was going to bed and not to call. I wanted to see his face when I confronted him.

The next morning I met Reese in the palatial lobby of Greater South Bank and Trust's headquarters. He had a huge smile when he walked in the door. I couldn't return it. I thrust my hand out, shook his hand, and formally said, "Good morning."

He cocked his eyebrows and shrugged it off. We had a meeting in a matter of minutes, and a security guard waiting to escort us up the elevator and to a conference room.

All through the day, I stayed cool and distant. I'm ashamed to say my behavior could be accurately described as passive aggressive. I didn't wait for him to open doors for me, sit next to him, or look at him unless I absolutely couldn't avoid it. I even found an excuse for not riding in a cab with him to the office.

"I left a file in the hotel. I'll meet you at the office." I didn't give him a chance to argue.

Reese sent me a text: *Are you mad at me?*

I texted back: *Yes.*

He responded: *What did I do?*

This was not something to be discussed via text messages, but the idea of making him squirm for the afternoon gave me pleasure.

I texted: *Cynthia Warren and I had a chat. Later.*

When I got to the office, Reese's smile seemed forced, and he sat stiffly in his chair. *Good. I hope he has a miserable afternoon.* I doubt anyone else noticed.

When we wrapped up our last meeting, I was antsy, knowing it wouldn't be long before Reese and I would be alone. I walked out of the conference room with Reese and Bill following behind me and found Cynthia loitering just outside in the hallway.

She was dressed to kill in a sexy blue dress, and beamed at Reese. "Well, hey there, Reese. I forgot you were supposed to be in town!"

I wanted to scream.

"Well, hello Cynthia. Good to see you again." Reese gave her a half hug and she winked to me behind his back. I tried to smile as if applauding her cunning. He backed away from her and stood next to me. "You remember Susan Sinclair."

"Yes, of course, nice to see you again, Susan." She smiled innocently at me.

I met her smile without flinching. "What a pleasant surprise to see you. What brings you to the office?"

"My father is taking me to dinner tonight."

"Reese, why don't you join us?" Bill invited.

"Thank you, but Susan and I have plans to debrief the day's meetings." Reese must have been sweating inside, but he kept his face smooth.

"Susan, I didn't mean to leave you out. Please, join us," Bill suggested politely.

Cynthia's eyes begged me to say no. I couldn't accept without making her suspicious. I faked a yawn and said, "Actually, I'm exhausted. Reese and I can catch up tomorrow. Right, Reese?"

Before he could respond, Bill seized the moment. "Well, now I feel like a third wheel. I'm actually a little tired myself." He sounded rehearsed and turned to Reese and Cynthia. "Why don't you two have dinner without me? You'll probably have more fun."

"Now, Daddy, you know that's not true," she answered as the daddy's little girl she was. "Shall we?" She looped her arm around Reese's elbow and started dragging him out the door.

He gave me a quick meaningful glance and left with the she-devil.

Stay calm ... I have to stay calm. Seeing Cynthia smiling smugly, having "bagged her man" made me want to puke. I didn't know what was going on between Reese and Cynthia, but obviously, something was.

A few minutes after they left Reese texted me: *See you ASAP. Room #?*

I thought about ignoring the text, but we'd had enough drama. I estimated it would be eight or nine o'clock before he would be able to break away so was taken off guard when there was an insistent knock at my door at seven.

I opened the door to Reese looking serious with brows creased. Then he took my face in his hands and tried to kiss me. I pushed him away. He followed me into the room and spun me back around.

"I don't know what you think is going on, but there is absolutely nothing between Cynthia Warren and me."

"Did you sleep with her?"

"God, no! Why would you think that?"

"She said after you dropped me at the airport, you *hooked up* with her. She mentioned your eyes and this 'amazing connection.' She told me you call her. She was waiting for you in the bar last night." My chest heaved and my face burned waiting for his answer.

"She told you that?"

"Yeesss."

He chuckled darkly before mumbling, "That little minx."

"Well? Is it true?"

"Only part of it. I had a drink with her when I got back to the hotel. She cornered me just like she did tonight. It was impossible to get away from her."

"Was that it? One drink?"

"When I went to leave, she grabbed me and kissed me. She practically attacked me. Susan, you have to believe me, I couldn't get away from her fast enough."

"Why do you call her?"

"I don't! She called me a couple times. I've been polite, but haven't encouraged her."

"How did she know you were staying in this hotel?"

"Lucky guess? We stayed here last time we were in Atlanta, or Bill could have asked Anne. I'll check with her." I wanted to believe him, but I'd become an expert liar. Maybe he had too. He pulled out his most persuasive tone, all deep and silky. "You saw how she is. That whole set up was embarrassingly transparent. I have zero interest. She's not my type."

He was convincing, but he was always convincing. "What's your type? A tall blond must be hard to resist."

He shook his head. "Too tall and angular. I'm addicted to this petite brunette with soft curves, much more snuggly—just like sleeping with a Teddy Bear." He looked at me with his big, warm brown eyes and I started to melt. "You believe me?"

"I guess." I let him enfold me in his arms and leaned against him. His crisply starched cotton shirt felt good on my face and the familiar scent of his cologne and skin made me weak. "How did you get out of dinner so fast?"

"We were here at the hotel restaurant. She tried to play footsy with me." He gave an involuntary shudder. "I told her I was seriously involved with someone, and she left as soon as her entrée was cleared." He laughed at the memory.

"That's not very funny. You probably broke her heart." It was easier to be generous towards the poor girl now that I knew Reese didn't have any feelings for her.

"I don't care. She's a lying, manipulative little minx. She deserves what she gets."

I couldn't have agreed more.

He took off his jacket and tie and tossed them over a chair. Then he slipped off his shoes and pulled me onto the bed next to him, wrapping his arms around me. I nestled into him.

"By the way, you owe me an apology," he murmured.

"I'm sorry I accused you of fooling around with Cynthia. I've no right to be jealous."

"I don't mind the jealousy; it's rather gratifying," he said a bit smug. "I'm referring to leaving me at the mercy of the Warrens."

"You should have seen the look Cynthia gave me. I didn't have a choice."

"What a piece of work … let's forget about her. Hey, look at me." He lifted my chin to look into his eyes. "I've missed you," he murmured.

I was lost in his liquid brown eyes. I ached for him and forgot all about my resolve to maintain a distance. Tracing his lips with my finger, I took in the beauty of his face. I wanted to memorize the curve of his lips and the exact shade of his eyelids. I ran my fingertips lightly across his eyelashes. An unconscious tear ran down my cheek.

"What's wrong?"

"My love for you has grown so much it's become almost painful. I want you. I want to feel your arms around me all the time. I don't want to leave you anymore."

He kissed me, and caressed me, and loved me. For the next hour, nothing and no one else existed in the world. He was my universe and I was his. After we were done making love, we clung to each other, our bodies still entangled. I thought of the bed in the hotel room as a little oasis, an island that was deserted, but for us. As long as we didn't leave the bed, we could be together and no one else mattered.

Then the phone rang, popping our bubble world. "Hello?" I answered.

"Hello? Is Reese there?" A female voice asked.

"I'm sorry. You must have the wrong room." The caller hung up and I turned to Reese. "I think that was Cynthia. She asked for you. Think she followed you?"

"There's no way, but I still don't like it. Why would she call your room?"

"Maybe she suspects 'the someone' you're involved with is me?"

"Doubt it. She probably called my room, and I wasn't there. She can't possibly know."

I had a sick feeling in my stomach. Hearing *thunk, thunk, thunk,* I jumped. Reese put his hand over my mouth, muffling my scream, but someone was knocking on the door. He whispered, "Don't panic. See who it is."

My heart raced as I made my way to the door. After sliding the security lock bar in place, I cracked open the door a sliver; then, asked as calmly as possible, "Who is it?"

"Hey, babe, it's me. I got the ice," a deep male voice answered.

"You have the wrong room."

"Oh, shit. Sorry."

I let out a nervous giggle and went back to the bed. Reese grinned at me, equally relieved. "Who was that? Your boyfriend?"

"Funny. Holy crap, that scared me. Reese, we shouldn't be staying in the same hotel."

"Come on, we've been through this. There's nothing suspect. No one knows about us—please, don't worry. You all right?"

"Other than having a minor heart attack? Yeah, I'm fine. I'm sure you're right."

"Good." He lifted my face towards his, looked me in the eyes, and softly asked, "What did you mean earlier when you said you don't want to leave me anymore?"

"Please, don't think I'm psycho, but it feels like there's a huge magnet in my chest. It throbs and pulls me towards you. When I'm with you, the throbbing stops and it's peaceful. It keeps getting stronger. It's harder to pull away each time I'm with you."

Reese didn't say anything.

"Think I'm crazy?"

"No, I feel it, too. Exactly the same." He took my face in his hands and gazed into my eyes. "I'm not crazy and neither are you." He pulled me closer to his chest, and I savored the strength of his arms around me, his warm skin against me. He whispered, "Stay with me."

"I can't. I have to go back. I don't know how to leave Matt or how to make things bearable for my boys. I need time to figure things out—"

"But you're willing to leave him?"

"I think I have to," I whispered. Saying it out loud made it real, and I started to shake.

Somehow, Reese managed to hold me closer. "I know it'll be hard, but we belong together. I'll make you happy."

"I can't just rip my family apart. You've got to give me time."

"Anything I can do to make things easier, I'll do—just let me know."

"I have to do this on my own. I have to finish things with Matt before you and I can even consider having an open relationship. And I—"

"Hey, it's okay. All I want is a promise that someday you'll be my wife to have and to hold and to organize my spices till death do we part."

I smiled against his chest, a bit embarrassed. "You noticed?"

"Yesterday. It made me laugh."

I pulled away as guilt erupted inside me. Things were moving too fast, like free falling without a parachute. "I can't talk about marriage yet. We only met five months ago and to be discussing me leaving Matt, getting married … it's too much—"

He stopped me. "I know it's been fast and intense. Nothing needs to happen tomorrow." He looked deeply into my eyes. "Say *yes* and we can go slowly from here."

"Yes," I whispered. "I love you so much, but I'm a mess and feel broken. I have to get myself together … and my boys—"

"You're not broken. If we're going to have a life together, you have to trust me and let me help you."

I wanted to come to Reese whole and clean, to make peace with myself, and come to terms with some of my own issues before I married again. I didn't want to make the same mistakes I'd made with Matt. All the love in world wasn't enough to make a marriage last. I could have stayed in love with Matt. If I had, I might never have been receptive to Reese. I needed time.

"I don't want to do anything or say anything to Matt until after the holidays; the boys deserve at least one more Christmas as a family." Thinking of their little faces and not spending holidays together, I choked on my tears. "I can't lose my children."

Reese held me, and softly murmured in my ear, "I won't let that happen."

He convinced me I should let him research divorce lawyers and make some discreet inquiries about California divorce laws and child custody. Painful as it was to discuss, he wanted to protect me as best he could under the circumstances. Researching an attorney was the only thing about which I was ready to agree.

The commitment we made to each other unleashed all of our passion. We clung to each other, not wanting to let go. I wanted to memorize every aspect of him: the particular scent of his cologne mingled with his sweat after the exertion of lovemaking, the taste and feel of him in my mouth, the line of his jaw when I looked up at him, the way he chuckled softly when he was amused, and mostly the way his eyes softened whenever he looked at me.

Neither of us felt shame when our eyes moistened at our parting. It would be two weeks before we would see each other again. The consolation was I would be back in New York and staying with Reese at his apartment.

Chapter 21

Reese monopolized my thoughts for the first few hours of the flight home from Atlanta. For the first time in my life, I had experienced love in an all-consuming, devastating way. Every cell in my body tingled in anticipation of his touch. I was attuned to the rhythm of his breathing and smell of his skin. Over and over his words, his taste, his scent, and the feel of his body against me replayed in my mind. I thought through various passages I had read describing great love, and the words of poets didn't seem extravagant any more.

My mind focused more on how to leave Matt the closer I got to home. No longer concerned with strengthening the thread keeping us together, guilt gave way to fear. I had to find a way out with the least amount of damage. My thoughts drifted to how Reese had sold Joe Benedetti on our new sales model. Reese had been so smooth that Joe was convinced all of the ideas were his own. Maybe I could find a way to make Matt think divorce was his idea.

Then another scenario occurred to me. I could see it all in my mind. *I would be in my home office and would receive a phone call from the police. "I'm sorry," a voice would say. "There's been an accident." Rushing to the emergency room, tears streaming, I would be too late. Matt would already be gone.*

Shame flooded me. I would never, *ever* allow myself consider such a thing again.

The very thought of Matt being dead sparked tenderness for him that almost had been extinguished. Despite everything, a part of my heart still belonged to him and always would. Love was still there, and I didn't want him hurt. Crazy as it sounds, the more fiercely I loved Reese the more desperate I was for Matt to love me. The reality of life without my family made me sick to my stomach and scared the hell out of me. A double bout of guilt hit me: guilt for wanting to leave my husband and guilt for not wanting my marriage to end.

Reese called after my plane landed.

"Miss you already," he said.

"Miss you, too." I meant it. My chest throbbed.

With a heavily divided heart, I hung up the phone. I was such a mess.

That night the boys were wound up. Halloween was just a few nights away, and they were bouncing with excitement.

"Are you going to finish my costume?" Jason asked with big, anxious eyes.

He wanted to be Harry Potter for Halloween, so I was making him a wizard's robe. "I promise I'll have it done even if I have to stay up all night." No way, would I let my little guy down. Micah was way past having me make him something. He wanted to go to the Halloween store and buy a Grim Reaper costume. Such a boy.

Both boys volunteered me to make a Halloween treat for their classroom parties. *Great. I have a first draft of a major proposal due on October 31. I need to finish Jason's costume, and now I'm baking treats for two classes.*

Matt read my mind. "You don't have to bake. Just buy something."

"Matt, I can't do that. The boys are counting on me to make something. Store bought is cheating."

"Yeah, Dad," Micah chimed in, "I want Mom to make sugar cookies."

"Mom, can we make popcorn balls for my class?" Jason asked.

"Sure. We'll make them ghost balls. How does that sound?"

Jason smiled, but Micah said, "That's just weird, Mom."

"You didn't think it was so weird when I did it for your class last year," I reminded him and winked at Jason. Jason giggled, Micah groaned, Matt smiled, and my heart swelled.

"Okay, tomorrow night Mom doesn't cook, and we'll help her. Right, guys?"

Matt considered my dedication to homemade costumes and treats as silly. He thought I didn't have time for these things, but it was important to me. I didn't want my boys to think I was too busy for them. It gave me a chance to do something special between us. I appreciated Matt volunteering to help and wondered what Halloween would be like next year. It was too much to think about. I put it out of my mind for the time being.

I stayed up sewing for a while before turning off the lights and meeting Matt in our bedroom. He was already in his pajamas, reading a *Great Outdoors* magazine in bed. He didn't look up when I entered the room. Nor did he look at me when I undressed and put on a nightgown. I crawled into bed and wanted to touch him, but I didn't know if he wanted to be touched. He didn't so much as kiss my cheek or squeeze my hand all night. I wondered if Reese's scent was on me and on some primordial level, it repelled Matt.

I studied his face as he read. He had a few wrinkles, but I still recognized the face I had fallen in love with all those years ago. He had been so grateful when I returned his love. How had gratitude grown to indifference? The crushing feeling on my chest returned. I rolled over with my back facing him. I didn't want him to know I was crying.

"Susan?" he whispered.

"Yes."

"Nothing … never mind."

I've missed you, too.

I could hear Matt put down his magazine and turn off the light. I hoped he would reach out to me, but he didn't. We went to sleep, still not touching.

The next day Reese called during our allotted time.

"How are you?" he asked, knowing the commitment I'd made to him would be emotionally taxing once I got home.

Shamelessly looking for sympathy, I said, "Other than missing you, I'm fine. I spent last night working on Jason's Halloween costume. I'll have to stay up late to finish it, and I have to bake cookies and make two dozen popcorn balls by tomorrow morning."

"And you need to finish the first draft of the Northern proposal."

Not what I wanted to hear. "Hey, I thought I was talking to my lover, not my boss."

"Dear heart, so sorry, but I'm the same person. Your lover sympathizes, but your boss can't let you blow it off."

"It'll all get done."

"Why don't you just buy something?" he asked.

"Ugh, I'm going to hang up. I don't want to have this conversation."

"Come on, don't hang up. I'm sorry. I know you just want to be a good mom. My mother used to do those things for me when I was growing up, and I loved her for it."

"I hope my boys love me for it. I hope they don't end up hating me."

"They are not going to hate you."

"You can't know that. Honestly, it scares the hell out of me."

"You love them so much there's no way they can hate you. Hey, I want to ask you something, and please, don't take this the wrong way." His voice was soft and intimate, the way it was when we rested on the same pillow. "Why don't you get a housekeeper? If it's the money, I'll—"

"It's not the money. I can afford help."

"Then, why do you do this to yourself?"

It was a good question. I had asked myself the same thing at least a hundred times, but I never wanted to admit the truth. Reese probably knew the answer before he asked. "Because if I didn't …" I choked back a sob. "If I didn't do these things, I don't know if they would need me." I wiped my cheek with the back of my hand.

"Sweetheart, your boys need you. You're their mother. No one cleaning a few toilets can replace you in their lives, but tell you what, I'll finish your proposal tonight, and then you can take tomorrow afternoon off."

"I can't let you do that."

"Why not?"

"Because we agreed we wouldn't let our relationship influence our work."

"You're not getting off so easy," he teased, "quid pro quo, just wait baby."

"Yes, sir." I laughed. "By the way, you're the best boss ever."

"No, your boss wouldn't do your work, but as your lover, I hope to be winning points."

Even though wrong and shameful to admit, that evening I derived a certain amount of guilty pleasure knowing I had two men running around helping me. Reese toiled in his office writing my proposal, while Matt washed dishes and cleaned up the cookie and popcorn ball mess in the kitchen. Thanks to their help, I finished Jason's costume and made it to bed by midnight. I couldn't help thinking this was an unexpected perk of being an adulteress.

My gratitude prompted me to reach out to Matt. "Thank you for your help tonight. I really appreciate you being supportive."

"You're welcome. I know it's important to the boys."

Is that why he did it? I should have known. *Matt cares about the boys, not me.*

The weight wasn't on my chest, but I felt something else, anger. I'd spent years trying to be a good wife and mother. Until my recent indiscretion, of which Matt was ignorant, I don't know what I did that made him care so little about me. I rolled over with my back facing him and another day ended with no physical contact. He hadn't so much as given me a hug or brushed his lips across my cheek in over a week. *Was I repulsive to him?*

Despite everything, I still wanted Matt to love me. When home, and away from Reese, I couldn't help thinking if Matt would only give me a little love, I wouldn't leave him. I just wanted a few hugs, a kiss goodnight, a little snuggling on the couch, a little conversation. I could live without mind-blowing sex. But what chance did we have if Matt wouldn't even touch me? He barely looked at me.

I picked up the boys after school the next day. Matt and I took them out for burgers and then trick-or-treating. When we got home, the boys counted their candy and swapped each other for their favorites. I read a chapter of *Harry Potter* to Jason, and finally got the boys to bed. I thought Matt and I would try to talk, but he slept on the couch.

As each day passed my love for Matt gasped for air. It was painful, as if a knife were stuck in my chest. Every day it inched out, but it sliced me along the way. There were times I just wanted to leave it, afraid of the hole it would create once out.

One week rolled to nine days and no touching. Day ten was a Sunday. Matt and I were exceedingly civil to each other. Everything was "please and thank you." There were no angry outbursts or accusatory looks. Verbal jabs were non-existent, but tension crackled the air. We each kept the appearance of normalcy, waiting for the other to crack

Sunday morning, we went to church as a family. I tried to focus, but couldn't absorb the sermon. Matt sat far enough from me in the pew to ensure he wouldn't bump my knee or brush my arm when he reached for the hymnal. At one point, I slid a little closer just to see what he would do. He silently inched away. Because we were in public, I held back my tears.

He kept a safe distance all day. The longer the day wore on, the more on edge I became. I could understand a day or two, but ten days? No. I couldn't take it any longer. I waited for the boys to go to bed. After they were out for the night, I went to the bedroom to confront Matt. He was already asleep, but it didn't stop me.

"Matt, Matt, wake up. I need to talk to you," I said, shaking him awake.

"What is it? Is something wrong with the boys?"

"No, we to need talk. I can't take it anymore. We can't keep going like this."

"Come on, I was asleep. What are you talking about?" he asked sitting up.

"I'm talking about the fact that you haven't touched me in days." His face grew pale, making me furious. He completely was aware, and yet acted as if it were nothing the whole time. "Why are you doing this to me? Is this supposed to be some sort of punishment?"

"No. I didn't think you wanted me to."

Passive aggressive bullshit. I struggled not to scream. "We had a huge fight, and I told you I needed you to love me more. You walked out of the room and have avoided physical contact with me for the last ten days and somehow it's my fault? This is bullshit!"

"Susan, keep your voice down. You'll wake the boys."

"Fine," I hissed. "What have you got to say?"

"I told you already."

"You must really hate me." I started to cry. How could he have been so consciously cruel? "If you loved me at all, you wouldn't be treating me this way."

"Please don't start with the melodrama."

"I can't live like this, Matt. I can't. I don't know what we're doing. I don't believe you love me anymore."

"What do you want from me? We're not newlyweds. I don't know what you expect."

"I expect more than this!"

"You want to be loved?" Matt grabbed me and tried to kiss me. I pushed him away repulsed. He jeered, "I thought that's what you wanted."

"It's not sex that I want. Is that all you want from me? Sex every Sunday night?"

"Of course not. I want to go back to the way we were before you took that promotion. You were home more and less edgy. We were happy."

"Matt, *you* were happy. I wasn't. I can't go back and pretend nothing's wrong. I told you before, things needed to change. It's as if you're punishing me for wanting you to love me. Admit it. You don't love me anymore." I was crying, but not hysterical.

Matt's face drained of color. He said barely audible, "I used to love you. I don't know when I stopped."

The knife ripped out of my chest, leaving a gaping hole. I curled up on the bed in too much pain to move or speak.

I heard Matt walk out and close the door. I'd half-expected him to deny it, but he didn't. He didn't love me. How was it possible? After all the years and life we built together, he'd stopped loving me somewhere along the line. Subconsciously, I had known. Why else had I been open to loving someone else? Matt didn't love me anymore. He didn't even like me. I'd felt it for months, but hearing him say it ripped my heart. I couldn't breathe or stop crying.

Matt walked silently back into the room, tears spilling over his eyes, too. It had been a long time since I'd seen him cry. He looked like a frightened, lost child. "I'm sorry." He grabbed me like a drowning man holding onto a life preserver. I didn't want him touching me, but I couldn't let go of him either. We held each other and cried, both of us grieving. We made love, but I don't know if it was out of desperation to hold onto what little bit of affection we had left or as a way of saying, *it's over.* Ironically, it was the best sex we've had in years. At least there was emotion. Afterwards we lay in bed and held each other for comfort, not out of love.

"Matt, what do you want to do?"

"I don't know …. You don't want me to leave, do you?"

"No. I think we can stay together while we figure things out."

"I don't hate you."

"I know. I don't hate you either."

That's where things ended for the night. No more love, but at least there was no hate. At least there was finally some honesty. I actually slept well.

Chapter 22

The next morning Matt and I continued with our normal morning routine: up at 5:00, morning workout, and home office at 6:00, Matt and the boys out the door at 8:00. Life went on. It seemed so bizarre to have such a momentous shift between us, but externally, nothing changed. If the boys were aware, they didn't say anything. Matt and I were conditioned to maintain appearances, but I didn't know how long he would want to keep up the façade.

I should have been happy, relieved Matt had confessed his true feelings; he might even suggest divorce first. I couldn't imagine he would want to stay in a loveless marriage. I wasn't happy or relieved. I was alternately stunned and horribly sad. If I could just have a good long week of crying, it would make it easier to move on.

I was dying to talk to Reese, but he had back-to-back meetings scheduled the entire day. It was more difficult than ever to hear his voice on a conference call, but not be able to talk to him. He broke free late afternoon and finally called.

"How's my love?" he asked.

"Desperate for you." I didn't want to launch right into my marital woes. I wanted to hear how much he loved me and missed me first.

"I miss you, too. I thought about you all weekend. I'm a man with *real physical needs*," he joked and then asked, "You're going to Chicago later this week, right?"

"Yep, arrive Wednesday evening and fly home Friday night."

"Could you stay an extra night?"

"Why? What's going on?"

"I can sneak out early Friday and meet you," he proposed.

I warmed at the suggestion, but Micah needed help with a school project and the boys had their last regular season soccer games on Saturday. "You know how much I love you—"

I heard a light tapping on my door and froze. It had to be Matt. How long had he been there? Had he been listening?

"Susan? You okay?" Reese asked with justifiable concern.

"I have to go." I hung up without ceremony and opened the door.

Matt wore the same pained expression as he had when he confessed that he didn't love me. My heart pounded. Even though our marriage was careening to an end, I didn't want him to know about Reese. Someday he would know, but not now, not this way.

"What are you doing home?"

"Susan …" He was too emotional to talk.

Oh, god, he'd heard me.

Matt wrapped his arms around me, pressing against me, holding me with a mixture of desperation and desire. He whispered, "I don't want our marriage to be over."

I owed him some honesty after he'd been honest with me. "It may be too late."

He pulled back far enough to take my face in his hands. He looked me in the eyes for the first time in years. I could see longing and sadness.

"I've been angry and confused, but I don't want to lose you," he said.

"Matt—"

He kissed me, kissed me passionately. I kissed him back. A separate part of me felt like I was betraying Reese. I'd committed to leaving Matt. This wasn't helping. Since Reese and I had become lovers, other than the prior night, I'd only had sex with Matt once, and it had been mechanical, muscle memory reflex.

Matt kissed me hungrily and my body responded. He lifted me off the ground, and I wrapped my legs around his waist. He walked us to our bedroom and lowered us to the bed. His body moved urgently against me, and we started undressing each other.

In the distance, my office phone rang, and then my cell phone, and then my office phone rang again and then my cell phone went off one last time. I was certain it was Reese. I kept kissing Matt. He was on fire, and he set me on fire. I didn't know he had it in him.

Afterwards Matt looked at me quite pleased and asked, "Feel more loved?"

I smiled at him and kissed him. I didn't want to hurt him, but I had to set the right expectations. My body had had a physical reaction to Matt's touch, but I had been keenly aware of an emotional disconnect. "One afternoon of great sex isn't going to save our marriage."

"At least it's a start."

Yes, it was a start. Matt and I got dressed. He left to pick up the boys, and I went back to my office to check my messages. All four calls were from Reese. I had to call him. He answered on the first ring.

"Susan, are you alright? What happened?"

"Matt came home early. I didn't hear him until he knocked on my door."

"What else happened?"

"Nothing."

"Damn it, don't lie to me. Why didn't you answer your phones?"

Why could he hear the lie in my voice when no one else could? I dodged him with a half-truth. "He just wanted to talk to me when the boys weren't home. That's it. Please, don't ask me to replay the demise of my marriage."

"I don't expect you to, but why do I have this sick feeling you were making love to him?"

He couldn't possibly know. "Why would you think that?"

"It's your voice; it always gets low and throaty afterwards."

I loved and hated that he knew me so well. I also hated when he got this way. I had never promised him I wouldn't sleep with Matt, but I understood the jealousy. I couldn't tell him he was right. I was actually sick with guilt for making love to my husband. My world had become unbelievably twisted.

"We argued. Maybe that's why I sound different. Why do you torture yourself?"

He sighed. "I don't know. I'm going a little crazy without you."

"I feel the same."

"Which reminds me, can you stay an extra night in Chicago?"

"I really can't—"

"Wait a second, you were about to say yes before Matt came home," he accused.

"Honestly, I wasn't. I need to be home."

"You haven't changed your mind about anything, have you?" he asked.

Hearing the anxiety in his voice, made my heart ache. "No, I'm sorry, but weekends have to be for my boys. It's my chance to spend time with them, and I have to get them ready for the week—laundry, grocery shopping—and Micah has his California Mission project due. I promised to help him."

"What's that?"

"He has to build a model sized replicate of a California Mission. He's counting on my mad craft skills. Besides, the boys have soccer games. It's their last matches before playoffs. Even if a client wanted to meet with me, I'd beg out."

"I'm sorry. I shouldn't have asked. Of course you should be there for them."

I had to work after dinner to make up for all the time I had spent with my men earlier in the afternoon. I fell exhausted into bed and habitually rolled on my side with my back facing Matt. I thought he was asleep, but he scooted next to me as soon as my head hit the pillow. He ran his hand up the side of my thigh and over my hip, pausing on my waist before cupping my breast. I didn't know where this was coming from, but decided to see where it was going.

We had sex the next night, too. It was as if we were trying to fuck the love back into our marriage. We even had a half way decent conversation about it.

I asked gently, wanting to be realistic, not discouraging, "You know just because we're having sex like newlyweds doesn't mean we're okay, right?"

"I know, but I do feel closer to you. Don't you feel closer to me?"

"Yes, but it's not just because of the sex. I'm grateful you're making an effort. It's been a long time. Why is that?"

"I didn't think you needed me. You work all the time and do your own thing. Sometimes I think you only tolerate me because of the boys."

"That's rather ironic. I thought you only cared about the boys. Sometimes I think you only keep me around for my paycheck and mad cleaning skills."

He didn't crack a smile at my attempt at a joke. He said, "I didn't know."

"That's because we don't talk."

"Hmmm," Matt mused.

How had we become so disconnected? I thought about Matt not feeling needed. I did need him, but in a different way than when we were first together. When we were dating and then engaged, Matt escorted me home every night. If I had a rehearsal that ended at nine o'clock, Matt would be waiting for me. If I was in a show and got out of the theater at eleven at night, Matt would be waiting for me. It didn't matter what time I finished; it didn't matter if Matt had to study or was working in the lab, Matt was always there waiting for me. He would give me a quick squeeze, put his arm possessively around me, as if declaring to the other actors I belonged to him, and usher me out the door. I used to call him my guardian. He would give me an embarrassed smile, but the title pleased him.

Our relationship had always been sedate—almost somber. Most nights we would go to his apartment. I'd fix us a little snack, and we would catch up for the day. He usually had more studying to do. While he worked, I'd tidy up his apartment and make his bed. I even did his laundry. I liked it. I liked folding his underwear and knowing what went in which drawer. In some ways, it had felt more intimate than having sex.

I had never experienced being that close to anyone before Matt. Whenever he finished studying for the night, we would make love. We made love almost every night, and then we'd curl up in his twin sized bed. Not having a choice, he had to sleep close to me then.

When we married, we bought a double bed. When Micah was born, we bought a queen. Now we had a king. "Maybe we should get a twin bed again."

He quietly laughed and put his arm around me. "It was a little crowded."

We were silent for the rest of the night. What neither of us cared to discuss was whether or not it was too late to save our marriage. There was no certainty from either one of us.

Chapter 23

B ack in the air Wednesday afternoon, I looked forward to being alone in Chicago. I needed time away from both Matt and Reese. I really wanted to stay an extra night just to think and clear my head, but I couldn't. Both men would have their own interpretations of why I stayed, and I had too many mom duties.

Matt's sudden desire to kick life back into our marriage changed the game. A week ago, I had been serious about leaving him. Undeniably, I was deeply in love with Reese. I could talk to him about anything and every-thing, and my desire for him almost scared me. If I were unattached, there would be no questions and no struggle. I would marry him in a heartbeat.

However, I was very much attached. Morally, what I was doing with Reese was wrong. There was no equivocation on that point. I had an obli-gation to my sons to stay with their father if there was even a sliver of a chance we could have a happy marriage again. I had to stay even if it meant breaking with Reese, even if it meant breaking both of our hearts.

I started thinking about the whole concept of being happy. I had been unfair to poor Reverend Jim when I'd accused him of being a simpleton about happiness. I had been the simpleton. Happiness was in my control. I remembered an article I'd read about the correlation between happiness and longevity. The gist of it was happy people live longer, and the commonality of all happy people was they had four or more close friendships. I didn't.

Matt hadn't cared for my theater friends. He never told me outright, but he'd be cool and distant whenever I returned from a cast party or made other plans with them. Instead of talking to him about it, I simply dropped them to please Matt. Part of "fixing me" required making friends. If Matt and I were going to make it, I had to have other companions.

Serena Jordan had been my roommate before I married. We had been good friends, but fell out of touch the last few years. The last time I spoke to her, she was making a living as an actress in Chicago. Thursday morning, I called the only number I had for her and got lucky. She was still in Chicago and her number hadn't changed.

"Oh my god, Susan, I'm so glad you called. How long are you in town?"

"I'm flying out after my meeting tomorrow. Any chance you're free tonight?"

"I'm in a show, but I can get you a comp and then we could go out for drinks."

"Love it. What are you in?"

"I'm playing Kate in *Shrew* at Shakespeare Rep."

"That's fantastic!" I was a little envious. I'd always wanted to play Kate.

"And you'll never guess who's playing Petruchio."

"Who?"

"Your old flame, Trent." I was even more envious. I'd always wanted to play Kate to Trent's Petruchio. "He's still single. I'm sure he'll want to join us for drinks."

"I bet he would." I laughed thinking about him.

When I hung up, we were both giggling. I really had missed her. She and I'd had some good times. She'd been my drinking buddy, and scoping-out-guys buddy—the kind of friend who held your hair back if you drank too much and found yourself bowing to the porcelain god.

I called Reese to check in after I'd finished my meetings for the day. As soon as we zipped through the business we had to discuss, Reese dropped his crisp business manner. He was home and safe to talk.

"Where are you staying?" he asked with his voice low and intimate.

"Whitehall again." I sighed at the memory of him holding me against the door and shaking with desire. He must have had similar thoughts.

"Nice … what are you wearing?"

"Why?"

"Quid pro quo. Time to pay up, baby," he said playfully.

I giggled. "Never in my life have I had phone sex."

"Really? Never? A little hussy like you?"

"Never. I'm a nice girl, remember?"

Reese turned on his seductive tone. "You are a nice girl, but even nice girls can be naughty. I could give you a lesson. Would you like that?"

I snickered. "I'll take a rain check. I've got to get ready to go."

"Oh, where are you going?" he asked with surprise.

"My ex-roommate is playing Kate in *Taming of the Shrew*. I'm going to the show and then we're going out for drinks."

"Sounds like fun."

"Should be and oh, do you remember me telling you about Trent?"

"The actor who was your boyfriend before Matt?"

"Yep. He's playing Petruchio."

"You sound pretty excited about this."

"I'm positively *atingle*. I haven't been out with theater people in ages. I might even have a shot of tequila!"

"Should I be jealous?" he asked jokingly, but he had an edge to his voice. I immediately regretted mentioning Trent.

"Reese, don't be ludicrous. If there were a reason to be jealous, I wouldn't have told you what I'm doing. Hey, I *love you*," I reminded him.

"Will you call me when you get in? I just want to make sure you're safe."

"If it'll make you feel better, but it'll be late, especially with the time difference."

It was so funny Reese wanted me to call him. What was that about? I decided not to worry about it. He probably sincerely wanted to make sure I was safe. He loved me after all.

The staging was a "concept" production set in modern day. Kate wore business suits, and Petruchio dressed like an auto mechanic. Not the way I'd stage it. I found the contemporary setting more distracting than enlightening. Of course, I shared none of this with Serena when I met her in the lobby after the show.

"Serena, you were great! I loved the show!"

"Cut the crap, Susan. The production isn't that good." she said with a laugh.

"Okay, but you were still great."

"Thanks. I'll take the compliment."

She suggested a bar on State Street, which was only a few blocks from both the theater and my hotel. As we walked, Serena caught me up on the ups and downs of her career and her love affairs. I laughed at her antics, but wasn't envious. She seemed to have developed a habit of changing lovers with each theater season.

When I told her what I did for a living, she said, "Wow, I can't believe how corporate you've become. I'd never have guessed. You were so dedicated to theater and acting."

"I know. Funny how life twists and turns, but I really love my job."

"I wish I loved a job that paid more money. You look fabulous by the way."

"Thanks."

"How's Matt?"

"He's fine, still the same, quiet Matt."

"I have to admit, I never thought you'd still be married."

"Really? Why's that?"

"Don't get me wrong, I know he's a sweetheart, but you always seemed like an odd couple. I always thought you would end up living in New York with some model handsome guy. Matt never seemed your type. You know, you changed after you got engaged. You became much more serious."

"I guess I did. My tequila days were over," I joked trying to get off the subject of my marriage before I admitted I'd met the model handsome guy living in New York.

"That's not such a bad thing, but I missed the good times we had. Remember that night at the Blue Lantern when we danced on the tables?"

We both busted up laughing. Serena and I had done an Isadora Duncan interpretative dance for the amusement of our friends. It'd been one of my wilder nights, which ended with Trent catching me as I tumbled off of the table. He had been my hero, and later that night Serena had faithfully held my hair while I'd lost the contents of my stomach.

Not long after we arrived at the small bar, the ten or so tables filled with other cast members and their friends. My head popped up when Trent walked in the door. I have to say, he looked good. He was buff, had a full head of hair, and he was grinning at me.

"Hey, Suzie-Q! You look just the same! How are you?" he called out in a booming stage voice as he crossed the room and swept me up in a bear hug. Some old feelings stirred inside me when he hugged me. I had forgotten how much I'd grown to dislike Trent's gregarious ways, but I smiled and actually was happy to see him, too.

"I'm good. You were great in the show tonight."

"Thanks. Hey, do you remember when we did the Kate/Petruchio fight scene in class?"

"Of course, I got to hit you."

"You connected for real a few times. For being so little you had a big punch." He grinned ear-to-ear and laughed. "Acting with you was fun. You were a good actress."

I laughed, too. We'd had an extremely physical and tempestuous relationship. Serena had observed on numerous occasions that all Trent and I did was "fight and fuck." Sometimes I think we fought knowing the make-up sex would follow. When we'd acted the scene in class, I'd been mad at him for flirting with another actress. I had really enjoyed socking him.

"Thanks, but it was a long time ago."

"Wasn't that long ago. How about a round of tequila shots for old time sake?" Trent grinned mischievously.

"Oooohhhh, no! I'm sure you remember how I get when I drink tequila."

"I do, which is why you need a shot," Trent pressed. "Take off that little banker's jacket and relax. You're with old friends."

Trent wasn't to be trusted, and I looked to Serena for help. She was no help. "Come on," she said. "You don't need to worry about being a good girl. We won't tell Matt."

"What the hell," I said feeling liberated.

After my second shot, my distrust of Trent numbed and I loved everyone. Trent always had a certain charm that was hard to resist. We laughed and laughed until tears rolled down my cheeks. Against my better judgment, I had a third shot and then one more.

It was no big deal for Trent and Serena. They didn't have a commitment until the next evening's performance, but I had a meeting with bankers. Sometime after midnight, I declined another round and called it a night. Trent insisted on escorting me safely to my hotel; he wasn't such a bad guy. It had been a long time since I drank so much, and it hit me rather hard.

When we arrived at the hotel, I said as soberly as possible, "Well, thanks for everything. It was good seeing you." My head spun, and I needed a bed.

"Good seeing you, too. You look even better than you did in college." He gave me a lopsided grin that used to make my knees weak. "I've thought about you off and on over the years. We had some good times, didn't we?"

I had to smile. We did have fun until I figured out he had fun with a lot of women. "Definitely, we had our moments."

"We had chemistry," he corrected, reaching for me.

I put my hands up, and they hit against his hard chest. "What are you doing?"

"I plan to kiss you, and then who knows ...," he said.

"I'm married, remember?"

"Doesn't bother me and no one else has to know." I pushed away from him. "Shit Suzie, you've been flirting with me all night."

"Goodnight, Trent."

I stumbled into the lobby and up to my room. What an egotistical jerk. Once a dog, always a dog. I so got the better man when I'd married Matt. Had I been flirting with him? I was drunk. Maybe I had flirted. The whole episode made me laugh. It had been a fun night. I tossed down a couple Tylenols, changed into my pajamas, and dropped into bed.

The hotel phone rang just as I was about to nod off. *Oh, crap. I was supposed to call Reese.* I grabbed the receiver.

"Susan? Where've you been? You didn't answer your Blackberry or your cell phone."

"Sorry. I must've not turned on the ringy thing after the show. How's my lover?"

"You sound drunk."

"Nope. I'm *inebriated*." I giggled at my joke. He didn't.

"How much did you drink?"

"Oh just one beer and four—no I think it was five—shots of tequila." I giggled again. "I had a good time."

"I bet. Did you howl at the moon?"

"Would've, but I was afraid of getting arrested."

"Was Trent there?"

"Uh-huh and he tried to seduce me. Can you believe it?"

"Huh," he grunted. "Were you flirting with him?"

"Uh, no, I don't think so."

"Are you alone?"

"Of course, silly man. Wanna know what I'm wearing?"

"You have a meeting tomorrow. I hope you're sober by then. Get some sleep."

He hung up without telling me he loved me. *Uh, oh. He's mad.*

When the alarm went off at six, my head still buzzed and my stomach wasn't happy. I would've killed for some chorizo and eggs. I called room service and settled for fried eggs and a diet coke. It wasn't perfect hangover food, but it would do. I went back to sleep while I waited.

The food arrived and I still wasn't ready to get up. Thank god, my meeting wasn't until eleven. I justified staying in bed until eight because it was actually only six in California. After I ate and showered, my head cleared. I'd be fine for the meeting.

Reese texted me: *Call me after your meeting.*

No please. He was mad. Didn't he trust me? Why was he checking up on me? Matt knew I was going out with Serena, and he didn't insist I call when I got in. Of course, I hadn't told Matt that I'd be seeing Trent. Matt definitely would have been less than pleased.

I delayed calling Reese until I'd checked in at the airport and found an empty gate. I wanted to make sure we could talk. He probably was still pissed, but so was I.

"How did the meeting go?" he asked stiffly.

"Other than having to hurl, it went fine. Thank God, everyone thought I'd eaten bad sushi. They were very sympathetic."

"Shit, please, tell me you're joking."

"*Joking.* I was not reeking of tequila, okay?"

"Funny girl," he said without a hint of humor.

"So, you're still mad at me?"

"Yes and disappointed. I can't believe you were out drinking knowing you had an important meeting this morning."

"Reese, come on. If you were only my boss, you wouldn't have known. You're the one who called me at twelve-thirty in the morning."

"I was worried; you didn't answer your phone."

"I just wanted one night to cut lose and have a little fun. Do you have any idea how long it's been since I've had a real night out with friends? Why are you making a big deal about it?"

"What the fuck? How did I become the bad guy? You're the one who got drunk and was out flirting with your ex-drama-and-passion-boyfriend!"

I hated when he raised his voice at me. "Exactly what I thought. You don't trust me."

"Not true."

"You think because I'm cheating on Matt, I'm capable of cheating on both of you."

He didn't deny it, but asked, "Why didn't you want me to meet you?"

"*Because I have to go home.* You know I do. Jeeze Reese, I called an old friend. It was a coincidence Trent was in the same show. I would never cheat on you."

"How do I know that?"

He actually said it, and damn did it hurt. I refused to cry. "Because you know me better than anyone. You know how much I love you, and what we're doing still sickens me."

There was a long pause, and I wondered if he could ever trust me after what I'd done to Matt. Then he said, "I'm sorry, I do trust you. It's just that I've been going crazy with this feeling you're slipping away from me. It scares me."

Hearing him say it scared me, too. The familiar throbbing beat in my chest, making me ache. Now wasn't the time to tell him our future was uncertain. For now, I just wanted him to feel better. I quoted Heathcliff's line from *Wuthering Heights*, "I cannot live without my life."

He finished the quote. "I cannot live without my soul." He chuckled softly. "English major. Remember?"

"Show off."

"Hey, I want you to do something for me. When you get home, look up Sonnet #57."

Chapter 24

When I walked in the door after my Chicago trip, the boys were already in bed and fast asleep, but Matt sat up waiting for me. I wasn't sure what to expect. He'd had time to think while I'd been away too. Matt could have decided our marriage wasn't worth saving.

Thankfully, he smiled. I was out of gas and not up for an argument. Matt gave me a quick squeeze and carried my luggage to our bedroom. He sat on the bed and watched me change into my pajamas.

After I hung up my clothes, I said, "You usually don't wait up for me."

"I thought we could talk," he said hesitantly.

"About what?"

"Nothing particular. You said we don't talk any more. I want to try." This was unexpected. "Would you like a glass of wine?" he offered.

"No thanks." More alcohol in my system wasn't appealing. I wasn't twenty-something anymore and to my dismay, it took much longer for my body to recover.

"Did you and Serena have a good time?"

"A little too good of a time."

"She didn't have you doing tequila shots, did she?"

"A few, but I didn't dance on any tables."

He chuckled good-naturedly. "I'm glad you had fun. You should stay in touch with her. You used to be good friends."

It was nice of him to say, considering he had never liked Serena. "We were. I really enjoyed seeing a play, too. I really miss theater." Matt's brows furrowed. "Don't worry. I don't want to start acting again." The truth was Matt had been more than pleased when I gave up acting. He didn't like me working late, or the lifestyle that went with it. "But I would like to go to the theater more often."

Matt's brow relaxed. "It was your life when we met. I'll go with you if you like."

"That's very sweet, but I know it isn't your thing. I'm a big girl. I can go by myself or find a friend to go with me."

He shrugged. "I don't mind."

He seemed more open than he had been in a long time. I wanted desperately to crawl into bed, but I didn't want to miss the opportunity for open dialogue. "Matt, I need to know something. We're being more honest with each other, right?"

"Yes."

"Why are you trying to fix our marriage? Is it for me or is it for the boys?"

"What do you mean?"

"Well, do you want to stay married because you want *me* or are you more concerned about staying together for the sake of the boys?" I'd tried to ask in a non-confrontational manner. I wanted him to be honest and had to know where I stood.

"I don't know how to answer. Does it matter?"

"Yes, Matt. It matters. I have to know and please, *please* be honest."

"It's not an easy question. We've been together for a long time … I don't love you the way I used to, but I want to be in love with you again."

"If we didn't have the boys, would you stay with me?"

"There's no point to the question. We have the boys. We need to make this work."

"Matt, please answer me."

"Probably not. I'm sorry." He couldn't look at me. The veracity of his answer was unquestionable. It was painful for him to say and painful for me to hear.

"Don't be, I'm glad you're being honest."

"Would you still be with me if we didn't have the boys?"

I answered the underlying question, "We can't stay together just for the boys. It's no way for either of us to live. It wouldn't be good for them either."

"You saying you want a divorce?"

"No, but if we can't find a way to love each other again, if we can't find a way for us both to be happy, then we shouldn't stay together." I couldn't hold back the tears any longer and let them roll down my cheeks.

He looked at me with an odd combination of deep sadness and hope. "We've drifted apart, but there was a time when we were in love and happy. I want to be that way again. I'm willing to try. Are you?"

Reese's face flashed in my mind. God knows how I loved him, but I couldn't say no to my husband. I couldn't say no to my children. If Matt was willing, I couldn't say no.

"Yes, I'm willing."

"Thank you." He was close to tears, too. I put my arms around him and we held each other for a few minutes before he said, "It's late and you're tired. Let's go to bed."

I got up early the next morning, wanting privacy when I looked up Sonnet #57. With coffee in hand, I went into my office, shut the door, pulled down my well-leafed copy of the complete works of Shakespeare, and read *Being your slave what should I do but tend, Upon the hours, and times of your desire?* Reading the sonnet made me ache for him and regret not staying the extra day in Chicago. Two lines particularly resonated with me: *Nor dare I question with jealous thought, Where you may be, or your affairs suppose.* I hadn't appreciated how difficult it must be for him to share me with another man. Dangling Trent in his face had been unkind. I wouldn't give him any more reasons to be jealous if I could help it. The sonnet ended with the sentiment his love has made him such a fool that no matter what I do, *"he thinks no ill."*

Heavy with fresh guilt, I wanted to call him, but was afraid someone would hear me. I sent him a text instead: *Am your sad slave too.*

He texted back: *Please call me.*

The house was silent except for the hum of the furnace. No one else was awake yet. I broke one of my rules and dialed his number. He picked up on the first ring.

"Hey, smart guy," I greeted. "How long have you been boning up on sonnets?"

"Your verb choice turns me on."

"You're so funny."

He chuckled. "I started after you stayed with me here. I was trying to figure out my feelings. I love you so deeply and completely, but I didn't know how to express it."

"You just did," I murmured.

"Mom?"

My heart stopped. Micah stood in the doorway of my office. *Don't panic. Whatever you do, do not panic.* I hadn't said anything incriminating. I held my hand up to Micah.

"Well, it's been nice chatting with you, Mom," I said in a cheery voice into the phone.

"Someone with you?"

"That's right."

"I understand. Call me later if you get a chance."

"Okay, Mom. Talk to you soon."

I hung up the phone and turned to Micah. He asked, "Why were you talking to Grandma this early?"

"No particular reason. Why are *you* up so early?"

"I dunno know." He shrugged. "Can you still help me build my California Mission this weekend?"

"Yep, we'll start working on it after your game. I was thinking we could build it out of sugar cubes. What do you think?"

"Sounds good." He hugged me. "I'm glad you're home."

"Me too." I squeezed him and kissed the top of his head.

He pushed away from me, making a face. "Mom, stop."

So typical. "Alright, let's get you some breakfast."

We headed to the kitchen with my heart beating double time. What a nerve-wracking reminder I always, *always* had to stick to my rule of no contact with Reese when someone else was home. I pushed thoughts of him aside. The day belonged to the other men in my life.

That night Matt arranged for the boys to have a sleep over with his parents. We had the house to ourselves until the next morning. Part of me didn't want to try; part of me wanted to say *enough. I'm in love with someone else. It's too late.* But what if it wasn't too late? I couldn't look in my boy's faces and tell them I was divorcing their father unless I tried.

Matt asked, "What would you like to do? Would you like to go to the theater?"

"No, I want to do something we can both enjoy," I said, wanting to be equally considerate. "How about we open a good bottle of wine, order a pizza, and watch a movie?"

"Can we agree on a movie?" he joked.

"I think so. I only have two conditions for the night. First, we don't talk about the boys. Let's pretend it's just you and me tonight. And no sex."

"I get not talking about the boys, but why no sex? We're alone."

"I don't want sex to be a band aid."

"But I feel closer to you when we make love."

"Well, I need to feel close to you before I want to make love."

Matt gave in first. "Okay, so how do I make you feel close to me?"

"Cuddle with me while we watch the movie."

Matt grinned. "What? You mean actually sit next to each other and hold hands?"

I snickered. "Shocking, but yes."

It started as a nice evening. Matt and I had a hard time not talking about the boys, but somehow we managed to make it through most of the night. Matt wasn't a cuddler but he either held my hand or kept his arm around me for most of the movie. I did feel a little closer to him. It was a baby step, but still a step back into a loving relationship.

When the movie was over, Matt kissed me. I let him, but when he started getting aroused, I pulled away. "You agreed to no sex," I reminded him.

"We just got done sitting together for two hours."

"That doesn't mean I want to sleep with you."

He sighed, pushed off the couch, and headed towards the door. Halfway across the room he stopped and turned back to face me. "I don't understand you. I really don't. One day you're upset because I don't touch you enough and now you don't want me. I've tried. I wanted to be a better lover for you. I thought I was."

When he put it in those terms, I sounded a little crazy even to me. "You were a better lover, but I want you to make love to me because you love me.

I don't want to make love knowing it would just be sex. That's all it was last week, and I can't do it anymore."

He snapped. "You're crazy! Do you know that?"

"Matt, I don't want to be with someone who has to try to love me. I want to be with someone who does love me!"

"Is there someone else?"

"What do you mean?" My heart pounded wildly.

"Have you met someone else?"

"How can you ask that?" *Stay calm, stay calm, for God's sake, stay calm.*

"You've been up and down, vacillating all over. You were the little seductress in Carmel and then the ice queen. You were damned enthusiastic last week and now you don't even want me to kiss you. None of this makes sense. So I'm asking, is there someone else?"

He glared at me, waiting for an answer. *Lie! He'll believe you. He wants to believe you.* Looking him in the eyes, I didn't flinch. "There isn't anyone else. There's never been anyone else. I loved you and gave you all I had to give and you stopped loving me. What do you expect? You've been breaking my heart for years." I started to cry. Only the first part was a lie; the rest was true.

"You broke my heart, too," he said in a quiet voice.

"How? What did I do?" I was bewildered. All I ever did was love him.

"You always made me feel like I should be grateful to be with you. When have you ever been grateful for me? Plenty of women would feel lucky to have me, but you never have. How do you think that makes me feel after all of these years?"

Matt trembled, and his raw pain cut me. I never knew he understood so much of what was never spoken. I had resented him for so many little things that I'd stopped appreciating him as a man. I appreciated him as a father, but not as a man. Had he sought comfort elsewhere?

My throat constricted and I asked, "Have you met someone else? Is that why you're questioning me?" I couldn't breathe while I waited for his answer.

He paused before confessing, "No, but sometimes I wish I did."

"My God, what's happened to us?"

"I don't know," he answered just above a whisper.

"You should leave, go stay with your mother. I need space. Please, *please* leave."

"I'm not going anywhere. If you need space, then you can sleep on the couch."

"Matt—"

"You are my wife until death do us part. I'm not going anywhere. You don't have to sleep with me, but I'm not leaving and neither are you."

"You can't make me stay."

"Oh yes I can. I won't let you have the boys if you leave."

"Are you threatening me?"

"No, I'm just letting you know the boys and I are a package deal. I know you. You won't leave them." He gulped for air and tears leaked out of his eyes. "I'm begging you not to split up our family. Please, we have to stay together."

I couldn't stand it. I couldn't stand seeing him in so much pain and comforted him the only way I knew how. I wrapped my arms around him and kissed away his tears. I didn't feel love and desire for him, but I did feel compassion. He clung to me.

"I won't ask you to leave," I murmured as his crying subsided. "I didn't know how unappreciated you felt. I'm sorry. I'm so sorry. I never wanted to hurt you."

"I didn't want to hurt you either. I'm sorry, too."

When Reese looked into my eyes, we connected. I could see and feel his love. It had been a long, long time since Matt and I had really looked at each other.

"I want you to look into my eyes."

"Why?"

"Please, just try."

His clear blue eyes were pools of pain, but beyond the hurt, in the depths, some love survived; enough to resuscitate some love for him. As we stared into each other's eyes, our severed bonds began to fuse. Our marriage didn't have to be over. However precarious and tenuous the bond, there was something holding us together—something on which to build.

"I want to feel close to you," he whispered.

I unbuttoned his shirt, rested my cheek against his chest, and then made love with him. He didn't kiss me in places and in a way I'd always wanted, but he made me feel wanted. He made me feel loved.

Afterwards Matt held me and whispered, "Deep down, I still love you. We'll keep trying, right? We can make our marriage work, right?"

I couldn't bring myself to tell him I loved him too. All I could think was *trying is not doing,* but said, "Yes, we'll keep trying."

I saw Reese's face in my mind. How was I ever going to explain all of this to him? If he knew about the vacillating affections I had for my husband, would he still think 'no ill' of me?

Chapter 25

Matt and I floated through the next two days, both trying to be considerate. He hugged me more and actually kissed me in front of the boys, which prompted vomiting sounds. I tried to notice and thank him for little things. We looked into each other's eyes a few times, too. Each of us grappled with a different kind of tension, but as long as Matt refused to give up, our marriage had a chance. The last couple of days were better than they'd been in a long time.

I regretted telling Reese I'd leave Matt and had no idea what to tell him. I'd felt so sure about it in the hotel room in Atlanta. Now, I doubted if I ever could. How could I, knowing Matt and I might be able to find a way back to each other? I decided my best course of action with him was inaction. If I could stall him until the first of the year, I'd have a better idea of where Matt and I stood.

God forgive me, but I saw Reese's face every time I closed my eyes. The longing in my chest throbbed harder the closer I got to being with him again. The night before I left for New York, even Matt noticed I wasn't myself.

"Are you okay?" he asked. "You seem sort of jumpy."

"I guess I'm a little nervous about my meetings in New York, that's all."

Matt gave me a hug and said reassuringly, "You'll do great. You always do. You know, I really am proud of you. You've worked so hard. You deserve your success."

"Thank you. It means a lot to me that you feel that way."

He smiled with genuine affection, and his eyes crinkled up the way I loved. The guilt beast in the pit of my stomach sprang to life. I buried my head against his chest, afraid he would see shame lurking in my eyes.

I left on the earliest flight available to New York the next morning. I had a non-stop landing me at JFK mid-afternoon and Reese's apartment key in my pocket. He'd meet me at his place as soon as he could slip out of the office for the day. We only had two nights together, but there was a good chance I'd get to see him again the following week in Boston.

As the plane approached, the more impatient I became to see him. I swear it took longer for the airplane to taxi to the gate than to fly cross-country, and then, an eternity for the doors to open and the people ahead of me to deplane. I silently screamed at the woman in front of me, *"Move your ass!"* I wanted time to freshen-up before Reese got home.

In my rush to get to the cab line, I almost missed a driver holding a sign for "S. Sinclair." I stopped, realizing he was there for me. The driver took my bag and led me to a black town car. Reese was waiting for me in the back seat. He smiled ear-to-ear and playfully ordered, "Come here, you little hussy."

I slid next to him and lifted my face to meet his kiss. "I hope you don't mind. I couldn't wait to see you," he said with his arms wrapped around me.

I leaned against him. Everywhere my body touched his was a taste of heaven. It wasn't enough. I twisted around to look at his face, his beautiful face, and his magnetic eyes. "You being here is the best surprise you could give me. God, I've missed you."

"I've missed you, too. I don't ever want to go this long again without being with you." He kissed me again, and I snuggled next to him as the driver started the engine and headed away from JFK. I loved the feel of his starched cotton dress shirt against my cheek and I deeply inhaled. The scent of his cologne mingled with his skin made my hormones rage, and I barely controlled an impulse to reach down and unzip his pants. I settled for hugging his waist tighter in an attempt to get a millimeter closer.

He asked, "Did you remember to pack a cocktail dress?"

"Yes, but what's on the agenda? Are we entertaining a client?"

"Nope. I'm wining and dining you." He had a playful, crooked grin and looked adorable. I wanted to eat him up.

"We're going out alone? Is that wise?"

"Stop frowning. It's a big city—we're safe. Trust me," he said with a kiss that led to another kiss and some serious groping. The only thing that stopped us from becoming completely obscene was the absence of a discreet window separating us from the driver.

As soon as we walked in the door of his apartment, he threw me over his shoulder fireman style and hauled me straight to his bedroom. Apparently, I wasn't the only one who was having problems controlling their hormones. He tossed me on the bed, both of us laughing, and pounced on top of me. We giddily ripped clothes off. Our lovemaking was joyous. There was no other word for it.

Afterwards, he only gave me a minute to catch my breath before he yanked me off the bed. "Come on, we need to get ready or we'll be late for our reservation."

"Do I have time for a shower?"

"Nope, you're going to have to smell like sex all night." He grinned wickedly.

"You're so bad. I'm at least washing up a bit."

After I cleaned up and dressed, I joined Reese in his living room. He looked handsome in his suit, but I still preferred seeing him in jeans. He eyed me up and down with a slight frown as I approached him.

"What's wrong?" I asked. "Is this dress inappropriate?"

"No, the dress is fine, and you look beautiful, but it's missing something," he said. "Turn around." I did as asked and felt cool metal against the base of my neck. He spun me back to face him and smiled. "Much better. Come have a look."

As he led me to a mirror, I reached up to touch the necklace and felt stones dangling from tear-drop shaped metal. Three to be exact. Looking in the mirror, I guessed the largest diamond to be at least two carats and the other two only slightly smaller.

"Reese, I don't know what to say. It's stunning, but ..." My heart was in my throat. I knew he was wealthy, but I didn't care about his money. "You don't need to sell me."

"Sweetheart, I am not *trying to sell you*. I wanted to give you something special. I liked picking it out for you. I actually got to tell someone I'm in love and got to talk to someone about you, even if it was just a sales girl. It made me happy, so don't, please don't ruin this for me."

His crushed expression made me feel even worse. "I'm sorry I questioned your motives. I love it. I really do, but you know I can't accept. I could never explain it to Matt."

"I'll keep it for you for the time being. You can wear it when you're with me."

"Reese, I—"

"You wear Matt's ring every day. I can't give you a ring yet, but I can give you this. Think of it as a promise of good things to come. Take it and wear it for me, please."

I worried about what the necklace symbolized, but as long as it remained with him, I could deal with it. I smiled at him and nodded. "It's beautiful. Thank you."

"I love you. It gives me pleasure to give you things."

I pirouetted for him. "So, do I pass inspection now?"

"Turn around one more time."

I did, hoping there wouldn't be any more surprises. He whistled. "Nice ass. Fuck me, you're sexy. Let's go before I toss you back in bed."

He whisked me out the door and we jumped in cab.

The dimly lit restaurant was designed for intimacy, a place where dining was a two hour leisurely event. Reese definitely had a talent for choosing settings. It was also very expensive. It felt wrong to allow Reese to spend so much money on me. The necklace, the restaurant, everything was overwhelming. It was hard to stop analyzing and just enjoy the experience.

"What are you thinking?" he asked, trying to read my expression.

"I'm thinking I'm head-over-heels in love, this restaurant is fabulously romantic, and you're spoiling me rotten."

"That's my plan." He took my hand and kissed it.

I had to ask, "Is there a reason for all of this?"

"What do you mean?"

"You're obviously sweeping me off my feet. You already know I love you. I was just wondering what your motivation is?"

"You're such a little cynic sometimes." He chuckled and shook his head. "I just want to make you feel special. Anything wrong with that?"

He looked at me with his warm chocolate eyes soft with love and I melted. "No, there's nothing wrong with it. I'm just not used to it. Thank you."

"You're welcome, and get used to it." He gazed at me a moment and chuckled.

"What?" I asked.

"I was just thinking about the day we met. You ran out before I even got a chance to find out your name; then there you were sitting in the conference room."

"Your first day at Global Security. I was so nervous sitting next to you all day."

He laughed. "It was excruciating. You bumped my knee at one point and I felt a jolt of electricity shoot through me."

"I remember that." We both grinned at the memory.

"Why were you such a stinker at first?"

"You tried to close me too soon."

"Ouch."

"Sorry, bad joke. I have a better answer." I smiled and quoted, *"Hard to seem won; but I was won, my lord, With the first glance ..."*

"I like it. What's that from?"

"Troilus and Cressida. Anyway, you were, are, my boss and I was attracted to you. I thought it would be better if I kept my distance considering we'd be spending so much time together—guess I was right. Here we are."

"Yep, here we are, eating and exchanging pleasantries." He took my hand, kissed the fleshy part of my palm, and winked. He was such a flirt.

I wished I could simply be happy basking in his attention. I loved him so much it was almost painful, and he was being the perfect Mr. Wonderful. If I were single and free, I would be thinking I was the luckiest woman in the world. As things stood, I felt more and more like the most selfish woman in the world.

"Susan, you just got the saddest expression. What's wrong?"

"Not sad … thoughtful," I lied, not wanting to sour the evening.

"Hey, you don't have to spare my feelings. What is it?"

"So much has happened in such a short amount of time. If it were just you and I …."

"I'm not going to pressure you. I promise we'll go at your pace."

"Thank you, I needed to hear that."

"I know."

Reese was so good to me and being with him was always heady. It was hard to think straight when I was with him. I did want to be with him for forever. He made me happy.

We had a lovely evening up until it was time to leave. Reese waited for me in front of the restaurant while I went to the ladies room. I was about to rejoin him when I noticed a man talking to him. Ducking back inside, I lingered a few minutes, but the man didn't leave. For all I knew he could've been a complete stranger. I mustered my nerve and walked out the door.

Reese's cool demeanor warned me to stay on guard. *Crap. I should have waited inside.*

"Susan, this is Gordon Bush. Gordon, Susan Sinclair. I'm not sure if you've met in person." Reese's manner was very formal.

I shook Gordon's hand and said, "Gordon, it's nice to finally match your name with a face. We've been exchanging e-mails over the last few months."

"Oh, you're Susan." He smiled and raised his eyebrows. "You're Reese's date?"

"Hardly a date," I laughed to keep things light, "working dinner."

"Ah, well, it's nice to meet you finally. I guess I'll see you in the office tomorrow."

Reese was silent during the entire cab ride back to his apartment. His silence made me nervous. I wasn't sure if he was mad at me, or the situation.

As soon as we walked into the apartment, he turned on me. "Fuck, I thought you would have had the sense to wait inside!"

"How was I supposed to know it was Gordon? Do you think he'll tell anyone?"

"Shit, let's hope not. That restaurant is definitely not a place for business and you look like you were on a date."

"You chose the restaurant and told me to wear a cocktail dress."

"So, this is my fault?"

"No, but it's not mine either. It was just a fluke run-in."

"You're right. I'm sorry." He exhaled heavily. "I want so badly to be able to hold your hand, or put my arm around you, or take you to any fucking restaurant and not worry about who might see us. Fuck, I hate having to sneak around."

"Me, too."

"Come here," he said pulling me into his arms. "I'm sorry. We get so little time together. I wanted tonight to be perfect."

I draped my arms around his neck. "Meeting me at the airport, the necklace, the wining and dining were all perfect. Being with you is perfect. Loving you is perfect."

His eyes smoldered. He was definitely forgetting about Gordon Bush, which was good with me. "This is just the beginning. I plan to make you happy for the rest of your life."

I didn't want to think or talk about the future, so I kissed him until he didn't want to talk anymore either.

Chapter 26

The next day passed without incident at the office. I saw Gordon. He was pleasant, and made no mention of having seen Reese and me the prior night. It probably helped that my meetings didn't include Reese. He spent most of the day in his office while I bounced between our legal department and product development, making sure we had a workable product. We were getting close to inking our first contract. The last thing we needed was the implementation going awry. Reese and I didn't even have lunch together.

He beat me home and had his living room glowing with candlelight and a cozy dinner laid out on his coffee table by the time I got there. I felt badly; I still had a couple hours of work ahead of me.

Reese asked, "Anything I can help you with?"

"I don't think so. I just need to bang it out."

"If you need some banging, I can definitely help," he joked and pulled me into his arms; then whispered seductively, "Ask your boss for the night off."

"He'd just say no."

"Try me." He kissed me just below my ear.

"Bank of Boston is expecting an implementation plan tomorrow. Based on what I discovered today, the timelines and sequences will have to change, consequently changing the billing." He let go of me. I asked rhetorically, "May I have the night off?"

"Shit." He flipped on lights and blew out the candles. "You can use my office."

Reese was lying on the couch reading when I finished. Exhausted, I laid on top of him.

"Are you done for the night?" he asked hopefully.

"Yes. I'll run it by Implementation in the morning and have it to the bank by noon."

"Not to sound like a nagging husband, but I hate that you had to work tonight."

"I'm sorry, but of all people you should understand."

"I do, but it still doesn't make me happy."

"What can I do to make you happy?"

His eyes lit up and he grinned. "You know what really turns me on?"

"I can think of more than a few things, but tell me anyway."

"Seeing you walk around the office all prim and proper in your little business suits."

"You have got to be kidding me."

His voice dripped low and thick. "It's kind of erotic watching you and knowing just how sexy you are underneath those clothes; knowing I'm the only one who really knows you."

He ran his hands over my body and I could feel what he wanted. "I'm so tired. Can you just hold me for a while?"

"Of course," he sighed.

He rubbed my back as he held me. I was very comfortable with his body warm and loving under me. My head rested on his chest, and I listened to the familiar rhythm of his heartbeat. He rubbed my back, soothing me, and he smelled good. He always smelled good.

"Susan? You're not falling asleep are you?"

"No, just relaxing."

The next thing I knew I woke up in his bed and looked at the clock. It was midnight, and Reese slept soundly beside me with his arm draped over my stomach. I carefully moved his arm so I could go to the bathroom.

When I reached the door, he asked sleepily, "Where are you going?"

"Just to the bathroom."

He had the bedside lamp turned on when I got back.

"I'm sorry. I didn't mean to wake you," I apologized.

"It's okay. I need to talk to you, but we didn't get a chance. Can we talk now?"

"Sure, something wrong?"

"Possibly. Joe called me into his office today to discuss you."

"Why?"

"He said there were rumors going around about the two of us. He was told by more than one source that we are 'very close', and he wanted to know if there was any truth to the gossip."

"What did you tell him?"

"I told him we work well together. I also told him you were very attractive, we're relatively the same age, and our travel requirements put us frequently together. The circumstances alone make us fodder for gossip. I didn't lie, but I didn't answer him directly."

I couldn't think with my heart beating so hard.

Reese caressed my cheek. "Sweetheart, you okay?"

"What do you think?"

"He can't do anything. He doesn't have any proof and even if he did, we're two consenting adults. Neither of us can be fired."

"No, but if Joe knew, he wouldn't let us work together. The policy about fraternization with subordinates is ambiguous. He could easily move me to another division."

"It's possible, but if we're careful, I don't think he will. You're critical to the success of mobile banking. I don't think he'll do anything unless something blatant happens."

"What should we do?"

"Keep a low profile."

"I thought we were."

I thought about the phone call in Atlanta from Cynthia Warren and bumping into Gordon Bush. Last summer, Curtis Pope had left us knowing we would be alone. Earlier that day, I'd caught Reese looking at me with an expression replete with meaning. Other people must have noticed, too. There had been times when he unconsciously placed his hand on my arm or my back as he guided me out of the elevator or opened the door for me. How much had Anne, his administrative assistant, caught?

"I shouldn't go with you to the meeting in Boston next week," he said.

"Probably not, but when will we see each other again? I'm on vacation the week of Thanksgiving. The next week I'm in LA, but there's no reason for you to be there, and then no one will want to meet with us until after the first of the year."

"There's the company holiday party."

"It's a month away." I was close to tears. He was upset, too.

"Hey, we'll figure out something."

"It's going to keep getting harder for us to be together."

"After you leave your husband, it'll be easier. Nothing has changed, has it?" He looked at me with a worried expression.

I flinched. I didn't want … wasn't ready to have that conversation. "This has nothing to do with my marriage. It has to do with work."

"I know, I know. Give me some time. I'll think of something."

He took me in his arms and kissed me. I wasn't tired any more. I didn't know when we would have a chance to be together again.

I had another hectic day. I wanted at least to have lunch with Reese, but there simply wasn't time. I wasn't even sure if I'd have an opportunity to say goodbye. A car service was picking me up at 4 p.m. to take me to JFK. I was in a conference room with Cutis Pope, when Reese caught up with me.

"Susan, I'd like to see you in my office before you leave," he said with a serious voice.

"Sure. How much time do you need?"

"About fifteen minutes."

"Okay, I'll be there in a few minutes."

Curtis raised his brows at me. "You in trouble?"

I wondered if he was really thinking about the night last summer when Reese and I had stayed late working alone in this very conference room.

Ten minutes later, I entered Reese's office. He sat behind his desk and asked me to shut the door. "Please, sit down," he requested. I started to sit in the guest chair, but he stopped me. "No, sit here," he said indicating his lap. A mischievous grin lit up his face. "You didn't really think I'd let you slip out without saying goodbye did you?"

"I wasn't sure, but I'm glad you didn't." We kissed and then I tried to get up, but he held me in place. "Come on, let me up. Anyone could walk in."

"We have fifteen minutes … no one will walk in without knocking first," he murmured as he slid his hand up my skirt and nibbled my neck.

"This is too risky."

"Slightly, not too … definitely worth it," he murmured.

"I'm getting up."

The next second Joe Benedetti opened the door without warning. I had just managed to get to the other side of the desk. *Who tipped him off?*

Joe's eyes darted from me to Reese and then back to me, all the while maintaining a poker face. Mine was firmly in place, but Reese visibly fumed.

"Oh, Susan, I didn't know you were still here," Joe said.

"I was just leaving."

"Did you stay with your friend again this trip?"

I smiled innocently. "As a matter of fact I did. We had a lovely time. Thank you for asking. Reese, as always, it was nice to see you. Joe, I hope to have some good news for you after next week's meeting in Boston."

"I understand you're very close to signatures."

"Yes, this should be our last presentation. I intend on leaving a final draft of the contract for the bank's legal team to review."

"Excellent. Good luck."

"Thank you. Well, goodbye."

It killed me to walk out without further contact with Reese.

He texted me: *Don't worry. Call me when you land.*

Chapter 27

Even though Reese told me not to worry, it was all I did the entire flight back to California. Ten seconds earlier and Joe would have caught me on Reese's lap. No amount of smooth prevaricating would have saved our asses. I was jeopardizing his career, and my own, for what? And what could I possibly tell Matt if I lost my job? *"I got caught snogging my boss in the office. So sorry."*

Where had my sense of morality, of right and wrong, gone? I took a hard look at myself and was sickened. How could I have done this to Matt? The lying and cheating. Matt was good and decent. I'd always feared deep down I wasn't a good person, not Matt's equal; that Mrs. Fowler had detected an inherent deficiency when she had tried to give me moral guidance as a child. Mrs. Fowler would be ashamed of me. I was ashamed of me. Thinking about Micah and Jason, put me over the edge. My boys deserved a mother and father together. Falling in love with Matt again was impossible as long as I was involved with Reese.

And how could I string Reese along while trying to fix things with Matt? It was wrong, wrong, wrong. It was bad enough he expected me to leave Matt. It would be even worse if our relationship cost him his career.

I had to do something before I completely lost control. As much as I loved Reese, as much as it would hurt, I had to let him go before something really, truly cataclysmic happened. Now would be the time. There would be no chance of seeing him for four weeks. It would give us both a little time to heal before we saw each other again.

Dazed, I stepped off the plane and took my time walking to my car in the parking garage. I settled into the driver's seat, braced myself, and with a shaking hand, hit his number.

"Susan?" he answered.

"Hi. Sorry if I woke you."

"You didn't. I was waiting for your call. I hated the way you had to leave."

"What happened when I left?"

"I let Joe know that when my door is closed, I don't want him or anyone else walking into my office without my invitation."

I respected Reese for not backing down, but he still didn't tell me what I wanted to know. "Did he say anything else about us?"

"No."

I exhaled, not realizing I'd been holding my breath. Although relieved, my pulse didn't slow. "I can't let you screw up your career for me."

"Sweetheart, nothing is being screwed up," he said soothingly.

"Today was too close; it's not only your career I'm worried about. My family counts on me … we have to stop seeing each other."

A sob broke from my chest, and there was deafening silence from the other end. Then, I heard Reese trying to catch his breath.

"Don't say that. It's late and you're tired. You don't mean it. I know you don't. I know you love me," he said with urgency.

"It doesn't matter; I almost cost you your career today."

"I ordered you into my office. You didn't do anything."

"But if we weren't seeing each other, it never would have happened."

"Love, you're upset, but you'll feel better tomorrow. We'll talk tomorrow, okay?"

I had to keep going. I didn't have the strength to do this again. "It's not just work. I'm not ready to leave Matt … I don't know if I ever can. I can't live with what I'm doing anymore."

I could hear him crying, too. "Don't do this, please … please, don't do this."

"I'm sorry. I'm so sorry. I have to go."

"This isn't over. You're just tired and upset. We'll discuss this tomorrow."

"Nothing is going to change."

"I love you and we're going to talk about it. Promise me … God damn it … Susan?"

"No, there's no point."

I hung up and sat in the car shaking and crying, unable to drive with my heart breaking. If it were only the two of us, I would give up anything to be with him. The one thing I couldn't sacrifice was my family. Taking a deep breath, I started the engine.

Everyone was asleep when I got home. I pulled a blanket out of the closet, poured a glass of wine, and curled up on the family room couch. My chest heaved and I fought to control my sobbing, terrified the noise would wake Matt. I knew this would happen. I knew there'd be no way our affair could end without someone getting hurt. At least, Reese and I were the only ones hurting. We were the guilty parties. At least, we still had our jobs, and I still had my family.

I fell asleep fully clothed on the couch. Matt woke me when he got up at seven.

"Why are you on the couch?" I'm sure he thought it had something to do with me not wanting to be in bed with him.

"I was wound up when I got home. I thought a glass of wine would help me sleep. Must've worked. I'm sorry. I'll make some coffee."

"Okay, thanks. You alright?"

"Just a little distracted. I should've been in my office an hour ago."

I started to walk to the kitchen. He stopped me and put his arms around me, holding me close. "I really missed you. I'm glad you're back." He said it as if he really meant it.

I'd made the right decision and pecked him on the lips. "Me, too."

I woke the boys and gave them good morning hugs and kisses. As soon as they left for the day, a black mood threatened to drown me. The weather matched my mindset, overcast with precipitation predicted later in the day. I wished I could call in sick and spend the day on the couch nursing my heartache, but other people were counting on me to review documents before they could proceed with their work. I poured coffee into my biggest mug and headed into my office. Whoever called earlier hadn't left a message.

With my laptop fired up and connected to VPN, I was ready to face whatever was on my e-mail, fully expecting to see something from Reese. There was nothing from Reese, which was odd. He usually sent half a dozen work related e-mails by this time most mornings.

I copied him on an e-mail to legal. An out-of-office response said he'd be unavailable until Monday. I pictured him lying on his purple couch, aching for me just as I ached for him. I almost called him, but decided it'd be kinder to leave him alone. He needed time, just as I did. I dove into work. It was my solace and the mental distraction kept my sorrow at bay.

Around one o'clock, I took a break knowing I should eat, but nothing seemed appetizing. I sat at the kitchen table and stared at the rain pouring down. Before long, my tears kept pace with the rain. The pain in my chest was so crushing I could barely breathe. I couldn't let go of the pain, so I embraced it. It kept me close to him. On the other side of the country, he was hurting, too. I could feel it as surely as I could feel my own heartbeat.

My muscles and my joints throbbed as if completing a two-hour work-out on no sleep.

A hot bath and a long soak always soothed me.

As I got into the tub, I could hear my home office phone ring. I thought about answering it, but it was Friday afternoon and already five o'clock on the East coast. Whoever it was could wait. Even if it was Reese, he could wait. I wasn't ready to talk to him. My emotions were still too raw, and I didn't trust myself to stay strong.

The hot water loosened my tense muscles and I sank deeper into the tub. My phone rang again. I immersed my head wanting to drown out the world and float in oblivion for a while. I involuntarily came up for air. My cell phone rang. I ignored it. Then my office phone started ringing again. I submerged my head again in an attempt to deafen the sound. Then my cell phone went off again. I couldn't ignore it. Somebody was determined to talk to me. Wrapping a towel around me, I ran to grab it.

"This is Susan Sinclair."

"Hi, it's me."

My heart stopped. I could barely get a breath. "Hi," was all I managed to say.

"We have to talk."

"I can't."

"Fuck! Don't give me this bullshit. We're going to talk and in person."

"In person?" Panic shot through me. "What do you mean? Where are you?"

"I'm at the SFO Marriott. Know where it is?"

"Yes, but what are you doing there? Are you insane?"

"You drive me insane; that's what I'm doing here. How soon can you get here?"

"Reese ..."

"You owe me this much." His voice was razor-sharp, and he added with an edge that frightened me, "I have to see you."

"I can be there in thirty minutes."

Crap, crap, crap! I'd counted on not seeing him and had to think of something to tell Matt. I wasn't sure if I could make it back before Matt and the boys got home for the day, and wracked my brain trying to think of something while I wrestled into my jeans and sweater.

I called Matt and told him a big wig from the East coast called at the last minute and wanted me to meet him in San Francisco for dinner. It wasn't a complete lie.

I glanced in the mirror. My hair was wet and I wasn't dressed for dinner in San Francisco. I changed again and quickly dried my hair.

On my way to the Marriott, I rehearsed my script. *I am very sorry, but we cannot see each other anymore. I am doing this for you. You deserve more than I can give you.* He'll argue with me, no doubt. *Don't look at his eyes. Don't let him touch you.* I hit traffic on highway 101 heading north. I already was late, and the rain didn't help. Reese called, worried I was no showing. Ten minutes later, I hesitated outside his hotel room, steeling myself before I knocked.

The door swung open. He looked like he hadn't slept at all the night before—unshaven, bloodshot eyes, and hair in disarray. I'd never seen him so disheveled. My heart wrenched as he pulled me into the room. Cupping my cheeks in his hands, he angled my face toward his. I tried to divert my eyes, but his hands held me like vises.

"Fucking *look* at me!"

The heat from his body and his touch weakened me. The pain in his eyes was my pain. Our eyes locked and a magnetic force held us together. I couldn't pull away, and I let him kiss me. His mouth was giving while his tongue was hungry and devouring, proving our need for each other. He pulled me tightly against the entire length of his body and whispered, "Don't ever do that to me again. I need you and you need me. You're in my blood and my bones. Don't ever do that to me again ... ever." As he held me firmly against him, I could hear the rain pouring outside and felt his cheek wet with our tears.

He took my hand, led me to the bed, and draped himself over my body. He rested his head on my breast, listening to my heartbeat, while I cradled him in my arms and his familiar scent filled my senses.

He whispered, "Sometimes, when you're away from me, I lie awake at night wanting you so much my whole body aches, and it feels like I'm literally going to die if I can't hold you."

I pulled him up my body and kissed him. "Closer," he said. "Hold me closer." I hooked my legs around his calves, held him tight, and welcomed the weight of his body. We laid in silence holding each other. The only sound was rain tapping against the window. After a while, our closeness couldn't be denied. We made love slowly and tenderly. Just like the first time, we became one body and one soul. That was why he had come to see me in person.

With our bodies still warm from lovemaking, we laid facing each other with our legs entwined. Reese rested his hand on my hip. "You can't ever leave me," he whispered. "Our souls are connected."

"You're not making it easy, but we have to stop."

"Love, don't start that again. Please, just talk to me. Tell me what you're afraid of."

"For starters, I don't want to derail your career. I know Joe can't prove anything, but it's changing his perception of you."

"My career isn't dependent on one man's opinion. Don't worry about me."

"Things could have been ugly yesterday."

He lightly caressed my hip while he talked. "The only thing ugly was Joe walking into my office unannounced. It won't happen again. I won't tolerate that kind of disrespect."

I untangled my legs from his, but his hand on my hip tightened, keeping me close. I purposely made my voice stern. "It's not only your career at stake."

"I haven't forgotten. I know your career is important to you, too."

"I have a mortgage; my boys go to a private school. Matt and I don't have huge savings. I can't jeopardize my position, and we'd agreed to keep a low profile." I shook my head, "I swear, sometimes I think you want us to get caught."

Reese let go of my hip, and I sat up. He sat up, too. "I understand why you feel that way. I'm truly sorry. I promise, no more risky games. We both have too much to lose."

"You've made promises before ... you've been sorry before. Your promises and apologies aren't enough this time."

"What am I supposed to say to that? I majorly fucked up. I *am* sorry. I'm sorry I put you in that position, but that's not really the issue, is it?"

I couldn't look at him. "No."

"You're not ready to leave Matt." It was a statement, not a question.

I nodded. "When we were in Atlanta, I was so certain my marriage was over. Matt and I weren't even touching." I stopped before I revealed more details, ashamed of exposing the most intimate aspects of my relationship with Matt. It felt like an extreme violation, an even bigger betrayal than sleeping with Reese. "The bottom line is he doesn't want a divorce. He said he and the boys are a package deal, and he won't let me leave." I looked up and met his eyes. "He claims he still loves me. He's been trying, and he wants me to try. I can't leave him."

Reese took a minute to digest what I told him before asking, "Do you still love him?"

"Not the way I used to, but I care about him. I don't want to hurt him, and underneath all the pain and anger, we're still connected."

His fingers lifted my chin to look him in the eyes. "Have you ever melted into him until you didn't know if it's your heart beating or his?" His voice was low and seductive and his eyes held me as his fingers caressed my cheek and brushed down my neck.

I whispered, "No."

"Does he think of you as his soul mate?"

I looked away. "He doesn't think in those terms."

His fingers ran lightly back up my neck and into my hair. Cupping the back of my head, he drew me into a soft and tender kiss. He murmured against my lips, "You love me more."

I was a heartbeat away from making love to him again. Instead, I shoved against his chest and scooted away. "I've never loved Matt as much I love you, and I don't think I ever can, but I can't be with you anymore."

Reese's game face replaced my lover's. "You once told me our life wasn't some nineteenth century novel. Why are you acting like it is? If I truly am the love of your life, you should be with me. Divorce isn't a taboo any more. I don't give a fuck what he says, he can't make you stay, and he can't keep your boys from you. Look, I found you an attorney. He told me California courts are very favorable towards mothers."

He had to be the most persistent man I had ever met. "Damn it Reese, it's over! It's not going to happen," I snapped. He winced, as if I caused him physical pain. "I'm sorry. I'd give up anything else for you. I'd give up my career and move to New York, but I can't give up my family. The boys and Matt, as a package, are my family."

"Did you know this when I gave you the necklace?"

"I wasn't certain about anything at that point. I knew I didn't want to lose you. After what happened, I was ashamed of how selfish I've been."

I couldn't look at him. It was too hard with my insides splitting open. He put his arms around me. I tried to push him away, but his arms tightened like iron bands. "As long as I know you love me, I'm not letting go. I told you I'm strong enough for the both of us and I am. You don't have to choose between us."

"You make it sound so simple, but I'm the one constantly nauseous with guilt."

"Don't you dare feel guilty because of me. I'm a grown man. I know what I'm doing."

"It's not just what I'm doing to you. Look at what I'm doing to my family. It's as if guilt is literally a living being eating my insides. Can't you understand why we have to end this? I can't split myself in two. This double life is killing me. I am asking, *begging* you to let me go."

He dropped his arms and his chest heaved. "Okay, I'll do what you need." I got up to get dressed, but he stopped me. "Can you stay a while?"

"Are you sure you want me to?"

"I want you with me as long as possible."

I got back in bed and molded against him, wanting to melt into him just as he had said. The rain had stopped and we gazed out the window, watching planes come and go.

After a while he asked, "When you come to New York next month, will you see me? You may feel differently after we've been apart for a while."

"You might feel differently, too."

"I won't. I know I won't … I'll always love you."

"I hope that's not true. We both need to let go."

He put his hand over my mouth, shushing me. "I don't want to talk about it anymore."

We didn't. We spent the rest of the afternoon and evening loving each other, both of us wanting to make the most of what little time we had left.

Chapter 28

The house was dark when I got home. I thought everyone was in bed, but Matt was watching television in the family room with the lights off. I popped my head in the room, not wanting to get close to him. I was afraid he would smell Reese on me.

"Hey, I'm home."

"How was dinner?"

"Uneventful."

"Want to watch a movie with me?"

"Sure, just let me take a shower first."

As I undressed, I swear I could smell Reese on my body. I lifted my arm, inhaled, and told myself it would be the last time I would come home with his scent mingled with my skin. I wanted to believe the hot water washed away his scent and his hold on me. I wanted to come back to Matt physically and spiritually clean. I thought of Mitzy Gaynor singing, *"I'm gonna wash that man right out of my hair... and send him on his way."* If only it were that easy. It made me chuckle. At least something did.

The movie distracted Matt. I was able to lay my head on his lap and let my thoughts stay with Reese. I fell asleep thinking of him, but Matt was the one who carried me to bed. Matt was the one who got in bed beside me, and Matt was the one who I woke up next to in the morning.

Both boys had their last soccer game of the year, and I had volunteered to organize the end-of-year party for Micah's team. The diversions helped me survive the weekend. We loaded into our minivan Saturday morning and left as a family. If I stayed with Reese, days like this would never happen again. I gave out a sigh of relief. I had actually ended the affair without Matt finding out; no one was murdered in the heat of passion; no one lost his job; nothing cataclysmic happened. Life went on as if my time with Reese had never occurred.

Jason's team lost. Micah's team won, and he scored two goals. He bounced up and down for the rest of the day. Matt was a very proud daddy. He took the boys to a movie while I went to the local pizza parlor to set up the team party with Tracy Roberts.

"Hey Susan, great game today! Micah must be very excited."

"I think Matt is more excited than Micah."

"Men and their boys," she joked.

We chatted as we hung a banner and streamers and set out party favors. She told me her husband, John, quit his job and was now a stay home dad.

"Wow. So how is it with him home?"

"Honestly, I wasn't too sure about it when he first suggested quitting. I didn't like the idea of doing without his income, but with both of us working it felt like we were always running. I didn't have time for him. He didn't have time for me. Know what I mean?"

"I do." It's the way Matt and I had been for years. However, Matt staying home would not be a solution for our marriage. He would never give up his work. Besides, he had no homemaker skills, and I was too picky about how I liked things done in the house.

"So it's been great. I can work late and focus without worrying about picking up kids or starting dinner. John is doing all the cooking and all the laundry. Neither one of us has been exhausted after our kids have gone to bed." She smiled and blushed slightly. Tracy was obviously enjoying a renewed sex life. Seeing another couple find a solution to their marital problems gave me hope for my own.

"It sounds great."

"It has its downside. Last week I ended up with all grey underwear. Can you believe he washed my lingerie with jeans?"

We both laughed. "What is it about men and laundry? I guess there are some things we just have to do ourselves," I said.

"Got that right, Sister. You travel a lot don't you?"

"Yeah."

"It must be nice. I would love to get away sometimes."

"Traveling has its perks." I thought of Reese and a pang rippled in my chest.

"So are you like that guy in that novel, *Up in the Air*?" The guy in the novel had an affair with a married woman. I wasn't sure what she was asking. "You know, do you have the gold cards and platinum memberships?"

My pulse normalized, and I laughed. "Oh, yeah, but it's not as exciting as it sounds."

"Never is." She laughed too and asked, "Hey, you want a beer? Bet we could get away with it before everyone shows up."

She was probably a bit of a party girl when she was younger. It was pleasant talking to Tracy, but I couldn't see her being more than an acquaintance. We were both moms and executives in large companies, but other than that, we didn't have too much in common.

"Susan, this was fun. We should have a girls' night sometime."

"We definitely should," I agreed even though I was almost certain we never would.

"I belong to an executive women's networking group for VPs and higher. We get together once a month. The meeting part can be deathly dull, but afterwards we go out for drinks. It's fun. Anyway, there's a meeting next week. Would you like to come?"

"I may be in Los Angeles, but I'll let you know."

What was wrong with me? Tracy was a nice, normal woman. Why couldn't we be friends? I had to make an effort, or I'd never have female friends. I resolved to follow up with Tracy. If I couldn't make the December meeting, I'd go the January event.

Sunday was harder to get through. There were no soccer games or team parties to distract me. Matt kept looking at me with his big blue eyes and "tried to make an effort," which only made me feel more guilty. More than anything, I wanted to be left alone. I told him I had to get some work done, which wasn't a lie. I checked my e-mail. There were a few from Reese, but they were all work related. I couldn't focus.

My stomach churned and my throat felt constricted. I wanted to escape my body and fly away, float in oblivion. I wanted to be free of the pain and the anxiety. I wanted to feel normal, not even necessarily happy; I would settle for peaceful. I couldn't remember the last perfectly peaceful day I'd had. I was happy with Reese, but never peaceful. There was always a varying quantity of anxiety fluttering around my stomach, and guilt, always guilt.

Reese was more than under my skin. I'd let him in the core of my being. I felt so entwined with him that I didn't know how to extricate him. Yet, I had to flush him out of my system and be free of him. I wanted to feel clean again. I tried soaking in a hot bath, but the boys kept banging on the door.

"Mom, I need to go to the bathroom," Jason declared.

"Use the other bathroom."

"What?"

"Use the other bathroom!"

Next, it was Micah. "Mom, Jason won't get out of my room."

"Micah, come on. He just wants to play with you."

"He's bugging me."

"Fine. Tell him I said to leave you alone."

Then Jason was back. "Mom, Micah punched me."

"What did you do to him?"

"Nothing."

"Tell him to come here."

A few minutes later I heard them screaming at each other. I got out of the tub and yelled at Matt, "Matt, please! I'm trying to take a bath."

Matt took care of it, but then he was knocking on the door. "Susan, sorry, but would you like me to start dinner?" Nice hint that he was getting hungry. Matt was a terrible cook. Why would I want him to start dinner? I gave up and got out of the bathtub.

I cooked a big dinner that night, and the boys were happy. Matt was quiet. I'm sure he knew something was wrong. He didn't ask, but he didn't try to touch me either, which was fine with me. I didn't want his touch, and I didn't want to hurt him with a rebuff.

Monday and Tuesday were even harder than Sunday. Reese and I had to discuss business and be on conference calls together. Hearing his voice was excruciating. It made my chest throb, and I had struggled to keep my voice steady. When I spoke to him, our conversations were stilted, but professional with no hint of double meanings.

I wanted to know how he was doing, but I didn't dare ask. I wanted to call him and tell him I'd changed my mind, but I didn't.

Wednesday I went to Boston, irrationally hoping he would throw caution to the wind and be there. He didn't. Being in the hotel room by myself, loneliness engulfed me. It was suffocating and a black hole in my heart threatened to suck me in. I almost called him, but called Matt instead.

Matt wasn't much of a talker in person. He was even worse on the phone. I indulged in a good cry and a hot shower.

On Thursday, the meeting was a success. We would have signatures on our first contract in a matter of weeks. I was elated and knew Reese would be ecstatic. I started to call him, but hung up before he answered. Instead, I sent him an e-mail from my Blackberry.

He sent me a one-word response: *Congrats.* That was it.

My heart was bleeding, and unsure I could survive without him, I seriously questioned my decision. How could I live when I couldn't breathe? When I got to the airport, I found a flight to New York that boarded in thirty minutes. I went so far as to get in line at the flight desk. My saner self got on the plane to San Francisco.

On Friday, I sent him an e-mail: *Friendly reminder, I will be on vacation next week. If you need me to reach me, call my personal cell.*

He e-mailed me back: *I'll be at my parent's house.* **Call my cell if you need me.**

I did need him, but I wouldn't call. He and I needed time and space. I tried not to think about him. It was impossible when my eyes hungered for the sight of him; my body ached for his touch; my tongue salivated for the taste of his skin, and every cell in my body craved him. I wanted to hear his voice and feel his warmth. I missed his scent. I missed him.

When I woke up Saturday morning, sunlight shined through the slates of the blinds. I opened them and let the sun in. I'd made it through a whole week without breaking.

The boys had the week off for Thanksgiving and Matt decided to take the week off, too. We needed the time to be a family. We watched movies, went bowling, and played games. The boys helped me make pies for Thanksgiving, and we spent the big day at Matt's parents' house.

I tried to participate fully, but it was hard. I floated and drifted through the week playing my part in the family events, but rarely being totally present. I didn't cry once, which was positive. One eye guided me through the motions of the day. I could play games with the boys, cook without burning food, and drive without accident. All the while, my other eye was turned inward, only seeing him, only wanting to see him. In rare moments I caught myself not thinking about him and hoped those moments would become more frequent.

The Friday after Thanksgiving, I received the official invitation for the company holiday party. This was the first year I'd had an important enough title to make the guest list. It was a black tie event and spouses were invited. I didn't think Matt would want to go. He didn't like parties, and I had never known him to wear a tuxedo, not even for our wedding.

He floored me when he announced, "I'll ask my mom to watch the boys for us."

"You want to go?"

"The invitation is to both of us."

It was a sweet gesture, and I tried to give him an easy out. "Honey, I appreciate the offer. I really do, but you don't have to go. I'm fine going by myself."

"Don't you want me to be your date?"

I most emphatically did not want him to be my date. The idea of Reese and Matt being in the same room was beyond terrifying. Besides, Reese expected me in New York sans Matt.

"Don't be silly. I'd love to show off my husband, but I know how uncomfortable you are with strangers. I'll have to be working the room. It won't upset me or hurt my feelings if you don't go. It's really okay."

"Your company should know you have a husband."

What did he mean by that comment? "They know."

"I've never met anyone."

"It's rather difficult when the company is based in New York."

"So, I'll go."

I gave him my last argument, "It's a black tie event. You'll need a tux."

"I'll rent one."

"You cannot wear a rented tux."

Matt gave me a befuddled look. "Why not?"

I pictured Reese decked out in impeccably tailored Armani, complemented with designer shoes. The image of Matt showing up in an ill-fitting rented tuxedo made me cringe. I envisioned some horrible prom look with lines at the bottom of the pant legs indicating where the hem had been for previous renters. Irrational and vain as it was, I wanted Matt looking his best when I introduced him to Reese.

After I thought about it, it didn't seem like such a bad idea. Matt may not be quite as handsome as Reese, but he was undeniably a bright and attractive man. It might be good for everyone at work to see my husband wasn't second rate. Maybe the gossip would stop.

"Matt, I know for a fact everyone will be wearing designer clothes. I'll buy you a tux."

"That's ridiculous for one night."

"It's not ridiculous. Maybe you'll be inspired to take me somewhere if you have the clothes," I teased. He looked at me with exasperated eyes, and I countered with my biggest puppy dog eyes. "Honey, please …." He shook his head in defeat. I smiled and pecked him on the cheek. "I'll take you to Saks' Men Store tomorrow and we'll get you a tuxedo and then you can help me pick out a dress."

"I hate shopping."

"Fine, we'll get your tux and then you can take a cable car to the Wharf while I find a dress. We can go to Max's for lunch."

"Let's bring the boys. The ice skating rink should be set up on Union Square."

Lord, he was exasperating sometimes. Shopping with the boys for Matt's black tie attire was not my idea of a good time. He had compromised, so I did too. "Okay."

I'd hoped Matt and I would grow closer over the course of the week, but we didn't. The drama of the past weeks had exhausted Matt's quiet soul. We slipped back into old habits and were much as we had been just before I met Reese. Matt didn't ignore me. The tension had subsided, but the passion that had flared a few weeks ago had already petered out. It worried me.

Spending time with the boys reinforced why I had to stick with my decision. If Matt and I had split, I wouldn't have had this amount of time with them. All week it was, "Mom, are you coming?" I always went. It was a good policy. I was afraid of being by myself. I was afraid of loneliness overcoming my reason and succumbing to my desire to call Reese. More than anything else being with the boys was the most therapeutic.

We went to church on Sunday. Not surprisingly, the sermon was about giving thanks, most specifically about giving thanks for the love of our families and the love of God. Listening to Reverend Jim's words, my heart filled with love for my family. I looked at my husband. Matt wore a contemplative expression. What was he thinking? His wide blue eyes met mine, and he squeezed my hand. Matt and the boys were my family, as a package.

Reese's face flashed in my mind. My heart rippled with pain, and the guilt beast fed ravenously on my stomach. There wasn't going to be any easy fix. I was still desperately and fervently in love with him. I had to find a way to stay strong for my family. During silent prayer, I dropped to my knees and silently begged for God's help.

Dear God, I have sinned against you and my husband. Please, forgive me and help me find the strength to resist future temptation. Help me let go of the love I have for another man and love only my husband. Give me the strength to do your bidding.

I hoped God was listening.

Matt had a soccer game that day. I hadn't watched him play in a while and offered to go.

"Are you sure you want to watch another f-ing game?" he quietly joked.

I cringed, ashamed of how I'd hurt him. "Sorry I said that. I like watching you play."

"I'll score a goal for you," he offered with a wink.

I remembered the first time I had watched him play. I had dragged Serena with me, wanting to show off my new crush. Serena had joked about how cute he was and wanted to know if there were any other hotties hiding in the biology lab. I don't remember much about the game except Matt scoring a goal and being powerfully attracted to his focus, his competitiveness, his aggression ... his maleness. As soon as the ball hit the net, he had turned to see if I'd been watching. Matt had smiled with his eyes crinkled up. I had blown him a kiss, but really had wanted to run up and jump his bones.

I still get a little turned on whenever he scores. I should start watching him play more.

Chapter 29

Monday morning I was back at work. I hadn't heard Reese's voice in over a week and was jittery knowing we would be interacting later in the day. I intensely wanted to know how he was handling everything. Was I the only one struggling to let go? Was he getting over me? If that were the case, would it be easier for me to move on?

We exchanged e-mails, but they were strictly work related. I listened to Reese lead a two-hour conference call, but couldn't decipher anything. I legitimately had to talk to him about issues that required his attention; after all, he was still my boss. I looked up his on-line calendar and sent a meeting invitation for the half hour he had open at eleven. He accepted, and I called his office at the appointed time.

Anne put me on hold and then got back on the phone, "Susan, I'm sorry, Reese is going to be a while. He wants to know if you're available at three-thirty."

"Eastern time?" *Damn.* I already had an anxiety-filled morning waiting for this time.

"Pacific. He actually has an opening earlier. Do you want me to check if he'll take your call in an hour?" she asked.

Knowing Reese, he wanted to talk privately. My guess was he would be calling me from his apartment. There was no point for Anne to attempt to schedule me earlier. Reese would decline. "No, three-thirty is fine. Please, let him know I'll be in my office."

"So, you two are back to late calls?"

"Reese is busy. I catch him when I can."

"Yes, you certainly do."

I didn't like her tone, but said nothing. There was no point.

Wanting to minimize my contact with him, I carefully reviewed my list and tried to anticipate anything that might come up later in the week. I started shaking when the meeting reminder popped up on my laptop screen. I hit the snooze twice, each time my stomach a little queasier. At exactly three-thirty, Reese's personal cell number lit up my caller id.

"This is Susan," I squeaked.

"Hi, it's me. How are you?" he asked with his voice seductively silky.

I didn't answer the question. Instead, I launched into my laundry list. Reese patiently and calmly talked through each item. When I was done, he asked, "Anything else?"

"No, that's it. I'll let you go," I said with a sigh.

"Please, don't hang up. I want to talk to you," he said. I couldn't answer. "Susan, are you still there?"

"Yes," I whispered.

"You never answered my question, *how are you?*"

"I'm fine."

"You sound far from fine to me."

I focused on keeping my voice steady. "If you must know, the last two weeks have been extremely difficult." I couldn't stop from asking, "How've you been?"

"Do you really want to know?"

I don't know. "Yes."

"At first, I couldn't sleep or eat. I couldn't stop thinking about you, about us together. Just breathing was hard. I tossed in bed every night hoping you would show up on my doorstep, regretting your decision. The night you were in Boston, I waited by my phone expecting you to call, but you didn't. Afterwards, I felt used and was furious for a day or two. I was so angry I could barely bring myself to congratulate you when you e-mailed me about the meeting."

"Reese, I'm sorry to have hurt you. Please, don't hate me."

"I'm much better now. I don't hate you, and I'm not angry anymore."

He didn't sound urgent, or horribly pained. Something had changed. He seemed at peace with everything. Maybe someday I would be, too. I got my answer.

"I'm glad to hear you're doing well and please, don't worry about me. I won't bother you more than is necessary for business. I should get back to work."

"Not yet. I want to tell you why I'm better."

I wasn't sure I wanted to know, but my curiosity won out. "Okay, tell me."

"I hadn't prayed in a long time, but I actually got on my knees. I was convinced God was punishing me. Proverbs 6:32: *He who commits adultery with a woman is void of understanding. He who does it destroys his own soul.* I felt destroyed, so I went to confession. Afterwards I should've been more at peace, but I wasn't. All I could think about was looking into your eyes and having your love reach so far into me that we became one. I'll never be whole again without you, and I know with dead certainty neither will you.

"I remembered a verse from Corinthians and had an epiphany. It says *'But now hope, faith and love remain—these three. The greatest of these is love.'* The Bible also says God is love. I can't believe God would punish me for loving you. Our suffering comes from denying our love, which is a gift. We're meant to be together and time won't alter our bond."

His voice remained silky smooth and calm all through his narration. So this was his new strategy? Unbelievable, using the Bible as evidence in favor of adultery.

"That was a very pretty speech. How long did you rehearse it?"

"Ouch! I thought it sounded more extemporaneous."

I chuckled and criticized ungenerously, "You might be good in front of a crowd but your acting lacks technique."

He chuckled too and taunted, seemingly unperturbed, "You are being a stinker. I'm getting to you. I can tell." I didn't respond and he continued in soft, loving tones, "Try not to be so cynical. What difference does it make if I planned what I had to say? It's still true."

"Why are you telling me this? It's doesn't change anything."

"I think it does. You can try to deny your love for me, but you won't be able to forever. It's only a matter of time and you'll come back to me. It may be next week, or it could be a year from now, but you won't be able to stay away. I can wait."

His audacity dumbfounded me. Underneath his gentle and loving voice was steely determination, so quintessential Reese.

"Wow! You're not worried about what I've said, or how I feel, or what I think?"

"No, I worry about those things. I want to know what you think."

"I think you're the cockiest, most persistent man I've ever met. Don't you ever give up?"

He laughed softly and said, "If I didn't know how much you love me, then I would; I almost did. Have you been happier or more peaceful without me? Is your marriage any better?"

"No, but there hasn't been enough time. Besides, it has nothing to do with how much you love me or I love you. I'm going to do the right thing and keep my family together," I answered with as much vehemence as I could muster.

"That's just it. I don't think you're doing the right thing," he argued. "I know how lonely you were, and I honestly think your marriage drowns you. If fading out of your life were the best thing for you, I'd do it. I'd do it in a heartbeat, but I don't think it's the answer. It'll only be a matter of time before you—"

"Enough," I said, cutting him off. "I know where you are going with this." Damn it, I started to cry again.

"I know the guilt is eating you alive. You have to stop blaming yourself for everything. Even if you and I hadn't met, what condition would your marriage be in today?"

"Not good, but—"

He pressed his advantage. "I think you should see a therapist to help you deal with all of this. I really think it'll help."

Gee, where have I heard that before? Matt and Reese each thought a therapist would advance their agendas. I was tempted to tell him that Matt wanted me to see a professional, too.

"Don't tell me. You already found me a therapist?"

"I have a short list for you."

"Of course you do."

He ignored my tone and stayed focused on his objective. "Will you try to see someone?"

Although his presumption and confidence irritated me, I desperately needed to confide in someone or I'd explode. "Yes. I'll make an appointment."

"Thank you." He let out a sigh of relief. "By the way, when are you due in New York?"

"A week from Friday."

"Have dinner with me." It was more of a statement than a question.

I cringed. "Matt will be with me." There was dead silence on the other end of the phone. Reese had been pumped and ready for this call. I imagined him deflating like a popped balloon. "I know it'll be awkward. I'm sorry. He insisted on coming."

"I guess I'll finally meet Mr. Sinclair." He sounded ruffled for the first time since he'd called. "You realize we'll be seated at the same table? Mobile Banking will have its own table."

"Crap."

"I think *fuck* is a better word for this occasion."

"Fuck, fuck, fuck!"

"That's right, Love. It feels good to say it sometimes."

I had to take a couple deep breaths to keep myself from panicking. "Reese, I don't want the two of you on the same coast, let alone across a table from each other."

"I guess seeing you alone won't be possible."

"No, it's still doable. He's leaving Sunday morning, but I'm staying through Monday and possibly Tuesday, depending on Bank of Boston."

"Then, I'll plan on spending Sunday with you," he declared, his confidence rebounding.

"I'll meet you for brunch, that's it. We're not meeting at your apartment or my hotel."

"Don't you trust yourself?"

"I trust myself. I don't trust you."

He conceded with a laugh, "Fair enough, my little spitfire."

"I'm not your 'little' anything."

"Okay, Sparky," he said in the same seductive voice he used when he called me his love.

I'd had enough of Reese's game playing. "I have to get back to work."

"Wait! Don't hang up," he interjected with humor still in his voice. "Number 116."

"What does that mean?"

He chuckled and teased, "You'll figure it out. And Susan ..."

"Yes?"

"I love you," he said in the softest, most genuine voice imaginable. I almost melted, but caught myself just before I reciprocated the sentiment.

After he hung up, it took me all of thirty seconds to decipher *116* was a sonnet. I didn't need to get down my Complete Works. I had committed it to memory years ago. It began, "*Let not the marriage of true minds, Admit impediments, love is not love, Which alters when it alteration finds...*" He was telling me that he would never give up. "*Love alters not with his brief hours and week, But bears it out even to the edge of doom.*"

Reese, Reese, Reese ... what am I going to do with you? If I didn't love him so deeply and completely, I would probably be freaked out by his unrelenting tenacity. His will power and determination were qualities I had found attractive. His self-assurance turned me on. It was an integral part of who he was and the reason why he was successful. Those qualities weren't as attractive when he was opposing my desires. I kept thinking about the line, "*That looks on tempests and is never shaken.*" It summed up his personality to me. Once he had determined on something, there was no shaking him from his "*ever fixed mark.*" I didn't know how to combat him. He would keep coming at me from different angles until he cornered me.

Over the next week, Reese played games with me. He used silky, seductive tones juxtaposed with facetious remarks and flirtatious double-entendres to keep me off balance. He kept his tone light and playful, always teasing. Sometimes he would text me a number. The number was always a sonnet he wanted me to read. The covert messages were how much he missed me, and the durability of his love.

My strategy was to dodge and weave. In the meantime, he was winning. The new game was fueled by sexual energy. It wound me up, pulling me out of my funk. It was hard to be sad while engaged in a game of cat and mouse.

Chapter 30

Exactly one week after Reese encouraged me to see a psychiatrist, I found myself waiting in Dr. Helen Morgan's reception room. I trusted Reese had thoroughly researched the doctors on his list. The other doctors were men, and God knows I didn't need another man in my life. Besides, a woman's perspective would be appreciated.

Knowing Reese, he would play it cool at the party, but would hit me with a full court press as soon as Matt left for California. I had to be prepared mentally and emotionally for whatever he tried. Since I wasn't in an abusive situation, I was confident any therapist would reinforce my decision to stay with Matt.

"Susan Sinclair?"

"Yes?"

"The doctor is ready to see you."

The receptionist showed me into the doctor's office. It wasn't what I'd expected. There were no couches to lie on or Rorschach prints on the wall. The office reminded me of my professors' offices in college.

The woman who sat in the chair facing me was not what I expected either. Dr. Morgan looked old enough to be my grandmother. I wished she were younger. The elderly looking woman intimidated me. How would I be able to tell her about my problems without dying of embarrassment?

She stood. "Hello, Susan. I'm Dr. Morgan." She reached out and shook my hand.

"It's nice to meet you."

Dr. Morgan smiled and said, "Please, sit down."

We both sat, and I crossed my legs looking expectantly at her. "I'm sorry. I'm a little nervous. I've never seen a therapist before, so I don't know what to expect."

"It's a natural response. Most people are nervous on their first visit. Why don't we start with why you decided to make an appointment?"

"Well, it's rather difficult to talk about," I replied already shaking with emotion.

"I imagine it is must be, or you wouldn't be here." She looked compassionately at me and waited.

"I've done something terrible, and I want to talk someone about it," I admitted, determined not to let tears run down my cheeks.

"Our conversations are confidential. I'm not here to judge you. I'm here to listen and help you come to terms with whatever it is."

"Thank you."

"Now, would you like to start by telling me what terrible thing you've done?"

"I've committed adultery with my boss." Looking down at my shoes, I felt like a four year old confessing a wrongdoing and prepared myself for her admonishment.

Dr. Morgan gave no reproof. Whatever she thought or felt about what I'd done was well hidden from me. "I see. Are you still seeing this other person?"

"No, I broke things off a few weeks ago, but he still wants to see me."

"Is he threatening you with your job?"

"No, but he has me confused. I don't know what the right thing to do is anymore."

"Well, let's start at the beginning, shall we? I think it would be helpful to understand how you found yourself in this situation. When did it start?"

"Last summer."

She leaned back in her chair. "Tell me about it."

Memories of the last six months poured out of me. For most of the session, I recounted the loneliness I had experienced, meeting Reese, and trying to save my marriage. She listened patiently, and occasionally nodded her head or interjected a question.

Dr. Morgan stopped me toward the end of the hour. "We're almost out of time. I have a few questions and observations before you go." She leaned forward and looked at me intently.

I exhaled slowly, apprehensive, but ready to hear her advice.

She smiled at me but seemed sad. She made *me* sad, and I braced for her prognosis. "First, it appears to me your relationship with Reese is more than a temporary fling. You seem genuinely in love with him."

"Yes. I love him more than I can tell you." The confession made my heart throb painfully with longing for him.

"I think you experienced depression because your marriage was no longer fulfilling. I question whether you still love your husband. Do you love Matt?"

She was sympathetic and nonjudgmental, her question legitimate, so I tried to answer truthfully. "I care about him. I suppose I love him as I would an old friend, but I'm not in love with him. I'm trying." I had to choke back tears. It was odd to be sharing intimate details of my heart with a complete stranger. I didn't want to cry in front of her, too.

"What has stopped you from leaving your marriage? Is it because you are afraid Reese won't want you if you're single?"

"Oh, no. Reese wants to marry me. He's quite adamant. He thinks we are more than soul mates. He believes our souls have become irrevocably joined."

"And what do you think?"

"I think people can intensely connect, but it doesn't mean we are united for life. I don't think any relationship is destined to last forever."

"Not any? Not even relationships between parents and children?"

"Not even with parents and children. Maybe that's why it frightens me so much to lose my boys." I felt callous confessing my personal philosophy, but it was what I truly believed.

"Interesting …." I didn't like the way she said that word. I wasn't a lab rat. "And why is it you've stayed with Matt?"

"I don't know if there is any one reason. I cling to different things at different times. Sometimes it's because I think I still love him. Other times, because it's morally the right thing to do. Maybe God will forgive me if I stay and make things right. I'm scared of what divorce will do to my boys. I don't want them growing up in a broken home. Starting my life over scares the hell out of me. I guess all of the above."

I expected her to ask more about my reasons, but she glanced at her notes and asked, "You said earlier you weren't sure 'what the right thing to do is anymore.' Can you elaborate?"

"I don't know if the right thing is to keep my family intact despite my loving someone else. I worry about what it will do to everyone long term. Will I make everyone miserable? Some day when the boys are grown, will I inevitably walk out? On the other hand, I can't shake the belief that leaving my husband for another man is fundamentally wrong. I already feel morally depraved. What if this is just a phase and I can fall in love with Matt again?"

"I want you to think about a few things before we meet again," she said.

I had hoped she would give an unequivocal answer, something concrete. All I had done the last couple weeks was think. Not knowing what else to say, I nodded.

"First, I want us to explore more deeply the reasons for your loneliness. Second, your infidelity is a symptom of your broken marriage, a primeval response to your loneliness, not the cause. Everyone needs love. If you left your husband, it would not be for another man. It would be because your marriage has become untenable, no longer giving you the emotional connection necessary to function healthily and causing acute emotional distress. Lastly, children do better in homes where their parents have a happy, loving relationship. Just think about these things."

I left without the guidance I'd hoped for, but feeling less guilty about my affair and love for Reese. It was a lot to consider. As I drove home from the appointment, my mind flew a hundred miles an hour. Luckily, I didn't have an accident.

I already had thought a lot about why I'd been lonely. I knew children had healthier upbringings in homes where their parents were happy and loving. Wasn't that why I had made the appointment? I wanted to be happy with Matt and sought a cure that didn't involve divorce. The part about everyone needing love gave me pause.

My guilt stemmed from the act of betrayal. Whether Matt was aware of it or not, I'd injured Matt and our family unit. For that, I was truly sorry, but I couldn't be sorry for the act of loving Reese. He gave me what Matt couldn't.

I had vowed always to love Matt. I broke that vow before I broke others. Maybe it was time to end the nauseating vacillation; accept that years ago I'd stopped loving Matt the way a wife should love her husband. I loved him because he was a good person and a good father. I cared about him, but I had never loved him with the passion and intense longing I had for Reese.

I never could. I felt guilty for never having loved Matt the way I should have, the way he deserved. He never loved me that way either. Yet, we both needed love.

Was staying fair to either one of us? Even if I fell in love with Matt again, would it be enough? Shouldn't he be given the chance to find the kind of love Reese and I shared?

When I got home, I sat in my car for a while thinking about Reese, how much we loved each other. Then, it hit me with numbing clarity he knew exactly what the outcome would be when he persuaded me to see a therapist. The visit had tipped the scales heavily in his favor. He had set me up. When Reese really wanted something, his actions were always well calculated.

It infuriated me how easily I had succumbed. The more I thought about it the angrier I became. I wasn't ready to give up on my marriage. I had made that abundantly clear, but Reese pushed me with the same single-ness of purpose he applied to advancing his career. I could see him writing down his goals: 1) Become CEO of Global Security. 2) Close Susan Sinclair.

The mind games had to stop. He knew how to push all of my buttons. My anger gave me courage to take action. I slammed the car door, stomped into my office, and called his home number. It took a few rings before he answered.

"Hello, Love. What a pleasant surprise."

"Maybe not so pleasant," I said, trying to stay under control.

"What's going on?"

"I've got something to say and this time you'd better be listening closely." My restraint was already slipping.

"I'm listening."

"I didn't like the therapist and I'm not going back."

"Sweetheart, why are you so upset? What happened?"

"You know exactly what happened; you planned it. I don't appreciate being manipulated, and I'm done game playing. I'm furious that you refuse to respect my wishes!"

"Whoa, Sweetheart, calm down."

"I WILL NOT CALM DOWN. YOU PISS ME OFF. Here's the deal: no more personal calls, no more calling me 'Love' or 'Sweetheart', no more texting me fucking sonnets to look up. I'm *done*. And by the way, in case you haven't figured it out, BRUNCH IS OFF."

"Anything else?" Reese asked in an infuriatingly relaxed voice.

"Yeah, one more thing. This time if you don't respect my wishes, I guarantee you'll regret it."

"What are you going to do? File a harassment case?" He had the nerve to laugh at me.

"No, but don't be surprised if a resignation letter lands on your desk." I managed to get that out in a calm voice. I wasn't fooling around. I meant it.

Reese stopped laughing. "Love, please. I'm sorry. I know I've been toying with you, but you liked it. Admit it. It turned you on."

"So what? All it proves is you know how to push my buttons."

"Sweetheart, please … I really don't know what Dr. Morgan told you."

"How did you know I saw Dr. Morgan?"

"You told me."

"No, I didn't."

"Really? I'm sure you did."

"Bullshit. I *know* I didn't."

"I guess I just assumed you'd want to see a woman."

"Funny. She was the only woman on the list. How do you know her?"

"I don't."

"Stop fucking with me! How do you know her?"

"I don't personally know her! I admit I read her book and some of her articles." He paused before he confessed, "I was pretty sure she'd advise you to leave Matt. In fairness, I had to do something sitting home by myself all those weekends when you were with him."

His last dig hurt. I pushed through the tears. "What was her book about?"

"Susan, it doesn't matter."

"Damn it, Reese, if you won't tell me, I'll just Google it."

"OKAY." He paused, then said, "It was about the effect of loneliness on couples when one spouse has a greater need of emotional connection. You and Matt fit the description of a textbook mismatch."

"And you and I seemed like the perfect match?"

"Yes, damn it … Susan, please, tell me what she said."

"You're actually frightening me."

"You have got to be fucking kidding."

My anger was spent. He'd crossed the line, and I was done, done, done with him. "I loved you and I almost left my husband for you, but I don't want to be with you. Even if I were single, I wouldn't want to be with you. You tried to manipulate me. You refused to respect my wishes. I can't love someone I don't trust, and I don't trust you. I'm staying with Matt. Don't ever call me again unless it's about business."

"Listen to me. I love—"

I hung up on him. Reese called me back.

"DON'T YOU FUCKING HANG UP ON ME. Baby, I've got something to say too! You were like a starving woman when I met you. How many times have I held you while you cried because of *him*? I loved you. I gave you attention. I bought you gifts. I gave you everything I have to give. I did everything I could think of to make you happy. I wanted to marry you, for Christ's sake! You have no fucking idea what it's been like for me

… waking up in the middle of the night wanting you, needing you, but knowing you were in another man's bed; knowing he could never give you what I give you … for fuck's sake, knowing he wasn't *capable* of giving you what you need. Waking up and not knowing if he had his dick in you. It makes me fucking crazy! You don't appreciate what I was willing to give up for you. Well, I'm done being used. This is it. If you walk away now, I won't be here three months from now when you're lonely again."

"You should remember that 'other man' you referenced is my husband! I love Matt—"

"I DON'T WANT TO FUCKING HEAR IT." I heard air rushing by, a crash and the phone went dead. Reese must have thrown the phone against the wall.

My heart pounded and my body shook. I had to calm down before Matt and the boys got home. I took a few deep breaths. Then, I unplugged my office phone and turned off my cell. I finally and conclusively ended things with Reese. This was my third attempt in three weeks. The third time had to be the charm.

I wished with all my being I could purge him out of my system. No matter how angry or hurt I was, he still occupied my heart. Reese was wrong about one thing. I did appreciate what he went through and what he was willing to do for me. It was part of why I couldn't see him anymore, why I couldn't stop loving him. I had to leave Global Security. It was my only hope of being completely free of him.

That night after the boys went to bed, I told Matt we really needed to talk. He followed me to our bedroom and closed the door.

"Susan, are you okay?"

"Not really. I've been thinking about things, and I saw a therapist this afternoon. She inadvertently helped me make a big decision."

Matt's eyes moistened and his brows furrowed. "I thought we were doing better."

"We are. Don't worry, I don't want a divorce."

Matt exhaled loudly and dropped to the bed. "You scared me. I thought that's why you wanted to talk."

"No, I'm sorry." I took his hand and gave it a squeeze. "Matt, you were right about something. I should quit my job."

"You serious?"

"Dead serious. I need a job that doesn't require constant overnight travel. I think I've been using work as an escape from our problems, but I just made things worse."

He squeezed my hand. "We want you home, you know."

"I know. There has to be a decent position in Silicon Valley for someone with my experience. What do you think?"

Genuine happiness shined from his eyes. "It tells me you really are committed to making our marriage work. Thank you." He kissed me, and then asked, "How soon?"

"If I stay through the end of the year, I'll get my bonus. It makes sense to finish out the year. I thought I would resign while I'm in New York next week. I'd like to do it in person." I was actually afraid Reese wouldn't accept my resignation. It would be safer to resign to Joe.

"Honey, I can't tell you how happy this makes me."

"I'm glad." I smiled at him. He really was one of the good guys. "Matt, will you do something for me? Will you look into my eyes and tell me you love me?"

He took my face in his hands and said tenderly, "I love you."

We made love for the first time in almost a month. It wasn't fire and passion, but it didn't have to be. It was enough that he wanted to be with me, and I wanted to be with him. If I couldn't have passion, I'd settle for contentment. Who knew if contentment was the most I could hope for had Reese and I been married thirteen years? Maybe, at the end of the day, contentment was the most anyone should expect after so many years of marriage.

The next morning I updated my resume and composed a resignation letter before I lost my nerve. I cited "family obligations" as my motive and used all the other "regrettable" clichés.

Once that was done, I put together a list of things I wanted to wrap up before leaving. After all the years with Global Security, I didn't want to leave on bad terms. Bank of Boston was a problem. They were ready to move. I was expected to be there for the signing and then take the key players to a lavish dinner as a "thank you for your business." I really wanted to be the one who picked up the first contract for Mobile Banking, but Reese was also expected to be there. It would be wise to bow out.

Reese got my message loud and clear. There were no after hour calls, no text messages, nothing inappropriate. We stuck to e-mail as much as possible. The few times I had to speak to him, he was ice cold. Even co-workers noticed his brusque comments whenever I said something on a conference call. It was embarrassing. Overnight, I had gone from his obvious favorite to the despised one. I'm sure the gossipmongers enjoyed the entertainment.

At least I wouldn't have to worry about him in New York. I didn't want to talk to him, and he didn't seem to want to talk to me. In a couple weeks, he would be completely out of my day-to-day life. If I were lucky, he'd be out of my heart by spring.

Chapter 31

E arly Friday morning Matt and I left for the airport together. After being accustomed to traveling solo, it was a bit disorienting to have Matt with me. Getting through security was routine for me, but Matt was sent back because he didn't take off his belt and then he left his cell phone in his pocket. I didn't think he was ever going to get through. Our plan was to arrive in New York early enough to have a nice dinner and walk around Time's Square at night. The next day we would Christmas shop, and I would have my hair styled for the party.

As a treat, I used my frequent flier points and upgraded us to first class. Matt was impressed and seemed genuinely excited about going to New York. I remembered what he'd said about not feeling appreciated. I looked at him seated next to me. He may have aged a bit, so had I for that matter, but he was still a cutie. He didn't like parties. He didn't necessarily like traveling. He didn't like leaving the boys. Despite all of that, he was on an airplane, traveling across the country to go to a party with me. He was a good guy.

He caught me eyeing him and asked, "What?"

"I was just thinking I'm lucky to have you for my husband."

He smiled happily and put his arm around me. He didn't leave it there for long, but it didn't upset me. It was enough that he was with me.

The closer we got to New York, the more jumpy I became. I hadn't laid eyes on Reese for almost a month. The last time I saw him was in the hotel room at the Marriott. We were both a bit of a mess that night. Now we weren't even on cordial terms. I worried Reese would make some caustic remark or be so unpleasant it would prompt Matt to be suspicious of my reasons for quitting. I never told Matt much about Reese. I always maintained I had no problems with my "new" boss and left it at that.

My anger had subsided. I was still in love with him and it hurt. The old longing thumped in my chest just knowing time moved me closer to him. If only I could turn off my love as easily as turning off a water faucet. It hit me in waves at unexpected moments. I was terrified of slipping in front of Matt and spent most of the first leg of our flight plotting a game plan while Matt dozed beside me.

When we landed in Chicago, I checked my messages. There was one from Reese. "Please, call my personal cell when you get a chance." He didn't sound angry or bitter, but he wanted me to call his personal cell. Not the office or his Blackberry. *Crap.* I told Matt I had to use the ladies room, found an empty gate, and ducked behind the flight desk.

I tried to keep my voice casual when he answered. "Hi, it's me. What's up?"

"Thanks for calling. I need to talk to you. Where are you?"

"I'm at O'Hare on a layover. I told Matt I was going to the ladies' room, but—"

"Before you say anything, give me one minute to apologize."

"Fine, one minute."

"What I did was manipulative and inexcusable. My only defense is I love you. I'd convinced myself I was acting in your best interest but I wasn't. I was fighting to keep you. I'm sorry. I'm truly sorry. I've been an asshole this week, and I'm sorry for that too. It's the first time I've ever been dumped and you did it pretty thoroughly." He chuckled self-consciously. "Anyway, I'll be on my best behavior tomorrow night. No more games."

His apology sounded sincere. Both his heart and ego had taken a beating. My traitor heart ached for him. "Apology accepted. Thank you. I'll see you tomorrow."

"Can you give me a few more minutes?"

I looked at my watch. I had time. It would be better to get this over with than wait for him to corner me somewhere. "I guess so."

"I did something stupid, and I want you to know ahead of time how sorry I am ...."

It wasn't like Reese to dance around a topic. "What exactly did you do?"

"Cynthia Warren will be my date tomorrow night. I was pissed and—"

"So you asked the one person who would hurt me the most?" Unbelievable. He'd warned me he was a sore loser. It was not his most attractive quality.

"It was an adolescent move. If it's any consolation, I regretted it the second she accepted."

"I can't believe I actually feel sorry for you." I imagined her hanging on his arm, convinced they would be married by spring. "Don't be surprised if she thinks this means you're serious about her. Is she flying up just for the party?"

"I'm not that stupid. She stopped into the office with her father yesterday. She was supposed to be *his* date," he explained, trying to make it appear less vindictive.

I had to hand it to him, he knew how to push my buttons. "Okay, you warned me. Anything else?"

"I don't want things to end this way. I want us to be at least friendly even if we can't be friends. Maybe someday we can be, but right now, it's too hard for me. I still hurt too much." His voice cracked, and I started to feel my own tears welling.

"We can be friendly."

It took a moment before he could talk again. "Will you still meet me for brunch on Sunday? I want to give you the necklace I bought you."

"Reese, I can't accept. It wouldn't be right. I'm sure you can return it."

"I refuse to go back and tell the sales girl I got dumped."

"Why? Is she cute?"

"Not as cute as you."

"Maybe you should take it back. You can ask her on a date."

"Funny girl. If you don't take it, I'm leaving it on a park bench. I swear I'll do it."

"Why is it so important to you?"

"It just is. I bought it for you. Call it closure." He paused and said softly, "I want you to have something personal to remember me by."

The man knew how to tug on my heart. "I don't need anything to remember you by. I'll never forget you, and I could never wear it. I'd have to hide it in a drawer."

He chuckled. "It'll be a great mystery when your grandchildren find it long after we're both dead. At least think about."

I couldn't help laughing at the thought. "I'll think about it."

He seemed to have accepted we were over, and I didn't want to end things on a bitter note. I told him where I was staying and when Matt was leaving. He said he'd call me Sunday morning and let me know where to meet him. Maybe things didn't have to end badly.

Matt didn't comment on how long I'd been gone. He gave me a little smile and went back to working his crossword puzzle.

Matt was so pleased by my decision to resign that he was agreeable to everything. He went shopping with me and waited patiently while I selected matching Christmas sweaters for the boys and presents for his parents. I told him he didn't have to, but he even accompanied me to the hair salon. I thanked him for being with me. Funny, when I was nicer to him, he was nicer to me. It seemed so logical, but much of the time, I didn't operate under that principle.

However, he put up a fuss when I tried to put gel in his hair for the party. I looked at him with the biggest puppy dog eyes I could muster. "Please, Matt ...."

He shrugged in defeat. "If it's so important to you, go ahead."

He looked great. I gave him a thank you kiss and shooed him to get dressed. He laughed quietly at me and walked out of the bathroom shaking his head.

I finished putting on my make-up just as he said, "I'm dressed." I walked out of the bathroom and almost didn't recognize the handsome, debonair man standing in front of me.

"Matt, you look good enough to eat."

He blushed, but was pleased. "Does this mean I'll get lucky tonight?"

I winked. "It's a distinct possibility."

He waited while I slipped into a Jean Harlow-looking brown satin evening gown, which was cut low in the back and hugged my curves until it flared flowingly just above my knees. I hadn't wanted a red or green dress. I'd wanted something sophisticated and subtly sexy. The color showed off my tan skin, and I had found the perfect pair of chocolate satin Kate Spade shoes to go with it. The design of the shoe was called *Lover*. I couldn't resist. My feet loved them. At the salon, I had my hair done in an old fashioned, Hollywood glam style. It was not my typical look, but opportunities to really dress up didn't come along very often.

Matt let out a low whistle. "You have never looked more beautiful. Come here." He grabbed me playfully and pulled me toward him.

"Matt stop! You'll mess up my make-up."

He kissed my neck before letting me go. "Alright, but you really do look stunning."

"Thank you. Does this mean I'll get lucky tonight?"

"Without a doubt," he said with his eyes twinkling.

I stayed reasonably composed until we got into the town car. I'd hired it for the evening because I didn't want to worry about hailing cabs wearing a flimsy dress in December. I started shaking knowing in minutes I'd see Reese, and he and Matt would meet.

"Are you nervous?" Matt asked with concern. "You're shaking."

"It's freezing."

He put his arm around me to warm me up.

I wasn't sure what to expect. The party was being held at a restaurant in Midtown. Eventually we figured out the cocktail portion was taking place in a private room in the basement. Regular diners were seated on the main floor, and we would occupy the top floor for dinner. The basement party room was festooned with gold and silver holiday decorations and lit with white Christmas lights. It was festive with a twist of glamour.

Matt and I had missed the coat check on the main floor, and he left me to run our coats back upstairs. I surveyed the room. I didn't see Reese, but waved to a few other people I knew.

Then I sensed a warm body behind me. I knew it was him even before I inhaled his scent and his familiar voice whispered in my ear, "Nice ass."

I spun around. Reese stood right in front of me looking like a movie star in his evening attire. I thought I was prepared for this moment, but I wasn't. I wanted to touch him to make sure he was real. Our eyes glued together, and it took a minute for me to regain my composure.

"You're supposed to be on your best behavior."

He grinned guiltily. "Sorry. I couldn't help it. You look absolutely ravishing."

"Thank you. You look quite ravishing yourself."

I couldn't stop looking at his eyes. They always had the power to mesmerize me. Electric currents shot between us. I forced myself to look away with my heart pounding. God forgive me, but I wanted to feel his arms around me. I wanted to hear his heartbeat. I wanted to taste him again. Tears welled up in my eyes. I missed him.

I asked, "Where's your date?"

"In the powder room. Where's your husband?"

"Checking our coats."

He looked at me with his soft loving eyes and started to say, "Susan—"

I cut him off with a furtive look and warned, "There's Matt now."

Matt walked to my side, and I introduced him to Reese. They shook hands and chatted cordially, all the while assessing each other. I could barely breathe and my pulse raced. The room was suddenly suffocating and hot. Matt looked back and forth between Reese and me a few times with a curious expression.

Reese studied Matt. He clearly was not what Reese had expected. I don't think I ever told him what Matt looked like. I am sure he thought Matt would be a dweeby looking scientist. Reese was thrown. Matt was as tall as Reese and slightly broader. In his evening attire and with his hair gelled, he looked almost as handsome and just as urbane.

I needed a drink.

Matt hugged his arm around my waist. He asked, "Shall we find you a glass of wine?"

Reese winced and I flinched, uncomfortable with Matt touching me in front of Reese. I hoped Matt hadn't noticed. I looked directly at Matt, attempting to draw his attention away from Reese. "Yes, please. Reese, please excuse us."

Matt took my hand a led me toward the drink station. About half way there, he whispered, "Why didn't you tell me about your boss?"

My heart started racing again and I tried to ask naively, "What do you mean?"

"You never told me he's young and looks like a movie star," he accused.

"I didn't think it was important," I lied.

He looked at me with disbelief. "You've been traveling with him for months."

"Honey, please. Can we talk about this later?"

He nodded in agreement. As I maneuvered him around the room, I made sure to maintain a healthy distance from Reese. It had been an uncomfortable meeting for everyone.

In typical Matt fashion, he followed quietly behind, my shadow, smiling politely, but not saying much. Untypically, Matt never let go of me. He alternated between clutching my hand and having his arm around my waist. He actually kissed my neck. He kissed it more than once. Matt never, I mean never, kissed me in public.

Every now and then, Reese's eyes reached across the room like a touch. Each time, I would turn and sure enough, he would be watching me. I prayed to God no one else noticed.

We worked our way to Joe Benedetti and I introduced Matt. Joe was effusive in his praise of what a handsome couple we made. He joked about me keeping Matt hidden.

"I've always been curious to meet the elusive Mr. Sinclair," he quipped.

Matt smiled tightly and answered, "I do exist."

"Have you had a chance to meet Reese yet?" he asked, raising his brow.

Matt glanced at Reese. "He's hard to miss."

Joe laughed and looked pointedly at me. "Will you be seeing your friend this trip?"

"I'm sure I will." I met his eyes without flinching. "How nice of you to remember."

"I try to keep up with my people," he rejoined with a knowing look.

I laughed it off. "That's why we love you, Joe." I extricated us from Joe's circle with the excuse I was ready for a second glass of wine. *That* was not a lie.

Matt asked as soon as we walked away, "Who's the friend he referred to?"

"Oh, I met Lara Jimenez for lunch the last time I was in town. You probably don't remember her, but she went to grad school with me."

I was more than relieved Matt let it go with a simple cover.

Now that Cynthia had joined Reese, I really, really tried to keep a wide berth. I had the satisfaction of knowing I looked better than she did. She might be tall and blond, but her red sequined dress was tacky. Knowing Reese's taste, I could only imagine what he thought.

I dreaded the end of the cocktail hour. Reese had warned me the seating charts had us at the same table. I was hopeful I could talk to the event planner and finagle a table change. I tried to move Matt ahead of the crowd, but he pulled me aside on the main dining level.

"Susan, your boss is making me uncomfortable," he said in a tense voice.

Dodge and weave. "What's he done?"

"He keeps staring at you."

"He's probably just checking to see who I'm talking to. He wanted me to treat this as an opportunity to do some networking."

Matt shook his head. "It's like he's obsessed with you."

"I think you're exaggerating," I said dismissively.

"No, I'm not. I did an experiment with him. Whenever I kissed you, he tensed."

"He probably thought it was unprofessional behavior. Please, let's just go upstairs."

Matt reluctantly agreed.

Somehow, I had to get Reese to stop. I'm sure he wasn't even aware of what he was doing. He wouldn't intentionally draw attention to us at a work function.

I left Matt, wound my way through a narrow hallway and back down the stairs. I slipped into the ladies' room planning to text Reese. I prayed he had his cell phone with him. It was not a brilliant move. There was a long line. Even worse, Cynthia was in line just ahead of me.

She smiled and greeted me with her honey dialect, "Hey, there Susan."

"Hi, Cynthia. Are you enjoying yourself?" I asked determined to be polite.

She smiled and gloated, "Oh, yes. I love being with the most handsome man in the room. Reese is being an absolute doll. I gather the two of you have been working very intimately?"

"He is my direct supervisor," I answered keeping my expression blank.

"I saw that you're with your husband this evening."

"Yes, I am."

"He's handsome," she said as if she didn't expect my husband to be handsome.

"Thank you."

"I think I'm sitting next to him at dinner. I'm looking forward to chatting with him," she subtly warned, but gave me a smile showing all of her perfect white teeth.

I distrusted her friendly smile and cut off our tête-à-tête with the first excuse that came to mind. "Goodness, this is a long line. I think I'll wait."

I hurriedly slipped back out. *I had to get Matt and I seated at a different table.* Who knew what that she-devil would say if she got a chance to speak to Matt.

I almost had my foot on the first step of the stairs when I literally ran into Reese. I bounced off his chest and started to fall backwards. He caught me. It caused us to do a half spin. His hands were on both of my arms, I was inches from his chest and he was leaning over me. At that exact moment, Matt rounded the corner. He paused at the top of the stairs. He didn't see I had been about to fall. All he saw was that Reese appeared to be pulling me close while I appeared to be backing away. Matt's face went pale and then colored with frightening anger.

Matt didn't shout. He growled, "Take your fucking hands off of my wife."

Reese immediately let go and I stumbled backward. Somebody pushed me upright. I didn't stop to see who it was or to check Reese's reaction. My eyes didn't leave Matt. He charged down the stairs towards Reese. I flew up the stairs as fast as I could and stopped him in the middle. It wasn't easy in an evening gown and three inch heels. I started to trip on my dress, but Matt caught me.

I rushed to explain, "It's not what you think. I fell. He caught me. That's it."

Matt took my hand, turned around, and practically dragged me up the rest of the steps. "We're leaving," he stated flatly and continued to pull me through the hallway towards the door.

Mortified, I waited by the front doors while Matt retrieved our coats and called the car service. Reese rounded a corner striding determinedly towards me. I shook my head.

He stopped and looked at me helplessly. He silently mouthed, "I'm sorry."

I nodded an acknowledgement and turned my back on him. I prayed he would be nowhere in sight when Matt returned with our coats.

Chapter 32

Matt helped me into my coat and led me by the elbow outside. We had to wait in the cold fifteen minutes before the town car arrived. The driver hadn't expected to pick us up for another two hours. Neither Matt nor I wanted to wait inside. It was too humiliating. Matt didn't say anything. He didn't say anything until we got to the hotel room.

Matt silently took off his jacket and tie. He was very calm. His equanimity unnerved me in contrast with the fury he displayed in the restaurant. He quietly asked, "Would you like to tell me what's going on?"

"Matt, I swear to you. I literally knocked into him and he caught me before I fell backward. I swear that's all that happened."

"I believe you. I don't think he would be blatantly indiscreet at a company function."

I exhaled deeply with relief. "Thank you."

"You still need to tell me everything."

"There's nothing to tell."

"When you left for the ladies room, I heard a couple men joking about him chasing after you. It's why I went looking for you."

"Maybe you misunderstood them."

"Stop. I'm not blind. I saw how he looks at you. Is he the real reason you're quitting?"

"I swear it's not the only reason. I want to be home for you and the boys."

"He wants you. You have to know that." He looked at me sympathetically. He didn't want to believe I had done anything wrong. He saw Reese as the villain. It was an easy out and I took it.

I nodded. "I know and … and … I can't work for him anymore."

"Why didn't you tell me?" he asked bewildered.

"I didn't see the point, and I thought I could handle it myself. It would only upset you for no justifiable reason." I kept prevaricating with half-truths. "None of this matters. I'm resigning. I'll be done with Global Security in a couple weeks."

"God damn him. Who the fuck does he think he is? I could literally kill him!" Matt exploded and started pacing. "No wonder you've been on edge for months … we should see an attorney." I started to cry, and he put his arms around me. "Honey, I'm so sorry this happened to you. He won't get away with it."

I turned away from him and confessed, "I can't pursue a harassment case against Reese."

"Why? What do you mean?"

I couldn't answer. I couldn't say it out loud, and he refused to see the truth staring him in the face. "I am so sorry."

Matt's eyes dazed as comprehension settled. "Oh, my God, you and *him*?"

I nodded. "It's over. I swear to you. It was very brief and it's over."

Matt sank onto the bed covering his face with his hands.

"I'm sorry. I am so sorry," I sobbed.

His body crumpled and he moaned in pain. I tried to touch him, but he slapped my hand away. "Don't fucking touch me." He shot into the bathroom and locked the door.

His muffled sobs vibrating through the door lacerated my heart. Not knowing what else to do, I changed into my pajamas. I wanted to do something, but I didn't know what. I sat at the foot of the bed, and cried while I waited.

Eventually there was silence. I heard the door squeak open and he quietly walked out. He was pale and his eyes blood shot. Every movement appeared to be an effort for him. He made his way to me and stood over me. "I want to know everything. No more lies."

"I promise, no lies."

"Your promises mean nothing."

"I know, but I'll tell you the truth."

He took a deep breath and started drilling me. "What is it about him? Is it because he's better looking or makes more money than me?"

"No. It was more about the way he paid attention to me."

"That's right. I didn't love you enough." He laughed bitterly.

I'd take my punishment, but he was part of the problem, too. "You told me that sometimes you wished you had met someone else. Can you understand a little bit how I felt?"

"I didn't have an affair. You did."

Shame flooded over me. "I'm sorry."

He paced, visibly fighting to control his emotions. "When did it start?"

"Nothing physical happened until late September."

"You went to Chicago for the weekend. Were you with him?"

"Yes."

He stopped pacing and asked, "Did you *fuck* him?"

I understood Matt's anger, but I couldn't help bristling. He made it sound so dirty. *Reese and I never fucked.* We had given ourselves to each other. There was nothing dirty about it.

He grabbed me by the shoulders and yanked me off the bed. His livid face held inches from mine. "I bet he fucked you hard, didn't he?" he demanded.

"Matt—"

"Did you put him in your mouth?"

"Matt, please, I—"

He shook me as if he wanted to break me. "DID YOU?"

"Yes, Matt. We had sex. We did what normal adults do. That's enough!"

"*I want to know everything*," he hissed and shook me again. "Did you enjoy it?"

His anger scared me. I jerked away and tried to escape to the bathroom. He grabbed me, spun me around, and then slammed me against the wall, pinning me against it.

Fear morphed to anger, and rage erupted from my center, spewing out of my mouth. "YES, I ENJOYED IT. Best sex of my life. Is that what you want to know? He's an incredible lover. Better than you. It was mind-blowing every time!"

He slapped me, making my head spin, and I tasted blood.

"Oh dear God, I'm … I'm sorry … I'll get some ice." He backed away and walked out.

My heart beat uncontrollably, and I was boiling hot. I threw water on my face in an attempt to calm down and winced wiping the blood off my face. Ice wasn't going to help. I already had a fat lip. My anger evaporated. I had deserved worse.

When Matt came back, he handed me an ice bucket with shaking hands. "I can't believe I hit you. I'm sorry … I'm so sorry."

"Please, don't."

I sat on the bed, wrapped ice in a towel, and held it to my mouth.

Matt pointedly sat in the desk chair, maintaining physical distance. Once he calmed, he stoically started his next round of questions.

"Were you with him every time you went out of town?"

"No, and not my last Chicago or Boston trips." I kept my emotions in check and my voice flat. I didn't want to antagonize him again.

"When did it end?"

"I called it off after my last New York trip. He came to see me the next day."

"He's the one you met in San Francisco?"

"Yes. It was the last time I saw him until tonight. He tried to talk me into staying with him, but I refused."

"He flew to San Francisco just to see you?"

My mind flooded with memories of Reese that day: the way he looked when he opened the door, him holding me tightly, making love to me for the last time. I struggled to hold myself together, and nodded yes.

"Unbelievable. What kind of man tries to take away a wife and a mother from her family?" he asked.

I couldn't answer. What was I supposed to tell him? A man desperately in love. A man who believes our souls are bound together. A man who gets lonely. A man who is relentless about getting what he wants. A good man who did a bad thing. All of the above.

"The way he looked at you disgusted me." He shook his head as though clearing his thoughts. "Did you fall in love with him?"

I paused. I considered lying again, but I had promised no more lies. I didn't want to break another promise. "Yes."

Tears started leaking from Matt's eyes. "Why did you end it then?"

"Because of you and the boys, us as a family. I couldn't leave you. Matt, I felt so alone. I was so painfully lonely, and he was there wanting me." I stared at him, trying to get him to understand why it happened, but he wouldn't look at me. "Later, I hoped if Reese were out of the picture, we could find our way back to each other. That's the real reason why I wanted to quit my job. I thought it would give us a better chance."

"I thought we had a good chance of being happy again, but … but you've broken my … my heart." His voice cracked and he began to tremble.

"Matt, please, I'm begging you to forgive me. I chose you."

"I can't believe you love him … that you let him in your body … I don't think I can get past that you love him," he said with his chest heaving and his eyes blinking back tears.

"Please, don't say that. We'll go home and get counseling—"

"Stop!" He took a couple deep breaths. "I don't want to look at you or hear your voice. I'm going home, and I'm filing for a divorce."

I wasn't going to get anywhere with him until he had a chance to think things through. He would feel differently in a day or two. "Your flight doesn't leave until mid-morning. Why don't you try to get some sleep?"

"I don't want to be in the same room with you."

"I'll leave," I offered.

"Why? So you can meet him?"

"No, I'll wait in the lobby."

"Don't bother. I'm going to try to get on the 6 a.m. flight."

I watched him change into jeans and pack his bag. As he was about to walk out the door, I said, "I know I've hurt you badly, but please, don't say anything to the boys until I get home."

"I won't, but don't come home for a few days. I'll call when I'm ready to see you."

I didn't argue. I wasn't in a position to argue.

After the door shut, I curled up in bed wishing everything that had happened were a bad dream, and I would wake in my own bed with Matt sleeping peacefully beside me. It wasn't a dream, and I couldn't sleep. My marriage was over. My career with Global Security was over.

What would my boys think of me when they found out? They would find out. Would they think their mother was a slut? A whore? How could I look them in the eyes? After all the years of believing I was different, I realized I was just like my mother. I had succumbed to *the mind of the flesh* and *God will judge the sexually immoral and adulterers.*

I broke Matt's heart. I broke Reese's heart. My heart was broken and bleeding and black holes were sucking me in. The weight on my chest was crushing, suffocating me. How could I hurt this badly without having a physical injury? I didn't know how to cure it.

I couldn't stop images from assaulting my mind. I imagined the snickers from co-workers who at one time had respected me, and Joe, who trusted me, shaking his head with deep disappointment. I visualized the pain I caused as some hideous, unstoppable disease spreading and growing until it assailed everyone I loved. I witnessed the pain on Matt's face and Reese's face. I could vividly imagine the faces of my boys, my parents, Matt's parents … and I had caused it all. I was the sick, malignant person who brought unhappiness to everyone.

And I was alone. After everything, here I was utterly alone in a hotel room in a city filled with millions of people. The hollowness inside me became unbearably painful.

If I were dead, I couldn't hurt anybody ever again. What would it be like? Would it be like floating in oblivion and finally being at peace?

Please, God, let me have some peace, let me feel nothing.

I don't think God listened to me anymore. He had given up on me.

A blade slicing through my wrists had to be less painful than the sorrow in my heart and the guilt beast gnashing on my insides. How long before I could float in oblivion, never thinking or feeling again? The pain in my chest would stop. The sickness in my stomach would stop.

I went into the bathroom and started filling the bathtub with hot water. While it filled, I pounded my plastic, disposable razor with the heel of my shoe until the blade was free. Then I stripped and sank into water so hot it scalded my skin. I didn't care. I breathed in and out slowly as my body became accustomed to the temperature. I sank deeper into the water and imagined cold, congealed blood warming and loosening, ready to flow freely. I took my ponytail holder and cinched it just above my wrist. The veins in my wrist popped up blue and thick. I stared at my wrist unsure which vein was the main artery.

Matt would know. He knew these things. If he were here, he'd say, *"Stop being so dramatic. Get some sleep."* He knows I'm hyper emotional when I'm tired.

I heard Reese admonishing me, *"Susan, this isn't some nineteenth century novel. It's late and you're tired."* Reese was right: I was more rational when I was well rested.

Hearing their voices snapped me out of my dark thoughts. I took the ponytail holder off my wrist and tossed the blade into the garbage. I sank back into the water and let it sooth me.

I wasn't alone. Love was in my heart. I still had people in my life who loved me … people I loved. As long as I had love, I would never be completely alone. Maybe God had listened. *Don't be afraid for I am with you … Yes, I will help you.*

My career at Global Security was over, but in the scope of my life, it wasn't important.

My marriage wasn't necessarily over. Matt was deeply hurt, but with time, he would forgive me. The life we built, our children bound us together. Eventually, he would take me back. But did I want to go back? What kind of a life would we have together? We were already struggling. Matt was Matt. There was no changing him. There was no changing what I needed. How long would it be before I found myself in the same place?

If I called Reese and told him I needed him, I knew with dead certainty he would be here in minutes. He would hold me all night and let me cry into his chest.

My boys would probably hate me for a while, but I was still their mother. They loved me and needed me. I couldn't be a coward. I had to face them even though I didn't know how I was going to explain what I'd done.

It was too much to think about without sleep. I'd think about it tomorrow. I got out of the tub, dried off, and put my pajamas back on.

I was alone in a city full of millions of people, but in my heart, I wasn't alone. Life would go on with or without me. I preferred with me. I was still breathing. The worst was over.

I turned off the light and closed my eyes.

Chapter 33

My cell phone ringing woke me the next morning. It had been almost dawn by the time I'd fallen asleep; consequently, waking was a struggle. Grabbing the phone, I expected it to be Matt. I don't know why. He should already have been on a flight back to the West Coast.

"Is he gone?" Reese, of course. I should have expected it to be him.

"Yeah. He left late last night."

"I really am so sorry." He sounded as bad as I felt. "I'm at the Starbucks around the corner from your hotel. May I come up and see you?"

My logical side warred with my emotional side. "Will you bring me coffee?"

"Skinny latte?"

"Venti with an extra shot, please."

"I'll be there in ten minutes."

I dragged myself out of bed and into the bathroom. I looked like crap with puffy eyes and a fat lip. I just managed get myself dressed and slightly presentable when Reese knocked.

I opened the door, grabbed my coffee, which I desperately needed, and made a quick turn. I wanted him all the way in the room and some caffeine in my system before he noticed my lip. I curled up on the bed and hid my mouth with the coffee cup.

He started to move in my direction. I shook my head, and he sat in the desk chair.

"Thanks for the coffee." I took a big gulp. The hot liquid felt good sliding down my throat, acting as an elixir and clearing the surreal fog of the last twelve hours.

His eyes blinked a couple times. I knew he was dying to be next to me and struggled to stay in the chair. He leaned forward and asked, "How much does Matt know?"

"Everything."

Reese nodded, absorbing the implications. "He knows we fell in love?"

"He knows everything." I had to confront him and asked, "Why did you keep staring? Did you follow me to the ladies room? Did you want Matt to find out?"

"Maybe subconsciously I wanted him to know about us … I don't know … I *was* jealous. Seeing him touch you made me crazy, but I couldn't stop watching you together either. He was taunting me, kissing your neck, and then looking at me. It drove me fucking crazy, but I swear I didn't do anything on purpose. I'm so, so sorry."

"God, Reese, you're always sorry. I am so fucking tired of hearing you're sorry. You're not sorry. You finally got what you want. Matt knows. He wants a divorce."

"You have to know I didn't want things to happen this way. Susan, please …"

Tears ran down my cheeks. It was too much for Reese. He moved next to me and put his arms around me. I put my cup down and buried my face against his chest. I wasn't even sure about which aspect of my life I was crying. Maybe I cried because the life I'd built was over, and I didn't have a plan. Maybe because it didn't seem to matter what Reese did, I still loved him. I missed him and the aching and the longing were breaking me. The only certainty was my heart was bleeding, and guilt threatened to swallow me whole. I wanted to escape my body, but Reese held me together. He held me and held me, and rocked me, letting me cry myself dry.

When my chest stopped heaving and my breathing normalized, my senses started operating again. I took in his familiar scent and the particular weight of his arms wrapped protectively, lovingly, around me. Everything about him comforted me. Everything about him felt exactly right. How could I stay mad at him? The warmth of his body soothed me, and I nestled deeper into him, lulled by the sound of his heartbeat.

I whispered, "Thank you for being here with me."

"I'll always be here if you need me," he said and tried to lift my chin to make me look at him, but I held it in place. "Hey, look at me," he gently ordered. Cringing, I lifted my face toward him, giving a full view of my mouth. His eyes flashed. "Did he hit you?"

"He slapped me," I said as neutrally as possible.

"That fucker," he grunted, jumping to his feet. "I knew I shouldn't have let you leave with him. I swear I'll fucking kill him!"

"I'm fine. I'm really fine," I continued with a level tone, trying to calm him.

"What happened? Has he hit you before?"

"He slapped me once. I swear he has never laid a hand on me before, and I had it coming. I told him sex with you was mind-blowing every time."

That took the wind out of his sails. "You told him that?"

"It just flew out of my mouth." I lowered my head. "I lost my temper, but he was crazed before I said it. He pushed me to say something that would justify hitting me. He wanted to hurt me as much as I'd hurt him. It's over. He's sorry and won't do it again."

"I don't give a shit what you said, he shouldn't have hit you. I still want to kill him."

"He's been hurt enough. Besides, he probably wants to kill you."

"I don't blame him if he does," he acknowledged. "Come here; let me get a closer look." I walked to him and lifted my face, letting him study my mouth. "No one will notice by tomorrow. You're still very kissable," he murmured. I turned away before he kissed me and sat on the bed. He sighed. "What are you two going to do?"

"Matt doesn't want me to come home for a few days. He said he's going to file for divorce, but he was furious and in shock. After he cools, we'll figure it out."

Reese paled. "I know you don't want to hear it, but I am sorry for what I've done to your life. Would it help if I talked to Matt? I'll tell him I was culpable for everything; I wouldn't leave you alone. I'll tell him anything you want."

"No. I have to take responsibility for what I did, but as sorry as I am for hurting him, I don't regret loving you. You helped me breathe again," I said with a little smile.

He grinned. "Glad I did something positive for you. Have you eaten? You missed dinner last night. You must be starving."

"Famished and I want to get out of this hotel room. It's suffocating."

He grabbed my hand and pulled me up. "Come on, let's get you some food, and then we can get our game plan together for tomorrow."

My heart started pounding again. "What happened after I left? I was so focused on Matt, I didn't notice who was watching. How bad was it?"

"Could've been worse. Joe was right behind you and saw the whole thing. Good news is he knows nothing happened. He saw you plow into me."

"Sorry about that. I was a little distracted."

"I know. Anyway, the bad news is he wants to see both of us in his office tomorrow morning at nine, but don't worry. No one is getting fired. I have a plan," he assured me. "We'll talk about it after we get you something to eat."

Reese and I walked a couple blocks to a little café with him holding my hand. I didn't care anymore if someone saw us. The fresh, cool air helped to clear my head and the buzzing voices in the restaurant were reassuring. Life was happening outside the confines of my over active brain. I devoured my cheese and bacon omelet. I had needed protein. Feeling fortified, I was ready to deal with the work discussion.

"Reese, I wrote a resignation letter last week. I'd planned on resigning before any of this happened. I'll make it easy on everyone and give it to you today."

He put down his fork. "God, I'm sorry." His voice was quiet. "I didn't know I'd made things so unbearable."

"It's not your fault. It's our whole situation. I couldn't keep working for you. It was too hard for both of us. Please believe me, I don't blame you."

He looked at me with pained eyes and practically ordered, "Don't resign."

"Cat's out of the bag. I can't work for Global after last night. I'm sorry, but I can't."

Reese went into business mode. "I understand, but let's hear what Joe has to say and then let me take the lead. I promised to take care of you. I'll get you the exit package you deserve. Can you trust me to handle Joe?"

Reese seemed confident, and I didn't want to walk without my bonus; I had worked hard and deserved it. Why I was uneasy? Squeezing his hand again, I said, "I trust you. Thank you."

He winked. "Anything for you, my lovely *Juliet*."

He had his share of charm. "Hey, what happened with Cynthia last night?"

"Hmm ... It's rather embarrassing. I don't think I want to tell you."

Now I really was curious. "Oh, come on, *tell me.*" I batted my eyes at him.

He grinned and caved. "Alright. After I followed you upstairs, the gossip eventually reached her—are you ready?" he asked, adding to the suspense.

"Yes." I giggled.

"She called me a cad."

"A *cad*?" I laughed.

"And threw her drink in my face."

"That's funny." I laughed some more.

He laughed too. "At least it was white wine and didn't stain my shirt."

"We're a rotten pair," I said only half-joking.

He stopped laughing and his eyes burned into mine. "We're not rotten all the time. We can be very good when it's just the two of us."

I might be strong enough to discuss work, but I wasn't up for a "feelings" conversation. I was afraid of confessing I still loved him. I looked away and announced, "I should go."

"You can't be worried about finishing Monday morning reports."

I chuckled. "No, the last thing I'm worried about is finishing a report for Mr. Kirkpatrick. Rumor is I won't be working for him after tomorrow."

He chuckled too, but with sadness. "No, you don't have to worry about that slave driver anymore. So, where are you going?"

It wouldn't be healthy to lie in bed wallowing in self-pity. I needed activity and to be around people. "Christmas shopping. I should finish up today since I don't know what will happen when I get home."

"May I come with you? I have excellent taste," he joked. "Besides, you need someone to carry your bags."

"Wanna be my bag boy?"

"Sure, I'll be your bag boy," he said with a small smile curving his lips.

He paid the check, because he always picked up the tab, and we spent the day together. Reese didn't tell me he loved me, nor did he attempt to kiss me on the lips. The only difference between two friends versus two lovers spending the day together was that I allowed him to touch me all he wanted. He spent the day holding my hand and draping his arm around my shoulder or waist. Occasionally, he wrapped his arms completely around me, and kissed the top of my head or cheek while we waited in line to make purchases.

It had long been his desire to do these things in public. It had been mine too. It was an unfulfilled part of our relationship, which we both wanted to experience even if it was only a one-day charade and meant nothing more than playing out a fantasy. The public display of affection that declared to the world we belonged together was deceptively satisfying. I didn't know if we would ever spend another day together, so I indulged him. I indulged myself.

When we returned to the hotel to deposit my purchases, the prospect of black holes sucking me in had me panicky. I couldn't handle another night alone sobbing into a pillow. I desperately wanted him to stay, but couldn't ask. He made it easy.

"May I stay with you—as your friend of course, no funny business?"

"I'd like that very much. Thank you."

Reese insisted I take a bath while he ran home to pick up a few things. As I soaked, I thought about him. He was at ease and didn't push all day. He was his most lovable when he relaxed. This really was what it would be like if we were married. Reese would relax. It would be so easy to stay with him, so easy to make love to him when he got back.

When I got out of the bathtub, I looked at the pajamas I had packed. There was the black negligee I had planned to wear for Matt and the pink flannels I had packed for the nights I'd be alone. I put on the flannels. Reese was resigned to being my friend. It would be best to keep things that way for the time being.

I called Matt's cell and left a message:

"*Matt, it's me. I am so, so sorry. I hope someday you'll forgive me. Listen, I'm resigning tomorrow and I want to come home. I want us to stay together at least through the holidays. Please, Matt. I'm not asking for me. I'm asking for Micah and Jason. I'll call you tomorrow. Please, tell the boys I love them.*"

When Reese returned, he laughed at my nightwear. "Nice try, but those pink flannels kind of do it for me."

I frowned.

"Don't worry. I brought my own flannels."

Reese started to undress and stopped. He went into the bathroom and came out wearing his pajamas. How many nights had I spent with him buck-naked? I had watched him shave and had once even plucked his nose hairs. He had even stopped shutting the bathroom door when he peed. Tonight he was being a supportive friend, with obvious undertones, but still a friend. He wore flannels, just like me. I guess changing in front of me would have been too personal. He didn't want to open himself up knowing I could still go back to Matt.

He didn't try to make love to me. He kissed my eyelids goodnight and held me.

I missed being held and nestled into him. His body was like a hot water bottle, warm and comforting. He smelled good and the rhythm of his heartbeat was my own personal lullaby.

"I've missed you," I whispered in the dark.

I could feel his chest heave. "I've missed you, too."

"Hold me closer."

He pulled me a little closer, held me a little tighter, and we went to sleep.

Chapter 34

The next morning I woke up to Reese's lips on my cheek. He wore an impeccably tailored Armani suit with his lucky platinum cufflinks poking out of the jacket sleeves. An ultimate bold stripe power tie completed the uniform. Game time.

"Morning, Sleeping Beauty," he said.

"Morning. What's the plan?"

"Don't speak to anyone. Go straight to Joe's office. I'll be there. Follow my lead, no matter what. Promise?"

He was an astute businessman. I trusted him. "I promise."

When I stepped out of the elevator and into the office, I wished Reese were by my side. As I braved the hallway gauntlet, snickers and whispers echoed around me. The whole office had heard about our little incident Saturday night.

I followed instructions and went straight to Joe's office. As planned, Reese was already there. He barely glanced at me and greeted with a clipped edge, "Susan."

I nodded; then, it hit me. *Oh, crap.* He didn't have to fall on a sword for me. I turned to stop him, but Joe's administrative assistant said, "Mr.

Benedetti is ready for you." With my pulse racing, I followed Reese into the judgment room.

Joe invited us to have a seat and scowled at us before asking, "I assume Reese has informed you why I wanted to see the two of you today?"

"Yes. He told me."

"Well then, there's no reason to beat around the bush. I'm very disappointed in the two of you. You were supposed to be my dream team. I carefully selected you both for this assignment. I thought you would complement each other. I didn't anticipate just how well I had matched you up. It has come to my attention you have been having an affair. I may be in an ivory tower, but I have a state of art good looking glass." Joe focused on me. "The *friend* you've been staying with is Reese. I know this for a fact."

He couldn't possibly know—unless he had the GPS in my Blackberry traced. He ignored my shocked look and continued, "I should fire you both." Joe's eyes shifted between Reese and me. "But I'm not. With that said, someone has to leave. I can't have you working together. I have no complaints about either of your work product. Your other behavior is the problem. You two have become an unproductive distraction for the business unit. I'm prepared to offer a recommendation and guarantee your annual bonus if you resign today."

Joe focused his eyes on me. *He wanted me to leave, but not Reese ... and* Reese must've known. At the end of the day, Global was still a boys' club. I'd been ready to quit, but not unfairly forced, not like this. "I would like to—"

"Susan, I know what you're going to say, and I'll save you the trouble," Reese interjected and then said to Joe, "Yes, we had an affair. I instigated it. When she tried to end it, I'm ashamed to admit I laughed at her and practically dared her to accuse me of harassment. I fully acknowledge creating a hostile work environment. She warned me if I didn't respect her wishes, she would resign. She prepared a resignation letter before coming to New

York with the intent of submitting it today. If you don't believe me, check the date the document was created on her laptop. Saturday night, her husband became aware of everything, and the situation has changed."

Joe's astute eyes pierced me. "Is this true?"

I looked at my hands, barely holding back tears, and said nothing.

"Susan, answer truthfully," Reese said.

Everything Reese said had layers of truth, but I only said and did those things after I'd fallen in love with him. I was still in love with him. I looked at Reese. His face was like stone, unreadable. I prayed he had a plan to save himself.

"Yes, it's true," I answered.

Reese asked, "Did I specifically use the term 'quid quo pro' in regard to our relations?"

Joe's face reddened. "Susan, this isn't a court of law, but I think you know the implications. I expect a truthful answer."

Reese had, but it had been a joke. Again, I said nothing.

"Just answer the question," Reese pressed.

"He did."

Joe looked away and mumbled "fuck" under his breath. Then he stared me down and asked point-blank. "What is it you want?"

Reese answered for me. "I took the liberty of speaking to Susan yesterday. She will waive all rights to future litigation provided she's given the annual bonus to which she's entitled, one hundred percent vestment of her stock options and grants, two years severance with full benefits, and a recommendation." Reese turned to me. "Did I miss anything?"

"No, that covers it." I was sick over the whole business.

Joe contemplated what Reese demanded on my behalf and then exploded, "Reese, this is fucking bullshit! What kind of game do you think you're playing?"

"No games. You should remember Susan was my direct subordinate and California is a litigious, employee friendly state. Global is getting off easy."

"What are you getting out of this?"

"Nothing."

"*Nothing?*"

"Nothing."

Both men glared at each other, not backing down, like a game of chicken. Joe broke first.

"Fucking hell. Reese, you'll be terminated effective immediately. I'll have no choice. I won't be able to give you a recommendation. You'll forfeit your bonus."

"I understand."

No! What are you doing? "I can't—" Reese shot me a murderous look, warning me to keep my mouth shut.

Joe looked at me. "Do you have something to share?"

I knew the answer Reese wanted me to give. "No."

Joe refocused his attention on Reese. "You understand what this will do to your career?"

"Yes."

I stared at Reese silently begging him to stop playing the romantic hero, to stop being foolish. I didn't care about the money. It wasn't worth sacrificing everything he had spent his entire adult life trying to achieve.

Joe stared at Reese bewildered and added, "I thought one day you'd be our CEO."

Remaining impassive, Reese didn't respond.

"Before I'm willing to meet these demands, I'll need you to submit a written statement. You'll be required to waive your right to pursue any future wrongful termination claim."

"I already have the documents prepared." Reese handed Joe a folder.

He gave the contents a quick glance. "Very well, then."

"Joe, for what it's worth, I'm sorry," Reese said. I could tell he truly meant it.

"I think you should save your apologies for Susan."

Reese's composure cracked, and he said sharply, "She knows how I feel."

It took all my strength to hold it together. I couldn't believe what Reese did for me. I would walk away with over a million dollars between bonus, stock, and severance. He would leave with nothing and forever have the blight on his resume that he'd been fired for harassment with his written statement on file. It wasn't fair, but I wasn't going to challenge him in front of Joe. Reese would perceive any contradiction by me as a slap in the face.

"Susan, I'm very sorry. Please, feel free to wait here while I have legal and HR draw up the documents." He turned to Reese. "I'll have security meet you in your office."

As they walked out the door together, I heard Joe ask Reese, "There are thousands of beautiful women in New York. Why did you do it?"

Reese paused and then confessed, "Because I love *her*."

Joe had to know the situation was complicated, but what was he going to do with Reese's statement in hand? I guess it didn't matter if Joe knew that tidbit of information. Maybe he wouldn't think as harshly of Reese.

"I'm sorry for you both," he said. I think he sincerely meant it.

I didn't watch Reese pack his personal things or witness him escorted out the door by security, but I ached for him. He had spent his life being the trophy-winning, record-setting, quota-busting superstar. He was *the Rainmaker*. It was an ignominious end to what had promised to be a long and illustrious career. I wished he hadn't done it, but there was no turning back. I knew it was over when the head of our Security Department stopped into Joe's office to inform me personally that I no longer had to worry about Reese Kirkpatrick.

Chapter 35

I did worry about Reese Kirkpatrick; I worried about him in ways no one but Reese Kirkpatrick could possibly fathom. As I sat waiting, thinking about the enormity of Reese's sacrifice, I was overwhelmed by what he'd been willing to do because he loved me.

About an hour later, Joe came back to the office with one of the attorneys. I reviewed the documents, signed, and briefed Joe on the terms of the Bank of Boston contract. He would pick up the signatures and host the dinner. After I relinquished my security badge, VPN fob, laptop, and Blackberry, it was my turn to be escorted out.

By the time I exited Joe's office, the entire floor buzzed over Reese's demise. Eyes turned toward me as if I was a freak on display. Curious eyes, accusatory eyes burned into me as I made my way to the elevator. I neared Anne, Reese's administrator. She was crying. I stopped, planning to apologize, but she mumbled, "Lying slut." Reese wouldn't want me to show emotion. I reined myself in for him and kept going.

Reese and I were both finished with Global Security by noon. As soon as I walked out of the building, I called him. I asked, "Why did you do it?"

"I have my reasons. Please, don't worry about me."

"I can't help it. I love you."

I heard a sharp intake of breath. He said with his voice shaking, "I didn't think I would ever hear you say that again. I love you, too. Where are you?"

"In front of the office. I'm going to the hotel to check out."

"I'll meet you there."

Reese walked into the lobby just as I stepped out of the hotel elevator. I went to him and flung my arms around him. Then I did something I'd been doing a lot.

"Susan, what am I going to do with you? Please, stop crying." He took a handkerchief out of his pocket and attempted to dry my eyes.

"I'm trying to." I took a breath, but it didn't help. "I can't believe what you did for me. I would've had a few choice words for Joe, but I would have resigned. You didn't have to do it."

"Hey, I knew what I was doing. Now, please stop crying." He wrapped his arms around me. "I fucked things up, but the company had made a huge investment bringing me on board, so Joe wanted you out. It wasn't fair, and I'd promised to take care of you."

"I was just as much at blame."

"But you never would've made the first move, and you didn't draw attention to us. I did, and I kept pursuing you even after you'd asked me to stop. You deserve the exit package. Please, just say thank you and let's move on. People are staring."

"Thank you."

"You're welcome. What time's your flight?"

"Not until six. Can we go somewhere to talk?"

"Let's go to my place," he suggested.

I felt at home when I walked through his door; Reese had been that welcoming. We'd made love on his couch and in his bed. I had cooked in his kitchen and worked in his office. I knew where to find extra sheets and toilet paper. I still had my key.

Feeling like road kill for the third day in a row, I dropped on the couch while Reese fetched me a glass of wine. He poured himself a scotch. It was the only indication he gave of just how trying the morning had been. He'd been the golden boy and now would be forever tarnished in the business world. Reese bore it without complaint. He did it for me. He didn't want me to see what the morning had cost him, but I knew.

Sitting in the chair across from me, Reese took a gulp and asked, "So what's next?"

"I'm going home to deal with Matt and see about my boys. I'm hopeful he'll let me come home at least through New Year's."

"Then what?"

"I want to start divorce proceedings."

He stared at his glass while he digested my decision. "Are you only saying it because Matt said he wants a divorce?"

For good or bad, my path was decided. I hoped God would forgive me; Matt would forgive me; my boys would forgive me; I could forgive myself. "No, if I give him enough time, he'll take me back. I can't do it though. I have to get out. I can't be the person he wants me to be anymore. He and I have hurt each other too much."

"It's been an emotional few days. You might change your mind once you're home."

He was right. There were no guarantees. "Not likely, but if I've learned anything, I really don't know what I'm capable of until I'm in the situation."

"Would you like the name of the attorney I tracked down for you? He went to Stanford Law. He's pricey, but he'll be worth it. He assured me he can get you custody of your boys."

"I'll talk to him, but I think Matt and I will only need a mediator."

For a while we just sat silently sipping our drinks, both of us stunned by the morning's events. For two people who were conditioned to work sixty, or more, hours a week, it was numbing. No cell phones or Blackberries ringing, no e-mail hitting an in box, and no conference calls. I would no longer have contact with people with whom I had interacted for eight years. I didn't even have an opportunity to say goodbye to my staff or clients.

For the first time in my adult life, I didn't have a job waiting for me. I didn't think I wanted to go back to the corporate world. I had played that role long enough, and it was soured for me. Life as I knew it was over … no husband, no job … single parent. Maybe my next career should be something creative, something closer to my true self. Thanks to Reese, I had a nest egg and time to sort out my life.

Reese leaned forward with his elbows on his thighs. His jaw twitched. He was rethinking his future too.

"I know why you did it," I said. He looked up at me. "You wanted me to have options."

He nodded. "I knew you'd never take money from me directly. I didn't want you stressed out over finances, and I wanted to buy you time to think over your next step."

"And I could leave Matt."

"You could."

"And retain a pricey attorney." I saw the full picture. "If things get ugly, I left Global due to harassment."

"You have legal documents supporting your claim."

Reese had thought everything through. He got up and refilled his scotch glass. He took a drink, and refilled it again. "Reese …" He turned to me with pain-filled eyes. I'd never loved him more than I did at that moment. "I've never stopped loving you."

He stilled. His only movement was to blink, making his lashes wet, but otherwise, he didn't respond.

I swallowed hard and kept going, "And I'm sorry for hurting you, but—"

"Don't say it. I know you have to go home and figure things out."

"I do, and I can't see you again as long as I'm married."

"I understand, and you should know I don't want to see you either unless you're free. From the moment I first saw you, I wanted you. I told you, it was love at first sight for me."

I smiled at his insistence. "Hadn't we agreed it'd been lust?"

"Sorry, I read a study scientifically proving love at first sight is a real phenomenon. It's more prevalent for men because the love area of the male brain is visually stimulated."

"Do you always have to be right?"

"Not always." The corners of his lips lifted. "Okay, most of the time." He took another sip of scotch. "Anyway here's the deal, I can't be just friends or a part-time lover. I wish I could, but I can't. I love you too much to go half-way. It has to be all in or nothing."

After all the turmoil and pain of the last few months, I didn't want to shred his love ragged by dragging him through more than I already had. I had to sort out my own life first and needed some distance to think clearly about him and our relationship. For now, Micah and Jason had to be my priority. Matt and I splitting up would be hard enough. Shoving another man into their lives at this stage would be too much, besides being even more hurtful to Matt. Once I was settled and had some perspective, once my boys adjusted, then maybe, but not now—and I didn't know how long it would take.

I had to let him go, and he knew it, too. "Then, it's goodbye for now?"

"It'll make negotiating a divorce and custody of your boys easier. It's best for you."

He moved next to me on the couch and settled me on his lap. Having his arms around me, listening to his heartbeat again, I didn't feel broken. I had to go back to California in a few hours, but leaving him this time would be different. I didn't feel like I was splitting myself in two. His love and friendship had nourished my soul back to health, and I knew the things I would have to do to keep from slipping back to that lonely place.

"The next year won't be easy," I said, breaking the silence, "but I'll take a few months to re-group and really consider what I want to do next. I think I'll reconnect with some old friends who might be able to help me. I'll spend time with my boys and help them get through it. They love me and need me. Matt won't keep them from me."

"Are you worried he'll get physical with you again?"

"He won't. I know he won't. Matt's a good man. You'd actually like him under other circumstances."

"Possibly, he has great taste in women."

I smiled up at him, and he kissed my nose. I asked, "Do you have any idea what you're going to do next?"

"I'm starting my own company. I always knew if you and I went public, staying at Global would be problematic, so I've been working on things for a while. Besides, living in New York was out for you. The best solution seemed to be my own company."

Until that moment, I had no idea he'd started plotting an entire future around me. "How far along are you?"

"I have a business plan and some serious backers. It's something I considered before joining Global, so I already had a lot of research and ground work done. I almost pulled the plug on everything after our fight last week.

Glad I didn't. Anyway, don't worry about me. Financially, I'm set and I'll land on my feet. There's only one problem."

"What's that?"

"I'd planned to base the business in California, but now I just don't know."

"When were you going to tell me?"

"Last week, but then everything derailed. Texas is actually more corporate friendly, and my backers prefer it, but being in the hub of Silicon Valley has its advantages."

I wasn't sure how I felt about it. On the one hand, I was once again blown-over by what Reese was willing to do for me. On the other, I wished he'd discussed it with me sooner, and I didn't want to worry about a random encounter at some restaurant or the mall. I also didn't want the responsibility of influencing his decisions more than I already had.

"You should do what's best for you and your business."

"I'll keep it in mind."

We spent the rest of the afternoon holding each other and quietly talking. Just before it was time for me to leave, Reese went to the bathroom. I took the opportunity to retrieve his apartment key from my purse and set it on his entrance table. Reese didn't notice, or if he had, he didn't say anything. He insisted on accompanying me to the airport. He even bought a ticket just so he could stay with me as long as possible.

No seats were available in the waiting area, so he leaned against a pillar and I leaned against him. When the intercom announced First Class boarding, he pulled me close and whispered, "I intend to move on with my life, and so should you, but no matter what happens or where we end up, I'll always love you." He cupped my face and kissed me—not a peck, but a deep, lingering kiss. Then he walked away without a word.

I reached into my purse for my boarding pass and noticed a small box. At some point, he must have dropped it into my bag. I thought it might be his apartment key, but it was the necklace he'd bought me. I turned to chase him down, but he was gone, leaving me to board the plane knowing he had vanished into the crowd and out of my life.

Chapter 36

I tried calling Matt's cell before my plane departed, but he didn't pick up. There was no way to know if he didn't answer on purpose or if he couldn't because of work. As soon as my flight landed in San Francisco I tried again and he answered.

"Matt, I'm at the airport, and I want to come home." I could hear him breathing so I knew he heard me. "For the boys. Please?"

Matt asked, "Is it really over with him?"

"I think it's better if we don't discuss this on the phone."

"I can't see you just yet."

"The boys expect me to make Christmas cookies this week, and we still haven't decorated our tree. Can you, please, put aside your anger at me for Micah and Jason? May I, please, come home? We need to talk. I know they're asleep."

"You can come home to talk, but don't plan on staying," he said and hung up.

When I walked in the door, Matt was waiting for me in the living room. He sat in his favorite reading chair with his head in his hands. I left my luggage in the entryway, and sat in the chair opposite him.

Matt asked, "Did you have a nice flight?"

"It was fine. Were you able to get an earlier flight yesterday?"

"Yes. I got on the six o'clock."

"Good … Matt, do the boys know anything yet?"

"No, I haven't told anyone."

I sighed with relief. "Thank you."

"So, you resigned?" he asked uncertainly.

"Not exactly, but I don't work for Global anymore." I told Matt the whole story, making sure he understood Reese's sacrifice.

Matt looked at me with disbelief and questioned, "He really did that for you?"

"He really did."

"I can't believe he threw all in," Matt muttered.

"What do you mean?"

"Don't be so naive. He was competing for you. I sensed it from the minute I shook his hand. He knew I was winning, and he was looking for a way to beat me."

"I'm not some prize for some guy competition thing. Don't belittle this."

"I can't believe you're so blind. He sized me up and decided the only way to win you was to throw all in. You saw him appraising me. Come on, Susan. How am I supposed to compete with what he did?"

"I don't expect anything from you."

"Why would you? He upped the ante and I can't match his bet. You're back with him, aren't you?"

"No, I'm not."

"And why's that?"

"Because I'm still your wife, and I need to focus on being a good mother right now."

"Well … good. It wasn't a fair fight, you know that, right? I didn't know what was happening until it was too late."

"In fairness, our problems started way before I met him. Reese—"

"Don't!" Matt's face hardened. "Don't you dare defend him or say his name."

I bristled, but the last thing I wanted was to provoke Matt further. "I won't." I waited for him to cool a bit before I said, "I agree to a divorce. It's the best thing for all of us."

He nodded. "Okay, if that's what you want."

"But I don't want the boys to know until after Christmas, and we have a plan for our separation. I want to make it as easy on them as possible. Can we do that for them? Please?"

"What's to plan? You're moving out and I'm keeping the boys. They stay with me. The boys and I are a package," he stated as if it were his final word.

"I'm not giving up Micah and Jason. Maybe you're the one who should move out."

"I'm not the one who fucked my boss!"

I choked back my retort and tried to appeal to his reason. "If you take that stance, it'll mean a long drawn out fight in court. Is that what you really want? Do you really want to put Micah and Jason through that?"

"You're putting us through this, not me. I'll fight for full custody and I'll win."

"I'm willing to be reasonable about the house, but don't threaten to take away the boys. You'd be hurting them as much as me. Do you even know who their dentist is? Do you know how to wash their clothes or cook a decent meal? I'm their mother and they need me."

Matt took a minute, stewing over what I'd said. "This is going to be hard for them. They love us both. I'm still angry with you, but I'm tired of fighting. I need peace."

"Thank you. I need some peace, too."

"I have a few conditions."

"What are they?"

"You sleep on the couch or in your office. I don't care which, just not our bed."

"Agreed. And the next?"

"No contact with *him* as long as we're married. You're still my wife."

"I have no plans to see him again. Anything else?"

"I don't want the boys to know I slapped you," he requested.

The soft spot in my heart reserved just for Matt throbbed. He would regret it for the rest of his life. I regretted telling Reese and vowed no one else would know. "I'll never tell anyone."

"You made me do it, you know."

Maybe I did, but he pushed me to say things I never would have. Maybe we were both looking for something that would be the final deal breaker. The final thing that would allow us both to walk away and be able to say our marriage wasn't fixable. I always thought a man hitting me would be it. I thought infidelity would be it, too. "I really want to be fair with you. I'm asking you to be the same with me. I don't want us to be ugly with each other."

"You should know I'm willing to wait about the divorce," he said with his eyes pooling. "If things really are over with that guy, I might be able to forgive you over time."

His tears tugged on my insides, weakening me, and a huge part of me wanted to remain a Sinclair. I couldn't do it. I didn't want to know what else we were capable of doing to each other. *Rip, rip, rip* went my heart. "I can't stay with you. I am so sorry for hurting you."

"I'm sorry you had to go to another man to get the love you needed."

My instinct was to wrap my arms around him and kiss his tears away. A part of me would always love him. I ached whenever he was in pain. I wanted to comfort him. I wanted to be comforted, but I restrained myself from touching him. He quietly stood and went to bed.

Tears ran down both our cheeks, but it was over.

I sat not moving for a while, thinking about what Matt had said. Matt could be very perceptive at times. I was fully aware of Reese sizing up Matt when they'd met, but Matt upped the ante himself that night. Matt had gauged Reese's reactions each time he put his arm around me and intentionally kissed me when he knew Reese was watching.

Why had Matt only wanted me when he thought he was going to lose me? I was the neglected toy he barely noticed until it was about to be taken away. He may not have known I was having an affair, but he knew things weren't right. Matt did fight, but he stopped as soon as he thought the crisis was over. The last few weeks I had been going back to being the neglected toy. I knew it and so did he.

Without question, Reese was prone to grand gestures: the key, the necklace, flying to San Francisco, the dramatic speeches. He couldn't have done anything bigger than sacrificing his career for me. I had lain in bed with him on many occasions and listened to him dream. I'd observed him day after day at work. Focused, driven, and charismatic, he'd been on his way to becoming the rock star of Global Security. As Matt put it, *he threw all in*. Matt insinuated it was all part of a game. I wished I could dismiss his observation as jealousy talking, but I had my own doubts. An obsessive drive to win was part of Reese's very nature.

Men that hazard all, Do it in hope of fair advantages. It was a line from *The Merchant of Venice.* Sometimes I wished I didn't know so much fricken Shakespeare. I shook my head in an effort to clear it. What did it matter if Reese's actions weren't completely selfless?

I didn't want to question Reese's motives any more. I couldn't. He loved me in a way Matt would never understand. What Reese did was out of love. Whether it was a parting gift for what we'd shared or as a final attempt to win me didn't matter. Either way he did it because he loved me. Either way he had freed me, and it was done.

I had never understood how my biological father could turn his back on me for the love of a woman. I still couldn't completely empathize, but now I had a fuller understanding of what love could make a person do. I now knew love had endless shades, degrees, and depths.

My stomach churned uneasily. Matt had been my safe harbor for so long, always calm, always reliable. Matt ... oh my God, Matt, what would life be like without you?

Susan Sinclair ... Susan Rosales. Susan *Sinclair* sounded better than Susan *Rosales*. I didn't have to go back to my maiden name. Maybe I'd keep Sinclair. It would make it easier for Micah and Jason if I kept the same last name.

If word of my infidelity got out, as these things often do, would I see looks of disapproval from other parents at the boys' school and soccer games? Would some of the mothers openly snub me? Would men look at me and wonder if I were easy? Do some of them have mistresses somewhere, or would they, if they thought they wouldn't get caught? Matt would be viewed as the victim, and I would be seen as the trashy cheater; but no one really knows what happens between a husband and wife in the privacy of their bedroom.

In all likelihood, my affair would stay a tightlipped matter. Matt was too private a person to air dirty laundry. He would never tell anyone; heaven knows I wouldn't, and my Global Security life didn't intersect with our personal acquaintances.

The adulteress and her lover were supposed to have a tragic ending. I chuckled darkly to myself. I'm lucky my life wasn't a nineteenth century novel; throwing myself in front of a train had never appealed to me.

Daddy, wherever you are, I forgive you.

Would God, or Matt, or Micah, or Jason ever forgive me? I got down on my knees and prayed. *Please, God, forgive me … please, please, please forgive me.*

Matt and I made no attempts to reconcile.

Two months later, I moved out.

Chapter 37

March, 2014

I walked out of the dressing room and into the backstage waiting area of San Francisco Repertory Theater, looking for Micah, Jason, and Matt. I'd been too nervous opening night to have them watch. Now that I had a few performances playing Beatrice under my belt, I was at ease and confident. Since it was a Friday night, most of the actors had friends and family in the audience; consequently, the waiting room was packed with well-wishers.

I said hello to a few people and then noticed the house manager ushering my boys to me. They seemed to get taller daily. Micah towered over me, and Jason had me beat ever since he turned twelve. Micah reached me first.

"You were great, mom." He bent over and kissed my cheek. "I thought I was going to be bored." Good to know our production of *Much Ado* could hold a teenage boy's attention.

Next Jason hugged me. "I loved it. You were almost as good as Emma Thompson."

I smiled at him, my actor in the making. He was already theater-crazed. "Thanks, buddy." I bowed to Emma Thompson. In my book, she was an acting goddess, and I would take "almost as good" as a huge compliment any day. "Where's your father?"

"He went to the parking garage to get the car. He's picking us up out front," Micah said.

Jason asked, "Can I say hello to Jeff?"

"Sure, I think you have time."

I started to lead them to my friend, Jeff, who played Benedict. Just before we reached him, a hand touched my arm and a hauntingly familiar voice said, "Susan?"

I looked up and stared at what appeared to be Reese's face gazing down at me. I blinked, thinking I must be hallucinating. His hair was shorter and his temples grey; otherwise, he looked the same. His eyes looked exactly as I had remembered, but it couldn't be him.

Feeling light-headed, I asked, "Is it really you?"

He held his arms out. "In the flesh."

I felt like I had the wind knocked out me. It was just such a shock to have him appear so completely out of the blue. I auto hugged him and asked, "What are you doing here?"

"I was in town on business and read your review in the *Examiner*. I couldn't resist seeing you on stage. You were fantastic. I always knew you would be, and you look great." He grinned, looking me over. "Haven't changed a bit."

That simply wasn't true. It'd been over seven years since I'd seen him. I'd gained a few pounds and few wrinkles, but said, "Thank you. It's sweet of you to say."

"Uh, Mom," Jason interrupted.

"Oh, sorry guys." Matt had kept silent about Reese, as had I—each of us for different reasons. My boys had no idea of the role he'd played in shaping our lives. "This is an old colleague of mine, Reese Kirkpatrick. Reese, these are my boys, Micah and Jason."

They shook his hand like grown-up gentlemen, and then Micah said, "We have to go. Dad texted me. He's out front."

"Sure, of course. I'll see you both tomorrow," I said and gave them quick hugs goodbye.

"They're nice looking boys," Reese said.

"Thank you. I'm very proud of them. They go to a Catholic prep school now and are doing really well. Micah was just accepted to Columbia University."

"Wow, that's great. And Matt?"

"He's good. He remarried a couple years ago. She's a nice woman. The boys like her."

"Hey Susan," my friend, Jeff called. "We're heading out. You coming?" A bunch of the cast members were going out for drinks. I had planned to go with them.

"Sorry, you have plans. I won't keep you," Reese volunteered. I could tell he didn't want me to go yet, and I was curious about him, too.

"Go ahead. I'll catch up," I called back, and then said to Reese, "How about walking me to my car? That is if you don't have someone waiting for you."

"I don't, and I'd be happy to walk you."

We exited the theater together, and I led him in the direction of the parking garage. I had so many questions for him, I didn't know where to begin. "Last I heard, you moved to Texas. Are you still there?"

"No, I missed New York too much. After a year, I moved back and then commuted to Dallas, but I sold the company a few months ago for a very nice profit."

"Good for you. Are you in town looking to launch a new venture?"

"Something like that." He chuckled. "So you're an actress again?"

"Well, more like a teacher who acts. Mainly, I teach theater at a community college."

"You seem happy."

"I am. I have some great friends and am at a really good place in my life."

"And you never remarried?"

We had just reached the garage. Something in his voice, more than the question, stopped me. My heart fluttered. An old ache woke in my chest and thumped softly. The first year we were apart I couldn't think about him without guilt, pain, and horrible yearning. Over the years, there were times when I ached to see his face and hear his voice. At first, I restrained myself because of my boys and a sense that not seeing him was penance for my sins. Later, after so much time had passed, I worried he may have deeply regretted his involvement with me and was happily building a life with someone else. I didn't want to know if he was married, nor to be an unwelcome intrusion. I never forgot him, but as each year passed, the aching lessened until eventually I thought he no longer had a hold on my heart. Standing inches from him shook my certainty. Our eyes locked, just as they'd used to. I battled an urge to touch his face and kiss his lips; for all I knew he was married or engaged. He could have children. I had no right.

"I've dated some," I said, "but that's it. How about you?"

"Same, nothing serious." He paused before he said, "I've never stopped loving you, but in my own way, I'd moved on. Then, I saw your picture in the paper this morning, and all these feelings came flooding back. I had to know … I had to see you."

As we stood on the sidewalk with people walking by and bright garage lights glaring, giving us no privacy, buried love pushed to the surface and palpable longing erupted between us. After seven years apart, I still loved him. I could never love anyone else the way I loved him.

I asked, "May I buy you a drink and introduce you to my friends?"

"Are you sure this is what you want?"

What I wanted was to take him home and hold him tight. I thought I'd lost him forever, but like a miracle, here he was. We were both free, my boys were settled, and I'd never felt so strong and grounded about my life. All in or nothing. It's what he'd told me years ago. I unwrapped my scarf to show him I was wearing the necklace he'd given me and smiled. The apprehension on his face gave way to a hint of a smile and then a full on ear-to-ear grin.

"Let's start with a drink," I said. "I wouldn't want you to think I'm easy."

He laughed and took my hand. "Let's go, you little hussy."

ACKNOWLEDGEMENTS

I would like to express my gratitude to Renee C. Fountain, Alan Rinzler, and Bob Pimm, all of whom provided invaluable professional insight, direction, and encouragement. Thanks as well to Lisa Haas for reading a very rough draft and the Blue Moon Writers group led by Scott Evans. A very heartfelt thanks to Adam Russ and David Sutton for sharing very necessary male perspectives and keen editing eyes. I'd also like to thank my dear friends Holly Adiele, Tori Schwab, and Sherri Maguire for reading first drafts and cheering me on.

Finally, many, many thanks to the three great loves of my life: Ted, Annie, and KatieMac. Without my family's love, patience, and support, I could never have written this story.